CHINESE THEATER
in the
Days of Kublai Khan

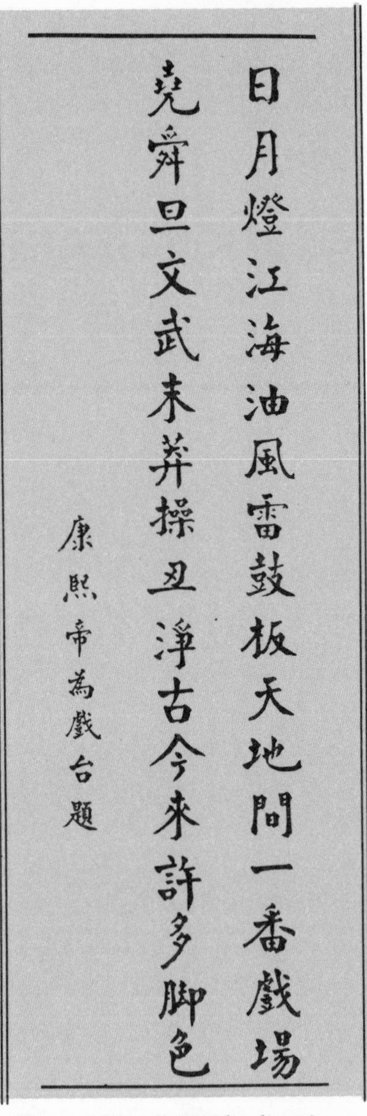
日月燈江海油風雷鼓板天地間一番戲場
堯舜旦文武末莽操丑淨古今來許多脚色
康熙帝為戲台題

"Teatrum Mundi," said to have been composed by the Emperor K'ang-hsi for the pillars of a playhouse

CHINESE THEATER in the Days of Kublai Khan

J. I. Crump

TEATRUM MUNDI

The sun and the moon were the footlights
(Their oil was the rivers and seas)
The drums were the wind and the thunder,
And all the sweep from the stars to the deep
the proscenium of their stage.

Yao and Shun were the heroines
(Wen and Wu, leading men)
The clowns were Wang Mang and Ts'ao Ts'ao,
While all mankind since time out of mind
has played out its predestined roles.

THE UNIVERSITY OF ARIZONA PRESS
TUCSON, ARIZONA

About the Author . . .

J. I. Crump went to the University of Michigan to teach Chinese language and literature in 1949 after he had finished his Ph.D. at Yale. His scholarly interests (as opposed to "serious pursuits" like fly-fishing and soaring) have been in the field of earliest Chinese fiction (Intrigues; Studies of the *Chan-kuo Ts'e,* Michigan 1964; *Chan-kuo Ts'e,* Oxford 1970) and in early drama (*Ballad of the Hidden Dragon,* Oxford 1971, and numerous articles). *Chinese Theater in the Days of Kublai Khan* is the result of some eighteen years of reading and writing about Yuan dynasty drama, which included periods of study in Japan, France, England, and Germany.

THE UNIVERSITY OF ARIZONA PRESS

Library of Congress Cataloging in Publication Data

Crump, James Irving, 1921–
Chinese theater in the days of Kublai Khan.

Bibliography: p.
Includes index.
1. Theater—China—History. 2. Chinese drama—Yüang dynasty, 1260–1368—Translations into English. 3. English drama—Translations from Chinese. I. Title.
PN2872.C7 792'.0951 79-20046

ISBN 0-8165-0697-3
ISBN 0-8165-0656-6 pbk.

For Chris and Jon

Contents

Part III. Program Notes

Illustrations

IMPORTANT NOTICE TO THE READER

(Hsieh-tzu)

Reader, I don't know what impelled you to borrow or buy this book, but let us suppose (and I like the thought) that you're simply possessed of a lively curiosity about the theater, about China, or about the Chinese theater. Let's further assume that you've never read one of the dramas which are the subject of this book. There are three good examples translated in Part II, with enough introductory material to make the plays more comprehensible and more fun to read. So, a sensible approach would be to read Part II first, including one or more of the plays, to enjoy the rest of the book in perspective. On the other hand, if you're like me (I don't take kindly to being told how to read, either), and would rather read a book, the first time at least, rather haphazardly—peering at the pictures, sampling the text, and using the glossary—get on with it.

Since almost all Yuan dramas (over 150 of the extant 162) consist of a "wedge" (hsieh-tzu), four acts (ti-yi through ti-ssu che), and occasionally an epilogue (san-ch'ang), it occurred to me that a book dedicated to this drama form might well take the same shape. Therefore, my notice to the reader is the "wedge," chapters one through four of Part I are my four acts, and I have composed an epilogue to Part I in the form we suppose it to have had in Yuan times.

For those acquainted with the dramas in the original I have included page numbers from *YCH* (e.g. 1130) and *WP* (e.g. *WP* 126) with all my citations. Occasionally I have identified a play by its position in these two collections (e.g. *YCH* #15). There is a Finding List in the Appendix which will get you from any page number to the play number and its romanized title, in case you prefer your citations that way. Items in the bibliography are alphabetized by the way they are referred to in text, whether author, title or abbreviation.

J. I. Crump

PART I

Behind the Scenes

1. The Society: The Barbarians and Chinese Drama

(Ti-yi che)

By a trick of historical perspective, Chinese classical drama (also called Yuan or Mongol theater) seems suddenly to appear on the literary horizon full grown. This complex, synthetic theater has a long history behind it, of course, but so many of the documents which should attest to it are lost that, when we discover the names of over a hundred playwright-composers and the titles of some five hundred plays which were mounted during the last fifty years of the thirteenth century, the effect is of a sudden aesthetic explosion at precisely the time it should least be expected. China had just been overwhelmed (as indeed had much of the rest of the world) by the Mongols, who were an alien people speaking an alien tongue and having every reason to reject Chinese values, aesthetic and otherwise. Yet it was during that period of subjugation that this Chinese musical poetic dramatic form reached its peak of formal and artistic perfection and its greatest popularity.

Another piece of *trompe-l'oeil* connected with the Mongol dynasty is brought about not because records are lacking but because, until quite recently, the West has not made intelligent use of Chinese documentation. I am referring to the vision that haunts history books, of hordes of malodorous Mongols in 1211 utterly destroying civilized China in spasms of rapine and butchery. These same history books, however, will also quote Marco Polo to indicate that scarcely fifty years later, when Kublai Khan took the throne, his administration was the marvel of all Europe and the Middle East. And, at a time when the prudent burgher of the West would not sell so much as a bodkin unless he could feel the reassuring weight and texture of the coin he bit or rang on his counter, not only were the Khan's armies accepting paper currency for their wages but there was such a stable system of credit throughout the Mongol empire that:

> When thus coined in large quantities, this paper currency is circulated in every part of the Great Khan's dominions; nor dares any person, at the peril of his life, refuse to accept it in payment. All his subjects receive it without hesitation, because, wherever their business may call them, they can dispose of it again in the purchase of merchandise they may require; such as pearls, gold, or silver. With it, in short, every article may be procured.[1*]

Common sense is offended by these unlikely contrasts taking place in such a short span of time, and this chapter is devoted to making the beginnings of the Yuan dynasty (and to some extent thereby, the Yuan theater) a bit more comprehensible by putting together the rather scanty material we have which bears on the lives of early Yuan playwrights and the most pertinent historical facts of the age in which they lived.

---

*Bibliographic notes are both helpful and necessary but are neither a pleasure to read or to write. I happen to be fond of the well-shod footnote laced with supplemental information, speculation, or curiosa. Throughout this book, notes of the latter type will be marked with some form of asterism, while numbers will always refer to notes which constitute the "scholarly apparatus." (I seem unable to suppress the image I always get from this term: an aged figure hunched reading a book and surrounded by Rube Goldberg contraptions which assist him in unimaginable ways.)

YUAN PLAYWRIGHTS AND THE *REGISTER OF GHOSTS*

Parcere subjectis et debellare superbos

Aeneid, VI, 1. 853

"To spare the submissive and beat down the haughty"

The sole contemporary source of information on Yuan dynasty playwrights is a nostalgic little book by one Chung Ssu-ch'eng called the *Register of Ghosts (Lu-kuei Pu).** Chung claims to have hailed from Pien-liang in the north, but he actually spent all his adult life in Hangchow. His preface to the *Register of Ghosts* is dated "the 6th day of the 8th month, 1330" (though several entries dated later than this indicate that he wrote the preface before he was finished writing the book), which means that he was writing about Yuan composers some sixty years after the most flourishing era of Yuan drama. His first section is headed, "Fifty six 'talents' of an earlier generation whose dramas are still with us." These all prove to be early and northern composers. Chapter II of the *Register* has (a) "Those talents (recently departed)† whom I knew," (b) "Those talents whom I know," and (c) "Those I have only heard of." Almost without exception, all of these prove to be late Yuan and southern. Indeed, among students of Chinese drama, the convention has arisen of treating all those names listed in Chapter I of the *Register* as early, and all those in Chapter II as late; one may read, for instance, that so-and-so was a dramatist of the late Yuan, though nothing at all is actually known of him save that he appears in Chapter II of the *Register.*

*"I have seen the not-yet-dead ghosts mourning those who are ghosts. . . . Do they not know that since the creation of heaven and the beginning of earth there have always been ghosts who remain deathless? The sage, the virtuous, the faithful and the filial have their deeds written in books . . . and they live on eternally." From Chung's preface; implying that he wrote his *Register* so that great talents might be remembered forever, be ghosts who never die.

†Chinese printers and book dealers were very insouciant about such niceties as text fidelity (except for the classics) and there are three editions of the *Register* which differ in such matters as arrangement, section headings, and play titles (the most helpful recension of the *Register* has a total of 1335 variorum notes!). In all cases I give a kind of composite translation of what's in all three versions of the work.

In what follows we shall be interested only in the fifty-six early composers found in Chapter I of the *Register* and listed alphabetically below:

Playwright	Place of Origin	Number of Dramas
Chi T'ien-hsiang	Tatu	6
Chiang Tse-min	Chen-ting	1
Fei Chun-hsiang	Tatu	1
Fei Tiang-ch'en	Tatu	3
Hou Cheng-ch'ing	Chen-ting	1
Hung-tzu Li-erh	Imp. City	3
K'ang Chin-chih	Li-chou	2
Kao Wen-hsiu	Tung-p'ing	32
Kuan Han-ch'ing	Tatu	58
Ku Chung-ch'ing	Tung-p'ing	1
K'ung Wen-ch'ing	P'ing-yang	1
Li Chih-fu	Te-hsing	11
Li Chin-chu	Ta-ming	2
Li Hao-ku	Pao-ting	3
Li Hsing-fu	Chiang-chou	1
Li K'uan-fu	Tatu	1
Li-lang	(see Hung-tzu above)	2
Li Shih-chung	Tatu	1
Li Shou-ch'ing	T'ai-yuan	9 (or 10)
Li Tzu-chung	Tatu	2
Li Wen-wei	Chen-ting	12
Liang Chin-chih	Tatu	2
Liu T'ang-ch'ing	T'ai-yuan	2
Lu Hsien-chih	Pien-liang	1
Ma Chih-yuan	Tatu	12
Meng Han-ch'ing	Po-chou	1
P'eng Po-ch'eng	Pao-ting	1
Po P'u, Jen-fu	Chen-ting	15
Shang Chung-hsien	Chen-ting	10
Shih-chiu San-jen	Chen-ting	1
Shih Chun-pao	P'ing-yang	10
Sun Chang-chang	Tatu	2
Shih Tzu-chang	Tatu	2
Tai Shan-fu	Chen-ting	5
Ti Chun-hou	P'ing-yang	1

Playwright	Place of Origin	Number of Dramas
Wang Chung-wen	Tatu	10
Wang Po-ch'eng	Cho-chou	2
Wang Shih-fu	Tatu	14
Wang T'ing-hsiu	Yi-tu	4
Wu Han-ch'en	Tsi-nan	10
Yao Shou-chung	Lo-yang	3
Yang Hsien-chih	Tatu	8
Yü Po-yuan	P'ing-yang	6
Yü Chi-fu	Tatu	15
Yüeh po-ch'uan	Tsi-nan	1

17 from Tatu
7 from Chen-ting
5 from P'ing-yang
4 from Tung-p'ing

Chung was obviously a theater buff. His *Register* was written to honor playwrights of the past and their works (he includes a list of titles attributed to each), and next to each famous name he writes a short panegyric in one of the verse forms used in Yuan drama itself. Under most of the composers' names he appends pitifully small scraps of biographical information. Here, for example, are the complete entries for three of the most famous and prolific early Yuan playwrights:

Kuan Han-ch'ing: a man of Tatu, clerk in the office of the Grand Physician. His sobriquet was "Old Man of Yi-chai."

Po Jen-fu: Son of Wen-chü. His given name was P'u and people called him Master of Lan-ku. He was from Chen-ting, was given the honorary rank of a *Chia-yi tai-fu* and the office of Minister in Charge of the Bureau of Protocol.

Kao Wen-hsiu: Scholar at Tung-p'ing-fu; died young. People called him the "lesser Kuan Han-ch'ing."

For almost all the remaining fifty-three "talents of days gone by" we get little more than a cryptic, "real name X; came from the capital."

The amount and character of the information the *Register* gives us on Yuan dynasty playwrights inevitably reminds me of the kind of harmless vagary indulged in by the author of the very famous and pioneering *Illustrated History of Chinese Literature (Ch'a-t'u-Pen Chung-kuo Wen-hsueh Shih)* where, facing page 214, there is a woodcut of a somewhat puffy-eyed Oriental gentleman staring into the middle distance.

Prince X Mr. Y Mr. Z

Reader (and I hope I am still talking to the same one I addressed in my Important Notice), this little nosegay of asterisks will be used throughout the book to indicate an attack of the digressions. The same mark, but with its stem pointing up instead of down, indicates the end of a spasm. When a similar device was used on other occasions, the more unkind among my critics insisted that it was a cross marking the place where my train of thought had died. In a sense, perhaps, they were right; I have always loved and fallen easy prey to digressions. I enjoyed them by lecturers when I went to college and by authors when I read, and find I perversely remember digressions long after I've forgotten the main thrust. With Laurence Sterne I feel "digressions incontestably are the sunshine;—they are the life, the soul of reading." However, I know that digressions are not everyone's cup of tea, so I feel called upon to signal those who are impatient with them. If you wish to get directly to the resumption of the argument instead of dawdling here with me, run your eye over the next couple of pages until you see the upside-down bouquet and begin.

The amount and placement of his facial hair would meet with approval only from the less amply endowed of today's (1974) youth. We are solemnly told by the caption that this is a picture of the famous literatus, Prince X.

Facing page 374 is the same chap—he is contemplating the horizon rather than the middle distance and the caption tells us it's Mr. Y; but it's the same chap.

Facing page 355: same chap again (he's trimmed his mustache); here he is called Mr. Z. Cheng Chen-to, author of this *Illustrated History,* was a collector and authority on old woodcuts as well as a literary historian, and there is certainly no reason why he should not have inserted these "portraits" into his text. They add nothing to our knowledge of the authors he is treating, but they mislead no one.

To the student of Yuan drama thirsting after information on the lives and personalities of the men who created these intricate musical plays, the exiguous biographical notes furnished by the *Register* seem as useless as the endless identical portraits in the *Illustrated History.* But whereas the imaginary woodcut iconography of the *History* was cut from the whole cloth (or whole wood?) and could only tell us something about the portraitist (and precious little about him), the distressingly brief notes in the *Register* actually are useful and, at the hands of Chinese and Japanese scholars, have been made to yield much information—if not on the playwright himself at least on the age in which he lived and worked, as I shall indicate later.

So little was and is known about Yuan dynasty dramatists, that admirers of Yuan drama have several times* lost their good sense and supplied fanciful (to use the kindest term) information

*The latest of these spasms involved the whole of mainland China. Kuan Han-ch'ing, whom we believe to be the most prolific and probably the best of the Yuan dramatists, was proclaimed "a people's writer" by those in charge of proclaiming such things, and the year 1958 was solemnly designated as the 700th anniversary of his birth. This was celebrated by prodigious quantities of publications—including variorum editions of "his works" and a biographical play "based on his life." Since

about the playwrights and their age. One such appears in the preface to the very important Ming dynasty (1368–1628) publication of one hundred Yuan plays now called the *Yuan-ch'ü Hsüan* (A Selection of Yuan Dramas), about which you will be reading a great deal in the chapters to follow. In the two prefaces to this drama anthology, the compiler, Tsang Mou-hsün (T. Chin-shu, *fl.* 1580–1621), becomes so carried away with the excellence of the dramas he edited that he succumbs to wishful thinking about how things *should* have been:

> Today southern drama is in the ascendancy. Everyone claims he is a playwright but no one seems to realize how far he falls short of his Yuan dynasty predecessors. In Yuan times, officials were examined and chosen on the basis of their dramatic compositions ... and even men of the stature of Kuan Han-ch'ing had to test their skills to the utmost in order to make their names.... This is why I have selected these one hundred *tsa-chü* (dramas) to show the marvels of Yuan dynasty plays and furnish those who work with the southern products of today something they can use as models.

If what Tsang wrote in A.D. 1615 were true, one could only conclude that the great Kuan Han-ch'ing's talents proved unequal to the challenge of civil service examinations, for the only post he is known to have held was that mentioned above (clerk in the office of the Grand Physician)—something about as lofty, it seems, as an orderly in the U.S. Naval Hospital at Bethesda, Maryland.

The truth is, the editor of *Yuan-ch'ü Hsüan (YCH)* could only imagine that the polished and literate dramas which flourished in Yuan times *must* have come from the hands of the intelligentry (as was actually the case with dramas composed during the Ming), and so he posited a civil service system in Yuan times which chose officials on the basis of their excellence as writers of musical

---

the only real information we have about him are the two lines from the *Register* quoted above, much commemorative commotion was made out of very little. As is sometimes the happy result of such self-conscious cultural hoopla, however, it stimulated the publication of some very solid scholarship on Yuan drama from which scholars East and West have benefited greatly. We also now have a breezy and fairly engaging "portrait of Kuan Han-ch'ing" (created out of even less information than are his "biographies") which future *Illustrated Histories of Chinese Literature* will doubtless eagerly add to their galleries! See Figure 1.

Fig. 1. The Thirteenth-Century Playwright Kuan Han-ch'ing as He "Appeared" in 1958

dramas.* This has caused no little mischief, because Tsang, his anthology, and his opinions later became greatly admired. It was not until the early decades of the twentieth century that more

*This hypothesis of Tsang's is not nearly so preposterous as it might seem to the Westerner unfamiliar with Chinese civil service examinations. Skill in popular verse forms often counted heavily in the selection of officials, especially during T'ang and Sung times. Whether or not this kind of examination helped to select the best men for government is debatable, but it certainly encouraged the composition of reams of poetry—mostly bad.

rigorous Chinese and Japanese scholarship finally convinced fans of Yuan theater that the composition of these plays was never part of any examination system and that none of the early dramatists (with one important exception) held a post more prestigious than general factotum for a small *yamen*.

The important exception is Po Jen-p'u (also known as Po P'u), the subject of the second sample entry from the *Register* given above. The entry notes that he was the son of Po Wen-chü. This immediately makes it clear that, unlike almost all the remaining fifty-five composers, Po P'u comes from a family influential in Chin* dynasty government: his grandfather had been a functionary in the powerful Bureau of Military Affairs and his father, Po Hua (T. Wen-chü), was a friend and contemporary of Yuan Hao-wen, the best known and most influential poet of the period just preceding the Mongol invasion. This justly famous poet addressed several verses to Po Jen-p'u's father, and the Yuan and Po families were related by literary interests and possibly by marriage.

With this for openers, Chinese and Japanese scholars (Cheng Ch'ien and Yoshikawa Kojirō in particular) have tracked down a good deal of information about Po Jen-p'u[2] and his circumstances. In doing so they have put in perspective the conditions under which many of the early Yuan playwrights lived during the Mongol invasions and the subsequent establishment of the Yuan dynasty.

It should be noted that in Po P'u's minuscule biography in the *Register of Ghosts* he is said to have hailed from Chen-ting: this is perhaps the most important fact in the entire *Register.*

The story of the enclave of Chen-ting (modern Shih-chia Chuang, a hundred or so miles south and west of Peking) begins with the first Mongol thrust into China (1211–15) which brought them up against Peking or Chung-tu (the Chin capital) whose walls they had not the siege machinery to break. They swarmed over the surrounding countryside, however, and many a place was made sharply aware of the difference between the way the Mongols treated inhabitants of towns which resisted and finally fell (their adult males were often put to the sword to the last man) and

*The dynasty (1115–1234) that preceded and was toppled by the Mongols; see below, "Chinese Entertainment Before the Mongols."

those towns whose "leaders" surrendered and cooperated with the Mongols. Most often these "leaders" were confirmed as heads of the areas in which they had always lived, and many Chinese and Khitan (few Chin) leaders from these areas were subsequently useful in persuading larger walled towns to surrender. These leaders and their men became a kind of auxiliary for the Mongols and were known as the Black Army or Han (i.e. Chinese) Army.

Igor De Rachewiltz distinguishes this first phase of the Mongol conquest from the second by the fall of Chung-tu and the return of Genghis to Mongolia. The Khan left reduction of tough Chin resistance to his generals Muqali and Böl, who in turn relied more and more on their Chinese auxiliaries to maintain supply lines and military administration over those districts nominally under the control of the Mongols. The Chinese generals in charge of these areas all were given the Golden Tiger Tablet with this formula engraved in Chinese:

> This is the sacred order of the Resplendent Emperor Chinggis, beloved of heaven: all commands to be executed in accordance with it.

They were plenipotentiary in their areas, and De Rachewiltz theorizes that the Mongol view of these Chinese "warlords" and their troops was identical with the older Mongol concept of *nököd,* "comrades-in-arms"—Mongol leaders who, with their followers, divorced themselves from local tribal concerns and devoted themselves to Genghis' cause. When these tribal leaders joined him, Genghis gave them their entire tribe as their share in the joint venture; those tribesmen were called *ayil,* "tents" or followers, not *injes* or "slaves." This is exactly what happened with the Chinese "defectors." They and their people were accepted as followers; the Mongols had already learned to welcome the help of many kinds of foreigners. On the other hand, those who resisted and were later captured were "slaves"; they were either killed or led into Mongolia to serve their conqueror.[3] So the treatment of conquered Chinese was very uneven. Those who lived within Chinese enclaves which had gone over to the Mongols under their own leaders must have made the transition into the new dynasty (always the most parlous time in Chinese history) relatively unscathed.

Certainly two of the most effective and impressive generals of the Chinese auxiliary army were Shih T'ien-ni and his younger brother T'ien-tse. Both of them were associated with the enclave at Chen-ting, but T'ien-ni did not live to enjoy the power and wealth of his area for long. In 1225 one of his subordinates had him assassinated at a banquet. T'ien-tse, captain of his brother's bodyguard, was away from Chen-ting at the time but, as soon as news of the revolt reached him, he mustered troops and crushed the affair. He went on to become an equal of Bayan, the supreme commander of all Mongol troops in China, and Chen-ting was always his pied-à-terre. He must have been a remarkable man: he stood about six-six and had a voice that "rang like a great bourdon." An incomparable archer and rider with prodigious strength, he was also known as one of the most assiduous and talented promoters of the gentler arts. In the *Register of Ghosts* there is a little paragraph of thirty-one names and posts of "those former worthies whose literary *ch'ü (yüeh-fu* or *yüeh-chang)* are still with us," which is a kind of preface to the main list of fifty-six early playwrights; and, in addition to Tu Shan-fu and Tung Chieh-yuan (of whom more later), the list contains the name of Shih T'ien-tse, Grand Minister of the Secretariat, or simply Grand Minister. Though his biography in the Yuan History (*K.M.* 6493.4) makes little of his erudition—mentioning only that he studied the *Tzu-chih T'ung-chien* (A Mirror for Government) and advised the Mongol emperor on policy he derived from that work—he seems to have been a poet himself (a writer of *ch'ü*), as well as a powerful patron of writers in the Chen-ting enclave. As will become clear later, it was fashionable among the educated in late Chin times to take the same sets of tunes to which playwrights wrote the arias of their dramas and create *san-ch'ü* or nondramatic *ch'ü* (literary verse) of their own.* It may or may not have been considered *déclassé* in Yuan times to have written for the stage, but there is no doubt that anyone who had pretensions to literary standing wrote these nondramatic *ch'ü*.

---

*Somewhat like taking the arias from *Aida,* say, and writing one's own lyrics to them for literary rather than operatic purposes. We know, however, that at least *some san-ch'ü* were sung, though not as commercial entertainment, perhaps.

Here we find all the clues which can make the rise of a great drama form during a period of external invasion and internal decay a good deal more comprehensible. The one man from the *Register of Ghosts* for whom we can find collateral information, Po Jen-p'u, we discover living in a Chinese enclave protected by a powerful and interested patron. He could have peacefully passed all his days there (though we know he did not) and continued writing through the entire early period of the Mongol dynasty. The *Register* lists six others who also hailed from Chen-ting, and we must suppose that they had secure, reasonably well-to-do audiences with, one presumes, ample leisure to become theater fans. Similar things were happening in places other than Chen-ting in Hopei. Another great Chinese general of the period was Yen Shih whose enclave was the city of Tung-p'ing in Shantung. The third entry from the *Register,* given above on page 6, concerns a certain Kao Wen-hsiu who is called a "scholar" at Tung-p'ing. This probably means he attended the school for Chinese ritual and music which the son of Yen Shih caused to be established within the city walls of Tung-p'ing*: once again, a combination of a protected Chinese enclave and encouragement of music and learning.

All of this makes a neat picture, doesn't it? But since we are dealing with human history, such dovetailing of facts should immediately raise the suspicions of the reader. Alas, for the tidiness of the theory! But it must be noted that in the list of the *Register*'s fifty-six names are seventeen from Tatu and five from P'ing-yang. Tatu is the name the Mongols gave to the Chin Chinese capital of Chung-tu (now Peking) after the Khans had built their own great enclosure on the northeast edge of it and made it their capital city. The story of the siege of Chung-tu is one of long blockade, starvation, and cannibalism within the city walls and, as the winter of 1214 trudged like a slow, black ox into the snows of January 1215, the city, still staunch, was deserted by its Chin leader, Mo-nien Chin-chung, who fled to K'aifeng, the southern capital of the

*We may have a clue to the musical and entertainment level of the enclave of Tung-p'ing in the fact that the ravishing Wang Chin-pang who so enthralled the young hero of *Huan-men Tzu-ti Ts'o Li-shen* is a "member of a troupe from Tung-p'ing" (*Yung-lo Ta-tien Hsi-wen San-chung,* p. 55).

Chin. His officers, who remained behind, lost heart and opened the gates to the Mongols. Then:

> Despite the city's submission, the besieging soldiers got out of hand, and unable to resist the lure of so gigantic a prize, sacked a great part of the capital and slew many thousands of its inhabitants. . . . (an embassy) which passed by Chung-tu a few months later reports that the bones of the slaughtered formed whole mountains. . . . the Imperial palace was set on fire and one learns that the part of the city in which the conflagration broke out burned a whole month.[4]

True, Chung-tu did surrender, so its citizens were spared the calculated butchery that would have been their lot had they resisted until reduced by arms; but one would scarce think of this as an auspicious beginning for what was to become, forty years later, the center of theatrical activity.

Because of the number of playwrights whose place of origin is given in the *Register* as Chung-tu (renamed Tatu by the Mongols), we must suppose that not only were the city's entertainers spared but its composers as well. In general, the Mongols took a dim view of "scribblers" and were largely unimpressed by their products. In contrast, the Khans were famous for their prompt and consistent use of non-Mongol technicians, artisans, carpenters, and the like. In Muqali's biography (*K.M.* 6420.3) we discover that entertainers were classed with technicians. Muqali's order for punishment of the perfidious towns of Kuang-ning and Yi-chou (which had gone over to the Chin again after having once surrendered and been well treated by Muqali) is phrased thus: "We cannot spare these rebels, for that would not warn off others who might later attempt [such treachery]. Therefore, let all the townspeople be put to death except artisans and entertainers." It seems possible to me that some of the early playwrights of Chung-tu Tatu may have identified themselves with the actors who performed their works and thus came under a specialized form of *parcere* *subjectis*. This may, in fact, have been the beginning of the rather close relationship which seems to have existed in Yuan times between the literate composer and the lowest member of Chinese society, the entertainer.* The actors and composers of Chung-tu could have been a special case, of course, not only because the city was the capital but because it did, after all, surrender.

But what of P'ing-yang? Five of the men on the *Register*'s list came from there and, as will become apparent in the next chapter, this city of 100,000 was a remarkably active focus for theatrical troupes and theaters. P'ing-yang never surrendered. It was reduced in 1214, given the Mongol treatment, and remained throughout all the early years of the Yuan dynasty one of the important military bases from which Mongol armies reduced the rest of China. Nevertheless, this town produced playwrights and acting troupes quite early in the Yuan dynasty. From such examples as Chung-tu and P'ing-yang, we can only conclude that theatrical entertainment could and did flourish under Mongol rule even at its harshest. As we will see in Chapter 2, there was in P'ing-yang and the hinterlands it influenced, a strong theater tradition which dated back at least to the Sung dynasty (960–1126) and which seems to have gained in strength all during the Mongol era.

The foregoing is just about all that can be wrung from the laconic entries in the *Register of Ghosts*† regarding the life and times of early Yuan playwrights. Scanty as they may be, it is not the

*A note in the *Register* appended to the drama called *Huang-liang Meng* (*YCH* #45) says: "One act of this was done by Ma Chih-yuan, one by Hung-tzu Li Erh, one by Hua Li-lang, and one by Li Shih-chung." Hua Li-lang and Li Erh were entertainers, and we know that Ma Chih-yuan held a minor office. By doing so, Ma was part of a universe vastly more respectable than any actor could hope to enter as a general rule. Yet here we seem to have evidence of cooperation between the intelligentry and entertainers. I say "seem to" because the form and origins of this note (like so much else in the exasperating and valuable *Register*) leave it open to question. See Fu Hsi-hua, p. 72, and Yoshikawa, p. 105.

†There are a few other bits of information that can be gathered and combined with controlled speculation which tell us a little more about eight or nine names listed in the *Register.* Certainly the most imaginative and interesting use of these crumbs can be found in Yoshikawa Kojirō's *Gen Zatsugeki Kenkyū* (Research on Yuan Drama).

brevity of the entries that is so distressing but our inability to use some of the information in them. If the reader will again look over the list of fifty-six early Yuan playwrights, he will see, entered after the composer's place of origin, the number of play titles noted by Chung Ssu-ch'eng as compositions of the man whose name precedes them. All told, Chapter I of the *Register* gives the titles of more than 320 *tsa-chü* (Yuan dramas, that is) from this early period. We today have two large collections of Yuan dramas: *Yuan-ch'ü Hsüan,* edited in 1615 (A Selection of Yuan Dramas—confusing though it may be, *tsa-chü* are often called simply *ch'ü* or "songs") and a later (edited in 1959) sequel called *Yuan-ch'ü Hsüan Wai-pien* (Additions to the Selection of Yuan Dramas). For all practical purposes we have in them a corpus of 162 Mongol dynasty dramas available to us today. The natural question is, are the titles we have today also found in the *Register*'s list? Unhappily, the answer is yes, no, and perhaps! For example, of the fourteen plays in existence today which are attributed to Kuan Han-ch'ing, some eight titles are to be found also in the *Register*'s list; but some of the things attributed to the Kuan today are not even mentioned in the *Register:* worse than that, some of the dramas we have left to us which claim Kuan as their composer are of such inferior quality that I find it very hard to believe they could have come from the same hand as those Kuan masterworks which still can be read today. The same situation pertains in a general way with all the other playwrights and their products noted in the *Register.* My opinion on the matter is that some of the scripts we have today are probably those referred to in the *Register of Ghosts,* but many are not. I would caution anyone against trying to synthesize an individual's style by simply analyzing all the plays we have today the titles of which are also found attributed to one man in the *Register.* It appears to me inevitable that many dramas were ascribed to famous men just to enhance their appeal. Furthermore, since so many Yuan dramas deal with well-known stories, a number of authors might each have had his own treatment of the same traditional subject matter and used approximately the same title. So, the *tsa-chü* we have today with a title similar to one appearing in the *Register:* was it done by Kuan Han-ch'ing or Kao Wen-hsiu, or was it in fact done by someone unknown and later? A ghost still unborn when the *Register* was compiled? There is no way of knowing. More important, it is certainly the wrong question to ask, "Is this the script the players in Tatu were following when they trod the boards in the days of Kublai Khan?" Professor Cheng Ch'ien of T'aiwan, one of the most astute and learned students of the Yuan dynasty drama today, has frequently pointed out that we have no reason to believe there *ever* were authorized versions of something so frivolous (in the Chinese view) as drama scripts. Generations of producers, collectors, and printers of the dramas that flourished so mightily in the days of Kublai Khan made additions, emendations, and alterations as they saw fit, and this process probably began just as soon as a play was mounted.

The *Register* is the best source we have: its pages have allowed us to reconstruct much that makes the age more comprehensible; but its seeming attribution of certain extant plays to particular authors must be used with the greatest restraint.*

If, with the help of the *Register* and other Chinese sources, my desires to counterbalance the usually apocalyptic Western view and the uniformly black Chinese view of the Mongols have made me appear to overemphasize both the peaceful transitions which

*In addition to the numerous vagaries in the several editions of the *Register* which make it an unreliable source for attribution, there is a fairly well-defined notation of *tz'u-pen, erh-pen, tan-pen,* and *mo-pen*. It seems certain that where *tan-* and *mo-pen* are noted it means there were versions of the same drama in which the star role was one sung by a female character in the play *(tan-pen)* or a male character *(mo-pen)*. It is my belief that Yuan playwrights enjoyed doing variations on traditional stories from different angles of vision by writing the singing part to fit various characters involved in them. This might account for as many as four plays on the same theme all different because the action was seen through the eyes of a different character. I believe that those critics who reprove the Yuan dramatists for choosing what the critic perceives as the wrong role for the singing part may be dispraising what is precisely the contribution of that particular playwright. The term *erh-pen* should mean "there are two versions" and the term *tz'u-pen* should mean something like "this is the second version." Now, even if we have riddled only half the terms right (see Sun K'ai-ti's *Ts'ang-chou Chi,* 399–405), they constitute clear evidence that the same stories were worked and reworked by several different men even within the rather limited population treated by the *Register.* Why should this not also have been the case with yet other playwrights unknown to the *Register*? Why, in any case, should we assume—except for theoretical purposes—that the scripts we have today are just those versions done by the best known composers listed in the *Register*?

took place inside the enclaves and Mongol tolerance of the Chinese theater, I do not mean in any way to minimize the impact of those invaders on China—or, indeed, on the whole of East Asia. The Mongols were brutal. But the Mongols were not so senselessly brutal as it would appear if one reads only Western and tendentious Chinese sources. For example, the scorched earth policy in which they did indulge from time to time was often a matter of seeing things through different eyes. The Mongols looked upon much of China as potentially splendid pasture land for horses, whose uses they understood very well indeed, but they found the land badly cluttered up with buildings and cultivated trees. If these were cleared away,* they reasoned, the yellow earth would become superlatively productive—of Mongol horses, naturally. However, to that Chinese family whose earth had been scorched the actual philosophy behind the deed was a matter of profound indifference.

Many of the people living in the Chinese enclaves had found their way to them through unimaginable terrors which had shaken them to the depths of their souls. Still others who lived in the relative safety of Chen-ting and Tung-p'ing had families which had been put to the sword (or worse) in less fortunate areas. Much poetry written during this period is called *sang-luan* verse, or "poetry of death and destruction," and *sang-luan* verse in many ways is a far more accurate measure of the emotional battering the Chinese underwent at the hands of the Mongols than any amount of historical documentation.

In June of 1223 Yuan Hao-wen, whom we have already mentioned as the poet friend of Po P'u's family, was taken captive and sent north into Shantung. Not all Chinese prisoners were exiled to Mongolia. He wrote three poems either during or about the trip which evoke the widespread sense of doom and dread among Chinese that civilized life itself was coming to an end:

*Regarding cultivated trees, the Chinese had early taken to planting dense groves of trees in sensitive border areas to slow down the horsemen from the steppes. The nomadic invaders often responded by cutting down the trees and dragging them with them to fill in city moats or defense works. (See Wittfogel and Feng, p. 563.) Trees, alas, are always early victims of war, both ancient and modern.

I

White bones strewn about like tangled hemp:
How soon will mulberries and catalpas of home
Be transformed into deserts of Dragon Sands?
All we know is, life has ended north of the river.
Ruined homes and sparse smoke
Number the families left.

II

So many of the sleeping dead on the verge of the road
Were prisoners bound hand and foot.
Past them the bannered chariots flowed like a river.
Red dust and the sound of weeping
Follow the Uigur horses.
For whom do they look back with each step they take?

III

Wooden Buddhas which went with our troops
Sell for less than kindling.
The city is scoured for the great bronze bells
Played in the court orchestra.
How long will the plunder last?
The question has no answer;
But great ships, heavy laden,
Are making for Pien-liang.[5]

The plight of those who avoided capture or exile was scarcely less hopeless:

The day soldiers left and people returned
flowers opened and snowy skies cleared,
field and stream were rank with old grasses
but new smoke stirred in the village;

hungry rats squealed in hollow walls
and starving crows pecked about in barren fields;
then the sound of people arguing—
the district officer was already pressing for payment.

As Professor Stephen West, who translated the last poem by Hsin Yuan, says on page 37 of his 1972 work:

> [Such poems] detail only too accurately the dilemma of many peasants in North China. Harried about the countryside by the hordes of Chinggis, not only did they face barren fields when they returned, they faced the ubiquitous tax man as well. They were victims of a vicious cycle during which the territory of Chin (i.e. China) shrank by about half while the size of the army grew out of proportion, in order to resist the Northern invaders.

So there is no blinking the fact that China did suffer at the hands of the invader even though in many ways the entertainer was peculiarly immune to some of the worse consequences of the Mongol conquest. Since the Chinese actor had no social status at all, he had none to lose in the great upheaval. The entertainer had seldom a square foot of earth to his name, so it was others' earth, not his, that was scorched. He had always to make a living by his wits from (or in spite of) other social classes, so it mattered very little to him when the hierarchy of classes was turned upside down. Last but not least, for whatever the reason, the Mongols seemed to look upon entertainers as people who had some desirable function in their scheme of things.*

*The situation is not without its analogies elsewhere in the world: "On the other hand, little as the barbarians [Attila and Co.] loved the theater, the *mimi* and *scurrae* of the conquered lands seem to have tickled their fancy as they sat over wine. At the banquet ... in 448 the guests were first moved to martial ardour ... and then stirred to laughter by the antics of a Scythian and a Moorish buffoon" (Chambers, vol. 1, p. 34).

But the above was during the tentative, wide-open days of the conquest and its immediate set of compromises; by the time Kublai had been on the throne a decade or so (looking more and more like a Chinese-style emperor), he or his bureaucrats began to treat the demimonde of entertainers and entertainment in much the same fashion his predecessors and successors to the Dragon Throne did:

PROHIBITION

1. All citizens not engaged in the pursuits proper to them and who in city or hamlet shall practice and sing musical entertainments *(tz'u-hua),* or teach or perform *tsa-chü* dramas, or bring together crowds for the purpose of lewd entertainments

SHALL BE PROHIBITED, and:

2. All animal trainers, snake charmers, puppeteers, performers of sleight-of-hand, player of cymbals, *tao-hua-ch'ien* (?) and Taoist drums, and those who deceive men and gather crowds for the purpose of practising quacksalving, will be prohibited and those who disobey

WILL BE SEVERELY PUNISHED

This prohibition is from the "Yuan laws"[6] but such attitudes and similar legislation can be found anywhere in the world and in nearly every age.[7]

CHINESE ENTERTAINMENT BEFORE THE MONGOLS

> The *doong-doong* of lizard drums blends with the sound of revels.
> The *ch'ing-ch'ing* chiming of pipes and strings melds words and tune.
> Nothing can match a Jurched banquet!
>
> *Chin An-shou,* Act IV (*YCH* #63)

Notwithstanding the well-attested terrors and devastations, we are presented with the ineluctable fact that the theater flourished during the early Yuan as never before in Chinese history; and a theatrical form, the *tsa-chü*—the musical, poetic drama which fixed Chinese taste in theater for all time, it would seem—grew to maturity and became overripe all within the 80-some years (1260–1345) the Mongol Khans ruled the Middle Kingdom. Anyone seriously interested in understanding the history of Chinese theater must try to account for this florescence even though the information available to him is more often suggestive than conclusive. It is all very well for me to have pointed out that several Chinese enclaves weathered the invasions of China well and the Mongols seem to have tolerated the theater in the heart of their earliest strongholds, but why should it have been the *theater* which fared so well? In theory might not the era and its circumstances just as well have stimulated the writing of biographies, say, or free verse, or even the making of pottery? It could, of course. The reason for the rapid rise during the Yuan dynasty of what is now considered classical Chinese drama is that the foundations for the Augustan Age of the theater (if such terminological miscegenation be allowed) had been laid before the Mongol invasions. This is as certain as it is paradoxical, because the dynasty which preceded and was destroyed by the Mongols was the Chin (1115–1234)—founded by Tatar invaders from the area of Manchuria who established their capital in Peking in 1151! So, by peeling off one layer of "barbarian" conquest we find yet another underneath. But the Chins were quite a different proposition. They had lived as a loose confederation of tribes on the northeast Chinese border for many years absorbing (and appreciating) much Chinese culture and many Chinese values. They were sinicized rapidly after their conquest of China, yet even during the piping days of Chin dynasty peace, during the reigns of Shih-tsung and Chang-tsung (1161–1208), when the court was as Chinese in form as any in the history of the Middle Kingdom, the Chins remained a more or less distinguishable minority in the midst of a huge Han Chinese population. But, says Professor West,[8] "like a certain American minority they were known for their dancing and singing." This description of them as a musical people, which West finds scattered through the Yuan dramas themselves, is repeated too often and in too many other sources to be dismissed as merely a theatrical stereotype. In fact, it is very likely that the founders of the Chin dynasty (who, as a tribe, were known as *nü-chen* or Jurcheds) were the proximate source of the kind of music around which the Yuan drama eventually organized itself. This music, the last echoes of which had fallen silent in the theaters and streets of China as early as 1600, was insistently modal in organization and certain melodies were traditionally grouped together in sets *(t'ao-shu),** all members of which were from the same mode. Chinese music had always been describable in terms of modes, but the Han Chinese themselves seem not to have been very interested in modal organization of tunes until the early twelfth century. Even then the interest was to be found in north China rather than the south:

> Ever since the invasions by the Chin and the Yuan, barbarian music has flourished to such an extent that only the instrumental music for the zither *(ch'in)* retains any melodies older than [Chin times]. The northern music of today probably descended from that brought in by the Liao and Chin as they invaded the border towns of the north: it was vigorous, powerful, and very savage—the songs of warriors on horseback. When it reached the heart of China, however, it had become the day-to-day music of the common folk. . . . Certainly southern music is not the equal of northern in the matter of organization by modes. . . . Though southern *ch'ü* (dramas) assuredly do not have modes there is an order to the sequence of songs in them and one must make his scene-suite out of "neighboring" sounds. . . .[9]

*In theatrical terms, this modal set or suite with its attendant dramatic apparatus (dialogue, stage business, etc.) constituted an act in Yuan drama. See Chapter 4 below.

Hsü Wei (1521–93), the eccentric playwright-critic who wrote these words in his *Nan-tz'u Hsü-lu* (Notes on Southern Music), was known as a musician of parts, and, though some of his conclusions are faulty, he is certainly right when he says that the typical northern modal music in China begins with the Chin and their near neighbors, the Liao. He is also quite right (though he somehow makes it sound like a contest in which the South was the loser) that southern theatrical compositions never show the kind of interest in modal grouping of their arias which is the basic convention of Chin and Mongol dynasty musical entertainments.

Hsü writes about the Jurcheds from a distance of almost 300 years after the fact, so his statements must be used with caution and buttressed by other information to corroborate them. A number of oblique references to the Jurched talent with music, which imply that music must have been of some importance to the tribe, will be discussed below. It must be remembered first, however, that Mongol dynasty dramas are most often spoken of by the Chinese as musical compositions.* Or, to put it another way, a person said to be skilled in music was assumed to be, in the Chin-Yuan period and to a lesser degree in the Ming, capable of composing dramas for the theater.

Possibly because of the geometric nature of their literary language, Chinese scholars like to play the numbers game in their writings: one hears constantly of the "five elements," "the three ways," the "seventy-two disciples," and the like. On the first page of *Ch'ang-lun* (On Singing)[10]—a short pamphlet by an anonymous late Yuan author who calls himself "Proprietor of the Iris hut"—there is a list of "Five emperors who truly knew music." The fifth on the list (the one closest in time to the author of *Ch'ang-lun*) is Emperor Chang-tsung of the Chin dynasty (*reg.* 1190–1209). This same emperor is given credit for the creation of a whole style of music named after one of his reign periods, the "*ch'eng-an* form" in the *T'ai-ho Cheng-yin P'u*[11] (The T'ai-ho Formulary for Correct Composition) compiled by the Ming dynasty's Prince Chu Ch'üan in the last years of the fourteenth century.

---

*Traditional Chinese theater is always spoken of this way by the Chinese; for example, even today one does not speak of going to see a Peking Opera, he says he's going to hear *(t'ing)* one.

Yoshikawa sums up the evidence from the histories and a number of stage compositions* and concludes, "everybody held the same view in Yuan and Ming times, that the Jurcheds were very accomplished singers and dancers."[12] But appreciation for the theater and music was not limited to the court, the capital city, or even to fellow Jurcheds. The following quotation from *Hsiao-heng Chi* indicates that the confraternity of players was both numerous and widespread during the Chin era, even in the provinces. The writer is describing a flight from the Mongols when the Chin moved its capital from Chung-tu south to Pien-liang:

> We had just reached the north bank of the Yellow River at Chi-yang when I noticed a fellow traveler who was also heading for the capital south of the Great River. He carried nothing, bore no goods, but he seemed well-fed; his speech was airy and even impudent. I was amazed and questioned him: "I'm an entertainer," said he, and then he continued, "I work together with those of the same profession and when we're on the road we share what we have with each other: working together gives us a sense of family and sharing with one another a sense of commiseration. So-and-so is an actor and he lives in this place, in another place there lives another actor—what do I need supplies for?†

*For example *YCH,* 901: Li Kuei, a Jurched, has an entrance verse in which he says "as a youth I could do both *yuan-pen* skits and *tsa-chü* dramas."

†Yoshikawa (p. 48) cites the above without cautioning the reader that the persona the writer is using is a "Master Upright" and the anecdote is a catapult to launch him on a homiletic flight. Yang Hung-tao may therefore have embroidered somewhat on the closeness of guild feeling among actors at the time: he would certainly have used a group, however, about whom such information would not seem ludicrous. The passage continues:

> When the actor had finished, a look of great contentment suffused his face. I was moved in my heart by this and said to myself: Men wish to become members of the gentry *(shih)* because they feel a moral life is more easily pursued by that class. But humaneness and righteousness are the basis of a moral life, are they not? Humaneness is desirable because it brings peace to others, and righteousness because it benefits others; the man who benefits and brings peace to his fellows, who has a sense of commiseration and kinship with mankind, is certainly beginning to lead a moral life. Actors are supposed only to hoax their audiences, but behold what they have achieved! Behold what they have achieved! (Yang Hung-tao's *Hsiao-heng Chi,* ch. 7, 27b.)

Nor were his fellows, it would seem, the only ones who welcomed the player in the provinces. When a Chin dynasty merchant's tomb in near perfect condition was excavated near the town of Hou-ma in Shansi province, it became evident that one of the enthusiasms this obviously wealthy man wanted to continue to indulge in the next world was the theater; for a model stage, complete with small glazed terracotta figurines of a troupe of five players on it, was found fitted into one wall. Not far from Hou-ma another Chin period tomb was unearthed in Yen-shih *hsien* equipped with three low-relief tiles picturing scenes and skits from the stage (see Figure 2). These too had presumably been worked into the interior of the tomb so its occupant could continue being as delighted in the next world by some kind of phantom theater as he obviously had been by the corporeal ones which surrounded him in Shansi in the late thirteenth century.

Fig. 2. Chin Dynasty Performers Redrawn from Tomb Tiles

Finally, there is quite a famous set of songs, done together in a modal suite form, and known as the "Jurched suite" which was incorporated with differing degrees of success into several Yuan dramas and about which Chou Te-ch'ing, author of the *Chung-yuan Yin-yün* (Sound and Rhymes of the Central Plains)[13] says:

> The ancients also cautioned us "when writing musical poetry take greatest care not to do violence to the musical requirements *(yin lü).*" This is to say, when doing something like the "Jurched suite" which begins with "Feng-liu T'i" you must sing it with Jurched words; for then, though the burden of the lyrics may be unclear, you will have succeeded if you cleave to the musical requirements.

Further search will show that when the Jurcheds took over north China they already had a lively interest in Han Chinese entertainment. The Mongols had Chinese (Chin?) entertainers* before they attacked China and, as we have said, very soon after the Mongol conquest of the Central Plains, theater underwent its greatest period of growth. At first hearing this does seem strange: how does an entertainer make a living trying to please those who speak another tongue and come from another land? The answer has already been given in part above: music seldom even pauses at national boundaries. As Chou Te-ch'ing says, "sing it with Jurched words . . . the . . . lyrics may be unclear but you will have succeeded if you do the music well." Instrumental and vocal *music* can be comprehensible and beguiling whatever your language.

The other part of the answer lies in the very synthetic nature of the Chinese theater: as more and more evidence accumulates, it becomes increasingly clear that Chinese theater always had a high component of other entertainment arts mixed in with it. Acrobatics, restrained or strenuous pantomime, dance, singing, musical and farce interludes seem always to have been as much a part of the Chinese stage as the dramatic story, the operatic production. Some scholars, e.g. Chou Yi-pai in *Chung-kuo Hsi-chü Shih Chiang-tso* (Lectures on the History of Chinese Drama, p. 105), even go so far as to claim that early association with these other entertainment forms was what makes the Chinese traditional theater what it is today, with its dance and gymnastic stage movements, its music and its song. However that may be, the ancillary entertainment forms embedded in Mongol era

*See Waley (1931), p. 81. "In Besh-balig (near modern Kucha in the Tarin basin) the musicians were all Chinese."

dramas are just those which most easily transcend national and cultural boundaries: the circus in Europe, for example, has never been geographically limited by anything except its means of transportation. All things being politically equal, the same circus is as welcome in Buda and Pest as it is in Bordeaux. The acrobat, the juggler, fire-eater, and slapstick clown are as nearly universal in their fascination as entertainment can be. Here history speaks to us in the imperative rather than the indicative mood: it must have been these entertainment skills that allowed the theater to survive (even thrive) while a generation of Mongol invaders grew up inside China proper, learning the language and something of Chinese ways. Those of us interested in theater as literature should always bear in mind what a sturdy rooftree the humble slapstick has proved to be throughout the world and how many delicate branches of theater arts have found shelter beneath it. Once acculturation had taken place, the Mongol court and the homes of their nobles welcomed the dramas which were shaped by music probably already familiar to them and which incorporated the less sophisticated arts that had always delighted them. Then it was that the golden age of Yuan drama began. As Yoshikawa says in the English preface to his 1954 edition of *Gen Zatsugeki Kenkyū:*

> The best of the plays were written in the second half of the thirteenth century, during the reign of Kubilai (1260–1294). This is earlier than Dr. Hu Shih has asserted, but later than some other scholars have supposed.

Yuan drama truly was the theater of the days of Kublai Khan, and men writing as late as the 1330s acknowledged that the era and its music were ultimately a heritage from the Jurched (Chin) dynasty:

> Chin songs delighted our first kings,
> White Chin fingers flew on the thirteen strings.
> Counsellor-actor Kuan Ch'ing of the Chin
> Offered his play *T'ang Heeds Yi-yin*.*

---

*Yoshikawa (p. 56) who discovered this verse hidden away in the works of a minor Yuan writer, Yang Wei-chen, says that the Kuan Ch'ing of the poem is probably meant to refer to Kuan Han-ch'ing, but since no such play as *T'ang Heeds Yi-yin* is mentioned in the *Register of Ghosts* he finds the information suspect. I see no reason why the poet might not have used Kuan's name as metonymy for Chin playwrights or early playwrights in general.

2. Stages and Theaters

(Ti-erh che)

Hsi-ch'ang hsiao t'ien-ti;
T'ien-ti ta hsi-ch'ang

"The stage is but a miniature world;
and the world only a vast stage."

Lu Hsün, *Ma-shang Jih-chi,* p. 311

STAGES

In the fall of 1934 a youthful Lawrence Sickman of the Nelson Gallery of Art in Kansas City was traveling along the arid Fen River valley in south central Shansi. The autumn rains—part of the complex monsoon climate of North Central China—had begun as he reached famous Kuang-sheng temple that lies at the foot of a spur of the 8,700-foot Mount Huo. A great spring gushes from the bottom of the mountain here, watering a miraculous strip of fresh green in the dry but fertile loess plain through which it flows. With the majesty of the peak and the wonder of a great fountain, this must always have seemed a spot beloved of the gods and, as far as can be determined, a temple—long since vanished—was built here as early as A.D. 147.

The temple compound closest to the flowing source is built around the Ming-ying Wang Tien (Hall of the Responsive and Perceptive Prince), a handsome shrine dedicated to the genie of locality who seems to have been both the spirit of the Huo mountains and of the bountiful spring itself. As befits such a benevolent god, his hall was lavishly decorated and contains some of the most impressive wall-paintings in all of North China. Dr. Sickman was there to photograph them:

> The hall itself ... is approximately thirty-five feet on a side, interior measurement. Around the hall is a covered veranda.... Both the roof of the hall and of the veranda have wide, sweeping eaves. The roof ridge is decorated in moulded tiles brilliantly glazed, typical of Shansi temple ornament. All four walls of the interior are covered with paintings. There is a brick wainscoting extending from the floor to a height of three feet. The paintings are continuous from here to the top of the walls. Those on the two sides are thirty-five feet long and reach to the top of the wall.

With lowering clouds of the autumn rains deepening the gloom of the temple room, Dr. Sickman worked as well as he could* with the cumbersome photographic equipment of the time in the faintly musty atmosphere always associated with dust which has long lain undisturbed:

> The largest ... inscription, I was unable to copy. This consists of a number of large characters ... running the entire length of the south walls. All the walls were heavily coated with dust and this portion was too high for the ray of my pocket flashlight. It was possible to obtain a few of the characters ... by the light of a candle tied to a long pole.... "Recorded in the great Yuan dynasty ... May 23, 1326 [*sic*]."[1]

*In a letter to me (3/9/73) Dr. Sickman recalls the day: "Photographing in the temple was almost impossible. It rained constantly and there was no light save from the open door, which was blocked by farmers from far and wide while I photographed. Moreover, it was in the days before electric flash. I had to use the old-fashioned flash powder. The only way I could focus on the wall paintings was by having my Chinese assistant hold a candle against the wall. I would focus on the candle, open the shutter, and set off the powder. I would give a good deal to know what the local gentry thought of these strange explosions going off in their temple."

Fig. 3. The Wall Painting from the Ming-ying Wang Tien, Shansi (from *Hsi-ch'u Yen-chiu*)

But the painting of greatest interest to us is on the

> Southeast wall. A single composition representing a scene from a theatrical performance approximately 12 feet wide. An actor in the official costume of the Sung dynasty holds the center of the tile-paved stage.... The stage is backed with a large curtain finished with a ruffle at the top.... The inscription which extends across the top of the picture is the ... 1326 one referred to above. [See Figure 3.]

Here the existence of a wall painting with undeniable Mongol dynasty credentials, depicting an actual performance of a drama of the time, was first brought to the attention of Western scholars. Dr. Sickman apologizes in the article[2] for the poor quality of his photographs, but the picture of the theatrical performance is quite clear enough to have made the heart of a student of Chinese drama leap—had any such organ existed in the West in 1937.

The curious thing is that if this mural could somehow have been reproduced in *seventeen* thirty-seven instead of 1937 it would have found an enthusiastic audience and the widest welcome. France from about 1730 and England from about 1740 to 1760 were in the throes of *chinoiserie.* This odd fad began as a very serious quarrel between the mother Church and the Jesuits. It was the latter's contention—to make simple what was a complicated era in the evolution of Christianity—that man's relationship with his God (for they viewed ethics and morality as inseparable from a belief in God) had actually been cloyed and subverted by the existence of a church. They reasoned that mankind in some distant land (and China was as distant as you could get), where he had not been already corrupted by an organized church, would exhibit just those praiseworthy human virtues which they felt the Church had debased in European men.

In 1615 works of the remarkable Matteo Ricci—the first European to have penetrated the intellectual life of China—began to appear, and the Jesuits published the first translation of part of the Confucian Canon in 1662. China rapidly became the model for many of the most restless thinkers and throughout the seventeenth and early eighteenth century exerted a considerable influence on such men as Montesquieu, Voltaire, and Liebnitz. The Physiocrats' economic and land theories were greatly influenced by Chinese concepts. These influences and concepts were initially based on some form of reality in China, but the Jesuits had a vested interest in selling the moral excellence of the Chinese. They were in favor of sinicizing Church doctrine as a way of converting the Chinese to Christianity, and, because the Church demurred, the Jesuit's reports on the natural morality of the Chinese became more glowing and more divorced not only from political realities but the truth in general.

However, by the late 1740s nothing of this church struggle's great seminal influence was left—in England at least—but a permanent love affair with tea and a kind of chi-chi dalliance with aesthetic matters "after the Chinese fashion." Anyone who has seen the whacking great pagoda sticking incongruously out of the midst of Kew Gardens* will have some idea of the tenor of the times. One of the few areas apparently most suited for things "after the Chinese fashion" was the stage, with its great masks and pageants, to which the English beau monde was then addicted. Now, upon this fertile ground there tumbled not one but two English translations of Jean Baptiste du Halde's *Description de la Chine.* The best known English version, done by Edward Cave, proprietor of the *Gentleman's Magazine,* promised in its prefatory material that the book contained "beſides the state of Philoſophy, Religion and the Sciences in China ... several curious Eſſays on Morality, Liberty and Government extracted from Chineſe Books." It was not noted in the preface that the *Description* also contained the first specimen of Yuan drama (translated by Father Joseph Prémare and vastly abridged) ever done in a Western language—*Chao-shih Ku-erh* (*YCH* #85) *The Orphan of Chao.* Du Halde's original *Description* and its English translation enjoyed instant and enormous popularity, and it took no time at all for the *Orphan* to become adapted for the English stage. William Hachett's *The Chinese Orphan: An Historical Tragedy* appeared in 1741. This was followed by adaptations in French and Italian by Voltaire and Metastasio. Arthur Murphey's *Orphan of China* (1756) was first staged in 1759, when it was an immediate success, and was revived in both Drury Lane and Covent Garden. In 1767 it was produced in the Southwark Theater, Philadelphia, Pennsylvania, and a year later at the John Street Theater in New York (where it was revived as late as 1842.)[3] Borne on the gauzy wings of *chinoiserie,* a badly mutilated and freely adapted Yuan drama had migrated all the way to the New World before the end of the eighteenth century. But after the 1740s interest in and knowledge of that dramatic form made no progress at all for almost a century, until Stanislaus Julien at College de France finally translated *The Orphan of Chao* in its entirety. And then another century passed before the first *English* translation of an entire *tsa-chü* appeared—in 1936 both S. I. Hsiung and Henry H. Hart published separate versions of *Hsi-hsiang Chi, The Western Chamber.*

*Or its more modest cousin, the *Chinesische Turm* in the Englischer Garten at Munich.

However, the second time this remarkable painting was made available to scholars East and West, there were a number of enthusiastic and trained students of the drama who saw its significance and gained insight from it. *Hsi-ch'ü Yen-chiu* (Drama Research) carried an article by Liu Nien-tzu, with the catchy subtitle "Notes on the Investigation of the Ming-ying Wang Temple's Yuan dynasty Wall Painting of a Theatrical Performance." Accompanying the article is a photograph of what seems to be a traced* reproduction of the painting (in full color and well printed) done by one Li Hsin. It has since been reproduced in many books including this one (Figure 3).

Grateful as we are for this priceless artifact, a question should spring to mind: what is a painting of what appears to be a secular theatrical performance doing in the Hall of the Responsive and Perceptive Prince when the other walls are covered with proper iconography depicting the god "dressed as a civil official and of fearsome aspect" and the service of worshippers and suppliants? In part, the answer is actually written on stone outside the temple itself.

Chinese civic and communal pride has often been chiseled skillfully on stone steles memorializing a collective effort, which are then set up somewhere near the buildings or sites they commemorate. Because of the distressing frequency with which large public structures in China went up in smoke, many times nothing at all is left of the place save the stele, which often makes note of what once existed there. Let me give some excerpts from Sickman's translation of the stele which celebrates the temple's restoration, dated August 21, 1319:

> The mountain is a rich treasury nurturing all things.... At appointed times the Emperor sends a special delegate to perform sacrifices....Consider the surroundings; it is truly a place where a god may descend....the benefits that the Prince gives to the people are so abundant that his abode should be a palace.

*This type of art work *(mo-hsieh)* is done with great skill on translucent Chinese paper by certain Chinese artists, but when one reflects that the overall size of this production runs to more than 250 square feet, the mind boggles: perhaps *mo-hsieh* (or *mo-hui*) simply means "to copy" in this case.

> The old people of the district say that formerly each year in the third month, from the 11th to the 20th day the people from all the districts made a festival. . . . From the cities and the villages far away and from the nearby hamlets the rich come in carriages and on horseback while the poor come walking, leaning on sticks. . . .
>
> Then the people from the Two Streams (of the spring) *contribute funds for a theatrical performance. . . . The crowds enjoyed themselves, sporting several days delighting in the best food.* . . . [Italics mine.]
>
> Originally the room of the great hall (was) completely adorned with paintings. What ill fortune! In the 7th year of Ta-te . . . (Sept. 6th 1305),* in the night, there was an earthquake east of the river. It was especially severe in this district—not a single thing was left! The upper and lower courses fell in and the (spring) water was unable to flow. . . .
>
> In the 11th month of this same year . . . the superintendent ordered . . . the District Magistrate to superintend the work of repair. . . .
>
> In the sixth year of Yen-yu (1319) the Superintendent . . . (and) workmen completed the walls, finishing them with fine sand.

And on the festive occasion which celebrated restoration of the Hall of the Responsive and Perceptive Prince, the grateful communicants, farmers from the Two Streams, subscribed to a fund to bring a well-known troupe to the temple's theater which used to stand somewhere across the compound facing the great hall (its rafters fell prey to wood rot and it was rebuilt in 1924 in a somewhat different way)[4] and which, we can tell from the wall painting, had a glazed tile stage floor and was probably made of brick. The celebrants were open-handed when they laid on the festivities, for they got a renowned actress and her company from the nearby metropolis of P'ing-yang (known in those days as Yao-tu) to help them celebrate the ten-day festival as they had in years gone by. But this time the theatricals were so exceptionally grand that the artist who was doing religious paintings for the other walls of the Great Hall saw fit to paint a performance from life, as it were, on the southeast wall. The players in the painting continued through the ages acting their silent tribute to the god who sat watching them from across the dim room.

Along the top of the gathered curtain which acts as a teaser or valance for the pictured stage, the artist painted the following:

*Should be 1303.

THE GREAT ACTRESS,*
ELEGANCE OF CHUNG-TU, PLAYED HERE

Beloved in Yao-tu	Days in the 4th month, 1324

Judging from this evidence alone, it would not be entirely clear whether the inscription appeared on the curtains owned by the troupe or was the painter's way of noting the date and greatness of the festive performances. Professor David Hawkes (1971, p. 74)[5] concludes that the inscription was on the troupe's curtains because:

> The wording on the pelmet which hangs across the whole width of the proscenium arch corresponds to the wording of the advertisement mentioned in the first act of *Lan Ts'ai-ho*.

This is true, in part. The text of Lan Ts'ai-ho's advertising flags and banners *(ch'i-p'ai)* reads: "On the stage at the Liang-yuan Theater the actor *(mo-ni)* Lan Ts'ai-ho is now performing." The Chinese language being uninflected for tense, "played here" and "is now playing" are both *tso-ch'ang*.† However, the text of the *tsa-chü* drama *Lan Ts'ai-ho,*[6] to which Hawkes alludes, does not force us to conclude that this advertising was written across the pelmet or teaser. In fact, the implication is otherwise. I must confess I found it hard to believe that "4th month 1324" was ever a part of any company's stage drapes. However, we might be quite unable to say with certainty that the inscription was done by the painter to celebrate the great event and was not on the troupe's hangings were it not that one of the stone pillars which was once part of a temple stage (in the village of Ku-shan in Wan-jung prefecture, Shansi) has an inscription that serves exactly the same

*In *Hsi-ch'ü Yen-chiu, ta-hang,* doubtless a short form of *ta hang-yuan* or *ta hang-shou,* "great performer" or "chef-de-troupe," was misunderstood as T'ai-hang, the name of a mountain range. At the time I thought it odd since the T'ai-hangs are not near Yao-tu. Ting Ming-yi (1972) set things straight. Shih (1976) perpetuates the 1957 *Hsi-ch'ü* error, however.

†For example, in the *Tu-ch'eng Chi-sheng,* p. 91, says, "There is a vacant space outside the wall of the government arsenal and all manner of entertainers play here." *(Tsai tz'u tso-ch'ang)*

purpose as our painting: it is carved to commemorate a great event in the temple's history; "The great actor* Chang Te-hao played here," it says, and then it gives the date "The *ch'ing-ming* Festival, 3rd month, 1301."[7]

Dr. Sickman translated (1937, p. 56) the large characters in the center inscription, "The Chung Pu-hsiu theatrical company played (?) here" which is a perfectly adequate translation (barring the typographical error, "Pu" for "tu") for all save those whose special interest is in the theater. On page 60 Sickman writes of the painting, "An actor in the official costume of the Sung dynasty holds the center of the tile-paved stage." It is scarcely surprising that he takes the epicene figure in the wide-winged hat to be a man, but in fact it can be none other than our "great actress" (she who was "beloved in Yao-tu") Chung-tu Hsiu or "Elegance of Chung-tu." There can be absolutely no doubt of her sex. In the *Ch'ing-lou Chi* (A Record of Painted Houses)† compiled by Hsia T'ing-chih (1316–137?) and prefaced 1366, are given the sobriquets of seventy-four famous courtesan-entertainers with brief sketches of their specialties (their public specialties, that is). The suffix *hsiu* appears in seventeen of these stage names and seems to have meant something like "Elegance." Thus we have T'ien-jan Hsiu (whose surname was actually Kao and who was called *Erh-mei*—little second sister—by her familiars). Her stage name must have meant something like "Natural (or Inborn) Elegance." She was much admired by Po Jen-fu (see Chapter 1, above), we are told, and she specialized in *tsa-chü* dramas about "women's quarters." In the drama *Lo Li-lang* (*YCH* #90, p. 1570) we find, "there is a new actress in town called Yi-shih Hsiu," which must have meant "Timely or Fashionable Elegance." Finally, in *Ch'ing-lou Chi* we have one Ta-tu Hsiu "Elegance from (the capital) Ta-tu" whose stage name exactly corresponds in form to our Chung-tu Hsiu. To be sure, I know of no

*There is nothing about this proper name that prevents it being translated "actress," but the given name has a more masculine than feminine flavor.

†Parts of this are translated under the title of "The Green Bower Collection" by Waley (1964).

place called Chung-tu,* but the use of toponyms for entertainers' stage names is very common. My favorite such from the *Ch'ing-lou chi* is the courtesan-actress P'ing-yang Nu, "The Slave from P'ing-yang" who, we are told, was "tatooed on all four limbs, specialized in robber-band parts and had a squint in one eye"! There must have been a limited number of parts she could perform on the stage, but I like to imagine that her private entertainment was much in demand if only for reasons of novelty.

Whether the artist added the inscription to the painting or it was done by the troupe on their own hangings, the most informative fact about the wall painting is that a great religious festival was accompanied by dramatic performances grand enough to have been commemorated on the wall of the god's shrine. There could hardly be a clearer example of the close connection between religion and drama, the temple and the stage. Even if there were no extant temples with their stages still intact today we would have to posit the widespread use of the temple stage as early as the Sung dynasty. Happily, however, there are many such temple stages left in China today, and the third stage type in Figure 4 is redrawn from a photograph of one taken by Dana Kalvodová-Diamantová of Charles University, Prague, in 1957. The stage structure is now the only part of this Hangchow temple compound left standing: the foundations indicate, however, that it was in the classical temple form of a hollow rectangle and the stage faced the main altar directly across an open inner courtyard. Almost without exception the main temple altar faces south; so, just as regularly, the stage faced north. Frequently there is a broad walkway from the stage to the main altar across the courtyard, and sometimes this thoroughfare is paved with large ashlars, as is the case with the

*One cannot help wondering, however, whether the *chung* of Chung-tu Hsiu is not simply a fancy version of *chung* "central." If this were so, the whole story would be clear because an old name for P'u-chou (an area controlled from P'ing-yang) was Chung-tu, "central capital."

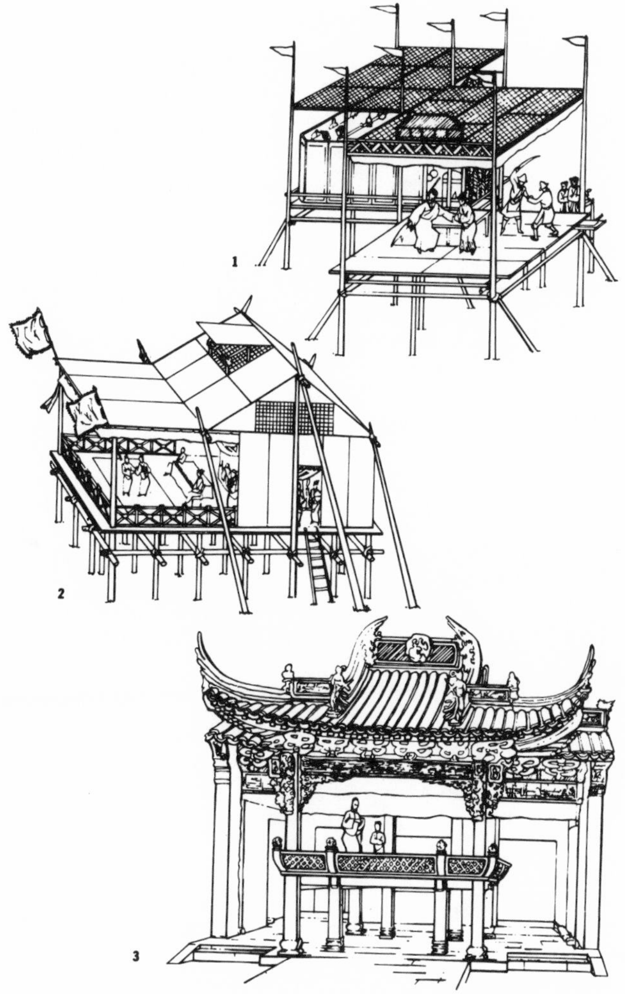

Fig. 4. Three Traditional Stage Types

Hangchow temple stage illustrated above. The very geography of the temple stage leaves no doubt that the performance was in fact an offering to the gods of the temple.*

*I'm not at all sure that it is significant, but it should be remembered that the painting in Kuang-sheng Ssu was on the south wall—the same general orientation as stage and shrine.

The association of some kind of performance with religious sites and activities in China must be unimaginably ancient. Probably the earliest documentary evidence of it appears (albeit obliquely) in the *Nine Songs* which seem to have been the verses sung during or about religious observances:

> The contents of these songs ... are self-explanatory. Male or female shamans ... dressed up in gorgeous costumes, sing and dance to the accompaniment of music, drawing the gods down from heaven in a sort of divine courtship. The religion of which these songs are the liturgy is frankly an erotic one. [D. Hawkes, *Ch'u-tz'u*, p. 35.]

During what era this association was first given structural expression in the temple stage is also lost in the mists of time, but the earliest notice of a temple stage structure (to my knowledge) is found not very far from either the Kuang-sheng temple with its remarkable wall paintings, or P'ing-yang, the city which favored our actress, Elegance of Chung-tu. In what used to be called Wan-ch'üan Prefecture, Shansi, is the little village of Upbridge (Shang-ch'iao Ts'un) where, until fairly recently, there was a rather large temple complex known as the Temple to the Earth Goddess *(Hou-t'u miao).* Today all that is left of it is the stele erected on the occasion of the temple's completion in the year 1020. Inscribed upon it are the circumstances of the building and a list of the men who built the Great Hall, the Temple to Erh-lang, the Niang-tzu shrine, etc. In the list is one "Li T'ing-hsün the Temple Master *(tu-wei na-t'ou)* and eighteen of his men who built *(hsiu)* the stage hall *(wu-t'ing).*"[8] Since this is by far the largest group to have been employed on any one unit of the temple complex, we may assume that the stage with its sheltering roof and walls was quite impressive and looked something like our stage 3.

From other facts carved in this stele one can put together information which makes it clear that the hall was actually begun in the year 1005; making this, "The earliest evidence of a wood-and-brick stage structure in the history of China" according to Ting Ming-yi.

Even though these early temple stages were doubtless set atop solid slab bases, rather than held aloft by columns as is the case with stage 3, Figure 4, the *wu-t'ing* (performing hall) and the *wu-t'ying* (performing structure) were rather ambitious undertakings with their masonry-and-timber walls and tiled roofs. We know they had much simpler origins even when built as part of the temples they served. One of those invaluable stone inscriptions found embedded in the foundation of what had once been the stage at the Temple of Prince Millet *(Chi-wang)* in the village of T'ai-yüeh, bearing the date 1271, reads in part:

> The main temple . . . long ago had its stage platform, but not for many years was it roofed over. Now this village . . . has subscribed the amount of two hundred strings of cash that a performing hall *(wu-t'ing)* may be built on it and this stone inscribed. . . .[9]

I read Comrade Ting's piece with a good deal of appreciation, took exception to his observation (p. 52) that because peasants and artisans worked on the temple stages they were "laying down the bases for culture," and then became bemused by one of his concluding paragraphs:

> The unfortunate thing is that so many of them [stages in Shansi] no longer exist as structures. Excepting those which were destroyed long ago by natural causes, a most important reason for their destruction was the foreign imperialists and reactionary groups inside the country. As far as we know, the stages of the Prince Millet Temple in T'ai-yueh village, the Hou-t'u Temple in Ssu-wang and the Tai-yüeh Temple in Hsi-ching were all destroyed by the Japanese imperialists during the war of resistance (1937–1947). The stage at the Temple of Wind and Rain in Wan-jung was destroyed by the bandit troops of Yen Hsi-shan during the same period. So all of these were crimes of invasion and cultural destruction by imperialist and reactionary forces. (p. 54)

One gets a vision from this of crazed hordes of Japanese and warlord troops attacking these inoffensive structures with firebrand and crowbar. While it is true that temples and churches tend to suffer during any armed struggle, I think I can suggest less dramatic (and politically less satisfying to Comrade Ting) causes for the destruction of Shansi stage structures.

Since these buildings were really only used during times of high festival they afforded for the rest of the year a dry, roofed-in communal space that was put to use holding newly reaped and drying shocks of grain and bundles of fodder, as well as the raw materials for such village industries as mat-weaving and basket- and sandal-making. Among the splendid photographs taken in China by Professor Dana Kalvodová in 1956–57 is one of the small stage on the canal in Shao-hsing (Chekiang) where Lu Hsün as a child watched performances from a boat—as he writes in his stories *She Hsi* and *Huo Wu-ch'ang*. Her picture shows this graceful little stage (set some distance away from the temple proper in order to offer the best view to a floating audience of boat-people)* stuffed half full of what appear to be drying sheaves of grain but may be straw or fodder. Since all of these commodities are inflammable and some of them are subject to spontaneous combustion, it does not strain my imagination to visualize one or more of the casualties mentioned above occurring during the decade of Sino-Japanese struggles from perfectly natural causes.

Not only did rural temple stages have humbler beginnings, even such a grand event as the performance given in the capital during the lantern festival (on the first full moon of the lunar year) for the emperor himself was conducted on a simple open platform:

---

*See also her "Village Theater of Shao-hsing in Lu Hsün's Work" (Kalvodová, 1976), especially p. 132 *ff*. She includes a woodcut by Shao K'o-p'ing (shown here as Figure 5) which depicts a performance going on in this small stage, the boat audience watching, and the temple to the right. The picture is done from the imagination but is probably quite accurate.

Fig. 5. Audience at Village Theater in Shao-hsing (from Kalvodová, 1976)

> . . . and at the foot of the tower (from which the emperor was going to view the lanterns) there was an open stage *(lu-t'ai)* made with timbers and laths with a festooned railing. Along two of its sides stood the imperial bodyguards . . . and facing it was the music tent. The musicians of the Imperial Academy and the players performed on it. . . . Thousands of commoners stood below the stage and watched: from time to time the players would lead them all in a "long live the emperor."[10]

But both the *wu-t'ai* (dance platform) and the *lu-t'ai* (open platform) were preceded by what is believed to have been a simple collapsible (?) fence or railing which could be set out on any convenient flat space to keep the spectators at a distance while the players performed inside the area enclosed by this railing or *kou-lan.*[11] This was probably the first secular "theater" and, since the term *kou-lan,* "railing," has been synonymous with the theater in China for at least seven hundred years, it seems proper here to turn to the subject of the theater itself: the reader will discover that I continue to speak from time to time of the performing area or stage but only as a part of a secular structure housing a theatrical troupe engaged in earning its daily bread.

THEATERS

> In the *li-wa* district are the Yaksha and the Elephant theaters. The latter is the largest and can hold several thousand.
>
> *Tung-ching Meng-hua Lu* (A.D. 1147), p. 14

As is apparent from the epigraph to this section, there were permanent theaters in the capital of K'ai-feng during the Southern Sung (a blessing on all rubbernecks who keep diaries!), and we have every reason to believe that in large cities of the North there were structures housing equally permanent enterprises. We have no illustrations of such playhouses but there are—in addition to those journals kept by sightseers in the capital—four documents from which we derive nearly all the knowledge we have of such establishments. The first is a Yuan drama about players (the first act of which is translated below), the second is a slightly humorous *san-t'ao* or "song" written about a country bumpkin going to the theater for the first time *(Chuang-chia Pu-shih Kou-lan)*[12] the translation of which is also included, the third is a southern play called *Huan-men Ti-tzu Ts'o li-shen* which title means something like "Young Man of Good Family Gets Off to Bad Start." However, since it is a southern drama, and theater practices there may have been somewhat different from Yuan theater, I use it cautiously and only as a secondary source. The last is the so-called *"?-tan hang-yuan"*[13] a *san-t'ao* by Kao An-tao which, as far as we understand this raddled text, confirms the first two but adds little that is new to our knowledge. This I also use with circumspection because I am not always certain I have read it aright. Now let me raise the curtain on our drama about players and show you how much information on the theater-as-a-performance-area is contained in its first act (somewhat abridged).

LAN TS'AI-HO (*WP* #159)

ACT I

(Enter CHUNG-LI CH'UAN *made up as secondary lead, recites.)*

CHUNG-LI:

(reciting)

Birth is my door as death is my gate:
Those who comprehend this, those I liberate.
To all at night comes doubt's small voice:
Salvation is his who dares to make the choice.

I am Chung-li Ch'uan, the Immortal known as Yün-fang, Master of The True Yang. Just now as I was returning from the Halls of Heaven I saw a straight shaft of blue vapor rising from the world below and piercing the Nine Layers of the firmament. I watched it for a long time and finally discovered that it came straight from a theater *(p'eng)* in the pleasure park of Liang in the city of Loyang. There, there is a man called Hsü Chien whose stage name is Lan Ts'ai-ho, whose destiny has already brought him halfway down the road to immortality. I have come straight to earth at Liang Park to bring this Lan Ts'ai-ho to salvation. Well, I must go into the theater now to:

Strike his name from the Books of the Dead,
Bring him to the Amethyst Halls instead.
Show him the path to Beyond-the-Sea
And guide him to travel the Way with me. *(exit)*

(Enter the female lead, the secondary female leading a child, and the two ching, WANG PA-SE *and* LI PAO-T'OU. *They speak.)*

WANG *and* LI:
We are Wang Pa-se and Li Pao-t'ou. Our big brother is Lan Ts'ai-ho and we are playing the theater in Liang Park. This is our sister-in-law. I must go and prepare the stage. First let me open the door to the theater and see if anyone is about.

*(*CHUNG-LI *enters.)*

CHUNG-LI:
I have come in person all the way from the cloud tops to go straight to the theater in Liang Park. In fact, here I am.

(He sees the "music-crib" (yüeh-ch'uang) *and sits down.* WANG PA-SE *sees him.)*

WANG:
Ah—Master Taoist? Would you mind sitting in either the "gods' tower" *(shen-lou)* or the orchestra *(yao-p'eng)* seats? You're now [*on the side of the stage*] where our women sit when they're "accompanying the spectacle" *(p'ai ch'ang).* You're not supposed to be here.

CHUNG-LI:
Is your star player, Hsü Chien, here?

WANG *or* LI:
If the Master will just wait a while, he'll be right back. You have something to talk to him about?

CHUNG-LI:
I'll just wait till he gets here and tell him.

WANG *or* LI:

Take a seat then, Master, he'll be right along.

(Enter the cheng-mo LAN TS'AI-HO.)

LAN:

I am Hsü Chien but I'm known best by my stage name Lan Ts'ai-ho.* My wife is Hsi Ch'ien-chin. I have a son, Hsiao Ts'ai-ho, and a married daughter, Lan Shan-ching. My two cousins are Turtle Wang† and Li Pao-t'ou. We are all playing an engagement at the Liang Park Theater. Yesterday I pasted up all our advertising banners *(hua chaoerh)* and my brothers have prepared the stage, so I'd better go into the theater. You know, the things we actors have to do are not easy to learn:

Tien-chiang Ch'un

(sings)

We take what is writ in Ancient Works
And bend it to the street players' ways.
I've grown practiced in the theater's styles
Of bawdy farce and Buddhist chant,
And exhausted all my meager skill
To learn where the reefs and shallows lie.

---

*This is meant to sound like a common and proper Chinese name, and it does, but it was a phrase used as a rhythmic nonsense unit in a type of Chinese verse, the way English in the past used such items as "hey-non-nonny."

†A *pa-se* is a kind of accompanist for performances, but by using the proper name Wang, the playwright has created a scurrilous pun which does not translate into English without crippling footnotes. I suspect Li Pao-t'ou also had a double meaning, but it is no longer comprehensible as a pun.

Hun-chiang Lung

See how close I've stitched my seams:*
We played one season at Liang Park
And were called back every year for twenty.
No doubt because we please them and
Because we treat our patrons well.
We do a new *yuan-pen* of love and hate
That urges piety and good,
And earns my feed-the-family-
Clothe-the-children wage.
We are better off here than anywhere.
Here, these few gifts of mine
Yield us more than would a valley full of fertile land.

(speaks)
Well, here I am in the theater—*(addresses* WANG *and* LI*)* has any audience shown up? Why, it's almost time.... let's get going with the cleaning up.

WANG:
Audience? Well, I just opened the door and this gentleman walked in and sat himself down in the music crib. I asked him to move to the gallery or the orchestra because our ladies sit here when they are not on stage *(p'ai-ch'ang)*, and he had the nerve to dress me down.

LAN:
Whatever the case, you probably offended him: I'll go talk to him *(pantomimes seeing* CHUNG-LI*)*. Greetings, Master.

*Sai Lien-hsiu ... in her middle years went blind, but her pantomime for entering and going outdoors as well as all her stage actions (lit. "stitching a fine seam") were perfect, no sighted actor was her equal *Lun-chu* p. 25. The term *pu-hsien hsing-chen* "stitching a fine seam" seems to have included any and all stage actions.

CHUNG-LI:
And where have you been disporting yourself?*

LAN:

[*aside*][14]

Oh, I'd like to have *this* fine gentleman paste up posters for me. *(to* CHUNG-LI*)* Why, I met some important gentlemen on the street and they asked me to take a cup of tea with them which is why I'm delayed.

CHUNG-LI:
I've been here half the day; "Better for the music to wait upon the customer than the customer to wait upon the music." I came to see you perform a *tsa-chü*. Which will you perform for me?

LAN:
What *tsa-chü* would you like, Master?

CHUNG-LI:
That's for *you* to tell *me;* let me hear what dramas you can do.

LAN:
Listen, Master, and I'll recite you the list:

Yu Hu-lu

(sings)

Let the noble official select the *tsa-chü*
dearest to his heart.

**San-tan* is a Taoist term and means to wander about; it is what the Taoist adept does by preference.

CHUNG-LI:
That's just a self-serving speech!

LAN:

(sings)

Can street players speak speeches of their own?
No, ours are new-made plays by talents of the *shu-hui.*

CHUNG-LI:
Well, since they're all done by gifted men, tell me the titles.

LAN:

(sings)

Let me do Yü Yu-chih's *T'i Hung-yuan at Chin Stream*
Or Chang Chung-tse's *Jade Lady's Sad Lute Song.*

CHUNG-LI:
Can you do "strip and fight" plays?

LAN:

(speaks)

Let me just name a few "strip and fight" thrillers we can do:

(sings)

I will play you *Lao Ling-kung Sword Against Sword*
Or sing *Hsiao Yü-ch'ih Mace Against Mace;*
Perhaps *Three Princes at Tiger Palace?*

CHUNG-LI:
I don't want them—name another.

LAN:

(sings)

Ah, none is the equal of *Black Whirlwind at*
Li-ch'un Garden.

CHUNG-LI:
No, another.

T'ien-hsia Lo

LAN:

(sings)
Perhaps I should do *Snow Closes Blue Pass?*

CHUNG-LI:
A different one!

LAN:

(sings)
Have pity, my lord, my talents are not that great.

(speaks)
Wang Pa-se, hang out the troupe banners *(ch'i p'ai),* swing the wall and eave drapes *(chang-ngo),* the rear curtains *(k'ao pei)* and backdrops *(shen-cheng).*

WANG:
I've already taken care of those.

LAN:

(sings)
Let the backdrops be swung in place.
Let our banners proclaim the troupe.

(speaks)
I want those who come from far and near to see and spread the word about that the actor Lan Ts'ai-ho is playing the theater in Liang Park.

(sings)
That my name may be on every tongue in the Empire.

(speaks)

Master, do take a seat in the orchestra, this is the place where our young women sit to accompany the performance.

CHUNG-LI:

I believe I'll just sit in the music crib anyway. . . .

LAN:

See here Mr. Taoist, I want you out of here! You've spoiled an entire day of performance.

CHUNG-LI:

I don't want to go, I'm going to see the play.

LAN:

All right! Wang Pa-se, since he won't leave, lock the door to the theater. . . . Now, I've locked up the theater—let me see you get out of there now! . . . and if you don't stop bothering me I'll keep it locked for a week and starve you to death!

I suppose the first thing that should strike the eye in this excerpt is the fact that Loyang had its entertainment district (Liang Park) just as K'ai-feng had its "tile markets"* and that there was an entertainment "season," since the play opens with the new advertising banners being pasted up and the theater being readied for what appears to be the first play of the new year; the troupe's twentieth. I have always supposed that Yuan troupes might have divided their time between the metropolitan areas in a fixed theater and traveling through rural areas during festival times, though I must admit there is little enough proof of this.

*There is some confusion here because the term "Liang's Park" in most traditional novels and plays refers to K'ai-feng Fu itself, for that is where Prince Hsiao of Liang is supposed to have had his pleasure park. However, in this piece Chung-li Ch'uan states very clearly that the light emanation comes from the Liang Park in Loyang. The explanation is probably that the amusement quarters in a number of cities was known as Liang Park but the one in the capital (K'ai-feng) became the most famous. What the position of the "tile markets" was in K'ai-feng is not clear.

The piece of information next in order is that the troupe is a family one. We could have surmised this from the frequency with which children appear on stage with speaking parts* (usually an anathema to actors because the kids either steal the show by mugging or blow the lines because they get bored or fractious), but it bolsters such conjectures to find all the troupe members we meet in the play *Lan Ts'ai-ho* are related by blood or marriage.

It may seem strange to the reader who knows only Western theater, but I find much reassurance in the fact that the star player is a male: most other sources (including, of course, our wall painting, Figure 3) concern themselves almost exclusively with star players who are women. Some scholars have wondered if *all* players were women in Yuan times.

The advertising banners *(hua-chaoerh)* must have been eye-catching objects, for the term *hua* usually means multicolored or decorated (*Country Cousin,* below, notes this as well). It also appears that putting them up all over the city was an arduous task but one which the manager-star felt he had to attend to himself—at least in this case.

The question of the position and use of the "music crib" has caused some difficulty. Some time ago Feng Yuan-chün suggested that it might be something like the Western "greenroom" but both *Lan Ts'ai-ho* and *Country Cousin* make it fairly plain that it was an area off one side of the stage where the women of the troupe sat when not actually performing. I confess that I have a less than perfect understanding of the term *p'ai-ch'ang* which I render "accompany the performance." It is used modernly to mean something like "surface appearance" or "visible show": certainly neither of those is applicable here. I get the impression that at the very least the women are on display while sitting in the "music crib" and Kao An-tao's piece confirms my suspicion:

> Sitting there accompanying the performance are all the women
> The music crib seems filled with the heads of wild beasts
> With gaping mouths and staring eyes—a most hideous sight.[15]

*They are frequently given considerable spoken parts. See 1010 and 490 for examples.

It is probable that they formed a kind of orchestra, sitting on an extension of the stage in the bigger establishments, or at the rear of the stage in smaller places. We do know that women played the clappers and several different types of drums and cymbals. There is no reason why they could not have been sitting and playing in the music crib until their cues came to perform individually or take part in a drama. But, given the fact that the second profession of women entertainers was prostitution, the music crib was also a way of displaying their wares.

A "song" sometimes titled "A Sigh for Hsiu-ying" (*CYSC,* p. 19)[16] makes it clear that the courtesan-performer sat there during the performance and also performed on the stage herself:

> The courtesan's life is all uncertainty—
> She contains her shame, stifles her embarrassment,
> Sits accompanying the performance;
> Chanting verse, playing clappers,
> Doing sketches, prologues *(k'ai-ah).*

And the song, "The Drum" (*CYSC,* p. 547), indicates that sitting in the music crib was a way for the performers to be in contact with likely clients for their other profession:

> The courtesans sitting on the stage *(tso p'ai-ch'ang)* stealing glances,
> Longing for the men on the street to come and take them by the hand.

The next, and without doubt the most important piece of information for the reconstruction of the Yuan dynasty playhouse, is the listing of drapes and hangings. These must have been the means a troupe used to limit and shape the open area of the plain stages on which they worked.* Hangings are certainly the most portable and

*It takes neither special knowledge nor a powerful imagination to arrive at this conclusion: after all, Hamlet skewers poor old Polonius with a rapier thrust through the arras not because such hangings were common hiding places in Danish castles (I fear one's feet might stick out in an embarrassing fashion) but because drapes were a regular feature of the Elizabethan stage.

versatile means of dividing and concealing. The simplest way of converting a platform to a stage is to hang a cloth drape on a scaffolding of bamboo poles lashed in various configurations.*

The passage talks of *ch'i-p'ai,* which by the look of the term were certainly some kind of sign-cum-banner that may have borne the name of the troupe or its star or both. Exactly where they were hung is difficult to say.

Chang-ngo I take to be a compound term meaning both vertical drapes and transverse hangings like the valance or teaser seen in the wall painting (see Figure 3). *Chang* is a fairly general term for hanging or tent and *ngo* basically means the "area above the eyebrows and below the hairline," which corresponds figuratively to the area just under the proscenium. How many of these hangings they had and how elaborate they were depended, I believe, on the size, affluence, and location of the troupe.

The *k'ao-pei* would seem to be a rear curtain of some sort, since the characters mean literally "to go along the rear," but the *shen-cheng*† must be identified somewhat tendentiously since the first part of the binom means "god" or "gods" and the second half, *cheng,* is *hapax legomenon;* the dictionaries (all of them) know it not. Judging by the character's phonetic it may belong to the word family having to do with "high, conspicuous, eye-catching." The sum of these circumstances certainly encourages one to identify the *shen-cheng* with the two hangings—obviously depicting mythological subjects—seen at the rear of the stage pictured in the wall painting (Figure 3) from the Temple of the Responsive and Perceptive Prince. Chou Yi-pai says:

---

*It should be noted that in Figure 4 the stages numbered 1 and 2 are entirely constructed of poles (probably bamboo) lashed together, so these would already be available to the troupe when they moved into the empty space provided by temple stages. In permanent theaters the scaffolding could be left in place throughout the entire season, then packed up and taken to any place the troupe might travel. We cannot see the interior of stage 2, so its drapes are not visible. Stage 1, on the other hand, seems to have solved the problem of space division in an entirely different manner and has only a single combined entrance-exit way. Both figures have been redrawn from scroll paintings known as *Ch'ing-ming Shang-ho T'u* (Festival Scenes Along the River) and may date anywhere from late eleventh century to late fifteenth century. The context of these stages in the paintings indicates that they were temporary structures there for the festival only.

†My romanization for the second character in this compound is entirely conjectural but probably correct. If not correct, the least that can be said for it is that it is certainly the sound a native speaker of Chinese would make on being confronted with it.

> The Yuan stage was not very different from the temple stage of today: at the rear of the forestage were hung what was called *shen-cheng* and *k'ao-pei* which were much like the *shou-chiu* of the present-day stage, but they were not made of a single piece of material; rather they were in sections, each one of which was like a hanging scroll or picture, and several of them were used [overlapping] each other.*

I think it highly likely that it was behind the pictorial *shen-cheng* that the cloth hangings came together and this (usually concealed) opening was utilized by the playwright and actors. In *The Character for Patience* (*YCH* #61, p. 1070), the monk Pu-tai is said to "enter secretly" *(an-shang)* into what is supposed to be the bedroom where a husband is accusing his wife of having had a lover. Several arias further on there is the stage direction "Pu-tai sneezes behind the hangings *(chang-man)*."† I feel fairly confident that the "secret" entrance was made by coming through the space between the drapes concealed by the one *shen-cheng* (pictorial hanging) and disappearing behind the other *shen-cheng,* where he later gives away his presence to the actors onstage by sneezing. The audience has already seen where he went and is expecting him to do something unusual since he did not enter by coming in, stage right, *around* the hangings in the normal fashion and is not therefore likely to announce himself in a normal way. I believe the generic term for hangings in Yuan theater was *chang-man,* and they were constantly used in various ingenious ways to augment the flexibility of the *mise-en-scène.* As might be expected, most notices of these uses have dropped out of the drama scripts we have today; probably the contexts in which they occurred never impinged on or altered the dialogue or arias, and so our literary texts tended to ignore them. There is one example still preserved, however, in this

*Though the tone of Chou's pronouncement here rings with confidence, he actually has no more information on the terms than can be guessed from the play *Lan Ts'ai-ho*. See Chou Yi-pai, p. 104.

†Li Tche-houa in his *Le signe de patience,* by which I have been instructed many times, translates this stage direction "Le Bonze éternue derrière le *rideau du lit*" (italics mine), despite the fact that the Chinese stage is innocent of both beds and curtains that go with them. This bedroom translation of his has forced an unworthy thought on me more than once: could it be that M. Li's long residence in France has given him a Gallic turn of mind?

same play about players that gives us much direct information on the theater. In the last act of that drama, Lan Ts'ai-ho, the singing role, has been enlightened about his own destiny by the Taoist Masters and the process seems to him to have taken only a short time. As the fourth act opens, the other members of the troupe "who have grown too old to make a living at their craft" now play the instruments (they tell us) for the younger ones. They are outside the theater when Lan Ts'ai-ho enters. He sees them and asks what troupe they belong to. They tell him they are of Lan Ts'ai-ho's company and he marvels that they should have grown so old:

LAN:
But I've only been gone three years!—How can you have become so old?

WANG:
That's because we *are* old people, but you are still in your middle years. Look, why not come to the theater with us and play some of your dramas for a few days?

LAN:

(sings)
Ah, in gestures I knew no match....
And I knew the pace and timing for the play.

WANG:
Brother, all the costumes you wore for the plays are still kept unharmed. Here, pull back the hangings *(chang-man)* and look at them.

LAN:

(sings)
The words delight me, I cannot hide
Smiles and laughter as I pull back the curtains to
look....

(LAN *pulls back hangings revealing the Taoist Masters* CHUNG-LI *and* TUNG-PIN *seated backstage.* CHUNG-LI *speaks.*)

CHUNG-LI:
Hsü Chien, you haven't lost all thought of the world of dust. . . .

This one surviving example hints at the almost unlimited uses to which divided hangings were doubtless put—the simple stage suddenly has doors to everywhere opening upon it and several levels of dramatic visibility with which to work.

Before trying to add a few more facts about the stage and its capabilities as gleaned from the dramas themselves, let me put before the reader a translation of the document that inadvertently tells most about the Yuan theater-as-a-structure:

Country Cousin at the Theater
(Chuang-chia Pu-shih Kou-lan)

(Shua hai-erh)

When the rains are in season and the wind sets fair
Nothing is better than the farmer's share.
Our grains had been reaped to the final stook
And the tax men had left us more than they took.
Since my village had a vow at the temple to pay
They sent me to redeem it on market day.
As I reached the highroad by the top of the town
I saw a paper banner they had just hung down.
On it was writing with designs in between,
And below it the biggest gaggle I had ever seen.

(sixth from Coda)
Among 'em was one who was working a door
Yelling, "This way, this way, pay your fee before
The whole place is full and you can't find a bench!
Our first act's a *Yuan-pen* called *Seductive Wench*.

This is followed by a short *yao-mo*
All about the actor Liu Shua-ho.
It's easy on the stage to make time go
But hard to get applause for doing so."

(fifth from Coda)
Then without a pause in his hullabaloo
He snapped up my coppers and shoved me through.
Now inside the door was a cliff made of wood
Where layers of people sat around or stood.
Like inside a bell-tower I would have said
When I stood at the bottom and lifted up my head.
But looking the other way it seemed as though
I was watching a whirlpool down below
Of people sitting everywhere.
And a bunch of women were sitting there
Watching a platform—it was not a god's day
But the drums and the cymbals were a-crashing away!

(fourth from Coda)
On the floor came a girl who capered, and then
Went off and led on a bunch of her men.
One of that gang you could tell right away
Spelled trouble if you met him whatever the day.
His head was wrapped in a jet black cloth
With some kind of brush-pen stuck in the swath.
(One look at him and you couldn't go wrong,
You knew right away how *he* got along.)
His whole face was limed an ashy white
With some black streaks on top of that—
Now there was a sight!
He wore on his body one of those kinds
Of tunics covered with bright designs.

(third from Coda)
Well he
Recited some verses and one or two rhymes
Then he spoke a kind of *fu* and sang a few times.
His mouth kept on goin' right through every verse!
He wasn't extra good, but I've heard a lot worse.
And the memory he'd got I wish I had—
To tell all those jokes and japes wouldn't be bad.
Then he came to the end: "That's all," he said,

Then he slapped his feet around a bit and he bowed
his head.
And that was all for one part so the music [?] played.

(second from Coda)
Now in comes "Little Brother" and "Squire Chang,"
The last tellin' the first one just where he's wrong.
They cross the stage and go round and roun'
All the time sayin' they're walking into town.
Then they say they're in town (though they
went nowhere!)
And they spy a young girl under the awning there.
Old Chang's got to have her if it costs him his life.
And he sets right out tryin' to get her to wife.
He's sure in a hurry and just that keen
That he teaches Little Brother how to be go-between.
But she wants silk and satin, millet and rice,
And ol' Squire Chang?—she won't look at him twice.

(first from Coda)
Squire Chang backs up 'cause forward won't do
And with his right foot in the air he hoists his left
one too!
Poor Chang is whipsawed fro and to
Til he's so hotted up he don't know what to do
So he
Bangs his meat-club on the ground and snaps it right
in half
And I nearly bust my sides while I double up and laugh.

(coda)
Now the lawsuits would start just as sure as there's rain
But I got such a bladder full I'm dyin' from the pain.
I keep hangin' on and hangin' round to see the
thing through
Just to listen to them talk and to watch what they
would do,
But my bladder is achin' so I can't catch my breath—
I just *had* to quit the place before I laughed myself
to death!

Again, as in *Lan Ts'ai-ho,* there is a seasonal aspect to the use of the theater structure: Country Cousin is in town* after the harvest and, since the author was a northerner, we can suppose that the theater was there in the fall and possibly during some harvest festival. In this song again the theater is a permanent structure with a door (stout enough to be locked with some hope of keeping a person prisoner according to *Lan Ts'ai-ho*)† and a barker-cashier guarding it. As in *Lan Ts'ai-ho* we find there are two levels of seats, but it seems the balcony, "god's tower," had a sloping floor (Country Cousin's "cliff of wood"). Does this not force us to visualize fixed benches in the balcony? Certainly not mats as the orchestra seats probably were.‡ Our actresses again are either sitting on or facing the stage in what we know from *Lan Ts'ai-ho* was the "music crib" and Country Cousin implies (by juxtaposition of the song's lines) that the women were playing drums and cymbals.

All the evidence indicates, then, that there were permanent structures in and around towns, that they held a substantial audience, seated them on benches in some cases, had them under roof, could charge admission fees, and raised the audience above the level of the stage. All this is in contrast to working from a raised platform (in rural areas, one supposes) where the troupe was either paid by a temple society or had to depend upon passing the hat among the viewers who could be melted away by the first drops of a rainstorm. The economics of acting in a permanent structure must have affected the amount and type of performance fare a troupe could offer and would certainly have tended to upgrade the cultural level of both the audience and the playwrights.

There is one final thing to be said about both the permanent and the mobile theater. A table and benches were a part of every production. The number of times someone is told to "bring in the table" (*WP* 174) or stage directions involve lifting, sitting at, or even

*The theater here seems to be in the main part of town and not in a "pleasure park" as in *Lan Ts'ai-ho.*

†Though I don't know the exact sense of *Country Cousin's ch'uan tso ti men,* "a door made of rafters," the implication here also seems to be that it was a sturdy affair.

‡Surely any incline capable of permitting better vision for those in the rear would create a fun-house effect with the mats in the back sliding (occupant and all) down upon the viewers toward the front of the balcony.

hiding under (1024) a table leaves no doubt that it was a permanent prop for all stages. Men put chess sets on the table (*WP* 248), a god strikes the table with his ivory scepter (1246), and a servant places flails and cudgels out on the table to intimidate a hapless prisoner (1208). But the uses of a table go much further. Actors are instructed by the stage directions to fall asleep standing at a "desk" which is the table, and I believe that to "pantomime sleeping and having a dream" may have been done by lying on a table (387) as was "falling out of bed and waking up" (301). It is my belief also that "pantomimes climbing atop the city wall" (1172) were done with the aid of a table, as is the spoken incident in which a child climbs a tree to fetch his kite (*WP* 71–72). There are fewer notices of benches (see 1037), but it is my opinion that when the actor says "bring me a seat *(tso)* and I will sit on it," for example (*WP* 118), he gets a bench, because the engineering needed to produce a reliable bench is simpler than that needed for a chair of similar dependability. It probably is more easily transported from one performing site to another and has greater versatility than a chair. I have little doubt that the bench was the first step in "climbing atop the city wall" noted above, and "sleeping and having a dream" or "falling out of bed and waking up" could have been done as easily with a bench as with a table. I presume that in less affluent companies the bench doubled as a bier (423) and perhaps was the bride's palanquin (1031), and certainly was the stretcher (503) used to carry Li of the Iron Crutch.*

Scholars are often hoisted on the petards of their own classification systems, which is one reason I provided myself with the bolt hole of digressions. I classify what follows as an attack of the digressions simply because I don't know where else to put it.

In Figure 6 the reader is treated to a woodblock carver's very fanciful depiction of an incident from "Judge Pao and the Ch'en-chou Famine Relief" (*Ch'en-chou T'iao-mi, YCH* #3). The Good

*It is not always this clear, when the verb *t'ai* (to carry by four corners) is used, that a stretcher is involved and I used to think they simply laid hold of the actor by his hands and feet and carried him. Now I believe that (though carrying by hand is done) most of the cases involve a stretcherlike device, namely the bench.

Fig. 6. Artist's Conception of Judge Pao Being "Strung Up"

Judge comes to Ch'en-chou to investigate illegal sale of relief grain by two scoundrels. For a number of engaging reasons[17] he finds them while he is acting the part of a menial. They send him out something to eat and Judge Pao tells them that he'd rather feed it to the ass he's tending than touch it himself. At which point the caitiff officials order him "strung up" *(tiao)* to a convenient catalpa tree to await their later flogging. The stage direction then reads "Tou-tzu pantomimes stringing up the singing role" (49). Judge Pao immediately thereafter begins singing his aria "Ah, that Liu Ya-nei who promoted his own son to high position." It must be obvious to anyone that the actor playing Judge Pao so far from being able to sing an aria while trussed up by the wrists as the artist has pictured him, would be hard put to utter much beyond an agonized groan. Stage instructions to "string him up" are to be found in six[18] different places in extant Yuan drama and, since all these are the result of a deliberately shaped plot, we must assume there were on the stage itself provisions for accomplishing it. We certainly cannot look to our anonymous artist for help; "play illustrations are always purely imaginary and bear little relationship to the actual performance," as David Hawkes notes.[19]

My guess on the matter is that, when the need came for stringing someone up, one of the hanging backdrops or side curtains was drawn aside exposing the lashed-up bamboo scaffolding from which I imagine the drapes to be depended. The actor's wrists were then tied to poles in convenient positions, but the actor's feet remained comfortably supporting his weight. He may have made a great show of writhing in torment, but I cannot believe even the most devoted and athletically inclined thespian would undertake to sing while all his body weight hung from his arms. Because of the number of times stringing up is called for, I am sure that there were splendid dramatic and performance possibilities to be exploited here and I should give a great deal to have seen it done.

3. The Actor's Art

(Ti-san che)

> "... The approach of a modern reader to a work from an alien milieu, ancient or modern, must depend to some extent on historical scholarship or what used to be called 'learning.' This learning ... should be used imaginatively, in order to bring the world of the reader and the author into as close an alignment as possible...."
>
> Scholes and Kellog, *The Nature of Narrative,* p. 83

At a conservative estimate actors have been practicing their art for two thousand years in the West and perhaps a thousand years in China, but until the last seven or eight decades, when photographic and electronic records of their artistry and stagecraft have become possible, the real arts of the actor, their motions, gestures, expressions, exploitation of the little universe that is the stage by nuance of voice and stylization of movement largely perished with the actor himself. In short, all those fascinations which are truly dramatic rather than belonging, at least in part, to some other form of art have been denied us. The best edited scripts in the world give only a pale image of the actor's performance and a faint reflection of the play's stagecraft, while those texts which have been preserved by literary men (and these preponderate) have more often than not left almost everything to the reader's imagination.

The loss to a play is great enough when the acting skills of Western artists are lost to us. But the traditional Chinese actor of today is singer, dancer, pantomimist, and often acrobat, and we have every reason to suspect that he was always thus.

We can judge from the poetic vitality of Yuan dramas that the actor did not dominate his material in the same sense that the Peking Opera actor of the nineteenth and twentieth centuries fleshed out his rather slim operatic scripts, but I believe all of us who have dealt with Yuan drama have assumed that the people who mounted the originals were actors who not only sang their play but inspirited it with dance movements, stylized pantomime, and a half-dozen other stage skills. For this reason a greater percentage of loss to the play is suffered when we are deprived of the Chinese actors' arts than would be the case in less synthetic or less stylized forms of drama. If you cannot read an early play script with a stage eye, an actor's eye, you have cut yourself off from the real satisfactions of drama, shorn a theatrical butterfly of its colorful wings, and consigned an example of the "lively arts" to the gray chrysalis of an old book.

In the sections of this chapter that follow I have tried to resurrect from the scripts something of the vivacity and color of the Yuan drama's *mise-en-scène,* and as much as I can of the performer's virtuosity and the variety of stage appeals he had at his command. From time to time I supplement what I find with the judicious use *of my own imagination.* This latter exercise would be both indefensible and uninstructive were it not for the fact that there is enough information on both the actors' arts and the stagecraft he used embedded in the scripts that my speculations about what was probably happening on stage are tolerably controlled. Furthermore, since the scripts we have left to us today were edited and redone sometimes hundreds of years after the death of the *tsa-chü* drama as popular theater—and in the course of their transmission as literary texts such things as stage directions have dropped out, been garbled, or ignored—the only way to do justice to the plays is to reconstitute the scripts as they *probably* were.* Let me give here one example of a very common kind of moth hole in the fabric of Yuan drama texts.

*Feng Yuan-chün (whose lucid and beautifully documented studies on Yuan drama made me her grateful slave 25 years ago) remarks (p. 89), "We should, when we deal with *YCH* and other drama collections as though we were directors of the dramas in them, add the obvious sound effects *as one of the supplements we make to the texts*" (italics mine).

In *YCH* #40 *(Hei Hsüan-feng)*, p. 694, Li K'uei, the violent Black Whirlwind, is enjoying the spring weather and singing of its beauty:

LI:

(sings)

See how the peach and apricot blossoms have bloomed
and fallen
In contrast to the silver leaves of the pear tree
just budded.

(PAI YA NEI *and the* CH'A-TAN *enter*.)

PAI:
Sister, let us get on.

LI:

(sings)

Here I stray and stroll
There he prates and prattles . . .
And I'm suddenly being dragged . . .

(YAMEN PAI *and the* CH'A-TAN *bump into* LI K'UEI)

PAI:
Oh, oh, that's bad, we must go, go, go! *(exit together)*

LI:

(sings)

. . . over the bare ground!

(speaks)

Now who were those two who sent me sprawling?! If I weren't busy with my brother's affairs you'd not get away with that!

Anyone can see that something like (LI K'UEI *regains his feet and shakes his fist after the couple)* would make for a more complete script if inserted after "sent me sprawling" (and we should heed Feng

Yuan-chün's injunction and insert it). But that is not the defect in the text I'm talking about. Here are Li K'uei's next lines:

LI:

(sings)

For I would clout that horse you're riding
Hoof over crupper with a crash.

Only at this point is the reader aware that the two bad guys came onstage on horseback*: a page further on, when Li K'uei is recounting the accident, we discover that they were both mounted on the *same* horse, and the full fascination of the encounter and how it might have been staged is finally borne home. It is bad enough not to be able to describe the acrobatic bravura with which the scene was certainly played, but for a scholar or translator not to supply at least such descriptive stage directions as will help overcome myopia of the mind's eye is simple dereliction of literary duty.

PANTOMIME

> . . . even more important was their command of gesture, an art carried to a high pitch in the ancient world, involving the active use of every limb (the *mimi* were often themselves acrobats).
>
> *Oxford Companion to the Theater,* p. 641

Stage directions in Yuan drama—obviously our most accessible source of information on the actors' art—invariably end with the word *k'o*. For example, "The young *mo* makes obeisance" (132 and *WP* 543) is in Chinese, *hsiao-mo tso pai k'o*. In the transla-

*The most frequent stage direction lapsus is failing to note that characters enter on horseback (either *ch'i-ma* "astride," or *shan-ma* "waddling"(?) . . . more on this under "Horses and Other Critters" below). I count fourteen places where our actor is unhorsed by a stage direction, including: 1096 and 282 in *YCH*, and 150, 156, 830, and *WP* 210. Next in frequency is failure to indicate that a character is accompanied by a servant of some sort (906 and *WP* 202, for example). In addition, the texts sometimes fail to indicate the existence of a prop that subsequently plays an important part in the scene: for example, a knife (*WP* 73), a lute (1150) and a faggot of thorns (*WP* 180).

tions appearing in this book I have consistently construed such directions as "young *mo* pantomimes doing obeisance" for the simple reason that there has never been a way to be certain how much stylization of movement went with it or how elaborate and prescribed movements on the stage were; the translation "pantomime" allows for any amount of either.

The term *k'o* in this context quite clearly means an action or a set of actions; but what about the "tone" of these actions? Stage business in any part of the world is somewhat artificial (if only because the audience is usually all on one side of the actors), but in the West we have for some time striven for the illusion of everyday life on our stages and it is conceivable that Yuan drama's stage directions simply called for an approximation of lifelike tone and motion. But common sense, history, and my own experience with the form convinces me that, in fact, all stage motions in Yuan drama were highly stylized and tended to be a kind of symbolic language, a form of acrobatic motion, or a dancelike movement. I cannot actually prove this to be so, but let me cite right here one example of the kind of thing that makes me believe as I do.* For reasons we can only guess at—I think in part it is precisely to enhance the choreographic effect of the *mise-en-scène*—all major speaking roles enter with one or more servants, factotums, soldiers, or maids. The stage is thus always equipped with two or more flunkies whenever two speaking roles are about to confront one another. The full form of the highly conventionalized confrontation can be seen in the following:

K'UAI:
You there, go and announce that K'uai Wen-t'ung is here.

SOLDIER:
Yessir. May I inform the general that K'uai Wen-t'ung is here.

HAN HSIN:
Send him in.

*Later on in this chapter under "From Here to There" and "Declamation Modes" I will further demonstrate the high degree of stylization that must have been part of Yuan drama.

SOLDIER:
Here he is.

(They pantomime seeing each other.) (74)

We cannot be sure what motions were used here, but that they constituted a conventional set of moves and gestures cannot be doubted, for there is another way of writing this kind of scene:

T'AO-KU:
Attendants! Announce that this unworthy official has arrived.

(They do the announcing-and-seeing pantomime.) (538, 978)

The directions for the scene have here been contracted to simply *pao, chien k'o* because this high-frequency situation was choreographed in movement and stylized in speech the same way each time. There are hundreds of such recurrent situations, and I believe each had a prescribed (within limits) set of motions and gestures which went with it. We can guess at only a few of these. For example, throughout the dramas, characters are said to "pantomime grief" *(tso pei k'o* or *ta pei k'o* 1138, *WP* 601). Here and there this is amplified: "pantomimes concealed crying" (1030). I believe that part of the stereotyped pantomime of sadness was the raising of one hand parallel to the eyebrows, palm turned inward with all fingers tightly together accompanied by a movement of the shoulders as if sobbing.[1] We can seldom describe the motions of other such units, but since we know that one of Yuan drama's ancestors was dramatic dance and can in a few cases observe how structured high-frequency actions are, we are certainly on firm ground suggesting that all high-frequency situations on stage were choreographed and stylized. For example, since all major entrances and very nearly all exits are accompanied by stylized, recited verses, we can be relatively sure that the acts of entering and exiting were done to prescribed gestures in a fashion probably much like that found on the Chinese traditional stage of today. So, from first entrance to final exit the audience must have witnessed unit after unit of prescribed motion or gesture, and the kinetics of the drama, if separated from song, must have appeared much like a dance. Let me just list a number of such recurrent units below while the reader tries to imagine how their pantomime might have been stylized and how balletic might be the result:

entering lovesick (179, 1154)
traveling (401, 1132, 1197)
shouting (244)
yawning (465)
sighing (1207)
having a coughing fit (271)
measuring out grain (36)
dropping money (17)
dropping cup (458)
setting out banquet (528)
writing characters (88, *WP* 188)
listening from outside the room (457)
receiving guests (1231)
rubbing eyes in disbelief (177)
hesitating (1208)
toasting with wine (31)
making apology (1241)
counting off on fingers (1393)
listening at door (*WP* 195)
opening door and feeling the cold (447)
sweeping the snow from lintel (447)
opening the skylight (window) (672)
assent (1235)
going to sleep and dreaming (221, 387)

These are all stage directions and all of them have the word *k'o** attached to them which, as I said, translates "to pantomime" and,

*Probably the most accurate translation for *k'o* in all cases is "an event" or "to take part in an event," but this would make for clumsy English and hardly serve the purposes of a translated playscript.

since all of the above involve some imaginable action, that translation serves well enough. But the term *k'o* is also applied to facial expressions and even offstage sounds.* "Pantomime" applied to the following would be misleading, I think:

> makes a bad face (875)
> shows annoyance (919)
> sticks his tongue out in surprise (1025)
> laughs sneeringly (1016)
> sighs as he lies on floor (238)
> makes an "angry mouth" (571)
> cocks his eyes one way, slants his mouth another (*WP* 783)

And so in my translations I don't refer to such things as pantomime. But when something involving facial expression is obviously accompanied by other motions and perhaps sounds, I do construe *k'o* as "pantomime." For example, the following instructions for instant crocodile tears (1137–38):

> FU-SENG:
> . . . But I can't cry.
>
> CHING:
> Here, my handkerchief has a corner soaked in fresh ginger juice. Just wipe your eyes with it and you'll cry like you were pissing through them.
>
> *(Hands the prop to* FU-SENG *who pantomimes weeping for his brother.)*

---

*For example:
cock crows (1025)
wild goose cries (12)
drums beat, cymbals sound (991)
fifth watch bell and cock crow (302)
comments from offstage (1130, *WP* 799)
donkey, horse and cow sounds (304)
See more under the digression called "Beyond the Gate of Ghosts," p. 150.

Tso-yi (erh)

There is one special combination of facial expression and pantomime which sometimes resists sensible translation because we are certain of neither its performance nor its purpose in some cases. Shao Tseng-ch'i (p. 28, n. 10) glosses the term *tso-yi* "a stage technique by which an actor expresses his feelings and thoughts through actions." Wu Hsiao-ling and committee (p. 260) have the following entry in their glossary: "*Tso-yi erh* is an actor using body motions and facial expressions to indicate spurious *(sic)* emotional excitement to arouse another actor." The first of these definitions suffers by being so general it could apply to any piece of stage business, the second by the fact that it applies too narrowly (and somewhat clumsily) to the one use of *tso-yi erh* there being glossed.

To my knowledge the term *tso-yi (erh)* occurs six times in the corpus of Yuan drama. Four of these *appear* to be related and reasonably straightforward. *YCH* 1664–65 has a heroine pretending to entice and seduce the villain. When she enters, the villain figuratively licks his chops as he says "what a woman" and proceeds to *tso-yi.* A page later in the text the heroine pretends that she can hardly wait to warm his bed for him: at this point *both* the villain and the heroine *tso-yi.* It would appear that a good translation for these cases would be *(villain leers)* or *(they leer at each other). YCH* 884, 1230, and *WP* 12 all have *tso-yi* as a stage direction under similar circumstances: in the first case two poets are eyeing a beautiful courtesan, in the second a husband and wife who have been separated from each other and dare not reveal their relationship are each directed to *tso-yi.* The third is from *Pai-yüeh T'ing,* which is preserved only in the bare *Yuan-k'an* edition and lacks context. In the aria which precedes the stage direction, however, the young woman sings of love and loneliness. It appears that in this group, whatever else the actors do when they *tso-yi,* they somehow indicate that they suffer pangs of the tender passion. But the problem proves to be more complicated.

The two cases below must be treated separately from the examples above. *YCH* 981 has a general who is surrounded and besieged in his own home by what seems to be an old friend turned traitor. When he realizes this, he *tso-yi.* His wife, who, in the singing role has been describing the siege, then says to him, "Sir, control your rage, I will go speak to our tormentor and straighten things out." It is clear that when the general *tso-yi* he was portraying wrath in some fashion for his wife's response remarks on it. Lastly, in *Hsi-hsiang Chi* (*WP* 289) the maid Hung-niang has brought a note back from Ying-ying's lover-to-be and put it on the mirror-stand for her mistress to see. Hung-niang sings her description of Ying-ying's gathering anger at the presumptuousness of the note and finally:

YING-YING:
Hung-niang!

(HUNG-NIANG *tso-yi*)

HUNG:
Oh, oh! Now I'm in for it!

This *tso-yi* might have been nothing more than a pert moue directed at the audience, but, whatever she did, it had no more to do with lovesickness than the general's anger.

There is not enough information on what constituted a *tso-yi k'o* (which literally should have meant something like "make one's emotions known") to give the reader any hard facts. One can only observe that there are elsewhere discreet and explicit stage directions for pantomiming anger (*tso nu k'o, WP* 148), for facial expressions (see pp. 73–74 above), for provocation (*pan-t'iao,* 456), for a villain embracing *(lou)* the heroine against her will *(WP 787),* and for both "loving congress" (*huan hui,* 1243) (which I suppose to be an embrace) and "consummation of marriage" (*ch'eng-ch'in, WP* 212) which I can only leave to the reader's imagination!

All of these stage directions except the last manage to be unequivocal about the emotion involved and the action required, but certainly the motions, facial expressions, and actions called for are ways "to make one's emotions known." What then could the seemingly vague *tso-yi k'o* refer to? It might have indicated that the actor went through a *series* of actions, postures, and the like; but we have at least one long stage direction that details actions done in a series; "pantomimes taking the wine, pouring it in his hat, pulling out bamboo bucket, filling it with wine and exiting" (956). So it is not likely that the term *tso-yi* meant a series of actions of *this* nature. For what it is worth, my guess is that calling for the actor to *tso-yi* ("make his emotions known") was to have him perform a Yuan version of one of those long, wordless *tours de force,* combinations of gestures, facial expressions, agility, and sometimes astounding acrobatics which are used on the Chinese stage to portray states of intense emotion. Here is one of them (a special entrance) that was still being played in the traditional Szechuan theater in 1956:

> EMPRESS TU:
> *(enters. A long somersault lands her in the very foreground. Everybody shrinks back. It is quiet as a tomb. She stands motionless, the long sleeves of her garment falling dejectedly down. Watched by the others she begins an uncertain staggering pace around the circle of people formed about her. She is like a lioness caught in a cage. Her breath quickens, her shoulders jerk . . . she grabs her own son and whips him madly. Exhausted she collapses in a chair. . . .)*[2]

Entrances and Exits

In every theater tradition entrances and exits are carefully staged and often are high points in the *mise-en-scène.* It only stands to reason that in a form-oriented musical drama like the Yuan *tsa-chü* they would be treated with conscious ceremony, stylized mime, and éclat; the existence of accompanying entrance and exit verses in Yuan drama itself would argue for such treatment even if there were no living tradition from which to draw analogies.

In traditional Chinese theater today, entrances have a formal pattern which is varied according to the solemnity of the scene or the dignity of the character portrayed. Each actor (even the clowns) enters audience-left and makes his way, with a gait that usually suggests his station, to a place downstage near right center called the *chiu-lung k'ou* (mouth of nine dragons) where he assumes a stance and performs one or more stylized sleeve and hand motions which usually include pretended adjustment of garments and headgear. It is only after this that he or she proceeds downstage center and begins his vocal performance. This process has a practical side to it (it serves to synchronize the music and the actor's performance), but its aesthetic symbolism is much more important. Judging from the Yuan dramatic scripts there is every reason to believe that some sort of measured and stylized movement accompanied at least those entrances (and exits) which are marked by declaimed verse.

However, in addition to the basic, formal entrance, Yuan drama has a variety of entrances and exits, ranging from what must have been an eye-filling but highly stylized appearance of generals with their banners and troops (*WP* 114 *ff.*) and the entry of civil officials announced by their attendants (1196), to some very chatty ones which are obviously staged for the contrastive effect of their "realism." The re-entrance of Li Wen-tao and Liu Yü-niang in *Mo-ho-lo,* Act II, translated in Part II of this book, is a good example of an entrance *in medias res.* As they enter Li Wen-tao is delivering a truncated line which is obviously part of a conversation supposed to have been held offstage and continued onstage:

LI:
. . . think it over.

LIU:
No, I want to see the magistrate!

A fair number of these "realistic" entrances exist cheek-by-jowl with the more frequent formal entrance (complete with declaimed verse and probably accompanied by choreographic movement) which indicates not only that the Yuan playwright was capable of mounting scenes consisting of plain speech and natural body motions, but that he probably used them to heighten and set off the more stately and measured entrances which, it would appear, seemed to him more fitting for use on stage—or such is my opinion, in any case.

Let me list below in some sort of order a number of entrances which fall between these two extremes. First, entrances involving a prop, and some of these properties would substantially alter the manner of entry:

Enter
plaiting flowers (*WP* 216)
carrying him on a stretcher (503)
two enter carrying mother on a sedan chair (987)
carrying wine (*WP* 186)
neighbors carrying him on a bier (962, 423)

Then entrance in a performing mode:

Enter
- playing drum and clappers (1055, 626, *WP* 890)
- singing satirical song *(ch'ao-ko)* (*WP* 776)

Entering while engaged in some other human activity:

Enter
- leaning into the wind (*WP* 134); against snow (*WP* 545)
- ill and supported by Mei-hsiang (713)
- leading two young children (340)
- lovesick (179, 1154)
- clapping his hands and exclaiming (*WP* 273)
- rushes onstage (591, 243)
- crawling, feigning madness (746)
- climbing pavilion (798)
- secretly (920)
- leaps wall and hides behind stone (162)
- convulsed with laughter (1019)

There are in addition some very special entrances which I would give a great deal to see:

> I'll come to earth from space and see what he says to that! *(pantomimes seeing* CHIN *who is startled).* (1099)

And "They enter in a boat" (1054) was probably a splendid piece of mime when done by accomplished artists (see p. 91 below).

Exits are rather less varied and less imaginative than entrances except for the so-called "empty exit" (described below) which is a canny exploitation of the bare Chinese stage. But there are:

- Exit two drunks supporting each other (102)
- Dies from anger and exits (560)
- Exit bearing woman off on her bier (423)
- Exit carrying the table (571)

After most onstage homicide (of which there is a considerable amount), the victim exits under his own power in some stylized fashion which simply removes him from the scene. This can be varied, however, by his jumping up and running off stage (1725) which the headsman who has just decapitated the man remarks as a grisly portent. (In fact, in the next scene the ghost appears carrying his own head—but that certainly belongs among "props" if anything does!)

The "Empty Exit"
hsü-hsia (or *shan-hsia*)

I am not altogether certain that this should be classed under pantomime but it certainly is a specialized and stylized form of exit.

Hu Chi (vol. 2, p. 31) glosses the term *hsü-hsia* as "the actor turns his back to the audience to indicate that he has temporarily left the scene." Chou Yi-pai (p. 60, n. 39) says: "anyone on stage who for the time being is not engaged in the *mise-en-scène* walks upstage and turns his back to the audience." Little as I like to find fault with my betters (notes and glosses by both these gentlemen have kept me from making ignorant errors more than once), their comments here give so little information that the reader cannot begin to imagine the kind of staging flexibility the "empty exit" gave Yuan dynasty players.

The first, and probably the most frequent use of the empty exit was, it seems to me, simply a way of portraying an exit from a room or some place which did not involve a door.* There is no doubt that when characters go out-of-doors they pantomime opening the door, stepping over the threshold, and closing the door again. But what if the action calls for simply passing from one room to another? At this time, I believe, the actor turns around, walks upstage, hesitates, and walks downstage again speaking the appropriate lines; he is then understood to be in another place. For example in *WP*, p. 212, the serving girl walks upstage *(hsü-hsia)* to remain there on the lookout for the lover's parents while the lovers themselves carry on downstage. There is a similar example in a Ming *tsa chü*,[3] where the majordomo is told to take someone to the great hall to rest for a time. They both go upstage *(hsü-hsia)* and,

*See 1708. *Mo* is in the open; he *hsü-hsia* to rest, *tan* enters and sings an aria, *mo* then comes downstage.

when the others have made their actual exits, they both come downstage again, but the scene is now taking place in the great hall. The same process can be used to suspend one or more characters in a state of invisibility until they are ready to resume the thread of their action. The best example of this is in *YCH* #10 (p. 161), where a comic-villain and a comic-villainness are interrupted in the process of contemplating a bit of hanky-panky by the entrance of the two main characters. They *hsü-hsia* until their interrupters have finished the next unit of the plot and made their exits, then the wicked pair reenter and declare their undying lechery to one another again. It may very well be, as Chou Yi-pai's note implies, that when this sort of empty exit is performed the players turn and walk upstage and keep their backs to the audience (thereby becoming "invisible") until they are ready to rejoin the action.

Now, what appears to me to be a natural evolutionary step in the use of the empty exit is the *hsü-hsia* which sets up a dream scene. The following (1100) is one of the most completely worked out.* Before it begins, Li of the Iron Crutch, a Taoist Immortal, has been trying to bring salvation to Chin An-shou and his wife Chiao-lan who, as is most often the case in "redemption plays," have forgotten they are actually immortals themselves, sentenced to spend some time in the "red dust" of this world because they fell from grace. But Iron Crutch cannot reach Chin An-shou directly, so he "makes passes with his hands" *(tso shou-chih k'o)* according to one edition or "performs a couple of actions" *(tso tso-yung k'o)* according to another. This suddenly enlightens Chiao-lan to the fact that she is an immortal (Jade Lady) come to earth and she goes to Iron Crutch though her husband tries to prevent her:

*(This particular asterism is directed, for a change, at the experts rather than the "interested layman" who may sit this one out with no regrets.) It is technically important to note that both the *Mai-wang Kuan* edition and *YCH* use the term *hsü-hsia* here. Since there is good reason to believe the *Mai-wang Kuan* is as much as forty years earlier than *YCH,* this demonstrates that the term and the concept of the "empty exit" was not a concoction by Tsang Chin-shu. This fact is crucial to my argument because in what follows I note that *hsü-hsia* is used in *YCH* several times where other editions have nothing but *"hsia."* I contend, none the less, that all editions are referring to the same stage phenomenon. If *hsü-hsia* never appeared elsewhere than in *YCH* it would considerably weaken my proposition. In point of fact all editions save *Yuan K'an-pen* use both *hsü-hsia* or *shan-hsia,* or both, but not with the consistency or the frequency of *YCH.* Tsang, whatever his faults, was a more careful editor than most.

CHIN:

(seizing CHIAO-LAN*)*

Where are you going? *(*CHIAO-LAN *pantomimes disregarding him.)* Why do I feel so sleepy I can't move? *(*CHIN *pantomimes falling asleep.)*

IRON CRUTCH:

Now he's asleep.

(Leads CHIAO-LAN *in an "empty exit")*

CHIN:

(pantomimes dreaming)

How strange . . . we were behind closed doors but this Taoist has taken Chiao-lan and disappeared—All about me I see nothing but a wilderness of tall mountains, dashing streams, and tangled forests.

(sings, pantomimes fear)

IRON CRUTCH:

(calling)

Chin An-shou.

CHIN:

(cocking his head)

Who is calling me:

(sings)

I hear a voice calling my name and stand
With bent head and folded hands.

IRON CRUTCH:

How came you here, Chin An-shou?

CHIN:

(sings)
Where is this eyrie
Of tumbled clouds and peaks,
Of streams and ancient trees?

IRON CRUTCH:
You are in the Heavenly Caverns of the Immortals who feed on the Peach of Longevity and drink the Honey Dew. Companions of the Gibbon and the Stork, they grow old with the green-haired, Ageless Tortoise.

CHIN:

(sings)
Ya! I'm in the Faerie Precincts—of Eternal Life.

(speaks)
But have you brought my love?

IRON CRUTCH:
Aye! but this karma-troubled animal is hard to enlighten! If I call up his own Mercurial Spirits, his Passion of Ape and Stallion and embody them, it will save me breath in the long run. *Chi!* (he gestures)* (MERCURY, CINNABAR, *an* APE *and a* STALLION *enter and pursue* CHIN. CHIN *pantomimes terror.*) Chin An-shou, cease being deceived (?) by elixirs, cast off the golden cangue and jade fetters of passion. Seek the way out. Cleave no longer to the path of error—

[Chin sings his reply but Iron Crutch is not satisfied.]

*This is Yuan period Chinese for "Abracadabra!" or "presto!" See *YCH,* 741. See also *Ping-Yao Chuan,* Chapter 1, where the Mysterious Maiden transforms the two magic pellets with the same cry.

IRON CRUTCH:
Chi! Seize him and bind him, Mercurial Spirits and Animal Passions!

CHIN:
All I see are high peaks, overhanging cliffs—they are right at my feet! What am I to do. *(pantomimes waking from his dream in terror)* How strange!—I dreamed and just as I plummeted into a mountain stream I awoke—

Yuan drama could readily handle two alternating scenes with two sets of characters in them on stage simultaneously. In Act IV of *Rain on the Hsiao-hsiang* (Part II, p. 290) Ts'ui-luan and her father, unbeknownst to one another, act out their individual griefs in separate parts of the same posthouse.* On page 1017 Shih Liu-chu's mother in her home (one side of the stage) by some mysterious means summons Shih Liu-chu out of an abandoned kiln miles away (the other side of the stage) just before it collapses. It may be that most or all of these scenes were handled by some form of "empty exit" but the placement of characters on the stage (blocking) is no longer a part of the literary drama texts we have today so we cannot know how these seriatim scenes were engineered.

In the *YCH* edition, which is what most of us read by choice, there are a number of places where an actor makes an empty exit and returns with one stage property or another (see 90, 223, 924). There are other incidents in *YCH* where someone suddenly appears to be using a stage property that has arrived on the scene unheralded. Furthermore, if one compares the pages given above from *YCH* with other editions he will find two (90, 223) cases are noted in the other edition simply as *"exits, returns with prop"* rather than calling for an "empty" exit. (In the case of 924 there are no stage directions at all in the other edition—clearly just a careless

*I always find myself visualizing this scene in the Western manner with the posthouse painted on a scrim and the porch where Ts'ui-luan and her escort-guard are sheltering done in three dimensions. When her father speaks or recites, you backlight the scrim showing him in his room resting. When Ts'ui-luan and her guard speak, sing, or recite, the backlighting is dimmed and the outside scene is spotlighted and brought up. This would be very effective, I'm certain; but note what a great deal of pother you've gone to by not having bare-stage conventions.

piece of editing.) As I remarked earlier, one can demonstrate that dozens of stage directions are missing* from the drama texts as we have them today and the greatest number of these have to do with stage properties. I am convinced many a *hsü-hsia* in which the actor returns immediately with a prop has been lost in successive transmissions of the text. This is unfortunate because I believe this empty-exit-and-return-with-prop indicates that on the Yuan dynasty stage, as on the traditional Chinese stage of the nineteenth century, the property man was alive and well and visible to the audience—equipping his actors with needed properties as they went upstage for their empty exits. The difficulty is that I simply do not have enough unequivocal examples to argue further for his presence at this point.

Finally, the empty exit is also used simply to indicate that time has passed: in the case of 680 a comic does an empty exit and returns immediately to report "there are no more dumplings." Minimum time has passed. In 223 not only does the comic actor come back with properties from his empty exit but describes how he has been engaged in peddling wares which resulted in his possession of the prop. In the latter case, anything from an hour to a day of imaginary time could have passed while the actors on stage simply held tableau awaiting the return of the comic.

In some examples of the empty exit it is not clear whether picking up the stage prop or allowing for the passage of time is the motivation. On 654 when the old boatman does an empty exit he returns with food for Wu Tzu-hsü but he also makes it clear that a measurable amount of time is supposed to have passed and Wu Tzu-hsü's pursuers are that much closer.

From Here to There

The Western stage wedded to realism is a boxlike affair into which the playwright must stuff his characters and invent plausible reasons for their being assembled there at a particular time. The playwright devoted to "realism" and *tranche-de-vie* drama limits the freedom of his cast to move except within "common sense"

*An example of what must be a missing *hsü-hsia* appears in 768 where the mother "exits" but on hearing her son's cries speaks lines without ever having reentered. She has done an "empty exit" and is speaking from upstage.

space and this has its drawbacks.* The Yuan theater with its conventions and simple but all-powerful symbolic motions is instantly prepared to shift from a small courtroom to a journey of a thousand leagues if the actor says the word. Act III and part of Act IV of *Rain on the Hsiao-hsiang* (Part II, pp. 280–93) are one continuous, rainsoaked journey, and through it there must have been intermittent stylized walking to indicate the extent of that trip.

On 401 there is a kind of travelogue done by the singing role. Three times there are stage directions saying *(pantomimes walking)*, three times he describes a bit of scenery he has just come to, and three times he sings arias which dilate upon their beauty.

Exactly how this walking was done we shall never know, but Professor Dana Kalvodová has reason to believe that, in Ming times at any rate, the actors described a figure eight or an oval across the stage and back as they portrayed a journey. Modifications of this kind of convention must always have been available to the Yuan stage. Time and again the dramas deliberately hold a tableau while one of the actors talks himself through what can be a considerable trip to fetch a person or an object that is to play a part when the tableau he has just left comes to life again. In *The Mo-ho-lo Doll*, Act IV (Part II, p. 365), the court bailiff is sent out once for the doll itself and once for its maker while the singing role silently awaits his return on stage. There are dozens of such examples in the surviving dramas; and since the traveler usually had to summon up his surroundings with speech, the texts we have today still reveal the action. For example, on 945 Chang Ch'ien is dispatched to search for a corpse with the following result:

> CHANG:
> Yessir, your honor. I go out the yamen door. Now I sally through this alley, now I wend around this bend, and here I am at Li Shun's house. H-m-m, not a soul here: I'll just slide softly into the courtyard and—! It's so quiet in here it gives a man the creeps!†

---

*Note G. B. Harrison's *Shakespeare*, p. 1221. "Only when *Antony and Cleopatra* is acted with speed on a bare stage in the Elizabethan convention are its magnificent planning and superb poetry fully revealed. Such an effect is quite impossible on any stage where scenery must be changed or where there is any attempt to give a realistic background."

†A complete translation of this scene will be found below (p. 93) under "Special Pantomime Scenes."

Sometimes the spoken "travel" is so intricate that I separate it from "Special Pantomime" (see below) only at the risk of seeming arbitrary. The example (616) given immediately below combines travel with several vocalized special actions:

(singing role pantomimes falling asleep)

TAPSTER:

I told you not to drink so much—but you wouldn't listen to me and now you're dead drunk and sleeping. [*to the audience*] What'll I do? This place of mine is plagued with evil spirits and they'll take his life. What to do? Well, I can try shouting him awake. *(pantomimes shouting at singing role)* Master! Get up! Really, this place is full of ghosts and you'll be killed! *(singing role pantomimes stirring but not wakening)* No, he's fast asleep and I can't waken him. What to do? Oh, well, I might as well go downstairs. Now I'm putting the wine vats away, lowering the wineship banner and shooting the bolt home on the door. Now I'm going upstairs again to shout him awake. Knock, knock.* Master if you don't get up and go you'll get eaten up by the ghosts—oh, well, it's no skin off my nose, I'm leaving. *(exit)*

These are rather special examples of getting from here to there. For the most part such locomotion is done with a couple of speeches to let the audience know the direction and purpose of the traveling and a stylized walk (see 679, 1017). Not only is travel from here to there pantomimed in a stylized walk but the lines which accompany it are more often than not quite conventional phrases. In the *Mo-ho-lo Doll* (Part II, p. 372) when Chang Ch'ien is sent to get the Mo-ho-lo statuette the following transpires:

CHANG:

(pantomimes traveling)

I go out this door, and to the Alley of the Vinegar Workers to ask directions of people. This is the house of Liu Yü-niang. I open the door and there on the altar shelf is the Mo-ho-lo. . . .

---

*In Chinese, *keh-poo, keh-poo.* I suspect he's rapping on the other's skull with his knuckles.

In this example the lines he speaks to accompany his travel are particularized. The audience knows that Li Yü-niang's residence is in the Alley of the Vinegar Workers and all the rest of Chang Ch'ien's speech as he travels is germane to this particular play. But statistically this is less often the case than the use of a set of conventional phrases to accompany the stylized walk. In fact, some of these conventional phrases were so thoroughly familiar to the audience that the actor could parody them and still expect the audience to understand.*

Indeed the player was so certain of his audience and their acceptance of his symbolic traveling and compartmentalized invisibility that he parodies these abstractions impudently (but apparently with impunity) on 206. In the opening "wedge" of *YCH* #13, (*Tung-t'ang Lao,* Elder of the Eastern Hall), Yang-chou Nu, a full-time ne'er-do-well, has been told by his father to go next door and ask the Elder to come over. Yang-chou Nu first tries to send someone else, then tries to get his horse saddled to ride the fifty feet to the neighbor's home, and finally:

YANG-CHOU:
... I can't understand how you can be my own father and still know so little about me. Don't you know that I won't even go to the outhouse unless I ride?

---

*On page 1051 can be found the straight form of what I take to be the highest frequency conventional "travel" speech; *"Chuan-kuo yü-t'ou, mo-kuo wu-chiao"* which means "I turn this street corner *(yü-t'ou)* and make my way around this house corner *(wu-chiao)*." (The most succinct form of the sentence is to be found on p. 317 of the Jenmin Wen-hsüeh ed. of *Hsi-yu Chi* where a description of travel appears as *chuan wan mo chiao,*" turning bends and getting round corners.")

But the familiarity of the audience with this pat Yuan drama "traveling" speech is such that it is parodied twice elsewhere (1132, 945) that I know of. In each case the sound of the two clauses is the same except for the next to last word in the statement which is changed to *kuo.* Now, the term *kuǒ-chiǎo* (instead of *wū-chiao)* could only be heard as "foot-binding cloth"—an object of considerable ridicule and rude humor with the Chinese. This, in turn, springs a catch in the mind of the hearer and the whole sentence is re-thought, at which time (I am convinced) the term *yü-t'ou* "corner" is re-heard as its homophone *yü t'ou* "dumbhead." So the high frequency line becomes a bit of nonsense, "I get around this dumbhead and I feel my way past the footbindings." The example on 1132 appears only in *YCH:* this is the only time I've caught the *YCH* editor with a pawky bit of humor that is not also found in the other editions.

FATHER:
Will you listen to this . . .?

YANG-CHOU:
All right! I'm going, I'm going. I've got you mad at me again, I guess. I go out the door. There's no one here. [*to the audience*] Oh, this one? This is my father, but he's not allowed to say a word so I can just knock him feet-to-sky—while I've been talking here I am at the gate of the Elder. . . .

I am certain that as part of his comic *shtick** he did indeed bowl his father over thereby parodying his own stage convention of invisibility. In any case it is obvious that the make-believe of the Yuan stage was not a fragile thing; the Chinese actor made it very clear in those days, as he continued to do for centuries, that he was a performer performing for an audience—the events taking place on the stage were not ever to be hampered by the trammels which control illusions of the "real world."

Special Pantomime Scenes

Having introduced the Yuan player's methods of talking himself from here to there, we are now in a better position to note and appreciate the role and mechanics of pantomime on the Yuan stage. Naturally, silent pantomime, of which there must have been abundant examples, could not have survived in our written scripts; but the Yuan dramas so frequently contrive to arrange scenes which carry a heavy freight of pantomime that the argument *a fortiori* for the important part pantomime played on the Yuan stage is overwhelming. As a simple example of deliberate structuring to allow for pantomime, I offer the following scene from *Yü Ch'iao Chi* (The Fisherman and the Woodcutter), *YCH* #50, 859–60:

*My authority for the spelling is Leo Rosten's *Joys of Yiddish*.

(Secondary role dressed as WANG AN-TAO *enters and recites.)*

WANG:

(recites)

The boat a floating leaf lashed to its willow oars.
(New-minced fish-sauce, fresh new wine.)
For more than twenty years I've fished these shores
And no other's hand has taken what was mine.

I am Wang An-tao from the Commandery of Kuei-chi and I make my livelihood by fishing the dike along the left bank of the Ts'ao-ngo River. I have two sworn brothers, Chu Mai-ch'en and Yang Hsiao-hsien, who are woodcutters. The former is very learned, but his luck is not as flourishing as his letters for he has yet to make a name for himself. He lives here as the son-in-law of Liu Erh-kung. Today in this winter dusk a heavy snow has begun to fall; my two brothers have been cutting faggots in the hills all day long, so I bought a jug of new wine and am waiting in this sheltered place to share it with them and drive away the chill. I think they are coming now.

[The two sworn brothers enter. After Chu Mai-ch'en has sung the frustrations of the poor scholar and Yang Hsiao-hsien has commiserated with him, Yang says:]

YANG:
What you say is true, brother.

CHU:
Isn't that our brother's boat moored there? Let me call him. *(pantomimes hailing)* Brother.

WANG:
Ah, it's you two, come aboard.

(They pantomime boarding the boat.)

Note that there was nothing in Wang An-tao's entrance verse nor anything in the subsequent dialogue and arias which would have made Wang's presence on the bank rather than on the river in any way odd; nothing in the situation or the demands of the rest of the play made it dramatically advisable for the two friends to board Wang's boat. Everything Wang has said up to this point puts him in verbal possession of the dike along the left bank of the Ts'ao-ngo River. (In fact, he later entertains everyone at his *house on the river-bank* in Act IV.) The stage directions are very clear on the matter, however: the men are to take part in the pantomime of boarding a small boat. Such things are done in the traditional Chinese stage with great panache. You can expect that the boat owner's body swayed and bobbed in a convincing manner as, one after another, the weight of the two other men rocked the boat while boarding it. As each visitor in turn leaves the solid shore and stands in the imaginary bobbing skiff, *his* body begins to bob and sway in a rhythm which is contrapuntal to Wang's because they are standing at opposite ends of this cranky little craft. I have seen this pantomime done so well that the outlines of a sampan sprang up on the stage as though projected there by *laterna magica.*

In case any doubt remains in the mind of the reader that Yuan players were particularly fond of doing boats (and expected plaudits for such nautical mimes from their audiences), let me refer him to *Rain on the Hsiao-hsiang* (Part II, p. 250), where all those on stage in the prologue are in a boat which founders as a result of the River God's jealous rage. I have no idea how this was presented, but it would have been simplicity itself to have done away with the scene and had the survivors simply appear and narrate for us what transpired in the storm.*

---

*Note also that all of Act III of *YCH* #18 and most of Act III *YCH* #17 are done in storm-tossed boats. On 624 two men get into a boat and one pushes the other overboard; 892 has directions that one boat be rowed closer to another; 1052–54 a boat is cast off, rowed, and finally the occupant leaps from it into the river; on 1194 a boat is caught and tied up and on the next page two characters exchange garments in this same boat.

Nor do deliberate arrangements for the inclusion of pantomime scenes stop at the water's edge, as it were. You may recall our two lecherous friends of the "empty exit." Well, undismayed by the interruption, they are seeking a suitable place for their illicit amours when the following little byplay develops:

> CH'A-TAN:
> *(tripping over something)* What was that? Ting Tu-kuan, close the door while I light the lantern. I'm tearing off a strip of paper from the window, now I'm twisting it into a spill to light this lantern. . . . (159)

Opportunity for pantomime is the only reason for the scene to be played this way. The *ch'a-tan* could as readily have entered with the lantern held up before her already lit. The same spoken pantomime gets a lamp lit on 394 and several other places throughout the dramas.

This lamp-lighting vignette is but a small elaboration beyond the high-frequency actions I asked the reader to imagine before (above, p. 73). Here I would like to list a few of the scenes I assume to have been deliberately included for their pantomime value in a roughly ascending scale of potential complexity and theatricality:

(230) Yen Ch'ing pantomimes being blind.
(541) Ch'in Juo-lan tries to dash herself to death against the steps.
(465) Wang the Horse-doctor pantomimes taking a leak.
(*WP* 227) Chang Liang climbs down and under a bridge to retrieve a sandal.
(*WP* 559) Ts'un Hsiao throws the corpse of a tiger across the stream then leaps across himself.
(790) Lü Tung-pin crosses and recrosses a mountain stream rescuing two children and
(791) He finally drops one child into the stream.
(*WP* 118) A spear with a hook on the end is used to fish a bucket out of a well.
(*WP* 76) A bailiff chases and finally catches a buzzing fly in the courtroom.

This last, it appears to me, has such potential for energetic and farcical acrobatics that I am sure any Chinese theatrical troupe worth its rice would have exploited it thoroughly.

In a sense, however, the reader has been obliged to take my word that the above were introduced into the dramas precisely for their mime value. But the scene translated below speaks for itself, I believe.

In the drama *Hou-t'ing Hua* (*YCH* #54) not one but two bodies have been disposed of by throwing them down wells. (It would appear from traditional Chinese fiction and drama that the well was the favored repository for corpses—either suicides or murder victims.) The Good Judge Pao knows that a young girl has been killed because her ghost has already visited a guest at the Lion Inn. He is not, however, aware of the fact that in a related murder the body of Li Shun has been dumped into his own well. The hapless Li Shun was killed by Wang Ch'ing abetted by Li Shun's own wife and the murder was witnessed by his young son. As this scene opens the Judge is about to question Li Shun's murderer—though he does not yet know that Wang Ch'ing has killed anyone:

(CHANG CH'IEN *leads* LIU T'IEN-YI *off and returns.)*

PAO:
Chang Ch'ien, bring Wang Ch'ing here.

CHANG:
Yes, your honor. (CHANG CH'IEN *leads* WANG CH'ING *on and he pantomimes seeing the Judge.)*

PAO:
Now, Wang Ch'ing, you were told to take the girl Ts'ui-luan and her mother to whom?

WANG:
The Minister told me to take them to see his wife; the minister's wife told me to have them killed. I told Li Shun to do it.

PAO:
All right. Since he told Li Shun to do it, Chang Ch'ien, fetch him here.

CHANG:
Li Shun's cleared out.

PAO:
Li Shun's cleared out—what next?! Chang Ch'ien, take Wang Ch'ing away. (CHANG CH'IEN *leads* WANG CH'ING *off and returns.)* Chang Ch'ien, he may have cleared out but go to his house; there must be someone over there. And while you're at it look in any irrigation ditch or tank or for any signs of a well, and drag them—

CHANG:
Yes, your honor. I go out the yamen door, now I sally through this alley and wend around this bend and here I am at Li Shun's. Hmmm, there's not a soul here: I'll just slip softly into the courtyard and—my, it's so still in here it gives a man the creeps—I'll open this back gate carefully—*(he trips and falls.)* A ghost! A ghost! *(He gets up cautiously.)* Humpf, it was nothing but this clothesline; but it sure scared a jump out of me! Now then, let me look again—Aha! Sure enough, a well. That old Judge Pao has brains between his ears, there's a well just like he said. And I have to investigate it—what an awful smell! I'd better go down it and see. But how do I get down there? Well how about that clothesline, then? I am tying this end to the well post and letting the other end down into the well *(pantomimes climbing down into the well and searching)*. Well now, here's a sack. I don't know what's in it but I'll tie my rope around it and when I get up to the top again I'll pull it up. *(pantomimes climbing back out of the well and pulling up sack.)* All right. Up comes the sack—I wonder what's in the thing?—and I'll take it back to his honor. *(Shoulders the sack and starts off.* CHILD *rushes on and seizes him.)*

CHANG:
What th—who's that holding on? *(pantomimes turning his head to get a view of* CHILD.*)* Oh, it's only a kid! Out of the way, boy! *(hits* CHILD *and pantomimes making his way back.)* Well, here I am at the yamen. *(pantomimes throwing down the sack.)* Let me tell you, your honor, you've got a head on top—there was a well, sure enough, and I went down it and searched around and found this sack. I wonder what's in it—open it, your honor.

PAO:
Very good! This rascal can do what you tell him. Open it up, Chang Ch'ien. (CHANG *pantomimes undoing the sack.*) It's a corpse! Chang Ch'ien, call in the woman who's missing her daughter. (CHANG *pantomimes looking at corpse.*)

MOTHER:
Your honor, this isn't my daughter; this corpse has whiskers.

PAO:
Now why on earth did you bring back a corpse with whiskers, Chang Ch'ien?!

CHANG:
But, your honor, this was all inside a well, how could I tell it had whiskers?

MOTHER:
Your honor, it is not my daughter.

PAO:
Chang Ch'ien, in whose well did you find it?

CHANG:
I got it from the well at Li Shun's house.

(Man ch'ing-ts'ai)

PAO:

(sings)

Then at Li Shun's must we seek more clues.

(speaks)

Chang Ch'ien, let me ask you further

(sings)

When you went to the bottom of that well,
Did no one see you there?

CHANG:
No, and I saw no one. I went into Li Shun's courtyard, saw this well, went down to the bottom, brought up this corpse and I carried it back here—Oh, that reminds me, though, I saw a little kid.

PAO:
Oh, so there was someone; then

(sings)

We must have him brought before us
We'll hear the tale from him
And get at least an inkling of the facts.

(speaks)

Chang Ch'ien, go look for the boy.

CHANG:
Yes, your honor. If the kid has gone, what'll I do? I go out the yamen door, walk a bit, and here I am back again in the rear courtyard of Li Shun's house. There's the well *(sees* CHILD*)*.

Oh, there you are, boy, still here. Come on, I'll carry you on my shoulders to see his honor *(pantomimes carrying* CHILD *and returning)*. Here we are, your honor, this was the kid.

PAO:
Careful, Chang Ch'ien, don't frighten the lad. You can tell he's already overwhelmed just being in the yamen: see those here-there-everywhere looks. Now, boy, come closer, I just want to ask you the name of your family. *(*CHILD *uses sign language with his hands.)* Why, he's a mute! Chang Ch'ien, this time you brought me back a mute!

CHANG:
But your honor, he's the one who lives at Li Shun's, how could I know he was a mute?!

PAO:
Look, boy, even though you can't talk, you seem bright enough. Do you recognize this dead person?

*(*CHILD *looks and weeps in pantomime.)*

PAO:
That's pitiful.

(Kan Ho-yeh)

(sings)
One glance and grief overwhelms him;
But this is strange—

(speaks)

Tell me, boy, who is this corpse to you? *(*CHILD *gestures in sign language.)* Oh dear, how best to do this?

(sings)

He defeats my hopes of understanding.
First his eyes grow dim with tears
Now his hands would double as a tongue.
How sad; "a mute cannot even tell his dreams":
It is enough to crack the stoutest heart.

(speaks)

Now, boy, I am going to ask you questions and when the answer is yes, nod your head; if no, you wave your hand, do you understand? *(*CHILD *pantomimes committing this to memory.)* Now; perhaps this is your father's younger brother? *(*CHILD *gives a negative wave.)* His older brother? *(*CHILD *gives a negative wave.)* Is it then your father himself? *(*CHILD *nods and does obeisance to the corpse.)*

PAO:

So, it is your father. Now, son, who killed him?

*(*CHILD *pantomimes sign-language as* PAO *translates.)*

PAO:

It was a big man—he seized—he seized your father by the clothes. He took out a sword—a sword—and killed him—and then ... and then threw him in the well! You poor child. Now look son, I'm going to ask you some more questions.

(Shang Hsiao-lou)

(sings)

Where may your mother be found?

(CHILD *points.*)

(sings)
He doubtless does not know
And cannot tell me till the day he dies.
But can I cease seeking any criminal
Who cut down a man in his prime?

(CHILD *seizes* CHANG, *and* CHANG *pantomimes terror.*)

PAO:

What is it, child? You mean to say Chang Ch'ien killed your father? (CHILD *gives negative wave.*) Oh, no, I understand now, you mean:

(sings)
You want to go with him and look for your mother?

CHANG:

You want me to go with you to find your mother? (CHILD *nods.*) You nearly scared me to death, boy!

PAO:

(sings)
As a filial son he thinks of both his parents.

(speaks)
Chang Ch'ien, go with him and look.

CHANG:

Yes, your honor. All right, boy, you lead the way. Out the gate we go and over there to find her.

(Ch'a-tan *make-up* CHILD'S MOTHER *enters, drunk.)*

CH'A:
It seems I've had a few and am drunk. *(*CHILD *grasps his mother and* CHANG *hits her.)* Brother, why hit me?

CHANG:
Because you're wanted at the K'aifeng yamen.

CH'A:
Well, I have done nothing; let's go there now. *(They both pantomime seeing* PAO.*)* Your lordship, I have done nothing, why do you call me?

PAO:
Woman, you're drunk! Can you identify this body?

CH'A:
(recognizes the corpse and pantomimes feigning tears) That's my husband, how can he be dead?

PAO:
[*sarcastically*] The death of a husband is something a wife should be informed about.

CH'A:
But I don't know how he died!

(Man-t'ing Fang)

PAO:

(sings)
Let's have no blaming of this
Or advising that.

Count us no Womanly Duties nor
Wifely Virtues,
Nor say,
"Blessed is that house
Which boasts a virtuous spouse."
A tile tossed in the air must fall
To earth somewhere.
Speak now and speak the truth.

(speaks)

Now, woman, let me ask you,

(sings)

Had there been some falling-out,
Some harsh words between you?

CH'A:

Never, your honor, never!

PAO:

(sings)

I don't suppose some bitter speech
Had caused a rift?

CH'A:

We always spoke well to each other, your honor.

PAO:

(sings)

Cease this piecemeal plea of innocence.
I'm only asking this—

(speaks)

Nothing else but this,

(sings)

Who is the murderer of this man?

(speaks)

Boy, who murdered your father? *(*CHILD *signals as before.)* You mean you know who it is? *(*CHILD *nods.)* Chang Ch'ien, take all these others over to one side and bring me the Graduate, Liu T'ien-yi. *(*LIU *is brought back and pantomimes seeing* PAO.) Now then, Liu T'ien-yi, I told you to ask the girl's ghost for some token to tell us who killed her. What did she give you?

LIU T'IEN-YI:

Just a peach blossom.

PAO:

Let me see it. *(*LIU *pantomimes taking it from his bosom and* PAO *takes it from him.)* Why, this is a peach blossom door charm, see here it says, "Long Life and Riches"! We have him!

(T'ang Hsiu-ts'ai)

(sings)

I cannot say just where he lives
But only that Ts'ui-luan was there
And on the gate will be
A peachwood charm to ward off demons;
To increase wealth and luck.
Oh, painted Gate Guard I can well conceive
The perjured report your owner gives to you this year.

(Tai Ku-t'ou)

But whatever falls his lot
He will have brought on by himself.

(speaks)

Chang Ch'ien,

(sings)

Bring that murdering devil here to me!

CHANG:
Who am I looking for?

PAO:

(sings)

Go, search for the gate that displays only:
"May They Follow You in the New Year,"
For in my hand I hold the other half—
These couplets which hint of
Bad cess and good,
This charm of peach which gives us
Earliest word of spring,
Can it hoodwink the King of Shades
Or Pao Tai-chih, Judge of Nan-ya!?

(speaks)

Chang Ch'ien, take this peach charm and seek its mate.

CHANG:
Yes, your honor. Now I sally through this alley. Now I wend around this bend, and here I am at this inn—but its gate couplets are complete. Now I walk to the Lion Inn gate. Let me see its door posts. Aha, there is "Follow You in the New Year," but no "Long Life and Riches." Now, let me compare the one that's there with this one *(pantomimes comparing).* I'll take 'em both back to his honor. *(Pantomimes seeing* PAO.*)* Here are the pair, your honor.

PAO:
Where do they come from?

CHANG:
The Lion Inn.

PAO:
All right, go to the Lion Inn and search about for me. If there is a well there, drag *it* too, and I'm sure you'll get results.

CHANG:
Out of the yamen and in no time here I am back at the Lion Inn. There is a well back here so I'll go down it and search. *(Pantomimes descending and bringing up corpse.)* Another corpse! I'll take it to his honor. *(Pantomimes seeing* PAO.*)* Your honor, another corpse.

PAO:

(sings)

Bring Wang Ch'ing to the foot of the dais
To hear my judgment.

(speaks)

Bring him here, Chang Ch'ien.

(WANG *enters.)*

WANG:
What did you summon me for?

PAO:
Wang Ch'ing, you'll be happy to know we have our murderer and it has nothing to do with you.

WANG:
But of course it wasn't me! I'm off for home.

(CHILD *enters and seizes* WANG.*)*

PAO:
This is the man who killed your father, is it not, boy!

CHILD:

(does sign language with his hands and speaks at the same time)

It is indeed! He and my mother did this and did that and then did the deed.

PAO:
Well, suddenly this one is no longer dumb!* Chang Ch'ien, bring Wang Ch'ing to me. . . .

Since Yuan drama was a popular, not a patron-supported, art form we must believe that Chang Ch'ien's *two* descents and his *four* round trips to the courtroom were so multiplied because they found favor in the eyes of the audience. These are not *burle,* the stock comic scenes of the *commedia dell'arte* (though Chang Ch'ien does get in his little comic *lazzi* with the clothesline and his fear that the child was accusing him); they are done because mime and movement are integral with the expectations Chinese audiences have always had of their stage presentations. The wholly unnecessary (for plot purposes) mute scenes are quite obviously opportunistic and gave the audience more of the kinetic display they expected when they attended the theater.

Acrobatics

One way of viewing the matter is to accept acrobatics as a particularly strenuous form of pantomime. Because it is convenient to do so, I am treating it under pantomime, but it should not be forgotten that a dancer and an acrobat have much in common; in the West there is a very hazy but jealously guarded line which separates the so-called "exotic" dancer and the woman gymnast from the *danseuse* properly considered. In China the line is indistinct in another way. The "performer" for most of China's history was a man or woman of many talents—juggler, contortionist, acrobat, dancer of a sort, actor, and, in later centuries at least, singer as well. Of course, these broke down into specialties but they seem not to have been nearly so exclusive as in European entertainment.

*The mute child suddenly becoming articulate may be in part because this is the beginning of the mandatory "happy ending"; but I am of the opinion that it's just the kind of audience-pleasing trick the Yuan actor favored. He would much rather surprise his audience with the unexpected filip than forego such an opportunity because of its possible destructive effect on the dramatic integrity of his story.

A Western actor on the legitimate stage (even those who used to be trained more rigorously in fencing and such things) has never been expected to enter stage right with a forward somersault or do a blind backward leap to straddle the arms of a chair and there support himself with only the chair arms pressing against the insides of his thighs; and he would take umbrage at being asked to attempt it. As a general rule on the traditional Chinese stage, however, neither of those moves would unduly tax an actor in his prime; most of the more exaggerated postures of *t'ai-chi ch'üan* are merely stock-in-trade for the traditional actor of military roles.

If the reader of Yuan drama will keep always in mind the probability that many commonplace moves called for in stage directions (for example, "kicks in door" or "vaults over garden wall") may actually have been prodigies of agility, he will be recreating for himself an experience more nearly congruent with that enjoyed by audiences in the days of Kublai Khan. It need hardly be added that anything involving a fist fight (or the Chinese equivalent) or sword- or cudgel-play, to judge by both history and the traditional Chinese stage of the twentieth century, was always accompanied by tumbling of a quality not to be scorned at a gymnastic meet.*

Acrobatics being even less often accompanied by speech than pantomime, they were even less likely to be noted in any way in the scripts we have today; but there are a few places where the text forces an acrobatic feat. My favorite has the villain and his victim taking shelter from a heavy downpour in an empty temple:

VILLAIN:
Here, wring out my shirt and then we'll conduct a little business.

VICTIM:
Brother, I can't wring it out.

---

*The same is true for several specialized roles as well. In the various versions of *Hsi-yu Chi* through history the character of Monkey has little else to do other than perform acrobatics and speak bawdy lines. See Dudbridge, pp. 82–83.

VILLAIN:
What? One little shirt? Here, take one end and you wring this way and I'll wring the other . . . wait a minute.

VICTIM:
Yes, Brother.

VILLAIN:
Never mind. You just stand there and hold your end still and *I'll* wring. (VILLAIN *twists and* VICTIM [*somersaults*] *and falls down.*)

VILLAIN:
You must have been cutting down on your food if you're this weak!

I have supplied the somersault above because it was certainly there when the scene was performed on the stage.

I am here arguing *a fortiori* again; but on 238, when Yen Ch'ing smites the villain Yang Ya-nei, the latter is specifically directed to turn a *chin-tou* (somersault); which in that case must have been a standing back flip. Far more often, however, there are either missing or incomplete stage directions at those points where there must have been acrobatic moves. For example, when Sung Chiang is warning the violent and bloody Black Whirlwind, Li K'uei, that he must not run amok among innocent citizens if allowed to go after a certain evil-doer, Li K'uei obviously does something quite physical twice and then the third time he hits Sung Chiang a tremendous blow. I leave bracketed space for the missing stage directions in the translation below:

SUNG:
Very well said, Hillock, but if I let you go down after him you must be forbearing and forgiving with everyone.

LI:
But brother, suppose someone bad-mouths me?

SUNG:
Forbear.

LI:
If someone spits on my face?

SUNG:
Ah, then you may give him something in return!

LI:
This much? [?]

SUNG:
Too little.

LI:
This much? [?]

SUNG:
Too little.

LI:
Ah, well, if I can give him back that much then what's to complain! *(Hits* SUNG CHIANG *a blow with his fist.)*

SUNG:
D'you want to kill me! Anyway, just don't get into such violent quarrels over what's right or wrong. (689)[4]

I believe that what Li K'uei does when Sung Chiang responds with "Too little" is to hit him a couple of stage taps and the third time he uncorks a wild one which sends Sung Chiang head over heels backward. I think such exaggerated moves were a part of every fight in Yuan drama (of which there are a fair number) and sometimes—if my guess is correct—even when an actor swings and misses he does somersaults and gymnastic pratfalls. This is what I believe is happening for example on 840 where the singing role is instructed by stage directions to "pantomime falling and hitting." I also imagine when the tiger knocks our comic Immortal down (*WP* 220)[5] or Yen Ch'ing is bowled over by a horse (233) each falls in the most spectacular way possible—realism is the last thing to be desired.

In a muscle-bound classic like "Liu Ch'ien Fights the One-horned Ox" (*WP* #148), it is safe to assume that the several contests between Donkey Snapper (who earned this charming sobriquet by seizing an ass by the head and the tail and breaking the hapless beast in two at the withers!) and the One-horned Ox, featured an almost endless display of acrobatic performance and pseudocombat. The wonder with such plays as these is that the performers could indulge in so much exertion and also manage to sing. Approximately the same observations can be made for all military dramas with the additional comment that complex and hair-raising mock sword fights or spear duels were the usual excuse for most of their acrobatic displays.

HORSES AND OTHER CRITTERS

> ...the hobbyhorse, whose epitaph is "For oh, for oh, the hobbyhorse is forgot."
>
> *Hamlet* III, ii, 1.145

Back in 1939 Sun K'ai-ti pointed out that traditional stage practice in the nineteenth and twentieth centuries had reduced the "horse prop" to a mere *(ma-pien)* riding crop,* but that there had once been a special object on stage in the Yuan theater which served as a horse. "What did this object look like?" he asks with a scarce-concealed note of triumph, "Just like the 'bamboo horse' of today!" Alas for us! The Chinese bamboo horse *(chu-ma)* of today is as unfamiliar as the *chu-ma* on the Yuan stage. I refuse to believe that Yuan playscripts could be referring simply to a stick (bamboo or not) such as a youngster might thrust between his legs, lash unmercifully and race about the yard in a two-legged version of a horse's four-legged gallop. The simple stick did not remain unembellished in the West so I cannot imagine that it did in China. I can

*See Scott (vol. 1, pp. 55–56 and note) for a complete description of the use of the switch and the body movement and postures which accompany the mounting, riding, and dismounting of a horse on the modern traditional stage. For Sun's article, see Sun K'ai-ti, pp. 381–83.

barely recall from my extreme youth one American elaboration of a stick wooden horse with a rather stiff silhouette of a horse's head attached to one end—I can't recall whether it was mine or some other child's. However, I can recall vividly when I was somewhat older seeing a picture of what must have been the Rolls Royce of wooden horses in some Edwardian publication devoted, I believe, to the fashions of English nannies and their charges. The stick not only boasted a handsome head with flaring nostrils and a mane, but there was a bridle and, as I recall, a tail—though that part is vague in my memory. However, the crowning touch in my opinion at the time, was a pair of small wheels attached to the nether end of the stick—the horse's rump. (I presume this was somehow expected to preserve the polished elegance of parquet floors?)

If the desire to embellish even children's casual toys was irresistible in the West, I assume that the traditional Chinese stage, which boasts some of the most elaborate costuming in the world, was not proof against the same urge.

As Sun points out, early stage directions for entering "astride a bamboo horse *(Ch'i chu-ma)*" (*WP* 583) are to be found in the so-called *Yuan-k'an pen* published in the Yuan dynasty; and similar, though more elaborate, directions exist later in a play written by a prince of the royal family of the Ming dynasty:

> [*The* mo *and* tan *pantomime summoning the servant boy to lead the horses over; servant boy enters with props; the* mo *and* tan *straddle the bamboo horse* (horses?).]

Though the *YCH* frequently neglects to mention the presence of a bamboo horse on stage (as noted above, pp. 69–70 and note) the creature nevertheless appeared very frequently in Yuan drama, and those riding it are said to be *ch'i-ma*, "astride,"[6] it. In addition to being astride *(ch'i)*, other stage directions have actors entering *hsi-ma* or *shan-ma*.* By the wave of a magical phonetic wand, Sun

*Unhappily there are a number of readings possible for both these characters and, since they are obsolete stage terms, no one can say that they were not variants of each other. To keep the record straight, I will give the reading *hsi* when the phonetic of the character is *li* and *shan* when it has the *ts'e* phonetic: *hsi*—233; 752; 967; *WP* 181, 859, and 93; *shan*—520; 1182; *WP* 105; 111; 116; 118; and 95. It should be noted that in the same play separated by only two pages of script we have both *hsi-ma* and *shan-ma* used when referring to the same action (or the same type of action).

concludes somehow that *hsi-ma, shan-ma* are the same as "straddling" *(ch'i)* a bamboo horse. I cannot prove that this is impossible, but the evidence he adduces in favor of the theory is weak.

At about the time of that spasm in modern China now known as the "Hundred Flowers" campaign, Chou Yi-pai[7] gave a series of lectures on the history of the Chinese theater and on page 105 of the published talks he addresses the question of our on-stage horses:

> One thing about the Yuan drama that differs from today is that every time someone comes on stage on horseback in Yuan drama he enters and acts while wearing a hobbyhorse frame *(chu-ma teng)*. This was very much like the later northern entertainment known as "running the mule" where the shape of the mule's forward half is fastened to the front of the performer and the rear half is fastened to his back. The riders in Yuan drama were actually wearing the front and rear parts of a hobbyhorse.

There is nothing particularly strange about the costume Chou suggests; in Europe it is as old as performance itself. Its continued use in Mayday morris dances makes it one of the very few survivors from the time when drama served ritual rather than entertainment functions.* It can be a very simple thing, like wearing a tub (bottom cut out) with the head and the tail of a horse fastened in appropriate spots. In what follows I shall call this apparatus a hobbyhorse and the straddled stick a wooden horse (corresponding to the Chinese *chu-ma teng* and *chu-ma*, respectively).

To return to Chou Yi-pai's speculation, however, if he had tried systematically to fit his hobbyhorse type of prop into every scene in which horse and rider appear, he would have soon discovered a number of places where it would be difficult to use. A simple example: many times the rider has to dismount from his horse during a scene and once (1180) he "falls from his horse." How is this to be done with Chou's hobby? In at least two cases *two* people *get on* the horse prop, whatever it may be, and that appears

*Chambers (vol. 1, p. 142, n. 2): "Douce gives a cut of a hobby horse, i.e. a man riding a pasteboard or wicker horse with his legs concealed beneath a footcloth. According to Du Meril ... the device is known throughout Europe. In France it is the *chevalet, cheval mallet* ... etc., in Germany the *Schimmel*."

to me very difficult with the equipment suggested by Chou Yi-pai. The bamboo stick horse illustrated in Figure 7, however, would serve well in either of these cases.*

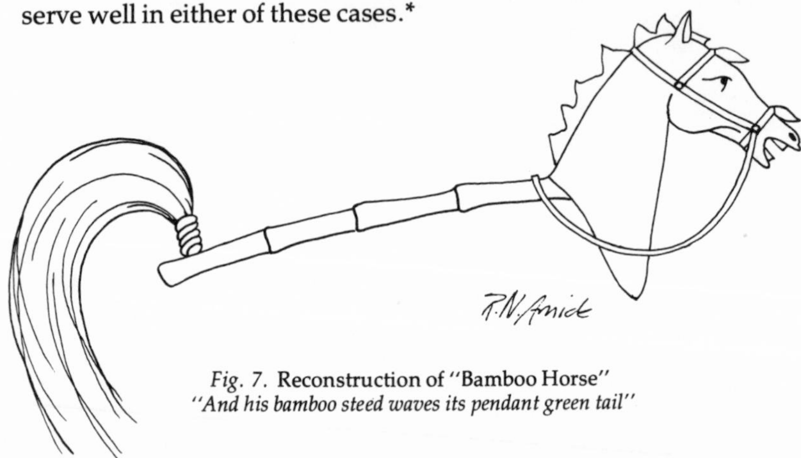

Fig. 7. Reconstruction of "Bamboo Horse"
"And his bamboo steed waves its pendant green tail"

My wholly imaginary wooden horse reconstruction above has some legitimate credentials. Admittedly, the T'ang style horse's head is there simply because I think it should be, but the bridle is attested to on 233 where the stage direction has an actor seizing the horse by the bridle; and my wooden horse's splendid tail is his courtesy of the line from Li Ho's poem given as caption to the picture. Frodsham believes the "green tail" refers to the bamboo's leaves; if that were so, the young prince would be riding a very unsatisfactory horse no thicker than a brush pen, for bamboo leaves do not sprout from the trunk of the tree. It is possible, of course, that Frodsham is right, but Li Ho is a poet almost obsessed with colors in odd contexts, and it would come as no surprise to me to find that he connected the word "green" in this poem with the glossy insouciance of youth as Shakespeare does: "In my salad days when my judgment was green.†" In any event, *my* stage *chu-ma* will retain his fine tail until archeology proves me wrong.

*On the other hand, in at least one scene (*YCH* #67, Act III) the hobby might be handier. Five men are all on stage at once *shan-ma,* wielding weapons, and seizing one another. Depending on what was involved with the hands it might have been easier to have a horse-prop suspended than straddled. In a pinch, though, I expect the stick horse could be held up by a strap (the reins) over the shoulders.

†Furthermore, in short "song" by Ma Chih-yuan (*CYSC,* p. 233) we find "my green hair is gone," meaning the glossy black of a youthful Chinese is now flecked with white.

In addition to these horse props which were "ridden" in some fashion, there are a number of examples of what appears to have been a costume which required a horse-head mask (1101, and see above under "Empty Exits"). Additionally, in scenes depicting the court of the king of Hell, that worthy is accompanied by horse- and ox-headed demons (502). But the most intriguing horse (as far as stagecraft is concerned) is the free-standing and unmounted stallion, Ti-lu (*WP* 150):

WANG SUN:
... I am under command from their Lordships to steal Liu Hsüan-te's mighty horse Ti-lu, so I might as well away.

(sings)
Having waited till the waterclock is spent
And sleeping souls will not awake,
I fear only that I may come upon some retainer
As I make my way to the stables.

I hope he will be tractable,
Well trained and docile.
To steal a warhorse is not simple burglary.
But I have been given my commission—

I have mixed half a manger of fodder
And he is more than half content.
Now to muffle my footfall and hide my tracks
As I unfasten his bridle and hobbles—

(He pantomimes stealing the horse.)

LIU PEI:
(Rushing onstage) ... I've come to get my horse away from here—you, there! who are you?

WANG SUN:
I see I must put Liu Pei to the sword if I would steal his mount ... (etc.)

In the event, however, Wang Sun is persuaded to hand over Ti-lu (the horse is presumably standing onstage as the dialogue takes place) to its proper owner. And at the end of the scene the stage directions instruct Liu Pei to "pantomime leaping the Sandalwood River." Since in the script it is implicit that he is mounted on Ti-lu, one wonders how it was managed.... I have no very good suggestions about how the effect was achieved, but the existence of a free-standing horse is not all that surprising. Anyone who has seen the two-man Chinese lion *(shih-tzu)* act knows with what charm and conviction that animal suit and mask (resembling nothing so much as a huge Pekinese dog wearing a fringed bed-cover) can be manipulated by a pair of agile performers. My guess is that Ti-lu, Liu Pei's famous steed, was created in a similar fashion.

It might be objected that this scene employs a unique effect called for only because the story happened to involve a horse as famous as Bucephalus. In order to dispel any such doubts, I feel I must introduce you to a beast with no claim to fame at all but who happens to be my favorite jackass. In the scene that follows, you should try to picture the (two-man?) donkey as he edges away from the distraught madam, perhaps grazing peacefully through the dialogue between the two humans and finally being ridden off by the madam with the Good Judge Pao—still incognito—holding its bridle. The deliberate construction of the scene leaves no doubt that the donkey was played on the stage as an independent character, not as a prop to be straddled or attached to the body of one of the human characters.

(Enter the ch'a-tan, WANG FEN-LIEN, *a madam, chasing her donkey on stage.)*

WANG:

I am Wang Fen-lien and I live at Dog-leg Bay in Nan-kuan. I am in the trade of selling smiles to gentlemen—which does keep bread in my mouth. Recently the Emperor sent us two officials, Yang Chin-wu and Liu Hsiao *ya-nei,* to open the granary and distribute grain to the people. They spend all their money at my establishment—very extravagant, offering ten times the asking price for everything they want. They're arrogant and self-important so when anybody else comes to the door they don't come back again. My establishment has been very solicitous of those two and they have now spent all their money there. A few days ago they pawned their Red-Gold Mace of Power with me. If they don't have enough money to redeem it, I'll have it cut up for rings and brooches —that ought to keep me quite comfortable for a while. Just now, a couple of my sisters-in-trade asked me over for a cup of tea, but that pair at my place sent one of their men with an ass for me to ride. Well, the man left and one never knows from the beginning the middle or the end of things, because as I was riding along I made some sort of sudden noise, lost the reins, fell from the beast and nearly broke my willowy waist! My, but that was painful! And here I am with no one to help me back on the creature. When I try to catch him myself he just moves again so I can't get to him. How am I to find someone who'll help me?

PAO:
There appears to be a woman of no great social standing. I think I shall just help her catch that ass and enquire of her about conditions here.

*(*PAO *pantomimes catching the ass,* WANG *pantomimes thanking him.)*

WANG:
I am much obliged to you, good sir.

PAO:
Daughter, where does your family hail from?

WANG:

(aside)

Now here's an old rustic for sure. He doesn't even know what I am. *(to* PAO*)* Why, I live at Dog-leg Bay.

PAO:
And what trade are you engaged in there?

WANG:
Good sir, guess, just try!

PAO:
Oh, trying is what judges do!*

WANG:
No, try and guess.

PAO:
You run an oil press.

WANG:
No.

PAO:
A pawnshop?

WANG:
No.

PAO:
A dry-goods store.

WANG:
Not that either.

*This exchange obviously involved a pun *(ts'ai tsa* and *shih ts'ai tsa)* but, since I don't know what the double meaning is, I cannot give an equivalent in the same subject area.

PAO:
Well, it seems you don't do anything. What is your business?

WANG:
My establishment sells plump quails! And where do you live?

PAO:
Well, daughter, I had only one wife and she's long dead: I have no children and so I just travel from place to place making what living I can.

WANG:
Old one, why don't you come with me, I could use you and there would always be enough to eat and drink for you.

PAO:
That would be fine, fine. Tell me, what would be my duties there?

WANG:
Oh, I'd dress you up in a brand new starched tunic, get you a new hat, a new light brown sash, a pair of clean, shiny new boots and a bench, and there you'll sit, a proper doorman for my establishment—wouldn't that be nice?

PAO:
Tell me, daughter, whom do you see at your place? Tell me all about the comings and goings.

WANG:
Well, we have the young blades and the traveling merchants, but none of those is as important as the two we've got there now. Both of them are granary officials, quite powerful and with lots of money—their father is a *very* important man in

the Capital. They're here getting ten tael in silver the peck measure of grain. Their ten-ounce dipper only holds eight ounces and the steelyard they use to weigh the grain won't budge until three ounces are in the pan. They've made their little pile all right, but I'm not asking for any of it!

PAO:
If you won't take their money, will you accept something from them as a gift, daughter?

WANG:
Their money I don't take, but they did give me their Red-Gold Mace. I tell you your eyes would pop out of your head and you'd perish if you saw it!

PAO:
[*with irony*] Now, how many times in my long life have I ever seen a Red-Gold Mace! Daughter, don't you suppose it would end all my bad luck and expiate all my sins just to have a look at it? My, that would be fine!

WANG:
Old one, I *do* think it would end your bad luck and cancel your sins just to look at it, so that you shall do. Come with me to my place and you shall see it.

PAO:
I will go with you.

WANG:
And have you eaten yet, old one?

PAO:
No, I have not.

WANG:
Well, come with me just up ahead. The two I told you about are waiting on me to start the banquet. There will be all you want to eat and drink there. Now help me onto that jackass.

(PAO *assists her to mount the ass.)*

PAO:
(aside) Ah, if the rest of the world could see Judge Pao, Judge of the Nan-ya, Magistrate of K'ai-feng, now in Ch'en-chou helping this woman catch her donkey.... It is very funny! *(exeunt)* (47*ff*.)

When they reach the madam's goal, the two bad officials have Judge Pao "strung-up" (see page 65 above). His servant eventually gets him cut down and then the madam, who has been inside all this time and knows nothing of what has happened, comes out and tells Pao that he can now help her on her ass again. Pao's servant flies at her, and with the pomposity of an underling in earshot of his master cries, "You'll be in hell before my master helps you on that ass!" Judge Pao merely says, "*T'uei!* Hush! Of course I'll hold your mount for you, daughter." In Yuan drama, officials and highly placed persons are too often simply stuffed shirts, but this one scene with its series of undignified events coupled with Judge Pao's laughter at himself helping a village madam onto her mount and his final dismissal of self-conscious dignity, makes him a very appealing character instead of simply an admirable one. The entire *mise-en-scène* is a fine piece of stagecraft —much of which is made possible by the donkey.

In addition to horses and donkey (however played), there were tigers on stage: one which knocks down and drags off the *ch'iao*, our bumbling Immortal (*WP* 220)*; a white one which rushes in and mauls La-mei (1035); and a third that rushes on stage and is

*The play which features the inept Immortal and his ill-trained tiger (*WP* #15) appears in an early Ming edition which includes quite complete notations of the props and costumes used in each scene. For this scene it is noted simply that a "tiger suit" *(hu-yi)* is needed, alas.

killed (*WP* 559). A white stag comes on stage only to be shot by an archer and go off with the arrow in its hide and its hunter in pursuit (*WP* 532). In *WP* on page 383 a red-headed crane (cranes?) dances; on the next page the Taoist gets on its back and is borne aloft *(ch'i ho shang sheng)*. There is no reason why (in the more elaborate theaters) the Chinese could not have had a hoist to accomplish this—I am sure the Greeks were not the only ones with a *mēkanē*. In any case, the considerable stage menagerie utilized by Yuan drama is yet another piece of evidence (if one were needed) of that entertainment form's devotion to colorful events, and a general theatrical liveliness.

PERFORMANCE MODES

> Generally speaking, when a play reaches a "cold" spot and there is little action on the stage, an interlude with the *ch'ou* and the *ching* will be greatly welcomed by the audience—and this, after all, is one of the objects of drama.
>
> *Ku-ch'ü Tsa-yen*, p. 141

Whatever Yuan drama may have lacked in scenery and other stage mechanisms, it more than made up for with its lavish array of performing modes. It is impossible even to guess at the voice quality, rhythm, or pace that distinguished some modes of presentation* so we must simply set them aside. But those which are left still constitute such a bewildering array that I have had to impose a kind of artificial order on them simply to keep them all in mind.

I have in the first place supposed that there were "norms" of singing *(ch'ang)*, reciting *(nien)*, and speaking *(pai)* which were used on stage so much of the time that the audience identified them as normal presentation. Now we are in a position to say that any deliberate alteration of these styles was a special performance mode. Let us assume further that there were certain levels of language speeds and rhythms proper to certain roles. These were

*For example, Chinese has five verbs which can mean "to chant": *yung, yin, nien, sung,* and *heng*. I am not certain what distinguished any of them. *Heng* is used to mean both wordless humming and a "hum" with lyrics—like Winnie the Pooh's compositions, one supposes.

"normal" because audiences were so used to them that when someone spoke very rapidly, or a number of lines were in a classical or archaic style, the impact on the audience would be that of a deviation from normal. Finally, I assume that there was a "normal" dramatic form: for example, actors when they spoke most often did so to each other and in character. I can therefore designate such things as asides, monologues, and conversations carried on with persons offstage as special performance modes. In what follows, I have tried to talk about this area of the performer's art within the provisions of the framework.

Singing Modes

The proper verb for the delivery of arias is *ch'ang* and normally the aria was addressed, as it were, to another actor on the stage.* Since almost every entrance by a singing or even secondary role was accompanied by some kind of servant, companion, or underling, as has been noted, there was always an ear present. This mode of presentation is the one least often altered. Even so we find the courtesan Chao P'an-erh (202) and the bride-to-be Sun An (1314) each singing an aria as an aside. Chang An-chu weeps and sings simultaneously (426), and on 390 the composer can even invert "stage reality" by having the singer pretend he cannot sing.

In this last situation, the singing role is a peddler who is being victimized by the villain. He sings of his troubles through most of a normal set of arias. Then, as another way of tormenting the luckless merchant, the bully demands that he sing a song *(ch'ang)* for him:

PEDDLER:
Oh, I can't sing—

VILLAIN:
Come on, sing a little, what harm could it do!

*I am hard put to decide whether the singer is statistically more often singing his own thoughts to himself or whether we should imagine him addressing another actor; both modes are common; other actors can feed lines to the singer on which he elaborates his song, but the singer can also feed them to himself. The latter is noted as *tai-yün* (included speech) in stage directions.

PEDDLER:
No, really, I can't sing at all—

VILLAIN:
(furious)
Sing or I'll—

PEDDLER:
(hastily)
Oh, I will, brother, I'll sing something or other while you have your drink.

VILLAIN:
Sing!

PEDDLER:
(passing VILLAIN *a winebowl)*
You have some more wine and I'll sing you—since this is the first time we've been together—"How Pleasant the Autumn Wind"—

VILLAIN:
Sing, sing, I'll drink.

PEDDLER:
(sings)
I cannot sleep but lie awake
Hearing the rustle of rain on the banana leaves,
The wind chimes sounding in the eaves.
Beyond the Nan-lou flies
The southering goose, I hear its cries—

(VILLAIN *pretends to have fallen asleep.*)

PEDDLER:
(speaks)
This is an awful situation! I've got to get out of here—

VILLAIN:
Shoo! Where do you think you're going?

PEDDLER:

(sings)
He did not sleep;
He but closed his eyes!

Singing this song (which does not belong to the same mode or key as the other, dramatic, arias he has performed so far), the peddler is pretending for the sake of the story to be singing for the first time and his choice of lyrics for the opening five lines has nothing whatever to do with the *mise-en-scène*. Then, as he tries to leave and the villain stops him, the song suddenly locks into place with the action of the drama and the last lines are directed once more toward the situation as it evolves on the stage.

Although singing *(ch'ang)* is traditionally the prerogative of the star, it would be strange to find a form like Yuan drama, so devoted to pleasing its audiences, unwilling to break with its own conventions. In fact, there are a good number of intrusive arias done by someone other than the singing role and in one case (*WP* 826) there is a sung parody of a serious aria which had just been performed.

(Wei-sheng)

LIU HUNG:

(sings)
All I want is to hear from you often
Let the two of us know how you are.
And if you have found anything lacking, forgive us.

CH'UN-LANG:
Oh, uncle, one day I will repay you for all this.

LIU HUNG:

(sings)
Whether you choose to repay me or even remember
Is entirely up to you.

[At this point the comic Wang Hsiu-ts'ai enters and berates Ch'un-lang for going off to the capital to sit for the exams and leaving him without support.]

CH'UN-LANG:
Brother—when I have gotten a post I will repay all I owe you.

WANG HSIU-TS'AI:
Oh, well, then! There's an end to it. Go! By all means, go!

(pantomimes singing Wei-sheng)
All I want is to hear from you often
Let Old Wang Hsiu-ts'ai know how you are
And whether you choose to repay me or even remember . . .
Dong-li-di da-li da li-li-li!

When he gets to the line which voiced unselfish sentiments in the original, he suddenly switches to the Yuan equivalent of "tum tiddy um tum." But he is obviously singing to the same tune and aping the words of the proper singing role.

Not only does the drama form break with its own conventions for this kind of supererogatory skit, but I am of the opinion that (far more frequently than our texts of today would have us believe) aria singing *(ch'ang)* was deliberately put in for players other than the singing role to satisfy the craving of actors for a little bit fatter part. *Rain on the Hsiao-hsiang* (see Part II, pp. 269 and 308) contains what I believe is one such example.

On page 1055 of *YCH,* three Taoist Immortals enter with a Taoist drum and clapper *(yü-ku* and *chien-pan).* When an entrance like this is made, the Taoist usually *recites* to accompaniment of his drum and clapper (see 626 for example), but he can also "sing a *tao-ch'ing* song" *(ch'ang tao-ch'ing ch'ü-erh).* A *tao-ch'ing ch'ü* seems to have been a song in any form, the burden of which glorifies the Taoist vision of transcendental realms. It appears that the melodies to which the *tao-ch'ing* words were sung were of several different types. On 1055 the songs Lieh-tzu the Immortal sings constitute a short subsuite of aria tunes related to one another and must have sounded much as though a *san-ch'ü* or literary song had been introduced at the beginning of the act's proper aria set *(t'ao-shu).* In *WP* 890, Niu Lin enters with the Taoist *yü-ku* and *chien-tzu* and sings what appear to be six songs with a basic seven-beat line; after the first, each is introduced by a stage direction, *yu* ("again"). Then he sings two arias in the *chung-lü* mode and two in *shuang tiao,* each set with differing rhymes. This whole performance is somewhat of a hotchpotch and, though he is not a *ching* or comic character, he is given a good deal of nonsense verse and even inserts a little horseplay in the middle of his first aria:

(Shih-erh Yüeh)

NIU LIN:

(sings)

My clothing is the simple hemp coat
And slippers made of grass—

(speaks)

P'ei! It should be "sandals made of grass" and I sang slippers—That's all right—No, but I sang it— All right, all right, I'll sing it over again from the beginning, "a team of horses cannot drag back one spoken word." If I don't fix it it'll look like I've no head for learning—

(sings)

My clothing is the simple hemp coat
And sandals made of grass.
But better than the most colorful robes. . . . *(etc.)*

I am not certain I understand the reason for this rather elaborate and shaggy interruption of the act, but in all cases I have just mentioned (and, I believe, for the reason I give), someone other than the singing role is given a chance to shine and sing bona fide arias in defiance of the Yuan dramatic convention that allows only one singing role in any given act.

In addition to singing arias *(ch'ang),* there are a number of places where as a part of the *mise-en-scène* one or another character sings a song *(ko).* In quite a few cases this takes the very old metrical form of *4-hsi-4.* Certainly the singing in *Hsi-hsiang Chi* of a *fu* supposed to have been written by Ssu-ma Hsiang-ju is meant to sound archaic (*WP* 284):

There was a young beauty, Oh,
Once seen could not be forgot.
Fail to see her a single day, Oh,
And madness is your lot.
The phoenix journeys far, Oh,
Everywhere to seek his mate,
But what can I do now, Oh,
My love's not at her gate. . . . *(etc.)*

But the same rhythm is sung *(ko)* in *WP* 206 and 1151,* where there is no reason at all for an archaic flavor. On the other hand, there is also a song *(ko)* on 819 over forty lines long in a basic seven-beat rhythm rather than *4-hsi-4.* There simply is no way of telling today what might have differentiated the mode of presentation known as *ch'ang* and that called *ko.*

Once again let me remind the reader that the composers of Yuan drama were first and foremost musicians, and like musicians in all parts of the world they were sensitive to the sounds of music in everything. They took obvious delight in incorporating all kinds of music into their compositions: in addition to the *tao-ch'ing* songs just mentioned, there is the "Jurched suite" mentioned in Chapter 1[8] and let me note here a very famous case where a set of nine "turns" or variations (?) on a peddlers' song-like ware-vending chant constitute almost all the arias for the last act of *Huo-lang Tan* (The Singer of Peddlers' Songs), *YCH* #94.†

For similar reasons, the playwright's ear for recitation forms and their sound effects was just as keen and just as eclectic. Not only do we have the poet Su Tung-p'o reciting his own composition, the Red Cliff *fu* (*WP* 778), in its entirety, for example, but Buddhist and Taoist chants, and prayers, and spells, enumeration of chess terms (*WP* 250) and acupuncture arcana (233); all of which

*Actually the rhythm on 1151 is variant: *3-hsi-3* and *4-hsi-3*.

†Peddlers' cries are used frequently in other contexts as well; see 872–73 and 876.

indicate a delighted wallowing in the sounds of words rather than concern with their import. In the section that follows, I have tried to bring a little order to the welter of recitation styles.

Recitation Modes

Shih-yün

Though we can say little or nothing about the voice timbre, rhythm, or emphasis proper to the various kinds of recitation, part of my complaint (lodged under the first asterism of this section) may be alleviated by weeding out synonyms.

The most general term for recitation of verse (or metrical delivery short of singing voice) is *nien;* but on 748 Pu Shang is said to "recite in *shih* verse" *(shih-yün)* and Sun-tzu responds with two more lines making a shared quatrain. Then the stage directions say that Pu Shang "recites again" *(yu nien).* In this case, of course, *nien* is being used to refer to the performance mode of "recitation in *shih* verse," so *nien* and *shih-yün* are synonymous.

On 926 we have the following:

LIANG:
All right then, you two, you must chant *(yin)*
me some of your verse—and if it's well done,
I'll let you off—if it's not, there's a hundred
strokes of the fuller's stick in it for you.

MA:
Oh, I have one you'll surely like—Me first!

(pantomimes reciting [*nien*]*)*
A jolly Graduate am I
I drink cold wine and eat hot pie,
I eat the latter down so fast
I've burnt my mouth awry!

LIANG:
Stupid! Beat him, men. . . .

Since Ma replies by *nien* when he was told to *yin,* we can assume that one form of the recitation mode *nien* was *yin*. Now, as I recall from my Euclid, if angles A and C both equal B, then angles A, B, and C are identical. Whatever *shih-yün* (recitation in *shih* verse) sounded like, when our script tells us that the person *yin* or *nien* it must have sounded the same as *shih-yün*.*

Certainly the most frequently occurring examples of *shih-yün* are to be found in the entrance and exit verses of all major characters. These are five- and seven-character quatrains much like the T'ang dynasty *ku-shih* and are easily recognized as imitations of this type of *shih*. For the most part, these quatrains are delivered by a single actor though there are enough examples of shared quatrains—in exit verse, seldom with entrance verses—to make the recitation duet a fairly common event.† (Minor characters, especially comic-villains [*ching*] are often given a rhyming or unrhymed couplet which may be nonsense or a reasonable statement, but these are never designated *shih-yün,* "recitation in *shih* verse.")

The playwright also indulged in all kinds of playfulness with *shih* poetry including a scandalously bad parody of Chang Chi's *chüeh-chü* verse, "Feng-ch'iao Yeh-po" (284) and entrance verse which is simply a pastiche of aria titles (91)—though it is not clear to me whether this latter is sung or recited. In dramas involving famous poets or "beautiful women and talented men," the characters frequently recite and write *shih* verses to one another.

*On 1650 an entertainer reads *(nien)* a document detailing the selling of a boy of her own family; the language is formal and literary to a degree. At first blush this use of *nien* seems to becloud the issue; but I think not permanently. My own view of the matter (though I have no evidence to pinpoint it) is that *nien* meant simply "to deliver in a formal style." In the case of verse, this probably included a mannered and even cadence; perhaps with a swaying of the head and perhaps with a hint of what we could call a chant. In the case of the legal document, *nien* probably meant to give equal stress and time to each word, which makes for a mannered delivery again, and which would sound quite different from normal spoken Chinese. The linguistically unsophisticated Chinese to this day will tend to make all his neutral *de*'s into full *dee*'s, his *le*'s into *liao*'s and his *hai*'s into *hwan*'s when he reads *(nien)* rather than speaks; even when what he's reading is supposed to be normal speech.

†See, for example, 53, 289, 316, 519, and 602.

Tz'u-yün

On *YCH* 976 there is an absolutely genuine *tz'u* (lyric) done to the pattern of "Ch'ang Hsiang-ssu" (3375//) and on 817 an equally genuine "lyric" to the pattern of *Che-ku T'ien* (7777 3377).* In these two cases (and a few others) when *YCH* has the stage direction *tz'u-yün* "recites in *tz'u* form," the editor is being accurate and descriptive. However, most of the time when the term *tz'u-yün* appears in *YCH,* it introduces a section done in a loose narrative verse with a basically seven-syllable line. The form bears no resemblance to the Sung style *tz'u* (lyric) and, of course, the *YCH* editor, Tsang Chin-shu, was perfectly aware of that fact. When he designates a section like this *tz'u-yün,* he merely means something like "recites with rhyme and rhythm."[9] Editors of the other editions seldom bother to indicate that any such passage is different from straightforward speech. As a result, one reads along and suddenly finds that the lines begin to have rhyme and meter. I for one then usually have to go back, discover where this started, and read it over again.

However clumsy the term Tsang uses, he is taking care to point out to the reader when an actor is using that remarkably flexible narrative verse form, apparently an invention of Chin and Yuan playwrights,[10] which supplies them with a verse vehicle as congenial to the genius of spoken Chinese as blank verse iambic is to English.†

Whereas the older forms of verse (T'ang-style *shih, fu,* and Sung-style *tz'u*) were for the most part keyed to the unisyllabic rhythms of the Chinese literary language, the narrative verse form in Yuan drama fully allows for and exploits the variety of multisyllable rhythms—brought about by unstressed and lightly stressed syllable groups—which had become a part of spoken (as opposed to literary) Chinese. This flexible narrative verse is used in the

---

*Note that Tsang identifies and names the *tz'u* patterns while editors of the other texts do not. Tsang was determined to be helpful. Note also (404) Ch'a-ch'a has a *tz'u* for her entrance verse, and on 1295 Chiang Liang recites a *Hsi-chiang Yueh* pattern (6676//).

†From here on I shall refer to this kind of recitation simply as "narrative verse" since there is no handy Chinese term for it.

majority of Yuan dramas for recapitulations,* final tableaux, and on occasion throughout the plays. The form takes well to comic monologue, lyric soliloquies, straight narrative, and both comic and serious dialogue.† And in at least one instance (*WP* 157, Act IV), the most important figure does nearly the entire act in narrative verse of one sort or another. Since he is a Ch'an (zen) master, much of it is in the form of *gāthās* or Buddhist homiletic chants. We are quite certain one of the forerunners of the Yuan drama was a kind of Chin dynasty entertainment known collectively as *yuan-pen* which included, among numerous other entertainment forms, the comic monologue. A number of little *yuan-pen* type acts can be found embedded in Yuan dramas, and one of the best known is performed in *WP* #52 on page 871 as an extended introductory verse by Chang Shih-kuei, a comic general—the Chinese *miles ingloriosus.*‡ He tells the audience what once transpired when he met another general intent on single combat:

> That day I met him he said not a word.
> (My weapon was the halberd, his, the two-edged sword.)
> We'd scarce engaged, when in a trice
> I'd lost from my left arm a tremendous slice!

---

*I am of the opinion that skillful use of it is something for which the critic should give the playwright high marks. Conversely, recapitulation in prose rather than narrative verse, for example, can indicate a failure by the dramatist to exploit the resources at his disposal.

†This last is rare. To the best of my knowledge the only full dialogue scene in which all the actors speak in narrative verse is in *Rain* (see Part II, pp. 296–301) where Ts'ui-luan, her gaoler, the hostel-keeper, and Ts'ui-luan's father all declaim in narrative verse and furthermore use an "u" rhyme, the same rhyme used in arias of that act. This is a rare piece of virtuoso handling of Yuan narrative verse. *WP* #155 has a large number of dramatis personae enter simply to declaim in narrative verse and exit. There, the verse is used to accompany and strengthen the pageantry—which is about all that *WP* #155 consists of.

‡Both Crump (1958) and Hu Chi (1964, pp. 314–16) consider this comic monologue, the skit of the bumbling Immortal in *WP* #15 (see note, page 119 above) and, of course, the *Two Physicians Raise Cain* (see p. 152 ff., below) to be vestiges of the old comic *yuan-pen* performances which are still incorporated in the later *tsa-chü* of Yuan dynasty times. Hu Chi even identifies the *miles gloriosus* monologue with a *yuan-pen* title preserved under the "soldier section" of the list given in *Cho-ken Lu*. There is a title there, "Needle and Thread," and I think it likely to have been very similar to the monologue above, though longer.

Needle and thread I got
From my kit
And made quick work of repairing it.
Now he had his pike and I my bow—
But he lopped off my right arm with a single blow!
Needle and thread I got
From my kit
And made quick work of repairing it.
Now I spun my broadsword; he whirled his axe—
Cut me and my horse in half with two great whacks.
Needle and thread I used
Once again.
In less than no time I repaired the twain.
We fought till I was stitches from head to toe
Then he cried in admiration as he stayed his blow,
"You can't fight worth a copper but you sure can sew!"

This is essentially a Munchausenesque tall story done in Yuan narrative verse. The sprung rhythm effects of groups of accentless syllables contributes greatly not only to the audible clarity of the tale but also to its comic lilt.

But narrative verse is in no way limited to the comic. Yuan dramatic form requires that a play resolve itself in a "happy ending." Many times this takes the form of rewards and punishments meted out in the final tableau of the fourth act by a high official or someone speaking in the name of the emperor. The texts of these epilogues are dignified and serious and the narrative verse form manages them very readily; even allowing the incorporation of proper names, official titles, and all manner of angular and poetically awkward items.

And on the upper end of the scale of artistry, the narrative verse form can be lyrical and evocative, as witness Chang T'ien-chüeh's lonely thoughts in the posthouse where he drowsed off and dreamt of his only daughter whom he fears may be drowned:*

*The reader will find this whole scene translated *in situ* in Part II.

First, because my heart was ill at ease,
Then because my mind was all uncertain,
As soon as my eyes closed, father and child were met again.
Even as I struggled to speak of those years of separation
Suddenly the startled dream fled.
From where came that cruel awakening sound; what was it?
—the chink-clank of iron horsemen?
I first thought it the
Cold, stiff thump of wet garments against a laundry block.
Then I guessed
The chittering of crickets in a deserted stairwell sounding
    through the west window
And conjured next the sight of
Geese returning to southern eddies from beyond the reach
    of heaven.
I now
Cease my chant and listen closely—
It is nothing but
The wild wind and rushing rain that summoned me awake.
I
Face this gray scene having lost all who were close to me.
What wonder then
Grief sours my heart and chills it more each day?
Oh, my child, do you still live the life I knew
Or have you come back to this mansion earth in
    another form?

Are you wealthy, honored? Or captive, slaved?

A white-haired father in the lonely hostel ponders,
    wonders—
Ah, heaven!
But his daughter in the bloom of her years is somewhere
    anguished!

Here I have noted the occurrence of lightly stressed groups which are sometimes called "extra-metrical syllables"—most of which occur in first position in the line—as hemistichs "I know," "it is nothing but," etc. "Ah, heaven!" *(t'ien-na)* is an apostrophe that stands by itself.

But the bread-and-butter duties* of narrative verse in Yuan drama are the recapitulations—to which this genre seems curiously addicted.† You may see two good examples on page 353 and 377 in Part II, but in order to have the various uses of narrative verse all assembled here in the section devoted to recitation modes, let me append one other recapitulation from *Shen Nu-erh* (*YCH* #33, p. 575). The child's ghost has just appeared to Good Judge Pao, and in this recapitulation in verse the ghost tells the judge the succession of events which led to his unavenged murder. As you will see, a great deal of narrative has been compressed into a small compass:

> Please sir, be not angry, I pray,
> But listen carefully to what I say:
> Because my aunt so hated my mother
> The families decided to part from each other.
> My aunt and uncle moved away.
> I came home from school that day
> And went out in the street to play.
> Our servant and I together went down
> To the Great Cross Roads at the center of town.
> There was a puppet-seller passing by
> And wanting one, I began to cry.
> The *yuan-kung* said, "I'll buy you one."
> I waited for him, but while he was gone
> My uncle came by and saw me there
> And took me back to *his* house, where
> My aunt slipped a rope noose over my head
> In a jealous rage, and strangled me dead.
> I've been a grieving ghost since then
> Weeping beyond the world of men.

---

*Or "rice and soy duties"?

†I have yet to see a convincing theory to account for the recaps in Yuan drama. Updating the audience is not the reason—most had known the stories since childhood—and why draw attention to the repeats by putting them in narrative verse? That playwrights could and did pass up recap opportunities is clear. See my note (Part II, p. 391 below) and the final words by Sung Chiang in *YCH* #14. As the other actors come onstage for the final summing up in *tz'u* he says: "I sent Tai Tsung down the mountain to find out the facts, so I know everything," thereby forestalling a recap. In Yang (1-12223) this is even more abrupt: "Yen-ch'ing, I know everything." Evidently this was too unlikely (dramatically) for the editor of *YCH*, and he has added his explanations.

The only hope that's left to me now
Is revenge and justice from honest Judge Pao.*

Finally,[11] a somewhat rarer use of Yuan drama's narrative verse resembles what we in the West call "invective." Human beings (regrettably, I suppose) seem to enjoy compositions which are characterized by malevolence and unbridled *ad hominem* vituperation—as witness the immense popularity of the English "Junius" (whoever he might have been) in the early nineteenth century—and the stage presents wonderful opportunities for capitalizing on this weakness. In Yuan drama, scurrilities uttered by comic characters are as common as mice in a granary, but these have no effect on the plot at all and were supposed to be forgotten as soon as they had gotten a laugh. The invectives I refer to here, on the other hand, are built into the play, have a prior cause in the story and a succeeding effect on the plot.

On 1007 Chang Yung, the singing role, has married a former courtesan who has just threatened to beat his son by a deceased wife. He pleads with her not to do it, but she pushes him out of the house. He then addresses the neighbors with an invective against prostitutes:

CHANG:

(reciting)

Hear me neighbors:
Cursed by the stars will be the man
Who takes unto himself a courtesan.
She'll squander his substance, scatter his friends
And use his wealth to further her ends—
He should know the painted face on her
Is only a whited sepulchre. . . . *(etc.)*

*In this latter translation (though the verse does not differ much in metrics from the father's lament), I have used rhyme and a good deal of enjambment to indicate the narrative speed with which this verse rehearses the action of the entire play. After years of messing about with Yuan drama, I have found that, when I want to capture a higher level of poetic diction and imagery, I do better by not opting to use rhyme. The simple, straightforward narrative use of the form invites enjambment (though almost all lines in the Chinese are end-stopped) and that in turn simplifies rhyming so much that one can approximate the frequency of rhyme in the original and yet not come up with crabbed English.

As a result of this invective, the concubine forebears to beat the child (for the time being) and the entire incident—pointed up by the invective in verse—is integrated into the plot the way a comic interlude would never be. Although some of the lines in this kind of verse are models of humorous vulgarity, they were not meant to be treated in the same fashion as transient humorous interjections. Below, the selection from 866 has many such lines, but the verse is meant to be taken seriously, and in the final act of the play it is made clear that the invective was spoken by Chu Mai-ch'en's wife only to shame him into making something of himself:

CHU:

But they told me next year I would become an official—then you would have rank and standing, manage official domiciles. . . .

WIFE:

Me run official domiciles
And now I'm treated like a case of piles!
Rank and standing? So many lies
Just farts to blow the sand in my eyes.

I wish you a palsy of the tongue because every time you move it there's more nonsense about official posts—why the only post you'll fill is a doorpost; with people knocking on one end and stepping on the other. As magistrate I suppose you might possibly manage to judge:

The river to be wet or a roof to be dry

The day they make you magistrate:

The sun will be red, the moon black in the sky,
Stars will wink out and the Dipper will sigh.
The day you're appointed to *anything*,
Dogs will pull coaches, snakes will sing,
Bugs and ants will wear felt hats,
And I'll expect to see leather shoes on gnats.

Queen Goddess of the West will sell onion cakes,

Men will sprout tails, rats will laugh 'til they trip on their legs.
And sparrows will fly around laying pigeon eggs—

Oh, no. I won't wait for your day to come. Write me a letter of divorcement now!

The invective goes on for another page; rhymed sections interspersed with straight lines and arias sung by Chu Mai-ch'en. This is a fine example of the options the playwright had in melding verse and prose rhythms, and the on-again-off-again quality of rhyme and meter gives one the sense of sporadic bursts of anger sweeping over Chu Mai-ch'en's wife.

Ch'en-yin (to chant or to ponder?)

Evidently the first time I learned the term *ch'en-yin* it was in a context which demanded the meaning "to chant in a low voice"; when I later came to read Yuan drama, I automatically thought of it in this way. Actually, *ch'en-yin* most often means to be "sunk in thought" or possibly "to mutter as in deep thought,"[12] though, of course, one of its meanings is "to chant." Somewhere I had subconsciously equated *ch'en-yin* with the sound of the Jewish prayer chanting known as *davining** and a few of the contexts in Yuan drama allowed me to cherish this equation:

HSÜ KU:
[*alone on stage*] I do not trust that Fan Chü: here we are ready to depart for home and he is at a banquet. I am a minister of Wei here as ambassador, and Fan is merely my follower—but he is feted. Had I not arrived on the scene I am sure he would have accepted the gold he was offered.

*The origins of *davin* "to say prayers" are obscure. See Rosten for one guess about its etymology.

> *(He pantomimes ch'en-yin, chants* (?).) It's not hard to see that Fan Chü has sold secrets of our state to the country of Ch'i and was greatly rewarded for his treachery. Ah, Fan Chü, you are unprincipled. *You* sit in a high place and *I* below the dais, yet you betray not the slightest unease. I shall store this away in my belly and when we return home, Fan Chü, there will be a reckoning and all will be spelled out very carefully. As they say: "small hatreds never made great men; no hero but what he has some poison in him!" *(exit)* (1206)

If Hsü Ku had intoned the last half of that soliloquy, it might have made a good contrast with the first—and that, in fact, is the way I used to construe it. But most of the rest of the uses of *ch'en-yin* do not back me up. See how the stage direction is used on 772, for example:

> WANG:
> What is this document?
>
> CLERK:
> This was drawn up against Yang Hsieh-tsu for betraying his brother and killing his sister-in-law.
>
> WANG:
> Yang Hsieh-tsu. Have I heard that name before? [*He ponders* ch'en-yin (mutters?) *and then suddenly remembers* (hsing).] I have! I have! One of the children of the Yang family from Hsi-chün village was named Yang Hsieh-tsu! (772)

Now, even supposing the second half of the soliloquy on 1206 was a complaint done in some kind of *davining* form, this latter surely could not be. It is more likely that Wang strikes some kind of pose that indicates deep thought (or perhaps he mutters unintelligibly) and then smites his brow (or the Yuan dynasty equivalent of that gesture) when he remembers. On 504 the stage directions say "he *ch'en-yin* (ponders it) and then speaks, aside. . . ."

This is probably what happens in 1206 as well, and see also 869 and 446. For whatever it may add to the case, the older, Hsi Chi-tzu ed. (Yang 1-3321) has no *ch'en-yin* as a stage direction for the example found in *YCH* 1206 at all, though the *Lai-chiang Chi* ed. (Yang 1-6286) agrees with *YCH* and has *ch'en-yin*. A question that interests me is how this "mutter" was distinguished from *pei-yün*, "asides," for example. See below, page 148.

Declamation Modes

Given this attention to the fascinations of song and recitation, one could predict that the Yuan playwright and actor would also neglect no speech mode that might enhance the theatricality of their productions. It may have occurred to the reader that some of the things I have included in this chapter on the actors' art were in fact the art of the composer-playwright. As I see it, there are areas where the two are inseparable; but when one finds the composer arranging for certain types of performance, it is perfectly clear that he has in mind what the actor habitually does well and is deliberately turning this to account. Whichever member of the partnership was responsible for it, no trick of presentation seems to have been missed: there is over-rapid speech, lofty and elegant speech (both apposite and inapposite), quotes from the classics, all manner of proverbs, sayings, maxims and saws, repeated tag-and-gag lines, monologues, asides, stage whispers, offstage lines and dialogue, direct address to audience, storytelling and dialect.*

An example (764) of modulation in speech speed for comic effect is given in the following excerpt:

*The last of these is hard to demonstrate with a nonalphabetic script like Chinese, but the playwrights were delighted to introduce what might be called "dog Ouigur" into the speech of a Mohammedan ambassador (*WP* 921) and into "southern" duets and trios (1666). Jurchen and Mongol terms abound, and the country bumpkin is such a standard fixture that I cannot imagine he came on without his rustic dialect.

BAILIFF:
All right, your honor, if you'll just stand aside I'll question the woman for you. Now then, woman, you are pleading here on behalf of this corpse?

MOTHER:
I am indeed.

BAILIFF:
Are you a relative of the decedent?

MOTHER:
I am.

BAILIFF:
Then you may give your deposition.

MOTHER:
[*high-speed speech*] Your-honor-have-pity-on-me-my-surname-is-Wang-and-I-come-from-Tung-shun-chuang-I-had-an-only-daughter-named-Spring—

BAILIFF:
Silence! Dammit woman, your mouth is flapping so fast you sound like a diarrhetic horse. D'you think I've got seven feet and eight hands?! Now once more and slowly!

MOTHER:
Your honor, have pity on me. My surname is Wang. . . . *(etc.)*

It is almost impossible to convert Chinese literary-elegant speech into anything congruent in English so the reader must be content with the knowledge that, in general, it is done in groups of six and four syllables, and in addition to the differences in vocabulary and grammar, its rhythms are more monotonous and grave.

There are good examples of this form of address on pages 1042 and 438, and in each case the conversations are supposed to be between learned men being very polite with each other. Quotations from the classics (you may see some used in the *Mo-ho-lo Doll,* p. 370 of Part II) are often in the same rhythm and style, but I imagine the quotes used in Yuan drama were so common that even with the antique grammar and odd vocabulary their gist was always understood by the audience.

The situation is similar with proverbs and maxims. The older proverbs tend to consist of two four-syllable groups which balance and which may rhyme the fourth and eighth. But the dramas use sayings that are three-by-three syllables, five-by-five,* and they may also consist of single seven- or five-syllable lines. We all tend to try and speak quotation marks around proverbs and maxims when we use them in everyday life. I am assuming that the Yuan actor used some kind of speech nuance to identify and elevate proverbs when he spoke them. Many times the situation is clarified because the proverb's preamble will be, "It is well said that ...," "Surely you have heard that...," etc. The contents of the sayings range from the pungent and pithy—"Who eats black rice will drop black stools" (of the company one keeps); "Sooner expect to get ivory from the mouth of dogs" (*WP* 130) (than to hope for reform of a ne'er-do-well)—to the fatuous; "wealth and honor are what all men desire." Some are poetic; "One hour of a spring night is worth more than a thousand in gold" (1150). Many are balanced; "The tongue is a sword to defend the state; verse is a ladder to ascend to the heavens" (1242); "Three cups compose all differences, one drunk will dissolve all sorrows" (1205). Some hit with a wallop; "One threat gets more done than a thousand requests" (1158); and some are elaborate, taking the form of what the Chinese call *hsieh-hou yü.* A *hsieh-hou yü* is a sort of riddle you ask and sometimes answer yourself:

> (to an unsuccessful fortune-teller) "Your art, sir, is like a tyke gnawing for fleas—sometimes he hits on one; more often not." (1020)

*When proverbial sayings consist of two groups of five syllables the 5th and 10th of which sometimes rhyme, it makes them look like two lines from a certain form of *shih* verse (see *WP* 184 for an example), and they may often in fact be.

Sometimes two clichés are put together so they balance; "Gold is man's courage; the mouth is calamity's gate" (932). And sometimes one feels that what he is reading is an *ad hoc* proverb (or *hsieh-hou yü*):

> (father has just warned daughter that the man she wants to marry has no money and not much future) "But he is like the flagpole in the grass, which is lower than anyone when it is down but towers over all when it is raised up." (916)

Often these sayings are done in plain speech first and then incorporated into an aria. The balanced meter of many proverbs fits admirably into several types of metric slots in the arias, and their conventional wisdom matches the tone of Yuan dramatic conventions very well.

The line between old saying and cliché is difficult to draw, but Yuan drama was hospitable to both.

It is perfectly obvious that the Yuan dramatist was *capable* of writing scenes in many different ways, but he chose (in nearly every case) to stick to conventional phrases for high-frequency scenes. For example, father calls daughter (who is not onstage), she enters, gives her entrance speech, and then says that she has been called by her father. Having done the pantomime for greeting him, she asks why he called her. The reply (whether it be by a father, a friend, or what-have-you) always begins *huan ni pu wei pieh shih*, "I've called you for no other reason than . . ." (921 *et ubique*). The signal in a play for new or further action is almost without exception: *chin-jih chi-jih liang-ch'en . . .*, "Today is an auspicious day and this is a favored hour so I will begin. . . ." And, of course, when any character enters and tells you he has nothing to do for the moment, then goes to the door to see if anyone is coming, you may be perfectly sure that lo, and behold! someone *is* coming. The incorporation of these well-worn speech pebbles into paths through the Yuan dramatist's garden of verses was part of his craft,* and since Yuan drama was extremely popular for over a half century, we can only assume the audiences both expected and enjoyed it.

*However, he may fairly be taken to task for overdoing it. *WP* 134 has *fen-fen yang-yang hsia-che hsüeh*, "the snow is falling in swirls and flurries," no less than three times on a single page of text!

Conventional phrases given under "From Here to There" (above) are not only more examples of stereotypes, they even include the tacit recognition that the Yuan playwrights' use of them was something susceptible to parody and humor. A phenomenon closely related to the constant use of identical phrases in declamation is the use and reuse of the same stanza or the same lines in entrance and exit verse. Using only the plays translated in Part II, note that the opening two lines of verse in *Li K'uei* are also to be found on 995; the tapster's entrance verse may also be found on 1008, 1717, *WP* 134 and 934. The "flour and water" verse recited by the clownish clerk in *Mo-ho-lo* can be found in three other plays (568, 671, and *WP* 132). The entire quatrain used to test Ts'ui T'ung's ability to cap verses in *Rain* may also be found in *WP* 144.

Once again, the playwrights were entirely capable of writing any amounts of new verse; but they chose the familiar chestnuts. We have to conclude that the audiences enjoyed the familiar, and I can imagine that these recurring bits of doggerel became household sayings and enjoyed great popularity for short periods of time. For what it's worth, let me offer an English analogy. At some time or another in some tearjerker, some actor said in all seriousness (and was taken seriously by the audience) to a fallen beauty, "What's a nice girl like you doing in a place like this?" I venture to guess that the line was used elsewhere again . . . and again . . . and again, and now it *cannot* be used in public entertainment without being greeted by titters; it has become a gag line which is used in ordinary social speech. It is my belief that something of the sort happened among the aficionados of Yuan drama when it was still living theater.

I believe we should keep firmly in mind that on balance, Yuan drama was faddishly popular in relatively lowbrow circles; the dramatists knew what their audiences liked and happily pandered to those tastes. I am convinced that the similarities and repetitions of plot, poem, and phrase were, in a sense, the playwrights' and actors' response to the old injunction, "never get off a winner." The fact that these dramas as literature are still admired centuries after they became a dead performance form is beside the point. They *are* pastiches and should be recognized as such (excessive piety about earlier literature has too often been responsible for critical fatuity). Not for a moment do I imply that Yuan dramas are unworthy literature and should not be given serious critical attention. On the contrary, they are remarkable for their formal perfection and the variety of their appeal, and, just as in the field of graphic arts there are collages which have artistic merit and those which do not, so there are good, better, and best among *tsa-chü*.

CHENG YUAN-HO:
(enters astride his horse leading CHANG CH'IEN*)* Chang Ch'ien, do you see those two ladies over there? Do you see that absolutely perfect creature; nothing could improve a beauty like hers. No makeup could help, no artist could capture that. . . . *(He drops his riding crop.)*

CHANG CH'IEN:
You dropped your crop, your honor.

CHENG:
So elegant, so completely desirable. *(He drops his crop again.)*

CHANG:
You dropped your crop, your honor.

CHENG:
I know . . . what a beautiful, beautiful woman. *(Drops crop again.)*

CHANG:
You dropped your crop, your honor.

CHENG:
I know.

I imagine that the first human to have discovered the comic potential of repetition had gone to his reward before they started building the pyramids. Western drama exploited it as soon as there was drama, and, as can be seen from the above, the Yuan playwright and actor also made the most of it. In addition to the sample given, one can find the stage direction "repeat the pantomime three times" (cf. 942, 528, 584) scattered throughout the dramas. It is perfectly apparent, therefore, that the Yuan dramatist had also hit upon the magic number of three repetitions to which we in the West have been partial for both rhetoric and comedy. There is even this further elaboration (942): the comic interrupts the witness telling the story of a crime three times until the judge finally gags him—and then he slips the gag and interrupts a fourth time. All of which merely demonstrates that when you have a good convention—the three times—it is made even better by depending on audience acceptance of it to transgress and draw yet another laugh.

Akin to repetition is the running gag line. Yuan drama uses it well. There is one miserly accountant who prefaces each of his speeches with a portion of the multiplication tables, and the pseudo-scholar who, from page 582 when he enters to the end of Act II, inserts the same idiot quotation from the *Analects of Confucius* every time he can. This is not only apposite for the character's profession, but its repeated syllables make a comic effect: "*chih-chih wei chih-chih; pu chih wei pu chih.*" In archaic Chinese this means something like "when you know something admit you know it, when you don't know, say you don't know." But in the context of the time and audience involved, it could only have sounded like a nonsensical "to know it is to know it; not to know it is not to know it" and fits perfectly with the clownish "scholar" who uses it. What is translated below is one of the few purely prose monologues I know of and it combines repetitions with the running gag—or rather the repeats are so predictable after a while that they amount to a running gag. To set the scene, the master and mistress of the household have just retired (probably still on stage) and then, enter a rather amateur but foresighted thief to rob them:

CHAO:
I am Chao T'ing-yü. My dear mother has passed away and I had no money to give her a funeral. But enough of that! I'm a man with a backbone, so there was nothing I could do but try

a little burglary. During the daylight hours I looked over this man's place so that, come nightfall, I could relieve him of a little money—just to bury mother, you understand, and show what a good son I am. By heaven, I *am* getting the hang of this burgling! Since there was nothing else I could do, I went to the stone mason's yard and lifted some lime. Now, you ask, what did he want with that lime? Tonight after I cut my way in through the wall, I'll leave a trail of lime on the ground. Now, if nobody raises a hue and cry, well and good, but if somebody hollers "stop thief," I fly along my little lime path and pop back through my hole in the wall.—By heaven, I *am* getting the hang of this burgling. Today, I also passed by a dumpling shop and lifted me a dumpling. Now what, you are saying, does he want with a dumpling? I got together a bunch of sharp, bent hairpins and stuffed them in the dumpling. Now if there's a dog about and he begins to bark, I slip him the dumpling and that'll pin his mouth so shut he won't be able to get off a single yap.—By heaven, I *am* getting the hang of this burgling! Well, here I am next to the wall, and it happens I carry this knife and I have now cut a fine fat hole in this wall—and now I'm going through it. *(He pantomimes scattering lime.)* And now I'm doing the lime. *(He looks about.)* There's this closed door; it so happens I have a little flask of oil on me and I'm pouring a good dollop into the doorpost holes so when I open it nobody will hear a sound.—By heaven, I *am* getting the hang of it!*

(offstage) All right! Now you're the granddaddy of burglars! (1130)

This monologue introduces the last three declamation modes I would like to make note of: direct address, narrative, and the use of offstage interjections.

It is, I suppose, inevitable in a theater so devoted to a "distancing effect" ("I am here on the stage performing for you there in the audience, and I'll keep you aware of it") that there should be a large amount of direct address to the audience. After all,

---

*In the Mai-wang Kuan version, the last repeat goes, "*Now* who's gotten the hang of this burgling?!"

each entrance and exit verse is in essence directed to the audience and not to any character on the stage. In addition, such address is seen fairly frequently in the same kind of context prevailing in the monologue above. "You're saying, 'why did he come on laughing'" (1018). "I kept them in jail but never questioned them once. Now, why did he do that, you are asking yourselves, well . . ." (432). However, one rare and very striking kind of across-the-footlights address is to be found in *WP* 125 where Li Ssu-Yüan "narrates" *(shuo)* the Parable of the Hen and the Ducklings. When a character in Yuan drama is speaking lines within the dramatic context (stage reality), the playscript says "so-and-so speaks *(yün),*" but this story narration *(shuo)* is obviously set up as a performance within a performance though we can't be certain that he is performing for the audience rather than for the *dramatis personae:*

SSU-YUAN:
I called him by his adoptive name and he didn't answer me. I'll try calling him by his child name. Wang A-san!

TS'UNG-K'E:
(pantomimes response and says) Yes, father, here I am.

SSU-YUAN:
Mother, did you see? I called him by his adoptive name and he said nothing. When I used his name as a child he answered. *(Narrates* (shuo) *the Parable of the Hen and Ducklings saying:)* This reminds us of the story. Once upon a time in the district of Wu-ling in Honan there lived a certain Goodman Wang whose home was on the banks of the Yellow River. One day Goodman Wang, walking along the grassy bank, came upon a nest containing more than a dozen duck eggs. Said he, "These duck eggs are doing no one any good here in the grass by the river," and so saying he took them back to his house. Now by chance his hen was brooding a clutch of eggs and when Goodman Wang slipped the duck eggs under her she happily warmed them too. In time the ducklings hatched and the hen led them about foraging for food. About a month later they fledged out and the hen took them to the river's edge looking for things to eat. Now, at the time some wild ducks were bobbing and sailing about in the river and when the ducklings on the bank saw them they promptly slipped

> into the water and went out to play with them. The mother hen on the river bank watched them go into the water and was certain they would perish. She hopped and fluttered, called and squawked. Just then Goodman Wang came from his house and realized that each of the creatures was responding to its own destiny. "Why cry out, mother hen?" he asked. "Your story is the same with humans who adopt another's child.—They may raise him how they will, but never will the child be theirs." And this parable was later called the Parable of the Hen and the Ducklings and became a warning for all men. There is a poem witness to this which goes:. . . .

Whatever Konrad Lorenz may think of the "imprinting" of the ducklings by the mother hen, there is no questioning the impression of storytellers' literature on this particular piece. Not only is Li Ssu-yüan instructed to "narrate" by the stage directions, but the final "there is a poem witness to this . . ." is the hallmark of storytellers' literature.

The whole history of Yuan drama shows it to be highly syncretic, having incorporated many different entertainment forms. It may be that the strong tendency for the actor to step outside the play and even speak of his own role in the third person is a vestige of an earlier entertainment form called *chu-kung-tiao* (a solo musical performance) which we know played an important part in the evolution of Yuan drama. This has been suggested by Feng Yuan-chün (pp. 365–66), and there is a certain persuasiveness about the theory. Nevertheless, it did not take any relationship to a narrative form for the pre-Romantic stage to develop both prologue and epilogue in which the actors step out of their roles and tell the audience what to expect of the play or remind them of the moral they might draw from what they have just seen played before them. All it takes for this sort of presentation to arise is a tacit understanding between the audience and the players that the stage is a stage, not life; that the play is a performance, it is art, not reality (however reality may be construed at the time). Classical Chinese drama of the Yuan dynasty and its audiences had this understanding very clearly before them always.*

---

*This did not, however, keep the actor from attempting illusions of life nor prevent the audiences from responding as though they were in the presence of something "real," as I shall attempt to show in the last chapter.

The dramatic aside must also be nearly as old as drama itself, and its close relative, the offstage addition to the play, almost as ancient as the stage. The former is used to make the audience privy to another level of "stage reality"—that level which exists only in the mind of a single actor, not in the *mise-en-scène*. For example, in 1156:

> YOUNG *Tan*:
> Sister, where are you going?
>
> FAN SU:
> The mistress asked me to inquire after Pai Ming-chung's illness.
>
> YOUNG *Tan*:
> What kind of illness?
>
> FAN SU:
> *(aside)* I'll exaggerate it a little. *(turns back)* Well, I'm afraid it is rather serious; in fact, he's gradually dying.
>
> YOUNG *Tan*:
> But how did he reach such a state?! Oh, dear, I would never dare ask him directly. Oh, what shall I do?
>
> FAN SU:
> *(aside)* Well, the young lady asks about it herself so she feels something. There could be no harm in letting her know more. *(turns back)* My dear, when I was visiting him to enquire after his health he gave me this paper with a few lines on it and said it was to go to you. I've no idea what it says. (See also 715.)

Here the audience has been informed of the well-intentioned guile lying behind Fan Su's speeches to the girl; but the young lady cannot hear them. This is a standard aside; but sometimes there are small holes in that soundproof curtain which isolates the speaker of the aside and the audience from the other actors on stage:

SINGER:
(aside) Oh-ho, this is the villain who seized and robbed the old official on Choubridge this morning!

VILLAIN:
What were you saying!? (*WP* 195)

Sometimes an actor can selectively turn his back on (that's the literal meaning of the term *pei* I have been translating "aside") some of the cast while being audible to one actor and the audience:

(Ying-ying's MOTHER *signals* CHANG *to drink.)*

CHANG:
I'm afraid I have little capacity for wine.

YING:
Hung-niang, take his cup.

MOTHER:
Yes, and give him another.

(HUNG-NIANG *passes cup.)*

HUNG:
(aside to YING-YING*)* Mistress, when will this agony end?* (*WP* 282)

Offstage lines had a number of different uses, the most common of which is to expand the tight little world of the stage:

*As mentioned before, it is sometimes difficult to know how a mode of performance like *ch'en-yin* was differentiated from several types of aside. Was it, in fact, the turning of the back for asides and remaining in the same position for the "mutterings"?

YÜEH:
My name is Yüeh Shou and I've come here to find my sister-in-law and her child; but I can't remember where she lives. I'd better ask someone. *(turns toward the* ku-men tao *and calls)* Brother! Please. Where may I find the home of Yüeh the *K'ung-mu*?

OFFSTAGE:
It's the house with the new-built gate tower. After Yüeh *K'ung-mu* died, Lord Han-Wei, recognizing that he was a worthy official, had a commemorative gate built for him.... They don't welcome peddlers and idlers there, though.... (507; see also *WP* 274)

A question originating in the *mise-en-scène* which is answered offstage is simply a way of saying, "there are people out here beyond where you can see, who are also taking part in our play." It is also a way of conserving a character or a costume which otherwise would have to be identified on stage. But the offstage addition can also be a way of incorporating and giving a voice to the audience. Note at the end of the thief's monologue above, the offstage interjection produces the dramatic and psychic effect of "I see you play-acting out there and I know what the audience feels like saying so I'm going to speak for them."

In addition to sound effects, answers, and comments from offstage, an entire dialogue can be carried on with a disembodied personality beyond the Gate of Ghosts* *(kuei-men tao)*.

Beyond the Gate of Ghosts

The term *kuei-men tao,* Gate of Ghosts (also called *ku-men tao* "gate of the drum" and *ku-men tao* "the ancient gate") simply refers to the entryway around the rear hangings. The "gate of the drum," it has been ventured, was the proper term for this entryway because it is where the great drum was stationed. This, I fear, is a bit

*See p. 158 for a complete quack doctor sketch carried on with offstage voice.

of backward rationalization, and from all I can gather, the Gate of Ghosts is the oldest of the three terms. I am partial to it because in all the comments and appreciations I've ever read by the Chinese on the classical Chinese theater, the authors were always deeply conscious of the power of the stage to resurrect the past and its ghosts. Witness also the title *Register of Ghosts* referred to so many times in Chapter 1.

What concerns this digression, however, is who was on what side of the Gate of Ghosts?

In 1960 Yen Tun-yi wrote a book *(Yuan chü Chen-yi)* on some special problems relating to Yuan drama which is an exasperating mixture of doctrinaire Marxian effluvia (and gaseous conclusions fed by this effluvia) and truly interesting insights. On page 162 he approaches the subject of this digression with these words:

> The strangest and by far the most interesting question of form (or perhaps style) of presentation I found in most abundant use in the play *The Gods Send Down Mulberries* [*WP* 144]. In it we come across the term *wai ch'eng ta, yün* or *wai-ch'eng k'o* ... some sixty times.... now the *ch'eng-ta* [comment?] is always said to be *wai* [from the outside?] and is always some kind of remark ... on the antics of the clown *(ching)* or on the character of the clown himself.... Now this *wai* does not refer to the role type known as *wai* but rather to *someone speaking who is not a member of the cast of characters.* [italics mine]

He goes on to gather evidence from both Yuan and early Ming *tsa-chü* and comes to the conclusion that this speaker who suddenly shows up on our stage and in our scripts and who is not in any way a member of the *mise-en-scène* should be one of the members of the orchestra. In 1958[13] I hazarded a guess that our intrusive *wai* with his *ch'eng ta* was none other than the prop man. I'm not entirely ready to give him up in return for Yen Tun-yi's orchestra member, and I will leave the reader to draw his own conclusions after having read the following section from *Gods Send Mulberries.* I include the entire translation here because the skit is a kind of dramatic coelacanth—an evolutionary survivor—an example of pre-Yuan theater as I will point out in the next chapter.*

*This is the horn-rimmed reason for including the skit; actually I want to simply because I think it is fun and a good sample of thirteenth century Chinese slapstick farce.

"Two Physicians Raise Cain"

(TOMBSTONE *enters made up as Grand Physician.)*

TOMB:
In the post of Grand Physician I am still quite embryonic, but nonetheless I know my texts, my pressure points and sundry kinds of tonic. When people summon me to treat their kin, I send them off to get a box that they can put their loved one in. My surname is Stone and my given name is Tomb. I was born to a family of medical men and trained by meticulous regimen—the results of this soon catch the eye; I can play the lute; I can sing up high; a dedicated drinker of wine am I—and hold the eating record for capon pie. When called by a patient I induce such a flux that the bad ones may live but the good ones die.

WAI *(ch'eng-ta):*
Obviously deserves the fame he's got—listen to him!

TOMB:
There is also living here a Dr. Head whose first name is Chuckle—his father's name is Turnip—and since his methods are every bit the equal of mine, I am his sworn brother. Should someone call a doctor now, neither would go without the other. While I make the diagnoses he prepares the proper doses; when my duty's his and his is mine, *I* compound the anodyne. We've sworn together a dreadful oath—equally binding on one or both—"on him who foreswears this partnership let there grow a hard chancre of the lower lip!" This very day Graduate Ts'ai of this town notified me that his mother was ill and I sent a man right off to tell my sworn brother so we could go treat the woman. Here I stand on Choubridge waiting for him.

(CHUCKLEHEAD, *the second* ching, *enters.)*

CHUCKLE:
With my healing arts, they survive and I thrive; I'm the high priest of hygiene. I so employed my drugs and brews and a similar preparation that I worked a cure on a calenture that assures my deification. The ancient physician, Pien Ch'iao of Lu, could be my great-grandson for all he knew. My drugs are possessed of such virtue that the feeble ones expire before I'm through.

WAI:
How about *this* lout!

CHUCKLE:
At your service here is Chucklehead, known to my friends as Number Eighteen. My forebears have physicked men for three whole generations (but while a student at the school I caused them consternation. My fingers couldn't read a pulse, nor my eyes the medication). When summoned to attend the sick I swill three cups, eight bowls and a tun—and top 'em all off with an onion bun. Such habits don't help a physician to think—but I'll bet there's not a man alive I can't outdrink!

WAI:
Now we're blessed with two of a kind!

CHUCKLE:
In the medical confraternity here there's one Tombstone. When he and I combine our skills we've half as many as anyone. So, though both of us were born to a different mother, I am sworn his younger and he my older brother. Two people wanted us to tend them sick abed, but they couldn't get a Head without a Stone nor a Stone without a Head. So while Head bled the man on the bed, Stone set the bone of the one who was prone.*

*I beg indulgence for the invention, but this Chinese *jeu* is not transmissable. His surname is Hu and he gives the syllable in all four tones. On those Wai comments, "He can recite rhyme classes too *(teng-yün)*."

WAI:
He even makes quack rhymes . . . that does it!

CHUCKLE:
The venerable Tombstone sent his man to me a while ago telling me that Graduate Ts'ai's mother was sick and wanted us to treat her—he said he'd wait for me on Choubridge, so off I go to see brother Tombstone. And here I am already. *(Pantomimes seeing* TOMBSTONE*)* Ah, brother—I know I'm a bit late, but I'm sure you won't take offense—thieves, not doctors, take fences.*

WAI:
How about that clown!

TOMB:
Still blabbering, Chucklehead!? You never were good for a thing. Here it is freezing weather and I've waited so long my thigh tendons have nearly got knots in 'em.

CHUCKLE:
Brother Tombstone, you mustn't be hard on me because I was late. I had a spasm of heart humors this morning. I got up a bit early, you see, and caught some kind of chill—I tell you the pain nearly killed me! My wife was in a panic, called the doctor, and he dosed me until the pain finally stopped so I could get here.

WAI:
But you're a doctor, why take another's medicine?

*I can only surmise that *ha-ma yang-te* "toad raised" has some such punning connection with *chien kuai* "to take offense."

CHUCKLE:
Oh, if I could've physicked myself and gotten here, I would've.

WAI:
Why couldn't you?

CHUCKLE:
Why, if I had taken my own stuff I'd have been dead two hours before it was time to leave.

WAI:
"Physician kill thyself,"* is that it? How about that one!

TOMB:
Little brother, ever since that law case, custom has been slow.

WAI:
Then why did you take a case to court?

TOMB:
Well, you see, little brother and I doctored a man to death, so—

WAI:
So the case went to court! What a brace of oily-mouths we have here!

---

*In Chinese the proverb is "The Physician of Lu can't cure himself," but it amounts in essence to our biblical (Luke IV:23) "Physician heal thyself."

TOMB:
Little brother, today Ts'ai the elder's wife has taken ill and we've been called to treat her. It's a wealthy house so we'll go there, and if she's one part ill we'll tell her it's ten parts and if she's ten parts ill we'll tell her it's a hundred parts. We'll do more than we ought with caut-er-y and puncture her soundly with acupuncture. We'll drug her extensively—if we make her well then well and good—and we'll bill them expensively; much more stiffly than we should. But on the slightest indication of a bad recuperation we'll pack our sacks and hide our tracks by heading for the wood.

WAI:
Those two!

CHUCKLE:
Brother, what thou'st said is well said.* Surely heaven knows the purity of our intentions and will vouchsafe us our daily rice.

WAI:
Ach!

TOMB:
Little brother, we're off! And here we are already. Lackey, report that the two most practiced practitioners are here.

SERVANT:
You wait here, I'll tell the master.
(pantomimes reporting) Master, the physicians are here.

TS'AI:
Tell them they are welcome and it is still early.

*Here he speaks a kind of pseudo-classical Chinese.

SERVANT:
You are welcome and early.

CHUCKLE:
Have a care, brother, you might slip.

WAI:
What!?

CHUCKLE:
They said we were welcome but it was oily.

WAI:
Oh, what drivel!

TOMB:
(bridling) I am physician to officials; when I come to someone's door I don't expect him to dispense entirely with paying respects; where is he?

WAI:
Have a heart, one of his family is ill—pay your own respects.

TOMB:
Very well, you dear boy, I'll go in just to save you embarrassment!

WAI:
He is too much!

TOMB:
After you, little brother.

CHUCKLE:
I would not dare accept. After you, older brother.

TOMB:
Most esteemed younger brother, you must go first, please.

CHUCKLE:
Oh, but you are mistaken. You seem to think I haven't read the books of Mencius and Confucius and so lack the slightest comprehension of what constitutes the conduct of Former Kings. But has it not been said in the Books of the Sages (and I almost quote), "He who walks slowly behind his senior is young-brotherly, he who hastens to pass a senior will never graduate.* As the plowman's field yields, so the traveler yields the road. Who is older is senior, who is younger, junior." You are senior and I am junior and this being so it is a question of seniority and juniority wherein one must distinguish between lowly and highly and in this matter the conduct of Former Kings was absolutely correct-when-they-say-and-I-quote, "I'll be a horse's ass if I go first!" —My goodness! *Don't* I have an oily mouth!

WAI:
And stuffed full of literary elegance, too!

CHUCKLE:
No, I dare not go first. Esteemed Elder Brother, you first.

TOMB:
Under no conditions—honored brother, you are a cultured and Superior Man whilst I am but a dolt. My brother is the most virtuous of men whilst I have scarce a half chaff-width

*This garbled quote from a book I doubt was ever written seems to be playing on the word *ti* which, as a noun, means "cadet," but as a negated verb it means "to fail in the examinations."

of ability. I have heard that my younger brother's practice of medicine makes one think the gods themselves were at work—the prescriptions you use in your treatments are effective without fail. My brother is the most accomplished of men and I am not worth a maggot's pelt. I'll be a gnawed dog's bone if I enter first!

WAI:
A plague on both of you! Shut up and go in!

TOMB:
Ah there, mother, feeling poor and ill affected?

CHUCKLE:
Our potions all diseases halt if taken as directed.

TOMB:
Now, both of us will take your pulse till symptoms are detected.

(each takes one of her hands)
(They sing, Nan Ch'ing-ker)

TOMB:
(holding her left wrist) To this home we have come, her eight pulses to interpellate.

CHUCKLE:
(holding her right wrist) I feel a thready tapping which is very delicate.

TOMB:
I must open up my drug pouch for the means to medicate—

CHUCKLE:

(speaking)

Dear me, a very poor pulse action.

TOMB:

We must hasten, hasten out to buy before it is too late—

CHUCKLE:

—Yes hasten, hasten out to buy before it is too late....

TS'AI:

What is it the physician must buy?

TOMB:

A coffin—do not hesitate!

CHUCKLE:

Yes, a coffin—do not hesitate!

(end Nan Ch'ing-ker)

WAI:

Don't they ever stop!?

(TOMB knocks over MOTHER with his drug pouch)

MOTHER:

He's killing me!

WAI:

That's the patient! What are you doing?

TOMB:
It's all right, she's still sensible. You see, she can still feel pain.

WAI:
If she didn't, she'd be dead, wouldn't she? That does it—

TOMB:
My dear Dr. Head, how would you diagnose the ailment?

CHUCKLE:
I don't like to inflate my skill but I took one look at her countenance, and—well, feel this side, how hot it is? Obviously then, caloric humors?

TOMB:
Now you're talking nonsense again! This pulse is leaping an inch—how can you even speak of a calenture? Look at this side, it's cold as ice. Clearly she's suffering from excessive gelidity!

CHUCKLE:
Dear brother, this presents no problem at all. We shall wind a carpenter's twine around the tip of her nose and let the plumb-bob fall straight to the ground where we shall pound in a peg and tie the twine. Then you will treat your left side which is suffering from a chill and I will treat the fevered right which is mine.

TOMB:
Excellent, excellent, excellent. We are in perfect agreement. But—what if the potion you give her should kill your right side?

CHUCKLE:
Well, that won't cast any stigma on your work with the chilly left.

TOMB:
Of course! How right you are.

CHUCKLE:
On the other hand, if you fix a potion and kill off your left side, what then?

TOMB:
That will not affect your reputation for curing the right.

CHUCKLE:
What if one of us should make a slip and kill the whole thing?

TOMB:
Why then, of course, *nobody* suffers.

WAI:
Will you two quacks ever stop?

TS'AI:
Grand Physician, have you decided on the medication?

TOMB:
Well, first dose will be the Pill That Snatches Life from Death, and the second the Pellet Which Encourages Immediate Demise.

TS'AI:
Why that combination?

TOMB:
Ah, you'd have no way of understanding, but I have a theory that once she has taken these two drugs she couldn't die if she wanted to or live if she wished it.

WAI:
Clown!

CHUCKLE:
Your honor, do you truly wish her to recover?

TS'AI:
But of course!

CHUCKLE:
Then I've a prescription that's much used at sea—but it requires a certain item—are you willing to supply it?

TS'AI:
Whatever it is, if it will cure my mother, I'll supply it.

CHUCKLE:
Well then, I'll take my scalpel and cut out both your eyeballs—she takes them with a cup of wine and she's cured!

TS'AI:
She's cured but what about me?

CHUCKLE:
Oh, you can use a cane.

WAI:
What drivel!

TS'AI:
Stop, stop, stop this idiotic argument! I want the best physician to treat her.

(The two alternate hitting each other with their drug pouches as they speak.)

TOMB:
I can put in order the rheums of all the seasons—

CHUCKLE:
And I, disorders brought on by diverse and sundry reasons.

TOMB:
But I cure children's rickets and infant diarrhea—

CHUCKLE:
And I, young ladies suffering with postpartum hy-ste-*ri*-a.

TOMB:
From every pulse I auscultate systolic circumvections—

CHUCKLE:
I physick all distempers found in human disaffections.

TOMB:
I cure the slow consumption or the fulminating phthisis.

CHUCKLE:
And I, right-handed palsy and left-handed pa-ra-*ly*-sis.

TOMB:
I cure thigh numbness and a weakness of the knees—

CHUCKLE:
But lassitude in all the limbs is something *I* can ease.

TOMB:
To puckermouth and bittertongue I bring expert attention—

CHUCKLE:
But I'll relieve your bellybloats and abdominal distension.

TOMB:
—spavined shoulders and yaws of the shin—

CHUCKLE:
—deafness without and dumbness within—

TOMB:
Remedies for fevers and chills—

CHUCKLE:
I alleviate mental ills—

TOMB:
—peccant humors, ethers of pain—

CHUCKLE:
—temples that throb, and acute migraine—

TOMB:
I remove papillomas from the breast—

CHUCKLE:
I excise soft chancres on request—

TOMB:
Come, come colleague, let us to the medication

CHUCKLE:
And help the poor woman achieve her expiration.

TOMB:
A draught of water, clear and chill,

CHUCKLE:
Some castor beans—let's say a gill—

TOMB:
This will tend
To blow the gut and bowels up

CHUCKLE:
To straighten every bend—

TOMB:
Mamma here will crap herself to death; but,
She'll be clean from end to end!

WAI:

(striking the two physicians)

Get out of here you two quacks! *(exeunt)*
(*WP* 428–31)*

It should be noted that until the last line when the *wai* "strikes the comics and [all] exit" it was never absolutely clear from the text whether or not the *wai* was on stage or beyond the Gate of Ghosts. A confusion exists with the terms *wai* "outside" and *nei* "inside." For the most part, whatever happens backstage of the Gate of Ghosts is labeled in the stage directions *nei* "inside."

LI:
(pantomimes calling toward the ku-men tao*)*
Brother, can you tell me where I can find the prison?

NEI [inside]:
It's the place with the high wall, the little gate, and it's set about with thorn trees.

But in one case, not in either *YCH* or *WP* because it is acknowledged to be an early Ming play, not Yuan, the following takes place:

ATTENDANT:
You back there, ask your mistress to come out, will you?

WAI [outside]:
Yes, I will.

*This translation was started in 1957, completed with Steve West in 1972, and received some cogent corrections from Cyril Birch in 1977. Altogether 20 years in the making; it is the proverbial mountain giving birth to a mouse!

And there is no doubt at all that he is shouting through the Gate of Ghosts and the servant girl is done by an offstage voice. Yet here it is referred to as *wai* (outside) rather than *nei* (inside). On 1229, the stage direction says "offstage *(nei)* music begins." Finally, the comment on the thief's monologue (above, p. 145) is said to have originated "offstage *(nei)*" in the *YCH* edition of the play, but in the Mai-wang Kuan edition (Yang 1–2846) of the same play, the stage direction says that the "*wai, ch'eng-ta* says":—exactly as the lines are labeled in the sketch of the two physicians. In short, there seems to be some kind of conflation here; but I find that quite understandable. We are, after all, lumping together as Yuan drama something over one hundred and fifty pieces which must have been mounted over five or six decades at the least. We know that some of the scripts we have were arranged (not written) by and for the royal players, and other scripts must reflect staging for much humbler companies. Stage terminology (which always verges on cant) doubtless changed through time; or it may have been that on large and permanent stages there was a lot of "inside" to be had backstage beyond the Gate of Ghosts (look at stage 2, Figure 4), while on the small unroofed raised platforms which often served for stages at more modest temples, there may have been precious little "inside" to be had backstage (or anywhere) so the supernumeraries, the orchestra, or the propman were all visible right there but by convention "outside" *(wai)* the *mise-en-scène*. The presence of the orchestra standing behind the players in Figure 3 may be yet another modification of the situation. It is clear that there is room (though not much, one imagines) behind the rear hangings, but there is no room off to the side of the stage for an orchestra or a "music crib" in which the young ladies were to sit and "accompany the performance." On the other hand, we cannot take what we see in the painting too literally: painters are expected to rearrange life into patterns which are pleasing and satisfactory to themselves and their patrons. Perhaps this particular iconographer wanted to commemorate the full glory of the festival, so he framed *all* the troupe onstage in his picture of the performance to give it the sense of lavishness he felt it deserved. The orchestra may indeed have been somewhere off the stage during the actual performance.

MAKEUP, COSTUMING, AND PAGEANTRY

> ....come, men, sound the cymbals, beat the drums, shout and wave your banners whilst I shoot three fire-arrows toward the prince's palace.
>
> *YCH,* p. 741

Those who have seen the elaborate and gorgeous *ta hua-lien* or "painted-face roles" of Peking opera troupes of the twentieth century tend automatically to think of this makeup as standard for Chinese dramatic performance; but such is not the case. A look at Figure 3 makes it immediately clear that there was a very restrained use of makeup during the Yuan dynasty. It was only with the advent of Ming drama that the complex and colorful elaborations developed which are with us still today. Of course, we are basing our conclusions for the most part on only one wall painting, but with the exception of the known black and white makeup of the *ching* roles (see p. 61 above) and an occasional reference to a "red-faced" bucko, Yuan makeup is subdued; there is no reason to think that the vivid and symbolic system of painted faces in Peking opera began any earlier than the fifteenth century. In the past there have also been assumptions that Chinese stage makeup (which covers the whole face) began its career as a mask. There is good evidence that Yuan drama used masks strictly for the roles of deities; the elaborate Ming makeup was *sui generis* and has in fact no mask in its family tree.

It is certain that a given role type had a particular kind of makeup: that is, a playgoer could probably look at the stage during the performance of any play and pick out the leading role, the villain, the tapster, or what have you—possibly on the basis of the makeup alone. It would appear, however, that the identifying maquillage consisted only of the rather restrained use of lamp-black, white lead (?), and cinnabar, each in some form of grease binder. The identification of role types was sometimes made complete by the use of false beards and costuming.

In the matter of costuming on the Yuan stage we have our temple wall painting which supplies only a small amount of information all of which is accurate. There also exists an edition of Yuan dramas which seems to have been used by early Ming dynasty Court Players. In this manuscript each play is provided with a scene by scene costume and prop list. This gives us a great deal more information and though it is a Ming dynasty edition, such authorities as Feng Yuan-chün (pp. 341–58) believe it reflects Yuan practices tolerably well.

Having what I always regarded as an average male obtuseness about dry goods and garment construction, I decided I must swot up on such subjects if I wanted to be at all informative about Yuan dynasty costuming. I gave it my best try: I can now theoretically tell the difference between shantung and pongee, and I know a slub from a selvedge. Unhappily, my efforts have proven to be of little help in trying to resurrect Yuan costumes in the mind's eye of the reader because the information in the Ming dynasty costume list is terse, and in the absence of copious illustrations not only would *I* have to know exactly what a certain kind of jacket looked like, but the reader would have to be quite well informed already to make sense of what I said. For example, there are no less than forty-six kinds of headgear listed for male roles. I could tell you the difference between a rabbit-horn cloth head-wrapper and a leather helmet (both of which are noted) but when it comes to "rolled corner" headgear and embroidered cap, "two eaved" headgear and small hats, fox hats, monks' hats, red felt hats, and the like, I could put all the words down here but neither I nor the reader would be left with a very clear picture of anything.

In addition to this embarrassingly rich selection of headgear there are over forty-seven garments listed, including "patched tunics," "round necks," *mang* jackets, Taoist jackets, "as-you-like-it" trousers, and something called a *ding-dong;* this latter, I am certain, would be my favorite item if only we knew what it was.

But I do not mean to whet the reader's appetite and then strand him miles from the nearest caravansery. Let me give you a fairly dependable description of a *mang* jacket as put together by Ch'en Chen-ai,[14] because it will at least summon up for the reader a dim reflection of the color and elegance of a kind of costume which has long been associated with the Chinese stage:

> The *mang* was worn by characters playing high civil and military officials. It has a round neck with a wide collar, "water-sleeves" falling as far as the feet. Under the sleeves was a decorated panel that featured either brocaded or embroidered dragons in frames or free traveling. The lower part

> of the garment was embroidered with the kind of water pattern known as "sea-waves and river cliffs" in which the waves could be either "sleeping or upright."

Now, although common sense tells us that the better troupes had more elaborate garments and the poorer outfits had less, the preoccupation with rich costuming has long been a feature of the Chinese stage, and there is no reason to believe the Yuan players differed from their descendants in that respect. What the Chinese stage may have lacked in scenery elaborations they made up for in exuberant garments. For example, the Great General's costume of the Peking opera (complete with four little flags sewn to the back to represent his army), including his fantastic headdress with its great long silver-pheasant tail feathers, is a masterpiece of the tailors' and trimmers' arts, costs a fortune, is a treasure of the troupe, and incidentally served to keep the troupe's repertory stable—no investment that large was liable to be used for only one season, let alone one play.

I am afraid that in the absence of illustrations (and to my knowledge no such thing exists) the reader will simply have to take my word for it that lavish and colorful costuming seems to have been as important to the traditional Chinese stage as scenery was unimportant. One of the chief reasons for this, of course, was Chinese theater's devotion to pageantry.

Let me begin speaking of spectacle by reminding the reader of something pointed out several times in the first two chapters: Theatricals were at the center of most festival celebrations. This not only accounts for the large number of extant dramas that deal with religious themes—Taoist salvation, tribulations of the gods and goddesses, and the intervention of various supernatural beings in the affairs of men—but these dramas furnished the prime vehicles for pageant and spectacle on the Yuan stage. In addition, the most colorful and imaginative use of costuming is to be found in these sacred, or semisacred, plays. Note the following stage directions:

> Dragon King and demons enter and save wife and child (285)
> Dragon King and sprites form battle line (1630)
> Gods and demons sing, dance and offer wine (*WP* 962)
> Female demons sing, dance and offer wine (*WP* 962)
> Tung-hua Ti-chün enters with Eight Immortals (793, 630, 1105, 1057, etc.)
> Seven Star Gods and little servant star enter and recite (1024)

In addition to this kind of opportunity for display, in plays of Taoist redemption one or more of the Immortals may appear to the backslider in a number of different disguises and the stage directions make note that he or she has "changed costume to become so-and-so" *(kai-pan)*. Where and how this was accomplished is not ever made clear, but some situations seem to call for the quick change artist; this sort of thing is still practiced in the traditional Chinese theater.[15]

Another very common reason for pageantry (and for costume virtuosity, one supposes) is the military play. In addition to skirmishes on horseback and battle scenes, there is opportunity for all sorts of confrontations of great leaders—which seem to have been conducted with the maximum number of *dramatis personae* on stage to add to the pageantry as much as possible. In one play, indeed (see *WP,* p. 473), no less than twenty-seven generals and attendants appear on stage at the same time. This was not something the average troupe could afford to do and we suspect this drama script was arranged for court performance. There are so many other places in Yuan drama where the entrance of a general and his army is followed only by a rhymed declamation and a formal exit that it appears certain no dramatic function other than pageantry is served. The military entrance or battle line are the most frequent excuses for pageant in the military play,[16] but there are variations on them:

Soldiers pantomime searching for Sun-tzu (749)
Generals form line of beaters for Li K'o-yung (*WP* 559)

Under the heading of "military plays" must also come the "strip and fight" types which feature so much mock combat. Sometimes (as in *WP* 1025) the kind of entertainment arranged for the principles on stage is to have four boxers and quarterstaff wielders perform before them. This I imagine was a lively sight but if they were not choreographed to move together it would have been as distracting as a three-ring circus with three separate acts.

Dramas which are laid in the palace or in wealthy homes always have their share of dancing and singing girls laid on to satisfy the audiences' love for spectacle.[17] But court scenes alone with their ambassadors (909), heralds, and ushers (983), and imperial progresses and levees accompanied by women and eunuchs (895), all of which were attended by high ministers as well, were spectacle enough in their own right.

Occasionally you get a clever amalgam of the spectacle with the dramatic requirements of the play. *WP* 600 has a crowd of youths follow and mock Yü Jang after he has ulcerated his flesh and reduced his voice to a croak by swallowing ashes. He does his arias in the face of this ridicule. The entire crowd of children is designated as "the *ching,*" the comic-villain. This I have never seen elsewhere. But a commoner use of spectacle is to be found in 1726 where "celebrants come on with musicians and open the scene." In their wake come two townspeople with speaking roles, and later all are frightened offstage by a headless ghost who has joined the throng. Since this opening festival crowd scene sets the time and the situation for the judgment play to follow, it is a good melding of spectacle and *mise-en-scène.*

However, the opportunities for spectacle I have spoken of so far were more or less dependent on the contents of particular dramas. But reckoning the amount of spectacle in Yuan theater we must also take into account the convention of Yuan drama's "happy ending" which is the occasion in nearly *every* play for a spectacle or tableau of some kind. Once again limiting ourselves simply to the three plays in Part II, note the final banquet scene in *Li K'uei,* the toasts to the reunited couple in *Rain,* and the distribution of rewards and punishments in *Mo-ho-lo.* The Yuan play is usually provided with some sort of final scene in the fourth act where all the *dramatis personae* assemble for the last tableau; this in turn generates the final declamations in narrative verse which bring the play to a close. Surely such a convention must be closely related to the audiences' desire for spectacle. Whether it also eventually harkens back to the dedication of performances given during festivals as offerings to one god or another is beside the point—the final tableau is a feature of all dramas, sacred or secular in the developed Yuan theater.

Let me conclude my attempts to breathe life into the ghosts of actors who plied their profession in the days of Kublai Khan by suggesting that there is still more information on stagecraft and the actors' arts to be wrung from the scripts as we have them today by dint of more careful reading and controlled imagination. Just to give one small example, I believe I can tell you how a jail scene was represented on the Yuan stage. Note the following:

(JAILER *opens door.)*

HICK:
Uncle, you still owe me for the straw you bought from me.

JAILER:
(relieved and laughing)
Why, y'know I was just on the point of looking for you. See here, plait me some of this straw into mats and I pay you for the whole thing. *(aside)* I'll trick this clown into a jail cell. *(He seizes the Hick's carrying pole and tosses it into the jail cell.)*

HICK:
Hey, wait, that's mine! *(starts toward cell and* JAILER *pushes him in)* Uncle, why is it so dark in here? (JAILER *opens skylight)* Eh-h-h? Uncle, did you know the floorboards in your house have sprouted heads. Don't they bite? Well, let me have the straw, I'll plait you some mats.

[*The* BAILIFF INSPECTOR *enters and wants to see the jail.*]

JAILER:
No need for you to bother with that, sir, that's Hu's job.

BAILIFF:
Nevertheless—what's this one in for?

JAILER:
He's a horsethief.

BAILIFF:
This one?

JAILER:
He's a pickpocket.

BAILIFF:
(*pointing to* HICK)
What's this one?

JAILER:
He's a dumbbell!

The hayseed's statement about the floorboards sprouting heads could only refer to the fact that there were other actors sitting on the stage with their heads in wooden cangues. Doesn't this in turn mean that when the action was going to take place in a jail or some place of punishment, the scene was set by having several people come on stage wearing prop cangues and seat themselves on the floor? The presence of at least two others on stage in the above is attested to by the inquiries of the bailiff.

This is the kind of thing that can be worked out with greater and greater precision the longer we study the texts of these remarkably rich dramas.

4. Background of the Plays

(Ti-ssu che)

> "Prose theater . . . usually lacks, as earlier drama does not, the element of play, of fun. . . . The awareness that a drama is a play and an actor a player . . . [earlier drama] asks that the audience participate in the world on the stage . . . and recognize that [it] is a sort of playful adult make-believe that illuminates our world yet vanishes when held against it."
>
> *The Genius of the Early English Theater,* p. 9, edited by Barnet, Berman, and Burto, 1972

Since this chapter is designed to give those who have never read a Yuan drama some kind of introduction to the nature of the genre and enough general background to enjoy the three plays in Part II, there must be repetition of material found in earlier chapters. Those already familiar with the form are invited to come along for the ride if only to see whether they think I have covered the ground adequately.

The first thing to get straight is that the Chinese traditional theater (all of it, not just the classical Yuan drama we treat in this book) is perhaps the most persistently musical stage medium in the history of the theater. That this is so often overlooked in the West is probably the result of the curious circumstances surrounding translations which came to be used in Western theaters. The best demonstration of persisting Western ignorance is to be found in a paragraph from *Burns Mantle* speaking of Will Irwin's script of *Lute Song* (a Ming dynasty play) which was produced at the Plymouth Theater in 1946:

> Following the first hearing, *Lute Song* was played at a number of universities, and notably at the University of Hawaii, where the actors were young American citizens of Chinese parentage. It was not until 1944 that producer Meyerberg, at suggestion of John Byram of Paramount, decided the play would do admirably as a starring vehicle for Mary Martin if a somewhat sketchy musical score could be added to it. This started a new chain of research, following which *everybody was delighted to discover that in the original fourteenth century production songs were also interspersed with the text.* [italics mine]

So a traditional Chinese drama finally assumed something like its proper shape as a musical only by virtue of the fact that Mary Martin was a singer!

Above all, Yuan drama is poetic drama written to elaborate musical requirements on which the playwright shaped his material. I will attempt only the sketchiest outline of these musical demands later. It will be sketchy because the music has been lost for over four centuries and the little we know about its nature is difficult for any save the musicologist to appreciate fully.[1]

The second misapprehension about traditional Chinese drama which persists in the West (and is somewhat related to the first) is the failure to recognize that Chinese theater is variety or synthetic theater. The traditional Chinese drama first evolved through variety and remained during its entire history essentially *variety* entertainment. We know that several kinds of dance, performed songs, skits and sketches, and at least one long (musical) narrative form entered into the evolution of what eventually became the developed musical performances we now call Yuan classical drama. In Chapter 3 above the reader can glimpse vestiges of many of Yuan drama's ancestors including the old farce sketch "Two Physicians Raise Cain" (which we believe to be pre-Yuan dynasty in date even though it is now preserved only in a rather late, we think, Yuan drama). It is sensible to believe that there used to be many such sketches and they were at first done separately but later incorporated into the musical plays which we know as Yuan *tsa-chü* or Yuan drama.*

The American theater (in particular the academic stage) has been very slow to realize the variety nature of traditional Chinese drama, has often been unaware of its musical origins, and has produced it either to get the maximum laugh out of its stage conventions, or has done it straight, as though they were working with a Western play and stage values. The former burlesque (and I suppose *The Yellow Jacket* is a good commercial example) wears very thin in no time, while the latter approach encourages audiences to wait in vain for psychological conflicts and memorable characterizations only to go away, in the end, greatly disappointed.

If we keep the basic facts about Yuan drama always in mind, we will neither take it to task for not being what it never tried to be nor underrate its very considerable strengths.

In order to make the nature of Chinese drama clearer to those who know it not, let me turn to a Western idiom for comparison. Shakespeare was related to his precursors in much the same fashion that the earliest traditional Chinese drama—Yuan or Mongol drama—was related to its predecessors.† Shakespearean drama owes much to the popular and rather low-brow Italian *commedia dell'arte.* He not only borrowed the *commedia* Guild's plot tricks—the twin brother-sister situations of *Twelfth Night,* most of *Midsummer Night,* and much of *Comedy of Errors*—but he was also the

---

*The term *tsa-chü* means "variety show," and even though the Yuan dramas we have now all are integrated around a dramatic story, it takes no great perspicacity to discern their synthetic character—equally hospitable to song, dance, comic skit, and dramatic story line.

†I am referring here especially to the debt owed by Yuan drama to the earlier (Chin dynasty) *yuan-pen* which were for the most part comic sketches of various sorts. (See *Two Physicians Raise Cain,* Chapter 3 above.) Figure 2, in Chapter 2 above, shows three impressions (by an unknown tilemaker) of Chin performances. The heavy-featured pair on the right (with their feet in approximately the ballet fifth position) are shown addressing a bird cage complete with bird. The one looking as though he had a fruit salad on his head is doing what we know was called the "barbarian whistle" *(hu-shao).* We have from Chin dynasty *yuan-pen* title lists an item called "Walking Brother Parrot." I believe that the drawing shows a performance of "Brother Parrot" and from the position of the performers' feet it is reasonable to conclude that it was a danced skit accompanied in some way by the piercing finger whistle known as *hu-shao.* Here is variety entertainment indeed.

legitimate heir (as was Molière) to the *Commedia's* concept of dramatic characters. Something of this "classical" (more accurately, "neo-classical") view of character and characterization and how it is opposed to what we must call the romantic conception, must be understood before we go on to Chinese theatrical practices.

Until the nineteenth century, there was in European theater a strongly marked traditional character typology; characters in Western plays were generally thought of in the Theophrastian sense: what we would now call stock characters, or the embodiments of sets of human characteristics, which each playwright had the privilege (perhaps duty is the word) of manipulating for his own purposes. For example, in the fifty scenarios from the *Commedia Dell'arte,* published in 1611 by Flaminio Scala, the duped father is *always* named Pantalone, the blustering bucko is Captain Spavento, Arlecchino is invariably the *zanni,* and they all had identifying masks. Such highly developed constellations of stock characters usually indicate the dominance of the actor over the script, and in the case of the *Commedia,* of course, we know the actors worked from bare scenarios and fleshed them out *ad libidem* on stage.

Shakespeare and Molière were clearly aware that using a limited number of already familiar type-characters in serious drama allowed the author to increase and compact the symbolic and dramatic powers of his play—this was a great artistic advance over the *Commedia's* hollow mannequins into which only the strutting players could breathe life. The "classical" character was one whose *general lineaments* were predictable and known to the audience to such a degree that the poetry of the lines they spoke often gained an extra dimension of universality. (It is this concept of characterization which informs the Mongol dynasty Chinese music drama as well.) Furthermore, remember that the English playwright of the seventeenth century had inherited a verse medium with which to write drama; any illusionist (as opposed to figurative or poetic) attempt at realism by the playwright was trammeled rather than transformed by the poetry of his lines. Only with the advent of prose drama and illusionist theater do we find the concept that "we must meet and know persons in art as we meet and know people in daily life" and the concomitant form of stage realism that such a conception engenders.

In traditional Chinese theater we have only to do with the "classical" concept of characters and characterization, not the romantic. Further than this, the majority of Chinese plays are "historical." That is, they deal with men who lived, and deeds which the Chinese themselves believe to have transpired in the past and with which even the illiterate seem to have been astonishingly conversant. Now, this fact has a further magnifying effect on the playwright's plots and personification: He may, for example, deal gently with a well-known historical character—a cruel general, let us say—which may be in contrast with folk knowledge of him and produce effects which the Westerner may miss; more important, he can depend upon his audience to accept the extravagances of his lines, in prose or verse, in just the manner the playwright intends, since both audience and playwright share roughly the same view of the *dramatis personae.* Chinese drama, in addition, always exists on a plane of abstraction and removal from "realism" one degree higher than even Shakespearean blank verse; for it is not only done in verse but this verse is invariably set to music, and the "tunes" to which the verses of the traditional Chinese drama are written were already familiar to its audiences who had doubtless heard them or versions of them hummed or played since childhood.

Yuan drama, in this respect, bears a superficial resemblance to the Western "Ballad Opera" since both are mixed speech-and-music forms using popular tunes to which, in each case, the playwright penned new lyrics to fit his particular play. The Chinese form is far more demanding than the English one, however, since, for example, each act of the former is written to a set of tunes from a certain mode and the order in which the tunes could be used was flexible only within limits. But the best known example of Western ballad opera, John Gay's *The Beggar's Opera,* utilizes song lyrics with poetic depth and dialogue having the dimensions of natural speech in the same general manner as Yuan drama. Both have literary values which greatly transcend the ordinary grand opera libretto. On a more philosophical level, however, "Yuan drama is clearly more serious emotionally than Gay's intellectual spoofing" as Henry W. Wells notes (p. 24).

There is more to the difference than that. The ballad opera, for all its swift rise to popularity, began life as a parody of Italian opera, and as parody it could hardly have made a strong appeal to serious playwrights as a form in which to cast their best efforts. The Yuan musical drama, on the other hand, was the evolutionary peak of Chinese entertainment tradition up to that time, and the best poetic talents of the age were engaged in exploiting this dramatic form for almost a century. Because of this, Yuan drama turns out to have many more dimensions than the English ballad opera with which it shares a number of formal features. Yuan drama not only encompasses all the vast world of Chinese folklore and myth but draws upon an elegantly polished literary tradition for its verse and utilizes the most pungent gutter idiom in dialogue or verse when it wishes contrast. It regularly includes song, declaimed verse, entrance and exit couplets and quatrains, slang, ordinary speech, rhythmic but unrhymed passages, and the whole gamut of theatrical accompaniments, including acrobatics, dance, lavish costuming, and stylized miming. Its tone ranges from farce through extravaganza to something akin to tragedy, and often these are combined in a single work. There are dramas of crime and the law, kings and courts, generals, Taoist and Buddhist eremetism and salvation, family dramas of "sorrowful partings and joyful reunions," tales of romantic love and a half-dozen other kinds of subject matter.

With this for a preamble, let me package the main features and conventions* of the genre in a kind of freeze-dried form below:

1. A poetic-musical drama	Included: song, dance, farce interludes, pantomime and verse recitation.
2. In four acts (rarely, five)	Option of one (rarely, two) demi-acts called "the wedge."
3. An "act" meant a set *(lien-t'ao)* of related songs (arias) with its ancillary dialogue and dramatic equipment.	All "songs" in one act were in a single mode or "key." An act must begin with a certain "tune" and end with a certain coda form. Same rhyme used throughout the act.

*There is actually more and better literature available (to the person who does not read Chinese) on the subject of form, convention, and development than any other aspect of Yuan drama. See Crump (1958), Crump (1970), Crump (1971) [the last noted is also published in Birch (1974)]. For musical conventions there is Johnson (1970). Shih (1976) has an extensive bibliography which is very useful, as well.

4. All lyrics were written for or adapted to "songs" already in the public domain.	Music not composed in the strictest sense. Dramatist's lyrics (to fit *his* story and *his* taste) set to groupings of conventional tunes somewhat in the manner of Western ballad opera.
5. Only one singing role in any one act (and limited cast in almost all cases).	Only "star" sang but he/she could act male part in Act I, for example, and female in Act III if need be.

About the first of these contents on the package label there is little more to say: to a large degree Chapter 3 on the Actor's Art was devoted to demonstrating this proposition.

Item two is one of the strongest of Yuan dramatic conventions: it has been conjectured that it goes back to the early days of protodrama when entertainers had to fit their offerings into the time and circumstances of a banquet. Why there should regularly have only been room for four acts between egg roll and fortune cookie has never been explained to my satisfaction: I regard the banquet origins of the four acts with suspicion.

This strong preference for four acts and the overall distribution of the weight of the play is one which led Chinese scholars in the past to rash and tendentious conclusions. In Chapter 1, I pointed out that Tsang Chin-shu, a Ming critic, who admired Yuan drama extravagantly, could not conceive that they had actually been composed by men of quite low standing. As a result of such social stereotypy he devised a wholly imaginary theory that the plays were written by playwrights because the civil service examinations, which he insists they took, required skill in this form of composition.

The trajectory of dramatic construction exhibited by Yuan dramas is a peaking of emotion (and singing) about three-quarters of the way to the end of the drama—the remainder of the play being devoted to a kind of winding down; a reaffirmation of social mores and general tapering off. Now the fact that this happens toward the end of the play may result in a slight statistical shortening of last acts (though no such shortening is visible in the three plays translated in Part II, for example). Whatever the case, Tsang thought he detected such a thing and came up with a ready theory as generous in intent as it was ill-founded in fact:

> Since men were chosen [by Chinese civil service] for what they could accomplish while seated "under the windy eaves" of the examination hall and during the "inch of time" given them by the tests, even the most renowned talents of the age . . . had lost their strength and impetus by the time they came to the fourth act of their dramatic verse.

The pitiful picture of the exhausted aspirant is all the more laughable if you are aware that the composers didn't write plays for examinations; they were for the most part professionals who wrote for their daily bread. However, the depiction of either an exam candidate or a professional playwright being so stupid as not to do the fourth act first if he felt he might fall prey to exhaustion just at a crucial point is one of those historical horsefeathers I cherish greatly. No, it is perfectly clear that the form and theatrical tradition called for this calm and gentle catastasis at the end of the drama—it was one of the things the good playwrights did best.

With item three the musical origins of Yuan drama become very distinct. Several kinds of earlier musical performance contributed to the growth of the "song-set" as a unit of division. In particular, the musical solo narrative form known as *chu-kung-tiao* (songs in various modes) which flourished during the Chin dynasty must have heavily influenced the final modal form of the Yuan drama "act." The modal grouping brought to a conclusion with a coda was the only overt indication the audience ever had that a unit (the act) was finished—there was no curtain to close, of course, and entrances and exits in mid-act often look much the same as those at the ends of acts. A few generalizations on modes and their use can be made: one of the nine popular modes became the standard one for the opening act of any drama, and there is a kind of statistical preference for a certain other mode to be used for the final act. We can also detect that four of the modes were much more popular in the composition of Yuan drama than were the other five though we have no idea why. Attempts have been made (e.g. by Brooks[2]) to relate the emotional content of acts and the mode chosen to compose it. I remain highly skeptical. However, Johnson is rethinking the whole problem with much more, and more reliable, material than Brooks used. What he concludes will have to be listened to with respect.

Still in regard to item three, we are now dealing with one of the most difficult aspects of the Yuan dramatic form to conceptualize. Note that I put the word "song" (and elsewhere, "tune") in quotations marks. There are literally hundreds of "song" titles which were available to the composers, but by and large they tended to use a rather limited group of the most popular ones with which to compose their dramas. A student of mine once complained that he was damned if he thought he'd go to see many musical dramas if he knew they were going to use the same tired melodies in each one. It does offend common sense, and I fear that we lack the proper nomenclature—and perhaps even the proper concepts—to make the immense popularity of Yuan drama *as music* comprehensible. The nearest I am able to come to an explanation is that the term I translate as "song" really stands for some kind of rhythmic-melodic matrix or pattern which not only could be varied and changed (while still remaining recognizable in some fashion) but the skill with which it was varied was somehow a test of the composer's genius. The reader should note as he reads the plays in Part II that, centered in parentheses and standing by itself at the head of each aria, is the romanized title of the "tune-pattern" to which the aria is composed. He should also note that all of *Mo-ho-lo* and the first three acts of *Rain* (Part II, pp. 277 to 313) have more or less complete scansion of these patterns appended; e.g.

(Hsien-lü [*mode name*], Tien chiang ch'un [*tune pattern*], 44345 [*scansion*].)

The numbers in this example are to be understood as indicating that there are five lines in that aria; the first two have four beats, the third has three beats, the fourth has four beats, and the fifth five beats. My English translation of the "song" will reflect this with the same number of English stresses per line as there are syllables demanded by the scansion. Now, your question should be, "How the devil can he know about beats, if the music (as he said) has been defunct these four hundred years." Fair enough. I used to be very doubtful that any such thing could be done, but the works of Cheng Ch'ien and Johnson have made a convert of me.

The problem is precisely that the music *is* defunct—we have nothing but the lyrics left to us today. We can tell (most of the time) from the rhyme where a line ended. We know the line consisted of extrametrical and "base" words. We can more often than not distinguish the former from the latter and clear them away so we are left with a base syllable (word) count. The same tune pattern in any of the dramas where it is found can be fairly convincingly shown to exhibit the same number of base words. Hence my scansion.* But this must mean that Yuan music had a rhythmic and syntactic relationship to its lyrics that is almost unheard of in Western music, where, for example, melisma can carry the single word "alleluia" through a hundred bars of music. So be it, then, Yuan music *was* that closely related to its lyrics—the evidence is too convincing to think otherwise.† Though we may not be able to conceive just how this sounded, it is clear that the argument in favor of some kind of term like "tune matrices" rather than "songs" is greatly strengthened. For this reason, since lyrics differ from one drama to the next, it would give the music of the same aria a somewhat different shape and sound (though still recognizable as the same pattern) in each drama where it was used. That in turn answers the complaint of my student: The playgoer would *not* be listening to the same tired tunes; each rendition of the tune pattern would be substantially different (in some fashion which I, for one, find difficult to conceptualize).

---

*The formulas are all taken from Johnson (1968) where he has worked out a sophisticated system of line-length mutations.

†For an interesting (but by no means conclusive) discussion of the peculiarities of Chinese operatic music see Crump and Malm.

Let me also point out to the reader here that I have tried to separate the "extrametricals" *(ch'en-tzu)* from the base words *(cheng-tzu)* by means of hemistichs in my translation in both the first three acts of *Rain* and all of *Mo-ho-lo,* thus:

As of now
I live my borrowed time each day.

But papa,
I still don't know if you swam or drowned.

Within the pulses of my heart dwell the sorrows of a
thousand years

And locked between my furrowed brows lie all the
world's miseries.

My gratitude, kindly fisherman who gave me love,

Who did not see me
As someone from the outside world

But took me
Straight to his breast as a natural child.

Most (but by no means all) extrametrics *(ch'en-tzu)* occur in initial position. The close-spaced "As of now," "But papa" indicate their presence in these two lines. The next three do not have any in them but the last two lines again have *ch'en-tzu* which I indicate by close-spaced "Who did not see me" and "But took me." This is merely a mechanical device by which to indicate something about the meter of the original.* I did not use it translating *Li K'uei* and I am not sure whether I have a net artistic gain or loss in the plays and acts where I have indicated *ch'en-tzu* in this fashion.

The very least the reader should be able to glean from the disquisition above is that Yuan drama is written to some of the most rococo musical conventions in the world and this in turn argues for a lengthy musical evolution preceding the developed Yuan dramatic form.

---

*When *Rain* was published in *Renditions* (no. 4, 1975), George Kao misunderstood what I was trying to do with the half-lines and close spacing, and so the *Renditions* version appears to be full of meaningless line divisions. Trying to explain what I meant was so slow and difficult (by mail to Hong Kong) that I gave up. Actually, the result doesn't look too bad.

The final item in the contents of our dehydrated packet*—a single singing role—is also believed to have been a legacy of the *chu-kung-tiao*. That kind of performance, you will remember, was a solo presentation (probably accompanied by drum, clapper, and possibly some melody instrument) in which a single individual (usually a woman) sang quite long and complex musical narrations. It may have been that the courtesan-entertainers who specialized in this *solo* performance somehow in later times became the nuclei for the small troupes which were all that were needed to perform the developed Yuan drama, and these performances still reflected her (his?) star role by having only one singing part in any one act of the drama. This would help to explain such facts as we seem to have about Yuan dramatic troupes: they centered around one performer (take our Elegance of Chung-tu in Chapter 2 for example), were often knit by family ties, and were essentially musicians.

There is perhaps one other dramatic convention with which the reader should be familiar in order to appreciate more of the peculiarities of Yuan dramatic form. All roles belong to one of five or six "role-types." There is the *tan* role (leading female and singing role), the *mo* (male singing lead), the *wai* (secondary male), and the *ching* (comic-villain). No matter what the story or who is being portrayed, each character is assigned one of these role-types and this (we believe) fixed the kind of makeup and in part the kind of costume he wore.† In addition to the main role-types there were the subtypes, for example: the *ch'a tan* (bad female), the *chung-mo* (more important than the *wai* but not so important as the *mo*?), the *ch'ou* (more clownish than villainous), and a half dozen other less often used designations. These are all as old as the Chinese stage and though there are numerous fanciful etymologies (usually pejorative) supplied for them by scholars, we have really no idea where the terms originated. The important fact about them is the further evidence they provide of the emphasis on generalized rather than individualized characters. (All maidservants are named Mei-hsiang, and all manservants Chang Ch'ien.) You will see later, however, that this generalizing tendency is actually contradicted in *Li K'uei,* the title role of which is quite vivid and idiosyncratic.

*There are, I hope, no harmful additives or artificial coloring.

†Note the similarity between the Chinese role-types and *commedia dell'arte* players.

So much for the list of stage conventions: nothing about them tells us anything of the artistic priorities of the genre; but reading even a single play will leave little doubt in anyone's mind about the artistic imperatives of this dramatic form. The Chinese love for and craftsmanship with lyric poetry (most particularly landscape and nature poetry) is the controlling literary factor in Yuan drama just as music was the overriding consideration in their performance. Yuan drama plots move swiftly along (sometimes with telegraphic brevity) until a place is reached for an aria on a subject that takes particularly well to Chinese style lyric elaboration, and there it stops to dwell on the matter with richness of poetic diction, word play, and ornamentation of detail—all ordered by some of the most Byzantine formal requirements in the history of poesy. Most of the time the aria subject is landscape or nature (either exterior or interior) but an astounding number of other matters can be well handled by this kind of verse. As an example, I simply draw your attention to the set of arias in *Mo-ho-lo* (Part II, pp. 354–55) where Chang Ting merely cites the cases-at-law in which he has been recently involved; the number and vividness of human vignettes he summons up in the mind of the hearer in a very brief time is remarkable.*

I trust it is clear that the Yuan drama's nature and genius is at the opposite end of the spectrum from the illusionist Western stage, and we in the West should compare it only with our own earlier poetic and musical drama if we are to make any sense at all. It is clear that whatever mirror Yuan drama held up to nature, it was as much a distorting speculum as was Shakespeare's.

It is difficult for me to guess at this point what further information the reader who has had no contact with traditional Chinese drama will find helpful or interesting, but it occurs to me that if I were such a reader I might have had enough of comparison with Western theater and now hanker to know something of what the Chinese themselves thought of their own traditional drama. Though I can only supply a limited amount of information on the subject (excluding strictly musical appreciations), I think the reader is entitled to it here.

---

*Incidentally, this aria regularly takes reprises *(yao-p'ien)* and the subject matter here is particularly suited to a series of repeated arias since the topic is essentially a series of imaginary court agendas: an example of aria form and subject matter match.

As might be expected (since the same attitude toward drama was frequently struck by Western clerics and other somber types) the Chinese intelligentry made much of the fact that the theater is a simulacrum of life: not "real," not "true." The general statement of opprobrium we get from them is that actors "hoax the multitudes" (see Chapter 1, p. 30, note). This was, in their minds, dishonest and therefore pernicious. But statements from those already ill-disposed toward drama cannot be expected to tell us as much about Chinese attitudes toward their own theater as do apologies written by enthusiasts. These latter fall roughly into two categories: the theater is a pleasant and harmless distraction; or, the theater should be used for social and moral reform. The former is seen as early as the Yuan dynasty and the latter becomes more and more common in late Ming and Ch'ing times. I submit one sample of each. In fairness to the second, so far as I know it was not supposed to be taken primarily as a piece of belles lettres; whereas the first, a fairly well-known writer's preface to a poem written for a famous courtesan-actress, is quite self-consciously belletristic.

Preface to the Poem for Madam Sung
(by Hu Ch'i-yu, 1227–93)[3]

Of all creatures man is the most intelligent, the most estimable, but also the most beset by sorrow and vexation. He ariseth at cock-crow, goes to his bed when night falls, and all the hours between are troubled and disturbed. If his sinews and bones are not at the beck of someone else, he racks his brain or bends his will on another's behalf. Apart from what he must do to sustain himself and put food in his mouth, he is forever serving some man or tending the needs of one barnyard beast or another. He either bears with his fate and buries his dead in some rustic town or rude hamlet; or pays his tax and serves his corvée in the magistrate's hall or at a frontier post. Out of every ten homes, need can be found in nine—brows are knit as often as hearts contract; anxiety weighs heavy on all and can seldom be dispelled. If he give rein to his emotions, eight times in ten he will do so with such want of restraint that he invites his own tears.

When he can get him an hour or two to lay his head upon the pillow, terrible dreams may visit him and he can find no peace even there. And so it passes: day and night, rising or resting, asleep or awake, man seldom knows ease for his heart or rest for his bones. Wherefore he moans and mourns even when in good health and becomes infirm before his two score years and ten are past. In that brief time had he nothing to loosen the toils of the world; nought to free him from his worries, to brighten things, lift his heart, show him some small pleasure with which to banish his burden of bitterness, it were hard to be a man at all!

This is why the Sages used music.... Musicians and players are equally precious to the ruler because the sounds of music match the harmonies of government, and the dramas of players can change to fit the ideals of any age. Presently, the plays of the Academy which were called *yuan-pen* have undergone a change and are become now what is known as *tsa-chü* or "varieties." They are aptly named. The variety of their subject matter may include the lofty and treat of power and the folly of kings, ministers and governance: or they may recount village matters and the improprieties of fathers, spouses, and friends. Nor do they fail to treat facts and feelings proper even to quacksalvers, and apothecaries, diviners, fortune-tellers, monks, merchants, peddlers, foreign customs and outlandish speech. No sentiment exists which these dramas are incapable of expressing nor is there behavior which they have not explored. And when one woman can act out the feats it took 10,000 men to accomplish, can do so in a manner which charms the ear and delights the fancy, surely the *tsa-chü* achieve something never attained on the stage before.

From *Chin Hsiang Shuo*[4]
(by Chin Chih)

In the places where they act these plays and create these characters they are able to move the emotions of the audience and make their spirits take flight—now startling them, now delighting them. It even comes to pass that those who act before the curtains and screens actually soak their sleeves with their own tears; as though they had lost all sense of the trumpery of the stage and took it to be present reality.

Now I believe that all lessons of the past are written in books that men may learn from them; but it would be so much easier to move men if we put those lessons in a play and acted it before them. For the "songs of the Pear Garden Academy" were not originally meant to amuse the ear and please the eye. If there be anyone whose ambition is to reform the people—who would truly amend the mores of our times—let him begin by reforming the drama!

And finally, something about the three plays in Part II: *Li K'uei* was first translated in its entirety in the winter of 1964 for the first volume of Cyril Birch's *Anthology.* It is in substantially the same form it was then (I've fixed a few errors). I would do it much the same way today only I would make almost all the lines of the arias end-stopped instead of having them run on as they do in the 1964 version.

Plays about the banditti of Liang-shan were very popular—there are nearly two dozen known titles which deal with the men of the mountain.* It appears, however, that no bandit was as loved by playgoers as the impetuous, bloodthirsty, but appealing Li K'uei.[5] The plot situation in which his head is forfeit to his own impetuosity is used in both *Li K'uei* and one other play that is usually known as *The Black Whirlwind* (*YCH* #40). I imagine that one index of Li K'uei's popularity is the number of sobriquets he has in the dramas: he is known as the Black Whirlwind *(Hei Hsüan-feng),* of course, but he is often called by his leader, Sung Chiang (whom Li K'uei idolizes), Hillock *(shan-erh),* Black Ox *(hei-niu),* and the Iron Ox *(t'ieh-niu).* Li K'uei refers to himself as Daddy Black *(Hei tieh-tieh)* and often ruefully notes the blackness of his complexion. He must have been a very distinctive character on stage with two broadaxes thrust in his belt, his "brown, bristling beard" and his black makeup.

All of these attributes should have barred Li K'uei from the singing roles *(cheng-mo),* since those were supposed to be done by much less violent and much more genteel personalities. However, conventions are man-made and are made to be broken by the same agent. Obviously Li K'uei, whatever his table manners, was good box office. The contrasts between Li K'uei's bloody ways and the poetry and tenderness he displays in his arias were something the playwright always exploited and, in *Li K'uei Carries Thorns* at least, with great success.

I am of the opinion that the two best known Li K'uei plays show so much similarity for the same reason that five or six so-called *kung-an* or "law-case" plays resemble each other: Yuan drama was above all a commercial and popular art form and, when it hit upon a formula which was well received, it stayed with it as long as it continued well received. To our great good fortune, in doing so Yuan playwrights turned out quantities of rich and appealing poetry which, above all else now, assures that their works will continue to delight us who must resurrect them for our mind's eye from between the covers of a book.

*These are the Robin Hood-like band best known to English readers through Pearl Buck's translation, *All Men are Brothers.*

Rain: The 162 *bona fide* Yuan *tsa-chü* dramas we have left to us include everything from undeniable masterworks to weak pastiches. During my more optimistic periods I believe we can arrange them fairly well according to their eras. In general we classify them from early—almost austere in tone, given to rather lean verse, few characters and compact in plot; to late—characterized by large casts, exuberant (often fulsome) verse, and complex plotting. *Rain on the Hsiao-Hsiang* is attributed to Yang Hsien-chih. As with all Yuan dynasty playwrights, we have only the scantiest information about him, but he is spoken of as a younger contemporary of Kuan Han-ch'ing—the most admired and prolific of all writers of *tsa-chü*—whose approximate dates lie somewhere between 1242 and 1323. If the attribution is correct, it would make *Rain* a product of the "earlier" age of Yuan theater (a time still characterized by close attention to classical form) but belonging to that period when the greatest talents flourished. There is nothing in the script to contradict this assumption and much to substantiate it—the accidental recrossing of the paths of daughter and father is easily accepted by the audience. There is a classical frugality with the number of characters used in all parts of the *mise-en-scène* except the finale (which is the one place Yuan drama is always lavish), and the whole piece is characterized by skillful exploitation of stage (rather than entirely literary) values. Act IV certainly contains one of the best and most playable scenes in the repertoire of Yuan theater. The lyric hopelessness and helplessness of the lost daughter outside the same posthouse in which her ageing and discouraged father mourns her loss would generate dramatic impact using either the scenery of the illusionist theater or the bare Chinese stage.

Another indication (in my view) of advanced technique used in *Rain* is the amount of declaimed verse it gives to all members of the cast and the way that that verse is organized into a kind of suite in Act IV. The classical form of Yuan drama demanded one and only one singing role in each act, as noted, but the evolutionary tendency of Chinese theater after Yuan was toward multiple singing roles and *Rain* is moving in that direction. In *Rain* we find two intrusive songs (Act II and Act IV) done by characters other than the singing role; but much more significant is the involvement of all the characters on stage in Act IV in rhymed and metrical exchanges. These verses all employ the same rhyme in Chinese, and one of the characteristics of song sets which comprise a single act of

Yuan drama is that all the songs in any one act will have the same rhyme throughout. In Act IV the playwright has created a *multi-voiced* and *spoken* set of verses which has most of the features of the *solo* and *sung* verses of the ordinary act. So far as I know, *Rain* is the only Yuan drama to do such a thorough job with declaimed verse, and it represents in my opinion uncommonly advanced composition technique for the time.

It was partly for this reason that I chose *Rain* to translate and precisely for this reason that I translated Act IV first (1966). Acts I through III were translated a couple of years after I had done Act IV and in this interim scholars improved our knowledge of Yuan dramatic metrics to such a degree that the songs in Acts I–III are translated to match closely the original, irregular meters of the Chinese verse, while those in Act IV still remain the impressionistic approximations they were in 1966.

The theatricality of the play—there must have been a great amount of involved and exciting pantomime, for example, during the foundering of the ferry and subsequent rescue of Ts'ui-luan—is nicely balanced by the simple lyric intensity of Act III which consists almost entirely of the delicate Ts'ui-luan's description of the miseries of her journey to a penal colony during the heavy autumn rains with the brusque but often sympathetic interjections of her guard providing excellent contrast.

The Yuan playwright often supplied himself with a journey to give free rein to his skills with landscape and nature poetry. There is certainly no wetter nor more miserable excursion in all literature than the one taken by Ts'ui-luan in Act III, yet it is an integral part of the dramatic mechanism, not something extraneous hauled in simply to give the composer an opportunity to demonstrate his lyric talents.

Another arresting aspect of *Rain* is the treatment of some of its lesser characters and scenes. In Yuan drama every servant, guard, or underling is either full of pawky impertinences or totally iniquitous, but Ts'ui-luan's guard during her painful journey is given unwonted dimensions. He beats her to make her move along but regrets the miscarriage of justice that has brought this upon her; he becomes exasperated with Ts'ui-luan but shares what little food he has with her—in fact, he seems to give it all to her in the end. This unusual underling is somewhat in keeping with the way *Rain* treats its final conventional scene. "Happy endings" being mandatory with Yuan dramatic form often led to the kind of hasty patching up of relationships at the last moment that can be seen in *Rain*. But almost always the irony of such finales is played with a bland countenance. This makes the line delivered by *Rain's* stock villainess (who has been condemned to be the heroine's serving maid for life) quite a shocker. "If I must be your maid then maid I will be—but let me warn you, a maid can go anywhere in a home a wife can, so do not imagine you will have a husband all to yourself!" Here, in the marshmallow and marzipan of the conventional happy ending, one suddenly comes upon a razor blade! The author of *Rain*, whoever he was, was not content simply to be an excellent craftsman within the demands of his genre, he was pushing its conventions to their limits and he must have succeeded in convincing his audiences that he was right to do so. This is often what distinguishes the genius from the simply talented.

A final note on the title of the play: I am not sure that the scenic valley where the Hsiao River meets the Hsiang in Hunan province is any wetter than most areas of central China, but "Night Rain on the Hsiao-Hsiang" was the name of an old song (also called "Man-chiang Hung") to the tune of which much sentimental poetry had been written. I imagine that the existence of such a song was as responsible for the setting of the play as was any meteorological peculiarity, even though the night rain was supposed to have been one of the "eight scenic wonders of the Hsiao-Hsiang area."

The Mo-ho-lo Doll: If your dramatic focus is to be the singing of lyric verse, then the various mechanisms used to move the story along to the next point where an aria can be employed to its best advantage must be concentrated in just those areas which are not sung. Dramatic movement cannot usefully be left in the singer's hands or you will eventually have simply a monologue performance in verse and prose.

A measure of the composer's stagecraft skills (and these may be totally independent of his power as a poet) is how and how well he handles those transitions, which are in many ways the essence of the dramatic. If believability and verisimilitude are important for your *mise-en-scène*—and strangely enough they are even for poetic drama in a peculiar way—a simple but extremely effective stage device is to create a secondary character who, because of his relatively detached position in the universe of the play, can carry the burden of narrative progress and shifting dramatic focus with little or no strain on the audience's willingly suspended disbelief. If this character's actions can be accounted for naturally, and, in addition the audience is always pleased to see him appear, the playwright has succeeded admirably, East or West. But in Chinese drama, which tends to be more fragmented than many types of Western theater, this character can serve yet another purpose by stringing the loosely connected episodes on the strand of his own personality.

Notice in *Mo-ho-lo* that Kao Shan is a prime mover, a solver of dramatic impasses as well as a mildly comic (but in all respects sympathetic) character.

If your vehicle is melodrama—and traditional Chinese drama may as well be called melodrama—the best mileage is gotten by forcing each emotional situation to such an extreme that every drop of drama is wrung from it. You must relieve your situation at the last moment, however, or you will have killed off your hero or heroine in the first act. The minor and moveable character who throughout the play becomes known to, and indeed a confidante of, most of the major characters can always be introduced to turn the dramatic climaxes so that they run along other lines. If, in addition to this you can arrange your plot so that this likable character is innocently carrying about with him that important knowledge which the audience knows will lead to dénouement, you have the dramatist's dream come true. This has been achieved many times in Western drama and the composer of *Mo-ho-lo* employs Kao Shan in this fashion with such ease and confidence that one can only conclude he had done similar things many times before.

For example, it was distressing to me, and I'm sure it will be to the reader, that in the last act Kao Shan is given what appears to us to be a totally arbitrary punishment for a concocted crime. (There is nothing illegal about making images of gods.) In part we are bothered because we have a strong feeling that we've missed some subtlety—and perhaps we have—but certainly the better part of our distress stems from the fact that Kao Shan is a good fellow and we like him. You see? The playwright has done just what he wanted to us!

Epilogue

*(san-ch'ang)**

(AUTHOR *in singing role pantomimes turning from typewriter and facing audience)*

(Hsien-lü, Hou-t'ing hua)

AUTHOR:

(sings)

Who would write an honest book
Must have an itch
That only writing one will ease.
My itch is scratched, my work is done,
And yet
I've only written half of one!

---

*Feng Yuan-chün (pp. 362–63) gives seven examples of something which was generally called, in the *Yuan-k'an* edition, "*san-ch'ang.*" Translated, this should mean something like "play-closer." Chao (p. 13) cites five examples of extant, dangling, partial song-sets at the ends of plays which he calls "post-play wedges" which is a contradiction in terms—somewhat like saying "final prologues." Cheng Ch'ien seems to be the first to have put two and two together and posit the existence of an "epilogue" *(san-ch'ang)* which appeared fairly frequently at the end of act four of Yuan *tsa-chü* just before the so-called *cheng-ming* and *t'i-mu.* Though he had formulated his ideas as early as 1944, his theory was first published in *Ts'ung Shih Tao Ch'ü* (1961) and in that work he still remains quite diffident about it. I find the theory convincing because epilogue-like units are such a regular part of non-illusionist Western drama and were widely experimented with in Chinese drama of the Ming dynasty. In any event, my effort above is written to Cheng's prescription (p. 203) and is respectfully dedicated to him.

(speaks)
All books (unlike Gaul) consist of two parts.

CHANG CH'IEN:
What's Caesar doing so far from home?

(Liu Yeh-erh)

AUTHOR:
(sings)
That book which lies unread,
However newly born,
Is all but dead
Until some Reader come
And crack its spine,
Smudge its page,
Dog-ear,
Underline . . .
And thereby make it whole.

(Yao-p'ien)

Reader, I have done my bit;
Do you likewise now,
And by your reading it
Make us both a whole and honest book!

(exeunt omnes leaving the stage to the READER*)*

Cheng-ming.
A Barbarian Emperor sits on the Dragon Throne above.

T'i-mu.
The Chinese Playwrights ply their trade in Liang Park below.

PART II

The Dramas

DRAMATIS PERSONAE

SUNG CHIANG,	*Leader of the Bandits*
WU HSUEH-CHIU,	*His follower*
LU CHIH-SHEN,	*Apostate monk and follower*
WANG LIN,	*Elderly tavern keeper*
MAN T'ANG-CH'IAO,	*His daughter*
SUNG KANG and LU CHIH-EN,	*Imposters, posing as the Bandit Leader and the Monk*
LI K'UEI,	*Bloody-handed and hard-drinking champion of justice*

The Bandits of Liang-shan Po and their activities have some slight historical basis as a group and a place where outlaws held out against the invading Chin troops. The place and the men had something about them, however, that appealed instantly and directly to the Chinese, and a cycle of stories was so well established among storytellers and playwrights by early Yuan times that publications of the earliest written version of the *Shui-hu Chuan* had begun to appear. The stories have been perennially popular ever since. The *Shui-hu Chuan* was the first traditional Chinese novel to be canonized by the present regime on mainland China and only now, as I write this, are they beginning to see and argue about the many implications in the stories which are totally inimical to Marxian theory and controls.

Li K'uei Carries Thorns *(YCH #87)*

(attributed to K'ang Chin-chih, *fl.* 1279)

ACT I

*(*SUNG CHIANG, WU HSUEH-CHIU, *and* LU CHIH-SHEN *enter with attendants.)*

SUNG:

(recites)

By the camp gate tumbles the quarreling mountain stream,
Wild flowers thrust aslant under sweat-stained headbands.
Black stroked words against the yellow banner's gleam:
"Delivering the people and aiding heaven's way."

I am Sung Chiang, also known as Sung Kung-ming, and called the Herald of Justice. Once I was a clerk in the yamen at Yün-ch'eng but, having killed the hag Yen P'o-hsi while I was drunk, I was sent to the prison garrison at Chiang-chou. Where the road passed near the foot of Mount Liang, I met brother Ch'ao Kai, who rescued me and brought me up here to the mountain. Afterwards, when Ch'ao Kai died during the three battles at Chu-chia village, the men made me their leader and I have brought together thirty-six great comrades, seventy-two lesser ones, and a host of followers. My power holds Shantung in awe and my orders are obeyed in Hopei.

Of all the festivals in the year the two I like best are the third of the third month, called *ch'ing-ming* and the ninth of the ninth month, called *ch'ung-yang*. Today is *ch'ing-ming* and I've given my men three days leave to visit the graves of their ancestors. When three days are up, all must return to the mountain and whoever disobeys the order will be beheaded.

(recites)

Who does not fear my strict command
And rigid limits to his leave,
But loiters longer half an hour
Returns to find there's no reprieve. *(exit)*

(Enter the elderly WANG LIN.*)*

WANG:

(recites)

The straw* hangs high on its springy staff,
A *p'i-p'a* sounds in the willows' shade.
Disciples of Kao-yang† linger with us
For mine host's wines are wondrously made.

My name is Wang Lin, I live in Hsing-hua Village where I run a little business in wines to make a living. Of the three in my family, my wife died long ago and left me and my daughter, Man-t'ang Ch'iao, who is now eighteen and as yet unbetrothed. My place is quite close to the foot of Mount Liang and the leaders of the band all buy their wine from my shop. I've got the wine vessel warmed, so I'll go see if anyone's coming.

---

*Bundles of straw and banners were used as wineshop signs.

†A warrior named Li Shih-ch'i tried to see the first emperor of Han while the latter was still battling for the throne. "What does this Li Shih-ch'i look like?" the emperor asked his aide. "A Confucianist," was the reply. "Send him off," said the emperor. Li Shih-ch'i heard the conversation and hooted, "I'm a disciple of Kao-yang chiu (i.e., the wine of Kao-yang), not Confucius," Almost the identical poem is used in a number of Yuan dramas when a tavern keeper appears on the stage. See *WP* #134.

(Enter SUNG KANG *and* LU CHIH-EN *in villain-clown makeup.)*

SUNG:
Firewood's cheap, rice isn't dear, and we're glib rascals, two to the pair!* I'm Sung Kang and the name of my mate here is Lu Chih-en. Because we come from around Mount Liang we're pretending to be from there. So I'm calling myself Sung Chiang and he's supposed to be Lu Chih-shen. We're here at old Wang Lin's wineshop in Hsing-hua Village to get a drink. *(He sees* WANG LIN.*)* Old Wang, is there any wine?

WANG:
There is indeed, brother, please be seated inside.

SUNG:
Give us five hundred coppers' worth. Old Wang, do you recognize the two of us?

WANG:
My old eyes are rather bad. I don't recognize you gentlemen.

SUNG:
Well, I'm Sung Chiang and this is Lu Chih-shen. A lot of our men from the mountain come to your place and cut up a bit. If any of them give you trouble, you come up the mountain and let me know. I'll take care of things for you.

WANG:
You men on the mountain are all good fellows, helping the way of heaven. No, there's been no trouble, but I hope you will forgive an old man for not recognizing your honor. If I had known it was you,

*This same quatrain is used by Lefty Dodge and Righty Hide. See *WP* 324.

I would have gone out to meet your honor. Very inhospitable, I hope you'll not hold it against me. Many thanks to you captains for patronizing my place. *(Hands him wine.)* Please, your honor, drink it down. *(*SUNG KANG *drinks.)* Here's more.

LU:

(drinking)

That's good wine, brother.

SUNG:

Are there any more in your family, old Wang?

WANG:

No one to speak of, your honor, only an eighteen-year-old unbetrothed daughter called Man-t'ang Ch'iao. Since I've no one else to do the honors, let me bring her out to pass your excellency his cup. It will show my respect.

SUNG:

Since she's not yet betrothed, perhaps you'd better not.

LU:

There's nothing wrong with that, brother, bring her out.

WANG:

(calls)

Man-t'ang Ch'iao, my child, come here.

MAN:

Why did you call me, Father?

WANG:

You may not realize it, but Sung Kung-ming from the mountain is here today in person. Come and serve him a cup.

MAN:
Wouldn't that be improper, Father?

WANG:
No harm. *(She sees the guests.)*

SUNG:
I've been afraid of the smell of makeup all my life. Back a little, please.

WANG:
Give the two gentlemen a cup, my child. *(She hands them wine.)*

SUNG:
And I'll give old Wang a cup of wine. *(He hands* WANG *a cup.)* My, an old gentleman like you shouldn't have holes in his clothes. Here, let me give you my red sash to patch them. *(*WANG *takes the sash.)*

LU:
Hah! you didn't know it, but the wine we handed you was the betrothal wine and the sash was the red wedding gift.* Now we'll just take your daughter with us to be mistress of Sung Kung-ming's fort. We'll borrow her for three days and we'll return her on the fourth. We're leaving for the mountain. *(They lead the girl off.)*

WANG:
My old eyes, my arms, lived only for my daughter. Oh, what shall I do now? *(weeps)*

(Enter LI K'UEI, *drunk)*

---

*A fine example of the Yuan playwright's scorn for "realistic" motivation. This same silly trick is used elsewhere (*YCH* 843) in the same fashion—simply to get on with the plot so that arias may be sung the sooner.

LI:

Drinking without getting drunk is worse than being sober. I am Li K'uei from the Liang-shan P'o. Because of my dark skin men call me the Black Whirlwind. Brother Sung Chiang has given us three days leave to enjoy ourselves and "dance among the new shoots"* so of course I had to come down from the mountain to buy a few pots from old Wang Lin and get rotten drunk.

(Tien-chiang-ch'un)

(sings)

The spirit of drink is hard to lay,
And laid, the intemperate ghost rises again.
Seeking wine in the village I asked of Wang Liu†

(recites)

Said I to him can you find me some wine?
But that rascal said nothing, only made a bee line
from my hand. So I yelled to him, whoa!
And I chased him and grabbed him so he couldn't go.
I lifted my hand just to tap him a bit,
then he splits his whiskers yelling, "Daddy, don't hit."

(sings)

Said Wang Liu, they have some over there,

(Hun-chiang Lung)

But this is the time of Ch'ing-ming.
The wind and rain are sadly tender with the flowers.
The soft breeze gently rises,
At evening the showers cease.
Yonder, half hid in willows, lies the tavern.

---

*This seems once to have been a peasant dance in the fields, but it means simply to enjoy the *ch'ing-ming* festival in most dramas where it appears.

†Here he interrupts his aria to deliver some kind of narrative verse in the same rhyme as his aria. Wang Liu is the Chinese equivalent of John Doe or Richard Roe.

From the bright blaze of peach blossoms peeks
The fisherman's little boat, blending with
Ripples in the green waters of spring.
Migrant swallows fly to and fro,
Sand gulls wheel far and near.

(speaks)
Who says we have no scenery at Liang-shan P'o? I'll knock his teeth out!

(Tsui-chung T'ien)

(sings)
For there green mountains stand in cloud-locked beauty
And willow isles lie caught in nets of mist.

(speaks)
There's a golden oriole peck, peck, pecking at a blossom on the peach tree and the petals are falling into the water. They're beautiful! Where did I hear something of that sort? Let me think—ah, it was brother Wu Hsüeh-chiu who said it.

(sings)
Light, impudent blossoms chasing the water's flow.

(speaks)
Let me pick up a petal and look at it. How red it is!

(laughing)
And how black the finger!

(sings)
But how its makeup glows through a coat of white powder.

(speaks)
Ah, but I take pity on you, little petal, and toss you back to join the others. And I'll follow you, chase you, eager to run after blossoms.

(sings)
And so I reach the shop at Meadowbridge hard by Willow-
ford.

(speaks)

This won't do! I'd be disobeying Sung Chiang's orders. I'd better go back.

(sings)

I try not to drink, but the waving of the wineshop
Flag has made my steps waver.
How it dances in the east wind atop its springy staff.

(speaks)

Wang Lin, have you any wine? And it won't be on the house, either. Look, gold chips, and they're yours if you'll bring me a drink.

WANG:

(wiping tears away)

What would I want with gold chips?

LI:

(laughing)

His mouth says what would I want with them, but see how fast he snugs them away in his bosom!* Bring me wine, Wang Lin.

WANG:

It's coming, coming *(strains the wine into a cup)*.

LI:

If I get this into my belly, I'll be back again and again. But if I don't drink I'll get drier.

(Yu Hu-lu)

(sings)

In former days I had wine debts everywhere I went;
Of every ten taverns nine carried my bill.

---

*This line appears almost verbatim on *WP* 936.

(speaks)

Old Wang,

(sings)

Your shop in Hsing-hua Village need not blush before the Hsieh pavilion.
Set me down your Ch'un-p'ei wine, smooth as warm oil,
Cook me up a fat lamb, the prize of your stock.
On one side cooking meat, on the other wine new-poured and fuming,
Make fragrance such as steals from spice bags yet unopened.
Now while the senses urge shall I drink three cups one upon another.

(T'ien-hsia Lo)

How true: "One cup dissolves a thousand woes."

(speaks)

Old Wang, I have finished the wine.

(sings)

All my cares are gone. Indeed, lost somewhere behind my brain.
And I have drunk the time away without a halt.

(speaks)

I *am* drunk!

(sings)

What matter if I fall by the road
Or sleep with my head on a wine vat?

(speaks)

I tell you old Wang Lin,*

(sings)

I'll pour it in till the vessel itself perishes!

**Lai Chiang-chi* ed. has it this way. *YCH* has "pantomimes vomiting."

(speaks)

Old Wang, this wine is cold. Heat me some more.

WANG:

Yes sir. *(changes the wine, weeping)* Oh, Man-t'ang Ch'iao—

LI:

Come, warm up the wine.

WANG:

(still weeping)

Oh, my Man-t'ang Ch'iao.

LI:

Old Wang, haven't I already given you the money? What's bothering you?

WANG:

It's not because of you, brother. It's just that I have troubles I can't hide. Please, drink your wine.

(Shang-hua Shih)

LI:

(sings)

Times past haven't we stood before the jug and talked quite readily?
Then why today do you feign to see me not at all?

WANG:

You don't understand, I've just given my daughter away—that's what troubles me.

LI:

(sings)

Ai! You addled old egg, how far you go in search of complaints.

(speaks)

If it bothers you so much, why did you marry her off in the first place?

WANG:

Aiya! My Man-t'ang Ch'iao.

LI:

(sings)

You should have kept her by you till her face was blue-veined
And her hair hoary white.

(speaks)

Don't you know there are three things in the world that cannot be kept as they are?

WANG:

What three?

LI:

A silkworm when it ages, a man when he ages, and

(sings)

You foolish old man, as it's often said,
A woman grown cannot be kept as she was.

(speaks)

But, tell me, who did your daughter marry?

WANG:
Oh my brother, if my daughter had married, do you think I would be troubled as I am? To my sorrow she has been carried off by a bandit.

LI:
Bandit is it! Next you'll be telling me I stole her!

(Chin Chan-erh)

(sings)
Here stand I staring with rage
And there he with his tricky tongue
And mouth all ready to open in gossip.
One instant of deceit now and I'll be stung to wrath.
A torch will change your little thatch gourd
To crumbling ashes, and its wine vats to shattered potsherds.

(speaks)
Up with my two broadaxes and

(sings)
Down come your fruit trees of the serpent roots
And your brown buffalo with flaring horns.

(speaks)
Listen, Old Wang, if what you say is true, that's an end of it. But if it is false, you will never get by me!

WANG:
Please, your honor! Rest your anger and its shouts and listen to an old man while he tells it all slowly. Two men came here for wine. One said he was Sung Chiang and the other was Lu Chih-shen. I said, since it's really two gentlemen from Liang-shan P'o, and I had no others to come pay their respects except an eighteen-year-old unbetrothed daughter, I would call her out to present herself and serve the gentlemen their wine, which would show my deference. Well, I called her out and she passed the wine and then Sung

Chiang passed me three cups and thrust a red sash into my bosom. Lu Chih-shen said the three cups were marriage wine and the red cloth was a wedding gift. He said Sung Chiang had one hundred and eight leaders under him and lacked only one thing. He said, take this eighteen-year-old girl as mistress of the fort. He said today was an auspicious day for such things so they would take her back to Liang-shan P'o. They said they would keep her for three days and then send her back to me. Then they left, taking her with them. And left me, an old man whose very eyes and arms exist only to look after that girl, to watch her led away in broad daylight. Oh, brother, would you still have me untroubled?

LI:
But what proof have you of this?

WANG:
Here's the red sash, that's proof.

LI:
I don't want to believe the story, but who among the gentry wears such things? Old Wang, you draw off a good crock of wine, slaughter a fine calf, and in three days I'll bring your daughter, Man-t'ang Ch'iao, back here just as nice as you please. How's that?

WANG:
Oh brother, if you can bring her home, a crock of wine, a slaughtered calf, even killing myself would be too little to repay you your kindness!

(Chuan-sha)

LI:

(sings)

I'll handle your enemies, but please
Spare me this string of oversworn vows
From a mouth as honest as a false-bottomed dipper!

(speaks)

Sung Chiang,

(sings)

Taking your pleasure you have done a grievous wrong.
I swear, though spilt water is water lost, yet I'll
Have reasons from you, not rubbish.
You'd best have your case by heart,
No substitution of what isn't for what is,
Only what happened, first first and last last.

(speaks)

Now I'm off to Sung Chiang to tell him his crimes. I'll have him take leave of his thirty-six comrades, seventy-two companions, and host of followers and bring him, along with Lu Chih-shen, down from the mountain to your village. And when I call you, don't you pull in your head like a turtle!

WANG:

If I don't see them I can say nothing. But I'll know the both of them if I do see them. And as for not identifying them—it will be strange if I don't bite a hole in that Sung Chiang!

LI:

Alas for poor Sung Chiang, what an awful death! Hey, Old Wang, I do believe that's brother Sung Chiang coming right now!

(WANG LIN *stares about him in fright.)**

No, it's not, old one, I do but tease you. However,

(sings)

Mind you don't become my spear with a point of wax. *(exit)*

---

*This stage direction does not appear in *YCH* but does in *Lai-chiang Chi.*

WANG:
Brother Li has left. I suppose I should straighten up the shop. Oh, Man-t'ang Ch'iao, I shall die of grief over you. *(exit)*

ACT II

(SUNG CHIANG, WU HSUEH-CHIU, *and* LU CHIH-SHEN *enter with attendants.)*

SUNG:

(recites)

Our flag is dyed in the blood of men
The oil of our lamps is fat from their brains.
The dogs we give their skulls and scalps
And the crows their livers and reins.

(speaks)

I am Sung Chiang. I've given my men three days leave for *ch'ing-ming* to leave the mountain, dance among the new shoots, and enjoy themselves. This is already the end of the third day. When the watch-drum sounds three times in the Hall of Justice the men must all assemble. Guards, to the main gates and watch for arrivals.

SOLDIER:
Yes sir.

(LI K'UEI *enters.)*

LI:
It is I, Li K'uei, and I carry the red sash to see Sung Chiang.

(Tuan-cheng Hao)

(sings)

Shaking black anger that bristles my brown beard.
Now no halt can be called. Crushing my hands together in eagerness,
Time and again I lose the battle against
Passions which assail my heart.
Oh Sung Chiang, why was this done? What reason
Was it, I wonder, what compelled him?
My anger swells like thunder.
But no matter who he is or I am, or that we have
Half a lifetime without a rift,
Today the sun and the moon reach eclipse!
Only a few words may pass between us,
Yet I fear the mark it can leave on our friendship.
Hesitation besets me again. . . .

(speaks)

Guard, report to Sung Chiang that Li K'uei has arrived.

SOLDIER:

Yes sir. *(reports to* SUNG CHIANG*)* Brother Li K'uei has arrived.

SUNG:

Send him in.

SOLDIER:

He is here.

LI:

Brother Hsüeh-chiu, "How bright the hat on the new groom, how tight fit the sleeves to welcome a new son-in-law." And where is our Sung Kung-ming? Come forth and exchange bows with me. I have a little silver here to send my new sister-in-law in salutation.

SUNG:
What impertinence the rascal has! He salutes Hsüeh-chiu and ignores me; and what drivel he's talking!

LI:

(sings)
Ai! To you my friend-till-death
Heartiest congratulations!

SUNG:
Congratulations . . . ?

LI:

(sings)
But where do I find the lady of our fortress?

(points to LU CHIH-SHEN, *speaking)*
Tonsured donkey, a fine deed you've done.

(sings)
You've kept your own bed-cover clean
But I'll not let you off.

SUNG:
What? Now he's after you, Chih-shen!

LI:

(sings)
Their eyes bulge with innocence as they stoutly deny it,
But we shall have it out right here.

SUNG:
Li K'uei, when you left the mountain something happened down there. Why don't you tell me exactly what? *(*LI K'UEI *stands mute and*

looking troubled.) Well, since you don't wish to tell me, tell it to brother Hsüeh-chiu from the beginning.

(Kun Hsin-ch'iu)

LI:

(sings)
If my brother wanted a wife
The bald one would make plans for him.

SUNG:
He says you make plans, Chih-shen. What plans?

LU:
The man has guzzled so much wine that he's whizzing around like a gadfly out of reach of the fly-whisk. Who can understand his bzz bzz?*

LI:

(sings)
So it is then. Liang-shan P'o's a heaven without a sun.

(snatches out his ax to chop the flagstaff)
Then I must bring our yellow banner down!

(everyone wrestles him for the ax)

SUNG:
You Iron Ox! Before anything is straightened out you draw your ax to cut down the yellow flag. What's the meaning of this?

---

*From *Lai-chiang Chi* ed.

WU:
Brother, you're too direct and violent.

LI:

(sings)

Too direct, you say, and violent.
Then I must dress the scene to please.

(calls to others)

Come here, all you men.

SUNG:
What should they come here for?

LI:

(sings)

To attend a banquet for the happy families.

SUNG:
A banquet?

LI:

(sings)

Yes, we'll not let you off so lightly,
Oh, noble matchmaker-monk, Oh veritable Tripitaka,
Nor you, radiant bridegroom, true Robber Chih.*

SUNG:
Brother, where did you go to drink when you left the mountain, and who did you meet? I think he must have said a good deal about me! Tell us from the beginning, but tell it clearly.

---

*The patron saint of robbers. Here he has acquired the surname Liu.

(T'ang Hsiu-ts'ai)

LI:

(sings)
Not only did you carry off his fair flower of spring,
You now abandon him to die of grief, that old, white head at Meadowbridge.

SUNG:
There must be something hidden in all this.

LI:

(sings)
Plainly was it hidden, this deed!
And such grief for him to be severed, living, from his life.

(speaks)
Oh, Sung Chiang,

(sings)
He has just grievance against you.

SUNG:
Ah, so it's old Wang Lin's girl; and you say I took her? No need to say I didn't, but if I had he should be happy, not grieved. But you tell me about it and I'll listen.

(T'ao-t'ao ling)

LI:

(sings)
Sometimes the old man weakly weeps in his thatched shop;

(speaks)
He looks toward our mountain, crying his hatred for Sung Chiang,

(sings)
He restlessly rises to his feet
Then whimpers with wrath outside his wicker door,

(speaks)
Crying, "Oh, Man-t'ang Ch'iao";

(sings)
And sighingly sobs his suffering.

SUNG:
What does he do with his sorrow?

LI:

(sings)
He then gloomily looms by his wine vats,

(speaks)
Picks up a dipper, takes the straw lid from the crock, dips up cold wine, and drinks it in gulps;

(sings)
Then dully, dizzily drunk,
Clutching his scrap of matting,
He listlessly lays it out on his brick bed.

(speaks)
He goes outside again to look; sees no sign of her, and then,

(sings)
He sadly sinks to his bed
And snuffles and whines to sleep.
This will not do, Oh no,
This will not do!

SUNG:
What does he mean now?

LI:

(sings)

The old man says there are no sweet waters on our mountain,
Nor honor in our men.

SUNG:

Brother Hsüeh-chiu, it seems some footpads have dared assume our names and have done this thing. But we cannot be sure. Our brother should have brought some proof so we could be certain.

LI:

But I have, I have! Isn't this red sash proof?

SUNG:

Li K'uei, I'll make a wager with you now. If it was I who took that girl you win my head, the seat of all my senses. Now, what will you be willing to lose?

LI:

My wager will be a whole banquet for you, brother.

SUNG:

A banquet indeed! That's good, that is. You must match my wager.

LI:

All right, all right! Brother, if it wasn't you, then I'll willingly give you my own bullhead.*

---

*The impetuous Li K'uei also wagers his head in the drama *The Black Whirlwind* (689).

SUNG:
Since that's settled, we'll write it down as part of our military oaths and Hsüeh-chiu will hold it.

LI:
Do you mean to say the Gay Monk is going to be let off?

LU:
Leave my bald head out of this: it would bring you bad luck!

(They write out the military form for the wager.)

(Yi-sha)

LI:

(sings)
My fate's in the hands of a man powdered prettily
On both sides. One whose words make true become false in an instant.
Who acts like a dog but thinks like a wolf. Tiger at one end,
Snake at the other. I make no twigs grow on twigs to form a maze,
Nor carry awls in a sack;
None made you steal another's child to ease your itch—

SUNG:
Hear the Black Ox becoming crude.

LI:

(sings)
You must forgive my crudities
Which raise a single hillock on the flat plain.

SUNG:
Since I didn't do the deed, how can I forgive you?

LI:

(sings)

Your finger at heaven or scratches on the earth
May fool the spirits, but posture and gesture as you will
You'll not deceive me—not that you don't do it well and cleverly.

SUNG:
We'll go down the mountain together—

LI:

(sings)

Yes, down from the fort to the wineshop.
We'll know the facts,
See the truth, then
I'll cut off your head to close your mouth.

SUNG:
The Iron Ox tries insolence now!

LI:

(sings)

No, not insolence; but since we've made this deadly wager
Am I likely to stick at anything?
What's more, I do it for thirty-six of my sworn brothers.

(speaks)

Come here, all you men!

SUNG:
Now what are you doing?

LI:
Men, I am now leaving with Sung Chiang and Lu Chih-shen to go to Hsing-hua Village. As soon as old Wang Lin has said "yes," then you, you matchmaking Gay Monk, need not be surprised when my ax cleaves your skull nicely into two bowls—who told you to make off with young Man-t'ang Ch'iao anyway? But Sung Chiang I will leave till last, for I would like to serve him prostrate.

SUNG:
What? You'll serve me prostrate?

LI:
Absolutely prostrate! I shall take your collar in one hand and your belt in the other and then, buckety-bump, you'll be flat as a bed-board with feet! While you're prostrate I'll serve you—by hopping on to your chest, raising my broadax and bringing it down on your neck, kerchop!

(sings)
Though all your ancestors to the seventh generation
Leap from their graves and beseech me not to do it. *(exit)*

SUNG:
Well, he's gone. Guard, prepare two horses. Brother Chih-shen and I will leave the camp together and go to confront old Wang Lin.

(recites)
Wang Lin has mischief on misdeed bred,
Li K'uei's confounded "yes" with "no";
Since one of us will lose his head
To Hsing-hua Village both must go.

ACT III

(WANG LIN *enters weeping.)*

WANG:
Oh, my Man-t'ang Ch'iao, worry over you will be the death of me. I am Wang Lin, whose daughter was carried away by the two bandits. Today is the third day. Yesterday brother Li K'uei went up Mount Liang to search for Sung Chiang and Lu Chih-shen to bring them here for me to identify as the ones who did this deed. I guess I'd better have something for them to eat when they arrive. *(weeps)* Oh, Man-t'ang Ch'iao. They said they'd return her on the third day but will they or won't they? I shall die of worry.

(SUNG CHIANG, LU CHIH-SHEN, *and* LI K'UEI *enter.)*

SUNG:
Brother Chih-shen, let us hurry a little. Look at our friend: when we go on ahead, he comes right behind us, when we hang back, he stays close in front of us. I dare say he thinks we'll escape.

LI:
Wait up for me! Thinking of getting to your in-law's makes you eager, eh?

SUNG:
There goes that devil with his riddles again, do you hear, brother Chih-shen? Never fear, when Wang Lin doesn't identify us, I'll take care of you, Li K'uei.

(Chi-hsien-pin)

LI:

(sings)
Skirting the blue-green foothills I see afar
The tavern's banner signaling in the wind, and think

(speaks)
No matter; I've come with you two to Hsing-hua Village and,

(Hsiao-yao Lo)

(sings)
I'll hew me a road as each mountain demands.

LU:
You should have said, "I'll build a bridge when I come to the river," brother.

LI:

(sings)
Ah, you who merely sailed a boat with the stream
Would not now let me burn my bridge when I've crossed it.

*(*SUNG CHIANG *advances.)*

He likes this ill and will throw his weight about.

SUNG:
Do you not remember the oath of brotherhood we swore on the mountain, the oath of eight salutations?

LI:

(sings)

You, my brother, mention our past bond,
Solemnized by the eightfold bow, that now seems
Only a bright bottle-gourd—all shell and no meat.
Scarce can I suppress scornful laughter.
What is it you wish? To match your talents with mine?*
To contest sensitivity and readiness to shame?

(speaks)

Here is Wang Lin's door. Brother, say nothing till I've called him out.

SUNG:

I understand.

LI:

(calling out)

Old Wang, Old Wang, open up. (WANG LIN *nods and dozes.)* Open up, I say. I've brought your daughter back!

WANG:

(waking with a start)

She's truly here? I'm opening the door!

(embraces LI K'UEI*)*

Oh, my Man-t'ang Ch'iao—ugh! It's not her!

(Ts'u Hu-lu)

LI:

(sings)

Poor fellow, once he earned the nickname "Half-barrel,"
Now here he is, stupid on just a spoonful.
'Tis just the loss of Man-t'ang Ch'iao
That's added such weight to his burden of years.

---

*Almost identical line on 926, including inversion for rhyme.

(speaks)

I called twice to open the door. The third time I said we'd brought his daughter. He threw open the door and hugged my black neck, crying Man-t'ang Ch'iao!

(sings)

Old one, you've been so constantly in grief.
And now I've got you rubbing your eyes,
Wiping your tears and sobbing again.

(speaks)

Brothers, go into the shop and be seated. *(They enter and sit.)* He's an old man. Don't you frighten him now. I'm going to have him identify you. Old Wang, come here and see if you recognize them.

WANG:

Yes, I want to.

SUNG:

Old man, come close. I am Sung Chiang, and I must tell you that Li K'uei and I have bet our heads on which one you will identify as the one who stole your daughter.

LI:

Go, look at him, old Wang: isn't he the one?

WANG:

(looking carefully at SUNG CHIANG*)*

No, it wasn't this one.

SUNG:

Just as I said!

LI:

Wait till he's taken a good look, brother; don't glare at him and scare him. How can he recognize you if he's scared? Come, old Wang, the two of us have bet our heads because of your daughter.

Isn't that one your "in-law," the stealer of Man-t'ang Ch'iao, Sung Chiang?

WANG:

(looking carefully again, wags his head)

No, he's not.

SUNG:

You see!

(Yao-p'ien)

LI:

(sings)

Why did you not sit still and bow your head?
What made you widen your eyes and stare him down?
You are so hard and haughty in your power, Sung Chiang,
That you must glare and scare him witless.
If this is aiding heaven's way, then I am happy
To leave mercy to my pitiless broadax.

(speaks)

Old Wang, come and look at this bald one. He's the go-between Lu Chih-shen. See if you don't recognize him.

LU:

Yes, and make it quick!

WANG:

(now looks carefully at LU*)*

No, no, he's not one. One of the two who did it was good looking and tall, but your Sung Chiang is dark and short. The other had a mangy scalp and sparse hair, but this one is a tonsured monk. No, no—

LU:

You see, brother, I was right.

LI:
You bald rascal, why did you have to yawp at him just as he was about to identify you?

(Yao-p'ien)

(sings)
Everyone knows you, Lu Chih-shen of Chen-kuan
And knows you took to the greenwood having left Mount Wu-t'ai.
If he but fingered your face in the dark he would know who it was.
When you bellowed your thunderclap
You turned the old simpleton's wits upside down.
Now he'd not remember any name.

(speaks)
He was just about to recognize you.

(sings)
See him now wagging his head and tilting his brain in wasted conjecture.

SUNG:
Since he has said we're not the ones who did it, brother Chih-shen, we'll return to the mountain and wait till the Iron Ox comes back to settle up.

LI:
Old Wang, my son, try again.

WANG:
I said they're not the ones and they're not. What good would another try be?

(LI K'UEI *raises his hand to strike* WANG LIN.)

Mercy, take pity or you'll kill an old man!

(Hou-t'ing Hua)

LI:

(sings)

I'll beat this old clod who asked for a purge when his guts were loose.
I'm bound I'll thump his pot and break his ladle.

SUNG:

Boy, bring the horses. Brother Lu and I are returning to the mountain.

LI:

You say let's return to the camp, but I say, brother, please sit a while and let him try again carefully.

(sings)

My brother cries ready the horses, back to camp—

(speaks)

Ai! Oh brother, this brings the shame home, but,

(sings)

Like one stuck on a plank-bridge with his mule
Here I stand and suffocate with rage—
But the sauce-pot's spilled. My rope's cut short at the windlass
And won't draw water from the well.
My barrel's empty, my dipper's smashed, my cleaver's broken in two.
Oh, but I long to hear the crackle of your thatched
Gourd burning down. You who lead men into pitfalls, enrage me so
I hop and bounce like a stranded minnow.

But how can I do what I want?
"The young must be protected, the aged respected."

SUNG:
Come, brother Chih-shen, back to camp.

(recites)
Head wagered in an empty cause
Ridiculous warrior, errant knight—
Return to the camp and stretch your neck
To meet my ax's heavy bite. *(exeunt)*

LI:
(with a sigh)
This time I was wrong.

(Lang li lai sha)

(sings)
And now I believe what is oftenest said,
"How hard to know the heart of a man;
For a lamp casts only shadows on its own base."
My eyes are opened now and see the difference between
The noble and the base.
Heedless, I wagered my head with Sung Chiang,
And now "the hope of three generations" has found
His own tongue heavy enough to cut off his head. *(exit)*

WANG:
Brother Li K'uei has left. To be sure, he brought two men to me to identify if I could—one was the real Sung Chiang and the other the actual Lu Chih-shen—but neither was one of those who took my daughter. May heaven smite those who did steal her!—Oh, how I long for you, Man-t'ang Ch'iao.

(Enter SUNG KANG, *sneezing, accompanied by* LU CHIH-EN *and the girl.)*

SUNG:

I'm sneezing and my ears are hot; someone must be talking about me. Well, here we are in Hsing-hua Village. Where is my "father-in-law"? You see, we promised to bring your daughter back in three days and here we are.

WANG:

(sees her, embraces her, and weeps)

Oh, Man-t'ang Ch'iao!

SUNG:

You see, we weren't lying. Exactly three days and your beloved daughter is back.

WANG:

Many thanks, your honor, accept my praises. Because this is a poor household and has been much upset, there is no wine ready to toast you. If you'll go to my daughter's room and have a drink of plain wine, I will kill a hen tomorrow and entertain you.

LU:

Old Wang, in our camp we've more than enough of meat and wine. I'll order one of the boys to bring you twenty or thirty fat lambs and forty or fifty loads of wine.

WANG:

Thank you, your honor. Unhappily I've no gift for the go-between: a dreadful thing.

SUNG:

Come, let us to the lady's room for a drink. *(exeunt)*

WANG:

So those two thieves aren't leaders from Liang-shan P'o. They stole my daughter and both of them have cracked her jug. Well, let that be. But what a pity brother Li K'uei, always a hot-hearted fellow, has bet his head on the matter. There is no time to dally. I'll fill two bowls, one with warm and one with cold wine, and help those two thieves get dead drunk. Then tonight I'll wait till they're asleep and quietly slip up Mount Liang, report the whole thing to Sung Chiang, and save Li K'uei. That ought to work.

(recites)

Why does Old Wang Lin walk by night
Up Liang-shan? Because he must requite
The kindnesses of Li K'uei.
Yet I fear
That false Sung Chiang's evil deeds
Will bring the valorous Li K'uei here
And send Man-t'ang Ch'iao untimely into widow's weeds.

ACT IV

(SUNG CHIANG, LU CHIH-SHEN, *and* WU HSUEH-CHIU *enter leading attendants.)*

SUNG:
I am Sung Chiang. Brother Hsüeh-chiu, the insolence of Li K'uei was insufferable. I bet my head against his, and now we've been to Hsing-hua Village and been identified as innocent of the abduction, brother Lu and I have returned to await Li K'uei's arrival—at which time he'll lose his head. Guard, go to the crest and keep a lookout. It's about time for Li K'uei to arrive.

(Enter LI K'UEI *carrying a fagot of thorn branches.)**

*See *YCH* 912 for another example of thorn-carrying as a ritual of apology.

LI:
Oh, Black Whirlwind, how needlessly you have acted, losing your life for another. Having no other way left to me, I have cut this fagot of thorns to carry back to camp and see brother Sung Chiang.

(Hsin-shui ling)

(sings)
I've arrived in my present plight only because
I pursued it. I needlessly wagered my head against
My brother.
I've thrown off my red coat and taken off my worn sandals.
I must think—

(speaks)
When I return to camp, my brother will want my head at once.

(Chu-ma t'ing)

(sings)
But how can I hand over this familiar old thing
Atop my neck?
I'd rather give up my body!

(speaks)
This steep green cliff overhanging the bottomless stream below. If I were to leap it would swallow me up—even ten Black Whirlwinds could disappear into it.

(sings)
Time and again I've thrown myself down that cliff,
But still the camp draws nearer.
Each step is the last one up to the altar of terrified souls.
When I am dead, who will fix a marker
On my tomb naming my native heath?
And who will chant beside my spirit tablet
To pray for me from the land of the quick?

Would that a man could be cut asunder, yet leave
A whole corpse for burial—
Ah, that would be the thing!

(Chiao Cheng-p'a)

I've come to the gates of the palisade and see within
The men drawn up in ranks like migrant geese.

(speaks)
Before, when I arrived

(sings)
The sentry stood to and hurried toward me,

(speaks)
But today,

(sings)
He acts the simpleton and stares right through me.

(peers surreptitiously about him)

(speaks)
Oh, brother Sung Kung-ming and all the men have gone to the hall.

(sings)
He faces the heroes assembled there.
Each and all sit gravely and with chins firm set.
I shall speak to the point and say: here stands a loutish
Lien P'o* to confess his crimes,
And he should die!

*A general of the Warring States period, and the most famous person to have used the ritual baring of the back to beg pardon.

*(*SUNG CHIANG *and* LI K'UEI *see each other.)*

SUNG:
You have arrived, brother, but what do you carry on your back?

LI:
My brother, I cut this bundle of thorny sticks to ask you to beat me for my moment of stupidity which caused this all to happen.

(Ch'en tsui Tung-feng)

(sings)
I call upon by brother, Herald of Justice,
To see to my punishment. Give Li K'uei a feast
Of thorns: first, because we are brothers, and second
To reduce my awful debt of blood and dissolution!
Say not that I fear death and burial, but rather,
If you don't thrash this stubborn fool until
The full moon rises, he'll never change his stripes!

SUNG:
We wagered our heads. There was no mention of beating. Guard, take Li K'uei to the Hall of Justice to be beheaded and report back to me!

LI:
Brother Hsüeh-chiu, intercede for me! Chih-shen, plead for me!

(They pantomime intercession for LI K'UEI.*)*

SUNG:
No! I will not beat him. This is a military oath. All I want is his head.

LI:
What did you say, brother?

SUNG:
I said I'll not beat you, I only want your head.

LI:
But are you sure, brother? Each blow causes pain in a flogging, but beheading—one stroke and it's over and isn't painful at all.

SUNG:
I won't beat you.

LI:
Well, if you won't, I thank you. *(starts to go)*

SUNG:
Where are you going?

LI:
My brother said he wouldn't beat me so I . . .

SUNG:
We wagered our heads and I will have your head, the seat of all senses!

LI:
Very well, then, so be it! But suicide is better than execution. If I may borrow my brother's sword I shall cut my throat.

SUNG:
All right. Guard, give him my sword.

LI:

(taking the sword)

Why, this was mine! Well I remember the day I was out with you driving game for the hunt. Alongside the highroad were people gathered saying that a snake lay across the path. I pushed my way to the front and found that it was no snake, but a perfect T'ai A* of a sword. And I gave it to you, brother, to hang at your waist. Some days ago I thought I heard the hum of a sword. I said to myself someone will be slain—never thinking that it might be me.

(Pu-pu chiao)

(sings)

My heart startled when I heard *leng-leng*
The cry of the sword.

(speaks)

And *what* a sword!

(sings)

To blow a hair against its edge is to cleave it†
Asunder. With such a weapon one would shear
A coin in half as he would a stalk of hemp.

(speaks)

I am remembering ten years of friendship and close feelings now ended.

(sings)

Enough of former feelings and off
With my well-beloved head.

(WANG LIN rushes on shouting.)

---

*A proper name for the sword which is as famous in China as Excalibur is in English-speaking countries.

†For the same cliché indicating keenness, see 904.

WANG:

Stay the knife! I have to report to your honor. Those two villains who stole my daughter have come back! I've got them soaking drunk at my place. I came straightway to tell you. Please be my champion against them.

SUNG:

Li K'uei, I'll let you go on this condition: if you take these two footpads, I'll use your merit in that to absolve you of the other matter. If you don't take them, you'll answer for both. Will you go?

LI:

(laughing)

Oh, this scratches just the place that itches! I'll take them like two turtles in a jug and bring them here in my hand.

WU:

Nonetheless, they have two horses ready. How could you take them both? If by chance you did not do it, the reputation of Liang-shan P'o would suffer. Brother Lu, go with Li K'uei and help.

LU:

He called me a bald go-between more times than once and had Wang Lin try to identify me time and again. What kind of an idea is this? If he can do it, let him go take them both himself. He'll wait a long time till I help him!

HSUEH:

Think of our watchword, "Assembled Justice," brother, and don't let a small grudge harm a greater goal.

SUNG:

That's the right of it. Brother Chih-shin, go with him and help bring in those two masquerading thieves.

LU:
If that is your order, I'll go with him. *(exeunt)*

*(*LI K'UEI, LU CHIH-SHEN, *and* WANG LIN *enter.)*

LU:
What wine! We were both drunk last night. The sun is already three rods high in the sky—I wonder where your "father-in-law" is. Was he stiff too?

LI:
You thieves! Here's your father-in-law. *(strikes* SUNG KANG*)*

SUNG:
We don't even know your name and you hit us!

LI:
When I do tell you, you'll wet your pants. I'm old Papa Black from Liang-shan P'o and this is the real Gay Monk, Lu Chih-shen. *(He hits them.)*

(Ch'iao P'ai-erh)

(sings)
Borrow the devil's name and buy his troubles.
Today heaven has caught you up!
Never will Man-t'ang Ch'iao be mistress of your
Lustful camp. And what is to be done is not
The fault of Papa Black's black anger.

SUNG:
These are the real ones! We haven't a chance, run, run!

LI:
Where are you going? *(catches up with them and hits them again)*

(sings)
I'll beat you curs till your skin's scragged,
Your bones broken and your flesh flayed.
And could you leap right through the blue
Veil of heaven, my hand would catch you
On the other side. You—you—you,
A fine Lu Chih-shen you are, who never abstain
From meat! And you, a Herald of Justice lost
To lechery! Now you'll confront those men themselves.
And from you let there be no cry of outrage;
Not brutality, but calamity of your own making
Has found you out. *(catches hold of both)*

(speaks)
Now we've got the thieves!

*(*WANG LIN *and his daughter bow deeply to* LI K'UEI.*)*

LU:
Save your bows, old one. Come to our camp and present them tomorrow to Sung Chiang, our leader. *(Exit* LU *and* LI *guarding the thieves.)*

WANG:
There they go, taking those villains with them, and we are rid of a mouthful of foul breath. Tomorrow, my child, we'll lead a lamb and carry wine up Liang-shan to thank Sung Chiang, the chief. *(Daughter pantomimes shaking with sobs.)* Come, my dear, don't carry on so. What good is a thief like that? Bide your time till I can pick out a good man to marry you to. *(exeunt)*

*(*SUNG CHIANG *and* WU HSUEH-CHIU *enter leading attendants.)*

SUNG:
Brother Li and Lu Chih-shen went to Hsing-hua Village a long time ago, my brother: I wonder why they haven't returned. Perhaps I'd best send someone from here to meet them.

HSUEH:
It won't matter where those thieves have gone, you won't have to send anyone else. They'll be here soon.

GUARD:
I beg to report, brother, two of our leaders have returned victorious.

(Enter LI K'UEI, LU CHIH-SHEN, SUNG KANG, *and* LU CHIH-EN.*)*

LI:
We've brought the two devils in and now wait for you to pronounce sentence, brother.

SUNG:
A fine Sung Chiang! A likely Lu Chih-shen! How dared you masquerade in our names and soil the honor of our families? Guards, bind them to the flagpole, cut out their hearts and livers and we'll have them with our wine. Then hang up their heads as a warning to all their kind.

GUARD:
Yes sir. *(exit taking the thieves)*

(Li-ting-yen Sha)

LI:

(sings)

In a green pool of shade the feast will be set
Beneath the flagpole, fat lambs
Will be carved. When cups are drained
They will fill again.
Their eyes are out, limbs hang useless,
Their hearts and livers torn grisly from them.

I snatched a bone from the maw of the tiger,
Plucked a pearl from the chin of the dragon
And took it upon myself to bring them ruin.

(speaks)

Brother Chih-shen,

(sings)

I must absolve you: never were you a go-between
Of violence.

(speaks)

Brother Sung-ming,

(sings)

I must let you off: no yearning to paint eyebrows
Possessed you.

SUNG:

Today we hold a feast in the Hall of Justice to reward Li K'uei and Lu Chih-shen for their deed.

(recites)

The will of heaven was served by Sung Chiang
And greenwood justice done by his men.
Li K'uei's sword was drawn in a cause,
Uniting Wang Lin and his child again.

T'I-MU. Wang Lin of Apricot Village asks justice.

CHENG-MING. The Black Whirlwind of Liang-shan P'o carries thorn fagots.*

*Couplets (called "the topic" and "the proper title") such as these appear at the end of nearly every Yuan playscript we have. There is much disagreement over what they were for and whether they were performed. For summary see Shih (1976), p. 31. Anyone wishing to stage a *tsa-chü* is at liberty to treat them any way he wishes.

DRAMATIS PERSONAE

CHANG T'IEN-CHUEH,	*Honest official in exile*
TS'UI-LUAN,	*His daughter from whom he is separated by shipwreck*
TS'UI WEN-YUAN,	*Old fisherman who rescues Ts'ui-luan*
TS'UI T'UNG,	*The old fisherman's nephew to whom he betroths Ts'ui-luan*
OFFICIAL,	*Imperial examiner who gives his daughter (the ch'a-tan) to Ts'ui T'ung to wed*
CH'A-TAN,	*The Official's daughter*

As with so many Yuan dramas this one is an amalgam of history and legend. There was a Chang T'ien-chueh exiled in Southern Sung times, but the tribulations that he and his daughter undergo here come partly from item #14 in the *Ch'ing-shih** (which revolves around some verse written on the wall of a posthouse by a young woman) and the composer's imagination. The story still remains popular, and there is an act in Peking opera of today called "At the Lin-chiang Posthouse" which is based on this Yuan drama.

---

*A collection of literary language fiction edited by Feng Meng-lung (ca 1620?).

Rain on the Hsiao-Hsiang (*YCH* #15)

(attributed to Yang Hsien-chih, *fl.* 1246)

(Mo, CHANG T'IEN-CHÜEH, *cheng-tan,* TS'UI-LUAN, *and household servant,* HSING-ERH, *enter.)*

CHANG:

(recites)

One heart devoted to work for home and state,
Two brows knit by care for temple and shrine.
Yet light and footless clouds the sun itself can't penetrate.
Exile from Ch'ang-an's saddened stauncher hearts than mine.

I am surnamed Chang. My given name is Shang-yang and my courtesy name, T'ien-chueh.* After I passed my examinations I was employed in successive posts until, thanks to the Sage Generosity, I achieved the office of Righteous Counsellor. Then, because those favorites who wore the highest hats—Yang Chien, T'ung Kuan, and Ts'ai Ching†—were oppressing the people I was faithful to by nature and convictions, I spoke openly against them.

---

*He also appears as a character in *WP* #113. In *Hsüan-ho Yi-shih,* a certain T'ien-chüeh is banished to Sheng-chou. See *Sung-jen P'ing-hua Ssu-chung* ed., p. 62. (ed. Yang Chia-lo, T'aipei, 1956).

†These are three of the four infamous counsellors of the last, weak emperor of Southern Sung, Hui-tsung.

My counsels were many times ignored and the Sage Presence has now sent me to "put my horse to pasture" in Chiang-chou. Unhappily, my wife died many years ago and left me an only daughter whose child-name is Ts'ui-luan. She is eighteen years of age and betrothed to no one.

Since we left the capital we have been wearied each day by our travels, but we have finally reached this ford on the river Huai. Since our time is limited, Hsing-erh, call the Guardian of the Ford for me.

HSING-ERH:
Very well sir.

(Enter ching *dressed as Guardian of the Ford.)*

CHING:

(recites)

All the hair is worn from my thighs,
But whiskers grow on my chops.
Fast as a shooting star or lightning flash,
I make my appointed stops
Along both banks, keeping watch and ward
For this is the duty of the Guard of the Ford.

I am the Ford Guard. The gentleman at the rest-house has called and I don't know what he wants of me but I'd better go see. Honored Uncle, report and say the Guardian has arrived.

*(*HSING-ERH *reports.)*

CHANG:
Bring him here.

HSING-ERH:
Here he is.

(They pantomime seeing one another.)

CHING:
Your honor called? I wait on your orders.

CHANG:
Guardian, I am under Imperial Orders to take myself and family to Chiang-chou where I am to reside. There are strict limits to the time of my travel. If you do not prepare me a boat, you will certainly cause me to exceed my allotted travel time. Whatever the circumstances, I must have a boat this very day.

CHING:
Your honor, the Spirit of the Huai differs from the genies of most places because he demands three animal sacrifices—cow, hog, and sheep, as well as paper gold, silver, and paper money. After you have burned your incantation to the God and you find he is pleased, you can set out by boat, but if he is not pleased, wild winds arise from every quarter, waves roll, and the billows tumble in such a way that no one dares launch a craft. May I inquire, your honor, have you performed the sacrifices?

TS'UI-LUAN:
If this is how things really are, papa, give him some money and have him arrange the sacrifices right away.*

CHANG:
Child, you don't understand. Your father is an appointed minister of the state and this is one of the official gods of the country; what need has it for more than the regular sacrifice? Have you not heard that "to deny the gods and then sacrifice to them is simply toadying"?†

(recites)

The empire of Sung is not the rude state of Ch'u
Nor was the clear Huai like the Mi-lo ever.
I wager my lifetime of faithful service
Will see me across this windy, tumbling river.‡

---

*Note the rare occurrence, where a character speaks a line before he or she has introduced himself to the audience.

†Not very apposite but pleasingly literary, it would seem.

‡This continues his demonstration of literary knowledge. The poem is by T'ang Chieh of Sung times and almost unaltered. The whole incident is based on T'ang's experience.

(speaks)
Guard, prepare me a boat this instant!

CHING:
I've got the boat; now don't blame me if something unexpected happens.

(pantomimes launching boat)

HSING-ERH:
Ya! The wind and waves are rising! What shall we do? The storm is sinking the boat—Help! Help!

*(*CHANG *exits.)*

CHING:
(rescuing the girl)
I've saved his daughter, now to reach his honor. *(exit)*

TS'UI-LUAN:
What terrible perils! Oh, papa, what trials! The Huai overturned our boat and if it hadn't been for the Ford Guard I would have perished. I don't even know if papa is still alive—the Guard has dived again and left me here by myself. What will I do?

(Supporting role, elderly male, TS'UI WEN-YUAN, *enters and sees* TS'UI-LUAN.*)*

WEN-YUAN:
Good heavens, young lady, where do you come from? And tell me who are you?

TS'UI-LUAN:

I am Chang T'ien-chüeh's daughter, Ts'ui-luan, and I am eighteen years old. Papa was sent to take residence in Chiang-chou so we had to make this crossing of the Huai. We did not heed the Ford Guard and made no sacrifice to the genie of the place, but directly launched our boat onto the river. As we had been warned they would, the waves and wind suddenly arose and overturned the boat. Had it not been for the Ford Guard rescuing me, I would never have survived.

WEN-YUAN:

As I watch this young lady it becomes plain that she has never known the sting of poverty and she is certainly from an official family. I will wait with you here for a while and if his honor your father is still alive I will return you to him immediately.

TS'UI-LUAN:

How long have we been waiting? Why doesn't the Guardian of the Ford return? For one thing, I can hardly stand these wet clothes on me any longer and, for another, it has gotten darker and I have no idea where papa has gone. Oh, heaven, am I destined to die here in distress?

WEN-YUAN:

Young lady, I am Ts'ui Wen-yuan, fisherman of the Huai river, and my home is not far from here. If you're willing to be my adopted daughter, then you are welcome to come live with me. Some other day we may locate his honor your father and I will see to it that father and daughter are reunited—how does that sound to you?

TS'UI-LUAN:

Good, kind sir, if you will not disdain me for accepting, I am very willing to become your daughter.

WEN-YUAN:

Since that's settled, follow me; we're going home.

(Hsien-lü, Tuan-cheng Hao 55755)

TS'UI-LUAN:
I wonder where my father is now?

(sings)

Just as I sink beneath the urgent flood
Desperate thrusts bring me to this strand.
Sodden, soaking wet and dripping garments head to foot.
Had there been no kindly fisher offering his home
Spiteful fate would have granted me no hope.

ACT I

*(*CHANG T'IEN-CHUEH *enters, leading* HSING-ERH.*)*

CHANG:

(recites)

A boat to ferry past the river Huai,
A heart too hasty hurrying its trip,
Could it have thought that wind and wave would rise
And call down grief enough to fill the sky?

I am Chang T'ien-chüeh who disregarded the Ford Guard and whose boat capsized in midcrossing. I do not know what happened to my daughter, Ts'ui-luan. I have set out in person to find her but the court's strict limits upon me press me left and right. What shall I do? For the present I will leave enquiries along my route saying that anyone who gives shelter to my daughter, Ts'ui-luan, will be rewarded with ten ounces of flower-marked silver. Then, when I have reached Chiang-chou I will send men back to search slowly over the route again—this surely makes good sense. Oh Ts'ui-luan, my child. I die of grief for you. *(exit)*

(*Enter* TS'UI WEN-YUAN.)

WEN-YUAN:
What did I know of joy before this morning? What passed as happiness before today? I am Ts'ui Wen-yuan and after I returned from a visit to my brother I found a young woman—the daughter of his honor Chang T'ien-chüeh—whose father was traveling to Chiang-chou to take up official residence. They reached the Huai crossing and paying no heed to the words of the Ford Guard, they did not sacrifice to the god. They launched their boat and in midstream a great wind arose and mighty waves surged up oversetting their craft. We don't know where her father has got to, but the child's destiny is somehow part of mine, so I adopted her, brought her to my home and we have become very close—a single family instead of two people. Each day, one way or another, we make out and I don't resent the fact that we're poor. This may be because I have done a good deed. Today I'll not go out to fish. I'll stay home and see who may come this way.

(TS'UI T'UNG *enters*.)

TS'UI T'UNG:
(*recites*)
Yellowed scrolls, a fusty scholar, beneath the flickering light,
The Nine Classics, the Triple Annals ready to recite.
When at last his name appears on the Golden List
Then squandering his manhood will finally seem right.

I am Ts'ui T'ung, also called Tien-shih, whose family has lived for generations in Honan. While still young I trained to be a scholar and read quite widely in the *Odes* and the *Book of History*—ten years spent cribbing and cramming to earn the pleasures and perquisites of one official post. I am on my way to the capital to sit for the examinations and now have got as far as the Huai River crossing. My father's elder brother, Ts'ui Wen-yuan, lives hereabouts. I might as well visit him now that I'm here. This is my uncle's gate—I'll call him. Is anyone there?

WEN-YUAN:
Who's calling? I'll open the door. *(pantomimes asking)* Who is it?

TS'UI T'UNG:
It's your nephew, Ts'ui Tien-shih. On my way to the imperial examinations, I stopped here on purpose to see you, uncle.

WEN-YUAN:
My dear boy, come right into the house! How is your father?

TS'UI T'UNG:
Thanks to you, uncle, he's very well.

WEN-YUAN:
Now don't you go running off. You must stay a couple of days.

TS'UI T'UNG:
Thank you, uncle.

WEN-YUAN:
Well now, are you married yet?

TS'UI T'UNG:
Ah, I'll have to quote you what the ancients say, uncle, "First a name and then a wife." In that case, you see, I couldn't have married yet.

WEN-YUAN::
The boy seems to have a bit of talent in him and i'm certain he'll get an official post. I've a mind to betroth my daughter to him. I wonder how she would like the idea. I'll call her and, when she's seen my nephew, I'll make my proposal. Ts'ui'luan, my child, come here.

(TS'UI-LUAN, *female lead, enters.*)

TS'UI-LUAN:
I am Ts'ui-luan and ever since I became separated from my father I have had no word of him. I owe Old Ts'ui much for adopting me—he has treated me as though I were his own daughter—but while I live here without the slightest worry I wonder each day where my father can be.

(Hsien-lü, Tien Chiang Ch'un 44345)

(sings)
I raise my eyes and worry fills them.
Father, now that you are gone,
Can I trace you?
Oh, the long, long river,
Has it drowned the years you had left to live?

(Hun-chiang Lung 4744773 (33))

Had it not been for
The fisherman who saved me
I might better
Have surrendered myself and floated east on the spring-swollen stream.
As of now
I live my borrowed time each day.
But papa,
I still don't know if you swam or drowned.
Within the pulses of my heart dwell the sorrows of a thousand years
And locked between my furrowed brows lie all the world's miseries.
My gratitude, kindly fisherman, who gave me love
Who did not see me
As someone from the outside world
But took me
Straight to his breast as his natural child.

(pantomimes seeing WEN-YUAN*)*

(speaks)
You called, father; what is it?

WEN-YUAN:
Child, I have a nephew, Ts'ui Tien-shih, who was on his way to the capital to make his name but, since the road lay by my door, he has stopped to visit me. Come over here and meet him.

TS'UI-LUAN:
Yes, father.

WEN-YUAN:
Nephew, you could not know this, but just recently I adopted a daughter whose name is Ts'ui-luan, and I have called her away from her quarters especially to meet you. Now don't you shy away! I want you to have a good look at her.

TS'UI T'UNG:
Call her over, I should be glad to meet her.

WEN-YUAN:
Ts'ui-luan, come here and present yourself properly to your elder brother.

TS'UI-LUAN:
A thousand blessings, brother.

TS'UI T'UNG:
(aside)
A fine woman!

(Yu Hu-lu 737773375)

TS'UI-LUAN:

(sings)

He clasps his delicate hands which will climb to the moon* or pluck the cassia.

TS'UI T'UNG:

Cousin, forgive my not recognizing you and paying my respects so seldom.

TS'UI-LUAN:

(sings)

I mean to go forward but retreat instead.†
The best I can do is
Make my flustered obeisance, only half-concealing a deep blush.

TS'UI T'UNG:

Cousin, I was destined for this meeting.

TS'UI-LUAN:

(sings)

I look and
See the elegant grace of his form, the delicate charm of his face.

TS'UI T'UNG:

Cousin, I cannot tell when we may meet again.

---

*Two euphemisms for succeeding in examinations.

†This is certainly four beats instead of the *cheng-ke's* three, but the *Ku ch'ü chai* edition and *Liu-chih* edition both have wording different from *YCH*.

TS'UI-LUAN:

(sings)

And see the warmth and goodness of his nature, the breadth and depth of his sentiments.
But stay such praise or
P'an An's face will be devoid of charm
And Ts'ao Tzu-chien*
Will be wanting in worth—
Even his
White scholar's shirt is smoothly stitched with love-duck clasps—
From head to toe
Nothing about him less than highest style.

TS'UI T'UNG:
Cousin, I came here first to find out how my uncle was and then bid him goodbye since I am off to sit for the imperial examinations.

(T'ien-hsia Lo 757555)

TS'UI-LUAN:

(sings)

Then I wish you may
Soon seize the highest rank; first place in the academy.
Elegant style
And good fortune to match!
A Graduate's Feast in Ch'iung-lin Gardens is the harvest of youth's ambition.
The name upon the roster exudes its own perfume,
The dress and how it's worn bespeak the lettered man
Who now prepares
To sport the palace flower and drink imperial wine.

---

*A man famous for his beauty and another for his talents.

WEN-YUAN:
I am already old and have no one but this girl that I've not got a husband for. My nephew is quite clever, I think, and I'm of a mind to give the girl to him to wife. I'll ask him about it. Tien-shih, have you married?

TS'UI T'UNG:
No. I've no wife—why do you keep asking, uncle?

WEN-YUAN:
Well, here I am at my age with only a daughter and I see that you're a serious type, intelligent and stylish, certain to get an official post; so I want to ask you to be my son-in-law and long after you've laid me to rest a little fame may come to my family. Tien-shih, let's say that she's the "virtuous young lady" who's a match for "the prince,"* eh? What do you say?

TS'UI T'UNG:
I respectfully obey your commands, uncle, and am much obliged to you.

TS'UI-LUAN:
Father, to have saved my life is quite enough. Why should you even want to arrange me a marriage?

(Tsui Chung T'ien 55756447)

(sings)
You not only
Rescued me from the maw of the river Huai
You now
"See me up the highest peak in Ch'u."

---

*Allusion to the first song in the *Book of Odes*.

(speaks, pantomimes turning aside, weeping)

Oh, my father,

(sings)

Your death or survival, even these remain clouded, impossible to know;
What hope, then,
That you could hear a go-between has made my alliance.

WEN-YUAN:

Why don't you say something to him, Ts'ui-luan? "Fate is fate in any season, Nothing happens save for a reason"—I wouldn't have you miss your chance, my child.

TS'UI-LUAN:

(sings)

Though you
Insist marriages are things of destiny,
Yet
It is difficult to answer in a single word
Because of my many
Storms of tears and clouds of worry.

WEN-YUAN::

Ts'ui-luan, this is a happy occasion, but you are crying. Stop that right now! Why, my nephew seems to have a whole head full of learning. He will certainly become an official. That's why I'm giving you to him. You know the saying, "A woman grown should not remain at home." How many young girls do you find taking care of the old bodies at home? No, you just do as I say. Today each of you must observe the ritual so that the betrothal will be completed.

(Chin Chan-erh 33655554)

TS'UI-LUAN:

(sings)

Always he has had
The greatest respect for scholars
And now he wants to
Bind me in marriage to one.
So he will
Risk the proverbial "trouble coming in through a mouth too often open."
He says, instead,
"A woman grown *should* leave home."
It seems he's given my promise for me.
Yet how can I lift my head and look at them?
For even though my heart agrees with him
My face still blushes wildly of itself.

WEN-YUAN:

(pantomimes pulling girl and boy into position to make obeisance)

There, this day is an auspicious one for the betrothal. Nephew, go now to the capital and take your examination for an official position, and just as soon as you have any sort of appointment and take up your post, remember where a bit of gratitude is due.

TS'UI-LUAN:

I thank you, father; I worry only that Master Ts'ui will go away and then forget us.

TS'UI T'UNG:

If I forget you, may the heavens refuse to cover me, the earth to support me, and sun and moon to shine upon me.

TS'UI-LUAN:
Master Ts'ui, since you must go, go, but write us as often as you can.

TS'UI T'UNG:
I understand, don't worry.

(Chuan-sha 555753447477)

TS'UI-LUAN:
(sings)
In his breast
Lie the Long and Huai rivers rolled up,
His
Sword flashes with stars from the Great Dipper;*
My father has
Mated me with a phoenix; matched me with a noble mate.
Thinking of you
Walking all alone a thousand li through mountain barriers
This night, how hard it will be to reach you by dream.
When you arrive at
The Hall of Complete Justice
And have
Won the coveted tortoise-head prize
I fear only that
You will swear never to return till the Golden Roster lists your name.
Oh, may it never happen
That your heart should forswear the oath of your mouth,
And don't quickly
Forsake kin and forget kindness.

(speaks)
Oh, Master Ts'ui,

---

*Clichés indicative of great talent. See *Chien-fu Pei, YCHS,* vol. 4, p. 14a, and *WP* #115, p. 223.

(sings)
Do not abandon me
To lean on my wicker gate and fix my stare on ships that never come home.

TS'UI T'UNG:
I will take my leave, now, uncle, for I've a long way to go. *(pantomimes bowing goodbye)*

WEN-YUAN:
Nephew, I wish only that you make a name for yourself soon, then fulfill your contract with my child, Ts'ui-luan, and make her mistress of an official's mansion.

(recites)
We shall wait till spring sends you home for new clothes—
To complete a good marriage takes but a moment of time.

TS'UI T'UNG:*

(recites)
Ch'ang Ngo, Moon Goddess, is fond of young men.
Should her great moon-palace be too hard to climb? *(exeunt)*

ACT II

(Enter Ching as the examination official, leading his servant.)

*Not in *Ku-ch'ü Chai* ed. which includes the next scene as part of Act I. *Ku-ch'ü Chai* often differs from all other editions of a playscript.

OFFICIAL:

(recites)

To the Spring Office,* they say, belong the peach and the pear,
Yet my gate garden craves a richer crop.
For composition I have little flair—
If my scale-pans still weigh gold, should I care?

(speaks)

My surname is Chao and my given name Ch'ien. A lot of busybodies call me by a sobriquet, Sun-li.† This year it falls to me to be the Imperial Examiner. I am completely and purely innocent of extorting cash from citizens; I purely and simply take their I.O.U.'s for everything. Well, it seems we have a candidate here whose surname is Ts'ui, whose name is T'ung and whose courtesy title is Tien-shih. He has handed in his petition for examination and I have decided he's to be number one on the list, though I haven't yet given him his preliminary exam. Attendants, summon candidate Ts'ui to me.

(Enter TS'UI T'UNG.*)*

TS'UI T'UNG:

I am Ts'ui T'ung and I have handed in my petition. The examiner of the day has summoned me, so I must go to him.

CHANG CH'IEN:‡

I report, your excellency, that candidate Ts'ui has arrived.

---

*A poetic (though historic) name for the Board of Rites which furnished examiners. This is the "flour and water" verse in *Ku-ch'ü Chai* ed.

†The first four surnames in the *Book of the Hundred Names* are Chao, Ch'ien, Sun, and Li. The passage is a type of plebeian, pedantic humor well liked by Yuan playwrights.

‡It appears the editors of *YCH* and *Liu-chih Chi* eds. have shortened the seeing and announcing formula. *Ku-ch'ü Chai* has: "Tell him I'm here," "Yes sir," and *then* Chang Ch'ien reports.

OFFICIAL:
Bring him here.

CHANG:
Here he is.

(They pantomime meeting.)

TS'UI T'UNG:
What did you call me for?

OFFICIAL:
You've handed in your petition but I haven't given you your preliminary examination. Can you read?

TS'UI T'UNG:
I'm a graduate, should I not be able to read, your honor? How many fish can't recognize water?

OFFICIAL:
How many graduates can't steal a dumpling on the Festival of the Ides? All right, I'll write the characters and you read them. I start it in the west and end it in the east, what is it?

TS'UI T'UNG:
That's the figure "one."

OFFICIAL:*
Ah hah! if you can recognize difficult things like that, I'll make no mistake putting you first on the list! Now, let me ask you, can you cap verses?

*In the *Ku-ch'ü Chai* ed. (Yang 1-2166) a *wai* has a *ch'eng-ta* interjection here, "What's so hard about that?"

TS'UI T'UNG:
I can.

OFFICIAL:
(recites)
Athwart the river lies the boat
Up the bank eight men draw the tows.

TS'UI T'UNG:
(recites)
Someone comes and cuts the ropes
And everyone of them falls on his nose.*

OFFICIAL:
Good, good! Let me try you on another verse.

(recites)
Here we have a mighty *ta-ch'ing* bowl
With rice all packed in tight

TS'UI T'UNG:
(recites)
If your honor could only eat all that
You'd be full from morning to night.

OFFICIAL:
Oh most excellent graduate! Why, with his literary talents I've half a mind to take him on as *my* teacher. Chang Ch'ien, ask the gentleman if he's married.

CHANG:
His honor asks if you are married or not.

---

*On *WP* 145, the comic general's entrance verse is the same quatrain.

TS'UI T'UNG:
If I am married, what then? Or what if I'm not married?

CHANG:
Your honor, he asks what if he is married and what if he isn't.

OFFICIAL:
If he is I'll send him off to Ch'in-ch'uan to take charge. If he isn't, I have an eighty-year-old daughter to give him to wife—

CHANG:*
Surely you mean eighteen-year-old!

OFFICIAL:
Yes, yes, eighteen-year-old.

CHANG:
Sir, my master says that, if you are married, he'll send you right off to take up duties in Ch'in-ch'uan, but, if you're not, he has a daughter and would like you for a son-in-law.

TS'UI T'UNG:
Hold on. Let me think. *(aside)* That girl at my uncle's, now, she wasn't raised by our family, so how do we know where she comes from? What do I want with her anyway? Besides, it's better to cheat the gods a little† than to let slip an opportunity. *(turns)* Actually, I am not married yet.

---

*This is said by the *wai* in *Ku-ch'ü Chai* and he says "*te-yeh-me*" after the official agrees.

†Referring to his oath in Act I.

OFFICIAL:
Since you have no wife I will have you as my son-in-law. Chang Ch'ien, tell Plum Blossom to bring my daughter here from the chimney corner.

CHANG:
Very well.

(Enter CH'A-TAN, *painted female role.)*

CH'A:
(recites)
This morning the good luck magpie cried,
Foretelling the arrival of my fate.
Should even a beggar walk inside,
I'd laugh and take him as a mate.

I am the daughter of the official in charge of this examination. My father has called me so I go to see him. *(pantomimes meeting)* Father, what did you call me for?

OFFICIAL:
I called you for no other reason than to get you a husband.

CH'A:
How many samples have you got?

OFFICIAL:
Only one, but look him over—wouldn't he make a good son-in-law?

TS'UI T'UNG:
Now there's a fine looking woman.

OFFICIAL:
How about your father-in-law?

TS'UI T'UNG:
Oh, he's a fine one too.

OFFICIAL:
(turning and looking at CHANG CH'IEN*)*
A good mother-in-law too, eh?

CHANG:
Flatterer!

OFFICIAL:
Ts'ui Tien-shih, I have made you magistrate of Ch'in-ch'uan county beginning today. You and my daughter must now go and take up duties. I have a bit of song called Tsui T'ai-p'ing which I will sing to see you on your way.

(Tsui T'ai-p'ing* 44737774)

(sings)
Because your
Every talent is as it should be—
Versed in the Classics and skilled in the Histories,
Capping poems, riddling characters, you understand entire—
I give
To you my daughter for your mate.
This kerchief,
Let me take it off and give it to you to wear now.

*The song is intrusive, of course. See also intrusive Tsui T'ai-p'ing in Act IV with which it is an exact parallel.

(pantomimes taking off kerchief)
This scholar's gown,
Let me take it off and give it to you to wear now.

(pantomimes taking off gown)
Now that I have stripped myself skinny-red naked. . . .*

(speaks)
Chang Ch'ien, come with me.

(sings)
I might as well go to the bathhouse and bathe.

TS'UI T'UNG:
Young lady, let us put everything in order today and leave to take up my post.

(recites)
We'll make our way past mountains far and rivers near.
Having bade farewell to the Gates of Peach and Pear.

CH'A:

(recites)
And though we've neither seal to wrap nor kerchief to unpack,
We'll stir a storm up here and shout the house down there.
(exeunt)

(Enter TS'UI-LUAN.*)*

TS'UI-LUAN:
I am Ts'ui-luan and after father Ts'ui adopted me as his daughter he betrothed me to Ts'ui Tien-shih, his nephew. Then his nephew left to sit for imperial examinations, but that has already been three years gone. They say he became magistrate of Ch'in-ch'uan, but he

*The line is a six beat, not seven.

has not come to fetch me. Now father Ts'ui has told me to gather what I need for travel and I have set forth for Ch'in-ch'uan to find Ts'ui Tien-shih. Since father wants awfully to see his nephew he will come later and visit me. *(sighs)* Hai! I fear that young graduates are fickle of heart.

(Nan-lü, Yi-chih Hua 553555777)

(sings)
When finally he
Climbed the moon-palace and plucked the cassia branch
And received his orders by the golden gate,
The wedding chamber should blaze in the candle-lit night.
When your name was placed on the gilded roster
Then for you
I abandoned family hearth and home
And sought my way down this long, long road.
(Resenting
Each ten-mile marker that does not appear in five.)
Now I feel
Silky threads of fall rain damping the red dust.
And oh how
Penetrating are the soughing gusts of autumn's metal wind.

(Liang-chou 6674444666662275 74)

(sings)
Now I watch
Defeated hosts of summer's leaves spiraling through windy space
And they are
Red gouts of blood staining the painted face of fall.
The chill and whirring western wind
Settles old scores with defiant chrysanthemums.*

*This line is from a poem by Chang Chu in *Kuei Ch'ien Chih*. See Yoshikawa, pp. 262–63. It is also used in the fourth acts of *YCH* #27 and #82.

As I look,
That patch of wood casts a shadow,
That ridge of hills grows slowly indistinct.
I have walked till
My mouth is dry and my tongue bitter,
My eyes swoon and my head throbs.
I cannot help
Wiping away tears and rubbing my eyes,
I cannot
Overcome the weakness at my back and thighs.
I, I, I
Gently, gently tighten the thongs on my sandals.
Now, now, now
Slowly, slowly settle my plaited hat.
Ai ya, ya, ya
Then I must slightly ease my waistband.
Then I think of that
False hearted,
That faithless man!
Now that you have
Gotten your post do you require no one to serve and none to comfort you?
Are you now so pressed
You could not fill even half a letter with news?
Because there must come a day when I shall see you once again.
I must search my thoughts carefully now.

(speaks)

But I have already reached Ch'in-ch'uan; I had better ask someone. *(turns toward the* ku-men* *and inquires)* Brother, if you would be so kind, where can I find the house of Ts'ui Tien-shih?

VOICE:

(from offstage)

It's the two-leafed "figure eight" wall door right ahead of you.

**I.e.* the stage exit—probably around the stage left side of the rear hanging. See above p. 150.

TS'UI-LUAN:
Sir, may I leave this bundle here while I go inquire of my family—I'll be right back for it.*

VOICE:
It'll be no trouble, go ahead.

TS'UI-LUAN:
Is anybody there at the gate? Will you go tell the master his wife is here?

SERVANT:
Lady, you must have the wrong place. He already has a wife.

TS'UI-LUAN:
What did you say?

SERVANT:
I said the master already has a wife.

(Mu-yang Kuan 334445555)

TS'UI-LUAN:

(cutting him off, sings)

That has to be
Only idle talk!
What can it mean?
He must be
"Sprouting twigs where none properly grow."
Three years have gone by since we parted,
But not for
One moment did I dream of being unfaithful.
I know he cannot
Have been willing to forsake the wife of his hardest years—

*Note that this plays absolutely no part in the rest of the script.

He has! He has!
Got himself a woman, some delicate slip of a girl
The better to destroy the hapless wife of his poverty.
Ai ya, ai ya, ai ya,
False-hearted, faithless indeed, Ts'ui Tien-shih!

(speaks)
Good brother gateman, will you report that I am here.

SERVANT:
(pantomiming report)
May it please your honor, your wife has arrived at the gate.

CH'A-TAN:
Here, you good-for-nothing, what are you saying?!

SERVANT:
That the master's wife is at the gate.

CH'A-TAN:
She's his wife? Then I'm the serving wench?!

TS'UI T'UNG:
This idiot must have a pair of left-hand ears.* Wife, leave us alone and wait inside. I'll go see her.

TS'UI-LUAN:
(pantomimes seeing him)
Oh, it's Ts'ui Tien-shih, how could you have been so faithless? Why didn't you send for me when you got your appointment?

---

*The *YCH t'ing-tso,* "hears left-handedly," undoubtedly should be *t'ing-ch'a,* "hears mistakenly." However this thought did not occur to me until many years after I had translated it as above, and now I am so fond of my two left ears that I refuse to change it. Sweet are the uses of adversity!

CH'A-TAN:

Now here's a fine thing! You said you had no wife—then how is it a second one has popped up? Why, you ass-brain! You animal! I shall surely die of rage. *(She pantomimes frothing with anger.)*

TS'UI T'UNG:

Now wife, calm yourself! She is nothing but my family's slave girl. She ran away from the house after she'd stolen a silver wine ewer and trivet, and I've been looking for her ever since without success. Now she's come to give herself up in the manner of a moth dashing itself against the flame. Attendants! Take her away, strip her and flog her for me!

(Servant pantomimes seizing TS'UI-LUAN *and she refuses to prostrate herself.)*

(Ke-wei *777227)**

TS'UI-LUAN:

(sings)

I did but wait
To be a wife who would follow her mate, who sings the lyrics for the lute he plays.
Could I know you had married without divorce and taken a trollop to wed?

CH'A-TAN:

(speaks angrily)

May heaven strike you down! Do you hear her revile me?

TS'UI T'UNG:

Well? Why aren't you beating her, you clowns?!

---

*This aria and its dialogue do not appear in the *Ku-ch'ü chai* edition.

TS'UI-LUAN:

(sings)

And so he would have me
Pulled standing or dragged prostrate down from his magistrate's dais.

(speaks)

Ts'ui Tien-shih,

(sings)

You must remember the time
We swore together
That solemn oath.

TS'UI T'UNG:

Nonsense! I never made any oath.

TS'UI-LUAN:

(sings)

Did you not say
"I will not be faithless, not be faithless," and swear upon heaven and earth?

TS'UI T'UNG:

(striking table repeatedly)

If you flunkies keep acting as though she were my wife—if you don't drag her off, strip her, and flog her good and proper—I'll show you some of my own handiwork and every last one of you will be conscripted! *(Servant pantomimes throwing* TS'UI-LUAN *to the ground and beating her.)*

(K'u Huang-tien 5555 4444(7)44)

TS'UI-LUAN:

(sings)

The pillar of my spine aches as though cut by knives!

The blows leave purple welts beside black bruises!
What a cold and savage rain falls now!
What hot, searing blows and lingering pain!
How can I bear that pitiless, pitiless stave
That strikes through skin to bone,
That crushes my brain, pierces my mind,
That shatters flesh and snaps sinew,
That lets blood and destroys the soul.
I am dying
I am dying
Of pain.
One thing I must ask
You, heartless Tien-shih.
Why have you
Thrust this nameless crime on me?

TS'UI T'UNG:
You're begging for a name to your crime? That I can give you. You, there, on her face tatoo the words "runaway slave," and have her sent under guard to Shamen Island.

SERVANT:
Yes, sir.

(Wu Yeh-t'i)*

TS'UI-LUAN:

(sings)

You scant-fated cutthroat
Whose reckless will would brand my face
And sentence me to penal transportation.
Has the world yet witnessed a more lawless act?

*This (Wu Yeh-t'i) is so abnormal in meter that noting the scansion would serve no purpose.

If I should cry till my breath moaned, my voice hissed,
I could not rid myself of the sobs that wring my breast.
If heaven is just
It must take pity on me.
I wish only that I could see
Your own blood-uncle appear this instant
So both of us could testify
(And he could judge where lies the truth)
And watch you, quick-lipped, slick-tongued,
Convince him some public or private crime was mine.

TS'UI T'UNG:
You men! Send for a strong-shanked, fleet-footed guard to transport this runaway slave to Shamen Island. Have him take her there and make the trip in such a way that she's more likely to arrive dead than alive.

TS'UI-LUAN:
Oh, Ts'ui Tien-shih, what malice!

(Huang-chung sha 77/33../47)

(sings)
Don't, don't, don't
I beg my lord do not carry out the scheme, the trick you plan!
For now, now, now
A new judge sits on sacred T'ai-shan in the court of speedy retribution.
That you, you, you,
Faithless man can believe there is a crime
Means my, my, my
Woman's frail auguries
Must have been at fault!
Haste, haste, haste then
To send me off today
To drive me from this place.

I shall go, go, go
And may someone pity her
Who journeys alone.
Fine, fine, fine
Will be the strands of thought in my heart
And dark my reflections on them.
Cruel, cruel, cruel
With only myself to turn to
How will I manage to live?
This must, must, must—
Cannot help but end
With a corpse lying across the road.

(pantomimes grief)
Aiyo! Heaven, when did my faithful Mo-lo* die
Who could have borne me away from here?

CH'A-TAN:
My lord, suppose she is your former wife, are we not doing a great wrong? Why not let her stay here as a slave. That will certainly keep people from talking.

TS'UI T'UNG:
Wife, stop fretting! Where would I have got another wife?

CH'A-TAN:
Just the same, she said she wants to stand by you face to face with your uncle—what about that?†

TS'UI T'UNG:
I do have an uncle and she was a slave in his house. He sold her to me. She's not at all bad to look at, but her fingers are light and her

---

*Name of the faithful K'un-lun slave who bore Ts'ui-sheng and his beloved away from all harm. See C. C. Wang, *Traditional Chinese Tales,* p. 94.

†Note the relatively rare occurrence of material introduced only in a song which is actually alluded to in the dialogue.

feet quick. She robbed me, and I looked all over for her. Now she's found me I hardly think I can pardon her. This trip she'll have to make through the damp autumn rains, and when they begin to work on the wounds left by her flogging she'll have no more chance of living than she deserves. Come. I'll go with you to the rear chambers and order some wine.

(recites)
Happy, this day! I caught a runaway slave!
And this trip she takes assures me her doom.

CH'A-TAN:

(recites)
But if truly you married her once long ago,
You'd better go look for a job as a groom! *(exeunt)*

ACT III

(Enter CHANG T'IEN-CHUEH *leading follower,* HSING-ERH.*)*

CHANG:

(recites)
The trip south to Chiang-chou gave me three views of spring,
To look back brings tears and a wrench at the heart.
Lonely, this night, with its cloud-blocked moon
Which lighted the hour that drove us apart.

I am Chang T'ien-chüeh, and it is already three years since my daughter and I capsized in the boat on the Huai. By the grace of my sovereign, it was decided that I was able and upright, frugal and firm, and that my thoughts were ever for my state and not my family. I have been given the post of Reviewer of Punishments and presented the sword of power and the gold seal of authority by which I may order summary executions without the need to memorialize the throne. It is the Sage Intent of his Majesty that I should discover debauched officers and their depraved subordinates and pass judgment on the obscurities in the laws. Aged and somewhat infirm, I still cannot shirk my duties. Grief and longing for my daughter Ts'ui-luan have grizzled the hair at my temples and my eyes have dimmed—I am not the same man who passed by here long ago!

Several years ago I sent men everywhere to search and inquire, but no word either for good or ill.—And now it has turned fall again. How will I stand its sharp wind and cold rains, its passing geese and the cry of insects. I look on the scene before me with never a companion to distract my fears and relieve my depression.

It has begun to cloud up and rain, Hsing-erh, let us be on our way.

(recites)

From the moment I became an officer of the court,
In every petty fashion vexed with bitterness,
My native heath lay dreamed of a thousand li away,
My horse's saddle beneath me dusted by three years of journey.
Parted from my own flesh by life,
My family's heritage blown away or drowned.
An autumn dusk like this will always summon up
Unbidden thoughts to crowd 'round about me.
Now hear the
Steady susurration of the rain
Matched by a
Thickening and coupling of the clouds.
Yellow chrysanthemums—the eyes of brazen beasts.
Red leaves—the scales of fire-dragons.
Plunging lines of the mountain range loom up.
Mumbling voices of the river swell loud.
My servant boy is wearied by the road untraveled—
All of him the picture of a soul overwhelmed.

(speaks)

Hsing-erh, what lies up ahead?

HSING-ERH:
The Lin-chiang posthouse is just a little further on, Master.

CHANG:
As soon as we reach it I am going to rest; it is true, "On the Long River the wind speeds a traveler; at the lonely posthouse rain delays the parting guest." *(exeunt)*

(TS'UI-LUAN *enters wearing cangue and followed by guard.)*

TS'UI-LUAN:
Oh, what rain!

(recites)

First in the women's halls my years were spent,
Then before judgment I stood alone.
Next, barred from home by banishment,
I endure the rain to reach my last imprisonment.

(speaks)
Brother, is your only concern to see that your staff can reach my back so you can beat me continually? I cannot believe your heart is so hard that there is not a spark of pity left in you. *(She pantomimes grief.)* Oh, heaven, heaven, I have a true grievance, I carry weighty wrong on my shoulders.

(Huang-chung, Tsui-hua yin 76545 (57))

(sings)
Suddenly I hear
The drums of a weird, uprooting wind
Which makes still worse
This violent rain pouring from giant, toppled caldrons.
Hobbled by pain, creeping down the road ahead
Pressed in turn by wind and rain.

Oh, when will these pelting raindrops cease?
For all to see
They put to trial and almost flogged to death a delicate girl,
Now who
In this wild and weary waste will stand against them as my advocate?

GUARD:
Move along faster, the rain grows worse all the time.

(Hsi Ch'ien-ying 574625734)

TS'UI-LUAN:
(sings)
So great
The rain I'll never reach a refuge.
(Who knows
Which of Hell's gates is found on Shamen Island?)
Alas, Alas!
The very air condenses into cloudy brume.
As I walk,
Drowned wheelruts work pitfalls to trap and seize my legs.
And soon will
Wrench a thighbone from its socket.
How will I stand either
The gleaming, streaming rain upon my head
Or the sliding, subsiding mud beneath my feet?

(pantomimes slipping and falling)

GUARD:
Now why did you fall?!

TS'UI-LUAN:
Brother, it's slippery here.

GUARD:
A thousand, no, ten thousand, people can walk for days on end without falling down once, but *you* have to fall on your face. Now I'm going to walk through there and if I slip I'll say no more, but if I don't, I'm going to break both of your legs in two so you can keep your balance on four short ones.

(He pantomimes walking past and falling down.)

Help me up! Young woman, you'd better walk around that way, this side seems a trifle slippery.*

(Ch'u Tui-tzu 45777)

TS'UI-LUAN:

(sings)

Now you have made me anxious over where to place my feet
Just as it grows so wet
That no sure place is left to step.
When we ate I dried these tattered rags before the fire,
When we took the road, rain drenched me through to the sash that binds my waist
When I fell I must have lost from there my comb of buckthorn wood.

GUARD:
What is it now?

TS'UI-LUAN:
I've dropped my buckthorn comb!

GUARD:
Let it lie! I'll buy you another up ahead.

*Another popular *shtick.* See *YCH* #64, p. 1122.

TS'UI-LUAN:
Brother, please look for it; when we get there you may want to comb your hair too.

GUARD:
You're enough to worry a man to death.

(He pantomimes stepping gingerly on something.)

I think I found your comb! Wash it off in that puddle—and then get a move on again, will you?

(Yao-p'ien 4577)

TS'UI-LUAN:

(sings)

In my
Heart I dread and brood as I think
Of the
Three things that can suddenly end my life.

GUARD:
What three things? I'll listen if you want to tell me.

TS'UI-LUAN:

(sings)

Those clouds. They can
Mask the sky and sun and blot out all signs of a city.
That wind. Now it appears violent enough
To wrench out rocks, spatter sand, and tear up tall trees.
That rain. Surely
Its straight shafts and slanting strands will drive me to a despondent death.

GUARD:
All right, now, if you're going to go, go. If you don't I'll just have to beat you.

TS'UI-LUAN:
(speaks)
Oh, good brother,

(Shan-p'o yang 443375(4 or 3))

(sings)
Please,
Please stop your angry shouts.
Do you imagine everything is solved
By thirty lines of insisting, tongue-twisting, lip-curling malediction?
The road shifts and toils,
The water frets and coils
And frightens me shivering, shaking, incapable of taking a forward step.
If you open my scars afresh
I'll be helpless to manage half a pace.

(speaks)
And then, good brother, though you beat me to death

(sings)
Would this add to your share of good luck?

GUARD:
Stop! You've too many tongues and too much mouth. This season the fall rain soaks everything and each day it's harder to travel than the last, so come on now, walk as I do!

(Kua-ti Feng 74744433455)

TS'UI-LUAN:
(sings)
See him stare and glare, bulge his eyes; call and rage

In puffing heaves that strain his breast.
But I
Am sodden with scarcely will enough to try the road ahead.
Aiya, I cannot
Move this poor, beaten body.

GUARD:
What? Not moving yet?

TS'UI-LUAN:
(sings)
Yes! Force one foot forward! Another foot now!
Whenever can I rest again?
Now! Step to this side! Step to that.
Everywhere lie lakes and streams.
Fortune's ill wind and evil wave
Have sent me bound to this place
Where every trace
Of fellow travelers has melted out of sight
In this empty
Watery fastness that mounts up the darkening night.

(speaks)
Oh, brother.

(sings)
Brother, how will you get me through this day?

GUARD:
Now what's the trouble?

TS'UI-LUAN:
Brother, the water's so deep and the mud's so clinging—how am I supposed to walk? Pity me, brother. Give me a hand, I beg of you, to help me across.

GUARD:
So help me! You're going to pester me to death for sure. Here, I'll help you across. Tell me, how did you happen to be a servant in his house and why did you take his money and anger him so that now he wants to see you dead?

TS'UI-LUAN:
I never was his servant and I stole no money—

(Ssu-men-tzu 55,55335 334)

(sings)
Let me tell you,
Good brother, my complaints one by one.
The Magistrate, your master, is my husband, he is truly.
Everything I've said is true—not falsified one wit.
I sought him out to reunite a family once again,
But he had wed another.
Then he foreswore himself by calling me a slave.
I give my oath,
I'm falsely charged and wrongly judged.

GUARD:
Hearing it told this way, our magistrate seems to have done a great wrong. But there's nothing I can do about it now. Come, move faster.

(Ku Shui-hsien-tzu 374456775)

TS'UI-LUAN:
(sings)
He, he, he has
Such a venomous sting.
Would, would, would
He not hoodwink his very soul to work some harm on me?

You, you, you are all
Savage, ravaging bailiffs and jailers.
I, I, I am just
A weak and meekly suffering convict
Ache, ache, aching from
The toll your staves took of fragile flesh.
And the cold, cold, cold
Metal fetters ringed stiffly 'round my neck.
And so, so, so
A person's driven to a hell on earth in innocence
And wronged, wronged, wronged,
He cannot plead in court in his own defense.

(speaks)

Brother,

(sings)

Come, come, come
With me—my only warrant against destruction!

GUARD:

It's growing dark. Move along now so we can find lodging for the night.

(Sui-wei 77?)

TS'UI-LUAN:

(sings)

The feelings of Heaven must be drawn by the heart strings of man
For here
Upon my face the many tracks of tears that overflowed my eyes.

(speaks)

Oh, heavens, heavens,

(sings)

And down them
Run teardrops as numerous as the drops of this autumn rain. *(exeunt)*

ACT IV

(Enter ching as posthouse KEEPER.*)*

KEEPER:

(reciting)

Back and forth to greet and send with never any stay.
Fetch and carry! Food and fodder! Guests are on their way!
The king's officials quarter here—with them I have no quarrel
But
To their boots and lackeys, grooms and squires, mine host is always prey.

I am the keeper of Lin-chiang posthouse and yesterday an outrider came to say that the great judge would be passing this way and I must not fail to clean up the hostel. Here is a gentleman coming now.

(Enter TS'UI WEN-YUAN.*)*

TS'UI WEN-YUAN:
I am Ts'ui Wen-yüan and I've not heard a word since I sent my adopted daughter, Ts'ui-luan, to find my nephew, so I have journeyed myself to Ch'in-ch'uan prefecture to see her. But since it is getting dark and raining I must stay overnight at this posthouse and continue early tomorrow.

KEEPER:
Ho there, old man, what are you doing?

WEN-YUAN:
The rain has become so great that it worries me, sir, and I've nowhere to stay further on. If you can find any place at all for me in this hostel, I will leave first thing tomorrow.

KEEPER:
Old man, you must understand that we will have a great judge staying with us so there can be no disturbance. You may rest in the cookshed.

WEN-YUAN:
Thank you very much.

(Enter CHANG T'IEN-CHUEH *leading* HSING-ERH *and attendants.)*

CHANG:
I am Chang T'ien-chüeh and I have reached the Lin-chiang posthouse. Hsing-erh, are you very wet?

HSING-ERH:
Master, this rain is so heavy it has soaked through every part of my clothing.

CHANG:
If that's the case, let us take shelter in the posthouse.

KEEPER:
(greeting them)
I am the keeper of the Lin-chiang posthouse and I bid you welcome to it. Please enter, my lord, and rest.

CHANG:
Hsing-erh, I am so weary from this entire day in the saddle that I must sleep for a while. Allow no one to disturb me for if I'm awakened I'll give you a beating. Tell the others what I have said.

HSING-ERH:
Yes, sir. Keeper, I order you to allow no disturbance, for my master

is going to rest and if he is awakened he'll beat me and I'll see you get yours.

KEEPER:
I could have guessed it!

(Enter TS'UI-LUAN *and* GUARD.*)*

TS'UI-LUAN:
Dear brother, my guard, all the rain in heaven is falling on us.

GUARD:
This much rain could just drown a man. I wouldn't mind resting a while myself—Shamen Island prison certainly takes a bit of walking to reach.

TS'UI-LUAN:
Brother, the rain gets worse.

(Cheng-kung, Tuan-cheng hao)

(sings)
So heavy the rain! Wind gusts as from a fan!
High in empty air they have twined together.
Neither heeds the traveler's woes, but buffet
His head and face.

(Kun Hsiu-ch'iu)

That day near the bank of the stream,
The rise of the shore,

What chance had we against that towering wind, that curling wave?
Our spirits chilled before their united forces.
The wind blew, piercing us with its arrows.
The rain fell, water pouring from a cistern.
This storm that I watch now I know bodes ill;
My destiny provokes punishments and summons calamity.
The water drenching this Hsiao-hsiang scenery
Is dark with the lampblack that wet clouds paint across the skies,
And tears drop from my eyes.

GUARD:
Here, here, now! Don't fuss so about it. We'll go to the Lin-chiang posthouse and spend the night. *(pantomimes calling at the door)* Keeper! Open up!

KEEPER:
Well, here's another one! Let me open the door. You two have a nerve with the great judge in here trying to rest! Now you stay outside and if you make a rumpus I'll break your legs for you. I'm closing the door.

GUARD:
What rotten luck! A great judge staying here so we can't even make a sound. Oh, well, I'll take off my jacket and try to wring it dry. *(pantomimes undressing)* Yah! I still have a biscuit in my sleeve pocket. Might as well eat that.

TS'UI-LUAN:
Brother, what are you eating?!

GUARD:
A biscuit.

TS'UI-LUAN:
Brother, could I have some?

GUARD:
Every time I'm eating something you're looking for something to eat. Oh well, take some.

TS'UI-LUAN:
Brother, could you give me a little more?

GUARD:
But it's only one biscuit! I give you some and it's not enough ... eh-h-h, I suppose I should give you the whole thing!

(Pan-tu-shu)

TS'UI-LUAN:
(sings)
I plead with my guard for food but
How impossible to explain to him the hunger in me.
He has taken this storm-swept journey by force and walked me
Till my sinews are slack, my strength is gone, and shudders of dizziness
Sweep my body, which is all pain and weary beyond reckoning.
I, I, I, sleep standing, and walk as I sleep.

(Hsiao Ho-sheng)

I, I, I, have pressed on through this night which has seemed a year.
I, I, I, have a grudge against heaven but
I, I, I, must be paying in full for some dread oath
Sworn in a former life. My, my, my eyes are wept dry.

My, my, my throat is cracked with sobs.
Come, come, come brother—How will I swallow this
Biscuit you have given me?

(speaks)

Aiya heaven! Here am I in this forsaken place; who knows where my father may be!?

CHANG:

Oh, Ts'ui-luan, my child, I shall die of grief over you. This moment through closed lids I saw my daughter before me. Just as she was telling me what happened to her years ago someone startled me awake.

*(recites)**

My evening years came long ago.
"My dream is broken, my spirit spent."
Soul wretched and hostel silent.
And the path in the sky has reached autumn;
The landscape is mournful.
Night is endless in this river town and
The sound of the watcher's bell vexes me:
It makes an old man chill with dread
Or simmer with impatience.
Crickets of the cold chirp,
Geese from the border fort cry,
The wind of metal soughs
And the rain rustles.

(speaks)

It may have been that heartless wind and rain which kept my eyes from closing.

(recites)

"Melancholy as all the water of the Hsiang which rolls on forever.
Like the rains of autumn—each drop the sound of grief itself."

*"six-four," *ao* rhyme, atonal.

(speaks)

But I just finished telling that worthless Hsing-erh not to allow any disturbance. He's been careless no doubt and should be given a beating.

HSING-ERH:

I gave the hosteler his orders but he paid no attention. I'll give him a beating. *(pantomimes beating the keeper)* You good-for-nothing, I told you there was to be no rumpus, but you've wakened my master and he's going to beat me: so I'll beat you.

KEEPER:

Uncle, stop! Go get some sleep yourself. It was all the fault of that prisoner's guard. I'm opening the door to beat that no-good. *(pantomimes beating the guard)* You, guard, I told you there would be no rumpus! You and your snuffling and crying have waked up his honor, and I've been taking a beating from his escort. Now you get yours!

GUARD:

But it was all the blubbering of this hard-case!

(recites in tz'u*)**

Oh, you are a fine Meng Ch'iang Nü carrying winter clothes a thousand li,
Or a filial Chao Chen-nü whose scarlet skirt was caked with earth.†
Though you weep more than empress Ngo-hwang,
Who would want *your* tears to dapple the bamboo?

TS'UI-LUAN:

(reciting in tz'u*)*‡

Let me speak, brother,

**u* rhyme.

†A standard allusion for a filial wife, referring to the woman who laboriously carried earth to build a tomb for her husband's parents. This story is the basis for *The Lute Song* of the Ming dynasty. She is alluded to in *YCH* #29, p. 501, as well.

‡*u* rhyme.

I am not allowed anger.
The wrongs I've suffered,
Who will plead them for me?
From this day forth, brother,
I shall swallow both bitterness and voice.
Never again will I wail or weep from pain.

(speaks)
Oh, father, how I miss you!

CHANG:
Oh, Ts'ui-luan, my child, how I ache for you. *(faces audience)* I was telling my child the things that happened to me after we were parted at Huai Ferry—but someone woke me from my dream.

(recites in tz'u*)**
First because my heart was ill at ease,
Next because my mind was all uncertain,
As soon as my eyes closed, father and child were met again.
Even as I struggled to speak of those years of separation,
Suddenly the startled dream fled.
From where came that cruel awakening sound; what was it?
—the chink-clank of armored horsemen?†
I first thought it the
Cold, stiff thump of wet garments against the laundry block.
Then I guessed
The chittering of crickets in a deserted stairwell sounding through the west window
And conjured next the sight of
Geese returning to southern eddies from beyond the reach of heaven.
I now
Cease my chant and listen closely—
It is nothing but
The wild wind and rushing rain that summoned me awake.

**u* rhyme, atonal.

†For the same set of images used to describe loneliness and regret, see *YCH* 362. They are phrased quite differently, however, since the set on 362 is an aria and literary, while those above are in a dignified kind of narrative verse.

I
Face this gray scene having lost all who were close to me.
What wonder then
Grief sours my heart and chills it more each day?
Oh, my child,
Do you still live the life I knew
Or have you come back to this mansion earth in another form?
Are you wealthy, honored?
Or captive, slaved?
A white-haired father in the lonely hostel ponders, wonders—
Ah, heaven!
But his
Daughter in the bloom of her years is somewhere anguished!

(speaks)

I told you, Hsing-erh, there was to be no noise! Now you've wakened me. *(pantomimes striking* HSING-ERH*)*

HSING-ERH:

Don't beat me, master, it was that damned hostel-keeper. *(He pantomimes going out and seeing keeper.)* You, keeper! I told you there would be no disturbance; what do you mean by waking my master?

(recites in tz'u*)**

I gave you
A thousand commands,
Ten thousand warnings
But you've allowed loud
Weeping and mournings.
And since my master beat
"aiyah!" from me
I shall thump an "Uncle!"
From thee!

**u* rhyme.

KEEPER:

It's all the fault of that prisoner's guard outside this door. I am opening it and I'll beat that good-for-nothing. See here, guard, I told you there was to be no disturbance and now you've wakened the judge, you whoreson!

(recites in tz'u*)**

What matter if
The rain has soaked you through and through
It gives you no call to weep
"Wu-hu"
And if his escort gives me mine
I will break your mother's spine!

GUARD:

(recites in tz'u*)†*

All I heard was a raised voice . . .
The door pops open in a rage at the noise.
Had you ever wandered you would always be kin
To the traveler. Instead, you begin
Without question to belabor someone
Cursed with
  a manacle-bearing
    cangue-wearing worry-minded
      tear-soaked stinking female
Who woke that posthouse-mounted
  gold-badge Panjandrum
    who first lops off a man's
      head and then asks him what he's done!‡

I've put up with hunger and suffered cold, because I've no love for the rod and now I find it's just as close to my skin as before. It would be a lot better to butt the wind and brave the rain on the highroad again to find some place else to spend the night.

**u* rhyme.

†*u* rhyme.

‡The line between the two rhymes "someone" and "done" is deliberately made to suffer metrical elephantiasis by the playwright for comic effect.

TS'UI-LUAN:

(recites in tz'u*)**

With this door between us, I beg you, brother,
Please hear my deepest feelings.
Find it in you to take pity on me
And you will mean as much to me as my blood parents.
Let's speak no more of further travel,
Of blistered feet, the ropes of rushing rain,
The arrow wind's wild thrumming.
You said we could find peace in your posthouse,
How can you drive us forth again by angry talk
And make us seek some barnyard inn or village public house?
But in this cavernous darkness who could find the place?
I would end my life in the jaws of wild beasts
Or the bellies of the river's fish.
In no time the temples' matin bells will ring.
Allow us, I beg you, to shelter here still,
Out of the night rain on the Hsiao-hsiang.

CHANG:

Well, dawn has come. Hsing-erh, go to the main door, find the person who has disturbed this whole night and bring him before me! *(*HSING-ERH *brings the guard and* TS'UI-LUAN.*)*

TS'UI-LUAN:

(recognizing her father)

It's my papa!

CHANG:

Ts'ui-luan, my child! Oh, where have you been these three years! What are you doing wearing cangue and manacles!

TS'UI-LUAN:

(weeping)

Oh papa! You had no way of knowing, but after we were separated

---

**u* rhyme.

I was adopted by Ts'ui the elder and he married me to his nephew, Ts'ui T'ung. Ts'ui T'ung went off to seek his fortune and was made magistrate of Ch'in-ch'uan prefecture. When he didn't send for me, I went to find him at Ts'ui the elder's bidding. But how could I even suspect he'd taken another wife? He accused me of being a runaway slave and sent me off under guard to Shamen Island. All the way here I would sooner have died than lived. Oh, papa, what will you do as my advocate?

CHANG:
Open the cangue and fetters! That faithless, worthless. . . . Where are my attendants? Quickly! Off to Ch'in-ch'uan prefecture and bring Ts'ui T'ung to me!

TS'UI-LUAN:
Papa, he is in charge at Ch'in-ch'uan. Just sending your men to take him will not vent my spleen. I must lead them to him and take him myself, to watch the perverse crab* with a cool eye while he ends his days in my cooking-pot!

(Exit with attendants.)

(Enter TS'UI T'UNG.*)*

TS'UI T'UNG:
I am Ts'ui T'ung and that woman the other day really was the one my uncle gave me to wife. I flogged her with enough clatter to get her tried as a runaway and sent to Shamen Island—having already told the guard that a dead prisoner would be better than a live one. I wonder why he's been gone so long and sent back no message? My wife has made enough noise at me about this already. *(pantomimes being startled)* Hello! My eyes are twitching like mad! I suppose that means she's coming over for another debate.

---

*This relatively harmless crustacean is a villain in Chinese simply because of his sidewise progress: the common Chinese term for perverse and tyrannical behavior is *heng-hsing* which, analyzed, means "sidewise movement, movement across the grain." Obviously a critter whose normal mode of locomotion is on the bias was not likely to be trusted by the Chinese.

(Enter TS'UI-LUAN *and attendants.)*

TS'UI-LUAN:

Here we are in Ch'in-ch'uan already. Attendants, open the door and go in. *(pantomimes seeing* TS'UI T'UNG*)* There is Ts'ui T'ung, men, take him for me!

TS'UI T'UNG:

Now this is queer! Where did you all come from?

ATTENDANT:

We arrest you by order of his honor the great judge.

TS'UI-LUAN:

Did you think I had come for an audience with you, Ts'ui T'ung! Strip off his cap and sash, you men, and lock him up tight.

TS'UI T'UNG:

Woman, take pity! Remember, "the Husband is the wife's heaven."

(K'uai-huo san)

TS'UI-LUAN:

(sings)

The moment I was dragged from here, drawn like a dying dog,
I knew "my husband was my heaven!"
But have faith in your flexible heart and glib tongue.

(speaks)

Move off!

(sings)

They will doubtless persuade my father to set you free!

TS'UI T'UNG:

Now that I know she's the daughter of a great judge, I'll remind him he's my father and everything will come out all right!

TS'UI-LUAN:
There is also a shrew around here; men, bring her out for me.

(Attendants drag out the CH'A-TAN.*)*

CH'A-TAN:
I am gently bred and the daughter of an officer. How dare you drag me about like a scullery wench! You know that a husband is liable for what his wife does, so none of this is any concern of mine; Ts'ui T'ung did it all.

TS'UI-LUAN:
(angrily)
Lock her up at once!

CH'A-TAN:
Don't yammer so! When my father was in office he especially liked to sing Tsui T'ai-p'ing;* I even got so I could do it. Dear lady, listen while I sing it for you.

(Tsui T'ai-p'ing)

(sings)
I see you are as brilliant as Wen-chün.
I see you are as beautiful as Hsi-shih.
Why should you have been light of hand,
Quick of foot and steal? Surely this was perjury by Ts'ui T'ung.

TS'UI-LUAN:
Attendants, lock her up!

*This aria is intrusive—i.e., not part of the song-set proper. One edition lacks it entirely, which is hardly surprising since the whole thing can be removed without losing anything. *Tsui T'ai-p'ing* is in the proper mode (cheng-kung) but it is out of its usual order and does not use the same rhyme as the rest of the arias in this act. See Act I, where her father does indeed sing this tune. Note that even the disrobing is parallel to the Act I song.

CH'A-TAN:
Aiya! Here am I, a bride still wearing her phoenix cap and sunset robe, about to be locked in a cangue! *(pantomimes removing of phoenix cap)*

(sings)
I take off my phoenix cap
With its Eight Treasures picked out in thread of gold;

(pantomimes taking off the sunset robe)
I unfasten my sunset robe;
These I bequeath to Lady Chang* as her dower;
I would be happy now simply to become her maid.

TS'UI-LUAN:
Attendants, they are locked up and in custody. Take them off to stand before my father! *(exeunt)*

(Enter CHANG T'IEN-CHUEH.*)*

CHANG:
I wonder why it's taking my child so long to manage the arrest of Ts'ui T'ung?

(Enter TS'UI-LUAN *with* TS'UI T'UNG *and the* CH'A-TAN *in custody.)*

TS'UI-LUAN:
Father, I have brought you the two villains.

CHANG:
You worthless wretch, how dared you behave as you did! When I write the court I will tell them that you, an official of the realm, did

*This, of course, is Ts'ui-luan's maiden name. Within the framework of the drama there was no way for the *Ch'a-tan* to know her by that name. The Yuan playwright often had a fine scorn for such niceties, but the Ming dynasty editor, Tsang Mou-hsün, usually picks them up and corrects them.

set aside your own wife and did take—as calm as you please—an illegal wife, and in doing so warped the laws and customs and called down upon your head the heaviest of penalties! For now, take them through the streets and then behead them.

TS'UI WEN-YUAN:

(enters excitedly)

Who is making all the fuss? I must go see. *(pantomimes recognition)* But it's Ts'ui-luan! My child, where have you been?

TS'UI-LUAN:

Oh, father,* when I found Ts'ui T'ung, he had taken another wife. Not only that, he swore I was one of his runaway slaves and he had me sent off under guard to Shamen Island. Luckily I met my papa, and now Ts'ui T'ung is going to be executed.

TS'UI WEN-YUAN:

(pleading)

Good lady, could you not spare his life for an old man? Could you consider it?

(Pao Lao-erh)

TS'UI-LUAN:

(sings)

Such an enemy was he in this life
That he must have wronged me in another.
I live only to offer his head on the altar of vengeance—

TS'UI T'UNG:

Uncle, ask her again. Tell her I'll divorce the other one this very day and be her husband again.

---

*She has been using *tieh-tieh* for her biological father, a form of address which translates directly into the English "daddy" as far as phonology is concerned. But "daddy" is too kittenish to be equivalent in tone and I have used "papa." Here she uses *fu-ch'in* to her adoptive father. This address is formal but not stilted.

TS'UI WEN-YUAN:
Good lady, spare him!

TS'UI-LUAN:

(sings)

What thrill of compassion could make me
Feel fondness again for him?
But can I turn my back on one
Who showed both these emotions for me?
I am fallen into anger here or resentment there.
Wounds upon the heart set the teeth against each other
And hurl wrath against the heavens.

(bringing TS'UI WEN-YUAN *before her father)*

(speaks)

Papa, this is Ts'ui Wen-yuan who saved my life and for his sake only let us let Ts'ui T'ung off.

CHANG:
I don't see why we should pardon Ts'ui T'ung!

TS'UI WEN-YUAN:
Your Honor, your daughter once was given, in all propriety, to my nephew as his wife. He now proposes to put aside the other woman and live with your daughter as a proper husband. Would this not be for the best?

CHANG:
Child, what is your opinion?

TS'UI-LUAN:
Well, marriage is the whole life of a woman, and it did occur to me that if Ts'ui T'ung is executed who can say whether I would get

another husband? All right, if you take the woman, have "shrew" tatooed on her face, and sentence her to be my servant, I'll agree.

CHANG:

Your decision is reasonable: attendants, bring the scoundrel over here. For the sake of Ts'ui Wen-yuan, I remit the death penalty. I will invite the man who saved you to live and be supported to the end of his days in my home. My daughter will become Ts'ui T'ung's wife again and that other woman will be spared the punishment of the tatoo because of the position her father holds on the Board of Rites; but she must become the serving maid of my daughter.

CH'A-TAN:

He's both the father and the magistrate. But his position is so high that my father will never be able to save me from this judgment. If I must be your maid, then maid I will be—but let me warn you, a maid can go anywhere in a home a wife can, so do not imagine you will have a husband all to yourself!

CHANG:

Bring the cap and sash and give them back to Ts'ui T'ung. When he has married my daughter, he will return to Ch'in-ch'uan to resume his duties.

*(*TS'UI-LUAN *and* TS'UI T'UNG *both receive the sash and cap.* CH'A-TAN, *dressed as servant, makes obeisance.)*

(Huo Lang-erh)

TS'UI-LUAN:

(sings)

Recalling the foundered ferry on the Huai
I know my destiny had run out.
Certain it was that remnants of a family
Would see the Yellow Springs.

But a levee-watcher saved a life,
Ts'ui the elder paired me with my destined mate,
Yet who could foresee this day—
Father and child united,
Husband and wife restored?

TS'UI T'UNG:
Heaven knows no sweeter event than the reunion of father and child or the reconciliation of husband and wife. I have the lamb slaughtered and the wine made ready to set out a banquet. I raise my cup to toast my father-in-law. *(pantomimes raising cup)*

(Tsui T'ai-p'ing)

TS'UI-LUAN:
(sings)
You, oh heartless Graduate, not only
Struck such a blow to the weak auguries of a tender girl
That the mirror of Princess Lo Ch'ang was barely made whole,
But undertook a trial which came to nought.
Oh, papa, you are so highly placed
Your hand is felt in the Sen-lo palace of the ruler of the dead.
Oh, Ts'ui T'ung, return happily to Ch'in-ch'uan;
Oh, Ts'ui-luan, endure and with firm step enter Wu-ling,
For all of this has transpired by the mercy of heaven.

(Wei-sha)

(sings)
Henceforth let the zither play, the lute thrum.
Nor will we speak again of braving wind and rain.

Let it be the phoenix taking her second mate!
Birds flown away from one another, twining
Their necks together in affection!
Let the plucked flower be a double lotus on a single stem;
If you will heed the plaint of *Pai-t'ou Yin*
I will be as dutiful as Meng Kuang—
Not that I remember only sweetness and forget the wrongs,
Only that my childish heart is all too soft.

CHANG:

(reciting)

First the ferry sank beneath the Huai,
They drifted apart, beneath an alien sky
And word of the other ceased without a trace,
Though their longing, hoping, time could not efface.
Wishes of the aged go usually unfulfilled,
But some god's compassion stirred and willed
A kindly fisherman to adopt my child as his.
Ts'ui the Younger soon was raised in rank
But as he was, my daughter's fortunes sank.
She swore to join her mate at any cost
And at his hands her life was nearly lost.
Far went my search, even to Ch'in-ch'uan.
Returned is the sword fallen in the dragon's den.
The mirror halves, on the phoenix-stand united again.
Bed candles this night shine on one another,
The couple's joy, they fear, belongs to dreams, not to men.

T'I-MU. A windy day on Breaker Rocks at the Huai crossing.

CHENG-MING. A rainy night on the Hsiao-hsiang at Lin-chiang posthouse.

DRAMATIS PERSONAE

LI YEN-SHIH,	*Eighty-year-old father of Li Wen-tao*
LI WEN-TAO,	*Wicked apothecary who lusts after the wife of Li Te-ch'ang*
LI TE-CH'ANG,	*Owner of dry-goods shop, husband of Li Yu-niang*
LIU YU-NIANG,	*Wife of Li Te-ch'ang, mother of Fo-liu*
FO-LIU,	*The Child*
KAO SHAN,	*Maker of Mo-ho-lo dolls*
CLERK HSIAO,	*Wicked and venal bailiff*
1ST JUDGE,	*Stupid and inept prefect*
PREFECT,	*Honest though unimaginative*
CHANG TING,	*His shrewd and competent head clerk*

The Indian demigod Mahoraga (Chinese, Mo-ho-lo) entered China in the modest position of one of the Buddhist boa demons described as "large bellied," but what happened to him *in* China was amazing. Beginning as a man-bodied snake-headed demon, he metamorphosed into a handsome youth with a serpent's head cap who became popular for his own good looks. What began the competitive lavishness of costumes for the image in the Sung dynasty is anyone's guess, but by that time the festival of the "Seventh of the Seventh" featured a figurine of Mo-ho-lo which celebrants (one suspects mostly women and children) decorated as profusely as their economics and talents allowed. This became subtly connected with prayers for skill in (womanly) arts of needlework and the like, and in the end the little figurine became a demonstration of the efficacy of the god himself as each celebrant tried to outdo the other in their decorative skills. That this should run to the same kinds of excesses that Christmas decorations do in the United States, or to the almost inconceivable lavishness of the dress and ornamentation of the famous Bambino de Prague, surprises no student of human nature. Mo-ho-lo no longer presides over the festivities of the Seventh of the Seventh; the Herd Boy and the Spinning Maid are the tutelary deities now, and have been for some centuries.

The Mo-Ho-Lo Doll *(YCH #79)*

(attributed to Meng Han-ch'ing, *fl.* 1279)

PROLOGUE

(LI YEN-SHIH *in* chung-mo *makeup enters with the* ching, LI WEN-TAO.)

LI YEN-SHIH:

*(recites)**

The waning moon that's passed the ides must find its light diminished;
The man who lives past middle years should find his tasks are finished.
One's offspring's trials will be the trials each offspring undergoes
So do not be their burden-beast to carry all their woes.

My surname is Li, my given name is Yen-shih, and I am listed with the Honan-fu bureau of records as living in Vinegar Maker's Alley. There are five of us in my family, and this is my son Li Wen-tao. In addition to him there is my nephew Li Te-ch'ang, his wife, Liu Yü-niang and their baby son called Fo-liu. It seems my nephew is about to leave here to sell his wares in Nan-ch'ang, and he told me he would come bid me farewell. I wonder why he's not here?

*See 879 for the identical entrance verse, and *WP* 902 for another occurrence of the last line of the quatrain.

(*Enter* LI TE-CH'ANG *as the* cheng-mo *leading* YU-NIANG, *the* tan, *and* CHILD.)

TE-CH'ANG:
I am Li Te-ch'ang, this is my wife Liu Yu-niang and my child Fo-liu. I have a dry-goods shop here, and across the street live my uncle and his son Li Wen-tao, who is a druggist. Up on the highroad I just had my fortune told and the teller said that for the next hundred days I would be in danger of calamity—but that if I put a thousand li or more between myself and here I would be safe.* I am about to set out now both to avoid calamity and sell my goods in Nan-ch'ang. Good wife, let us go over with the child so I may take my leave of uncle.

YU-NIANG:
Yes, we should.

(TE-CH'ANG *pantomimes seeing* LI YEN-SHIH.)

TE-CH'ANG:
Uncle, I'm going to Nan-ch'ang to sell my cloth and to avoid calamity. Since this is an auspicious day for travel, I came to bid you goodbye.

YEN-SHIH:
Since you must go, my boy, be careful along the way.

TE-CH'ANG:
(*turning to* LI WEN-TAO)
Take good care of our home, brother.

---

*A favorite story device: see *YCH* #23, #80, and #99. See also *All Men Are Brothers*, p. 1091, and *Ching-p'ing Shan-t'ang Hua-pen* #15, "Lan-lu Hu." All of these employ the same plot motive.

WEN-TAO:
And you, elder brother, return as soon as you can.

TE-CH'ANG:
Uncle, I'd best begin my long journey. *(pantomimes going through door)*

YU-NIANG:
Since you are off today, I have something I want to tell you. Do I dare?

TE-CH'ANG:
What is it?

YU-NIANG:
Your cousin has made advances to me.

TE-CH'ANG:
Silence! All the time I have been home you said nothing. Now on the day of departure you tell me something like this. Wife, do not bring it up again! Your job is simply to take care of our family and to see to it you put your heart in it.

(Hsien-lu, Shang-hua Shih 77545)

(sings)
Just because brother and sister-in-law have shown some temperament,
Must I start peacemaking now?

YU-NIANG:
(sadly)
But what will I do when you're gone!

TE-CH'ANG:

(sings)

You must shed your fears and forget your grief.
Simply tend to our home outside and in.

(speaks)

Everything else is unimportant.

(sings)

You must heed only the welfare of our son.

YU-NIANG:

I understand that, of course, but I want you to prosper, too—

TE-CH'ANG:

(sings)

It's just because
A man must earn his salt to be a man
That I
Leave you now to sell my wares in distant counties.

YU-NIANG:

Please come back soon.

TE-CH'ANG:

(sings)

Mind those tears don't overflow the cup of your cheek
For I'll be gone but six months or a year
And when I've turned a profit I'll be back. *(exeunt)*

YEN-SHIH:

Li Wen-tao, your cousin's gone to peddle his wares. Make sure you don't show up at your sister-in-law's house on some pretext. If I find out about it you'll not get off lightly.

(recites)

A brother must be above suspicion with his brother's wife.
Now he is in Chiang-nan you must take more care
And never cross her threshold if you've no business there,
Or the thrashing you will get will be the soundest of your life. *(exeunt)*

ACT I

(YU-NIANG *enters)*

YU-NIANG:

I am Liu Yü-niang and my husband Li Te-ch'ang has left to sell his wares in Nan-ch'ang. Since I've nothing else to do now I will open up the shop and see who comes.

(Enter ching, LI WEN-TAO.*)*

WEN-TAO:

I am Li Wen-tao, owner of that herb shop. People all speak of me as the "Equal of the physician Pien-ch'iao." My older cousin has gone to sell in Nan-ch'ang leaving only my sister-in-law at home. I have always wanted her; my father has forbidden me even to go in the direction of her house. But now I've fooled him and I think I'll go and see if I can make out with her. "Whatever you choose I've nothing to lose." I'll just go into the shop ... *(sees* YU-NIANG*)* Sister, I've seen nothing of you since my cousin left.

YU-NIANG:

Since your cousin isn't here, why have you come?

WEN-TAO:
I've just come to visit and have a cup of tea with you. There's no harm in that.

YU-NIANG:
This fellow has come for no good so I'll call his father. Father!

(*Enter* LI YEN-SHIH.)

YEN-SHIH:
Who called me?

YU-NIANG:
I did, father.

YEN-SHIH:
What is it, my child?

YU-NIANG:
My cousin came over and began to annoy me so I thought I should tell you.

(YEN-SHIH *pantomimes seeing* WEN-TAO.)

YEN-SHIH:
What are you doing here? (*beats* WEN-TAO *who exits*) If that good-for-nothing comes here again just tell me and he'll not get off as lightly as this time. I'll go and beat that whelp again now. (*exit*)

YU-NIANG:
If things go on this way, how will it end? I'll go close up the store. Oh, Li Te-ch'ang, will you come back before I die of loneliness? (*exit*)

(*Enter* TE-CH'ANG *with carrying-pole and burdens.*)

TE-CH'ANG:
This is quite a rain.

(Hsien-lü Tien-chiang Ch'un 44345)

(sings)
The Seventh Month is scarce begun
And Earliest Autumn carries still
The heat of summer days.
But wearing
Light clothes of summer's weight
Can ill protect me from these swooping strands of rain.

(Hun-chiang Lung 474477 (4344))

Cloud joins cloud relentlessly.
The countryside grows indistinct, as seen through wavering depths of water.
I watched the rain conceal the peaks
And clouds lock up the open blue.

(speaks)
This *is* a heavy storm!

(sings)
Its cloudy heights as deep as the Eastern Sea,
The press of its rains as heavy as Tung-t'ing Lake,
And
Haze and scud deceive my eye
And hide the road I took.
Black blinding
Clouds on every hand
Dim shimmering
Mists across my path.

(speaks)
Now it's raining even harder!

(Yu Hu-lu 737773375)

(sings)
It is as though
I had become painted into an ink-and-water sketch of the Hsiao-hsiang
Where I am
Soaked through and through.
But all is made worse
By these funneling, tunneling rills scoring their runnels,
See their rash spattering dash along the wave paved road.
Hear the wind's
Lush-sussurous brush through the mist-glistening trees.
How can I pass by you,
  Loose oozy pool of
  Grime slimy mud
Unless I step
  Step trippingly tiptoe
  Shuffle softly and slow?
For I must
Teeter myself upright just to totter on ahead.

(T'ien-hsia Lo 7237335)

Now in my scrambling haste I've broken the latchet on both my shoes.
How that
Hinders my steps*
And
Defies my least repair!
I must tear
A strip from my hamper's hempen cloth and bind my sandals on.

---

*Often the two characters in this verse of T'ien-hsia Lo are split by the song-syllables, *yeh-p'o*.

So wet am I that
I can neither raise my head
Nor
Rest my weary feet
And
This has made me bleary-eyed and hopeless.

(Na-ch'a ling 242424334)*

I begrudge
Eight paces as though they were seven miles.
Can I afford
To stop thrice to rest once?
I know I must suffer
A hundred trials, a thousand woes,
And my
Mind is vexed,
My
Heart dismayed.
Will I ever know comfort again?

(Ch'üeh t'a chih 334466)

Nothing but
A close, steep slope
Lies along the road.
But now I've raised my head I see
A building in that grove of trees.
Surely that's a temple there—perhaps a shrine.
Whichever, I can stay awhile and shelter from the rain.

---

*The arias Na-ch'a ling and Ch'üeh t'a chih appear in the Yuan k'an edition only. The first three two-beat lines are missing in this form of Na-ch'a ling.

(speaks)

Way off there is an old temple I can use to get out of the rain. *(pantomimes putting down carrying pole and hampers)* Now I've put down my load I see it is a temple to the Lord Commander of the Five Ways* and long ago gone to ruin. —What a lonely place!

(Tsui-chung T'ien 5575646)

(sings)

The sagging altar table does crowd the door ajar.
Wild grass has wedged its way into the temple's porch.

(speaks)

Good Lord of the Five Ways, this is Li Te-ch'ang returned from selling his wares who hopes for your protection.

(sings)

This pinch of earth will be my incense, I'll draw its holder upon the ground.
Having made my bows, I raise respectful eyes:
My thanks, good spirit, for your holy protection.
I pray
Your golden whip will point me my path
And see me without mischance quickly back home.

(speaks)

It certainly did rain! My clothes and burden are all wet. I must undress and try to dry my garments.

(Tsui fu kuei 557565)

---

*On the *Lord of the Five Ways,* note the following from *Religion in Chinese Society* by C. K. Yang (Berkeley, 1961, p. 31): "A typical [funerary] act ... was the immediate reporting of ... the death to the proper governing authority in the underworld which might be ... Wu-tao (The God of the Five Roads) ... under the belief that ... such gods ... guard the underworld portals." (The Chinese way with bureaucracy followed them even to the underworld!)

(sings)

Let me
Wring the water out of my light leggings
And spread the soaking garments here to dry.

(speaks)

Why is everything so wet here? Oh—the temple hall is partly fallen in and the roof is leaking. Well, I must see to my goods-packs.

(sings)

I fear the oiled paper atop the hampers may have leaked,
So I must sort the bundles from the bottom up.

(speaks)

Here's reason for happiness, nothing at all has gotten wet! But why is it dripping so in here?

(sings)

How strange!
Thrice I've wiped my brow but still the water drips!

(speaks)

How can this be? Oh, you addled egg! Don't you see—

(sings)

You've clean forgot
That soaking headband wound about your hair!

(speaks)

I must take off the rest of these things to dry, then go to the door and see how the sky looks. *(pantomimes undressing and going out the door)* Aiya! Suddenly I've both chills and fever. What's happening to me!

(Yi-pan'erh 77737)

(sings)

It's as though
A tiny fawn were thrashing, dashing itself on the cage of my breast.

And then
As though a tongue of flaring flame had licked the lining of my lungs.

(speaks)

Could it be there's something impure about me and I have offended the god? (I ask the guidance of thy bronze flail, the protection of thy hand, oh lord.)

(sings)

Perhaps
The evil odor of corrupt humanity gives offense to immortal senses?

(speaks)

But no, Li Te-ch'ang, the very state of godhood forbids concern with mortal foibles.

(sings)

As I think about it now

(speaks)

It's clear I've caught a chill

(sings)

In part because the wind's to blame, in part because of rain.*

(speaks)

And how can I get anyone to pass by here so that I may send a message to my wife and ask her to come and help me? Oh, well, I had better rest for now.

(Enter KAO SHAN *shouldering carrying poles.)*

---

*Yi-pan'erh, the title of the aria, means "one half" or "one part" and the requirement for using this song is that the composer (in addition to fitting his lyrics to its meter, of course) end the last line with the phrases "In part X and in part Y," a curious and delightful type of formal *jeu d'esprit* for which I know no counterpart in the West.

KAO:

Aiya! What a rain! At least I got me as far as the Temple to the Commander of the Five Ways so I can get out of it for a while. *(sets down his burden)* I am Kao Shan of Dragongate. There are only two of us in my family, myself and my wife. Each year on the Seventh of the Seventh I go into the city with a load of Mo-ho-lo figurines to sell. I had hardly got out my door this time when the clouds gathered and the heavens emptied. If my wife hadn't made me take along two sheets of oiled paper, my whole stock would've been ruined. I'd better take a look at them anyway. Thank heaven, not one damaged! But my little drum that earns my daily bread has become all slack with the rain. Let's drum it a bit.—Well, it still makes sound!

TE-CH'ANG:

Someone has come! How wonderful!

(Chin Chan-erh 3377555)

(sings)

So wet from the rain
My mind cannot compose itself*
Then a sudden sound and
The furrows leave my brow.
But where is the
P'u-lang-lang of that little snakeskin tambour coming from?
I go to the door and look: he seems spry and quick of wit.
He has some hair-clips of soft metal
And combs to hold back temple locks.†
Ah, he sells
The dolls they pray to for clever fingers;
Figurines to wile away the long nights.

---

*I follow *Yuan-k'an* here, but I am not certain of *hsin-su*.

†Perng Ching-Hsi suggested to me that these may all be articles Kao Shan peddles in addition to the Mo-ho-lo dolls. I was of the opinion that they were things he wore, but that makes less sense.

(TE-CH'ANG *moves softly* [pan]* *across stage and bows.)*

TE-CH'ANG:
Greetings, old one.

KAO:
(terrified)
Gods help me! A ghost!

TE-CH'ANG:
I am no ghost, I'm a man.

KAO:
If you're a man, you shouldn't startle people like that! Call out so a man can tell you're human. But sneaking over and giving greetings right in my ear—in this old temple—with no one about—well, you're lucky it was me, anyone else would have been scared to death!

(KAO *reaches down and picks up a pinch of mud.)*

TE-CH'ANG:
What are you doing?

KAO:
You scared me so bad my fontanel has opened up.†

TE-CH'ANG:
Old one, you know I'm a peddler too. Won't you come in and sit with me?

---

*The character used here (probably pronounced *pan*) is not to be found in any dictionary. Aoki suggests that it is a form of *pan* "to move."

†There was a belief that when a young child was badly frightened his fontanel opened up and could be ritually plugged by sticking a daub of mud atop it.

KAO:
I will, but what have you got your kerchief tied around you like that for?*

TE-CH'ANG:
Well, you see I came into this ruined temple to escape the rain and I took off my clothes to dry them—too soon, I suppose, so I caught this chill. —Old one, where are you bound for now?

KAO:
I'm going to the city to sell my wares.

TE-CH'ANG:
Would you take a message for me?

KAO:
Good brother, there are three things I've forbidden myself to do all my life: one, to be a go-between for anyone; two, go security for anyone; and three, to deliver anyone's message!

TE-CH'ANG:
Look, I'm from the Vinegar Worker's alley in Ho-nan Fu, my family name is Li, and I am called Te-ch'ang. There are three of us in my family, my wife Yü-niang, my son Fo-liu, and myself. I went to Nan-ch'ang to sell and I've come back with a hundredfold profit—

KAO:
Stop, stop, stop! *(He goes out the door to look; shouts.)* All of you who've come in out of the rain, let's get together and talk a while! What, nobody here? *(Comes back in door and looks at* TE-CH'ANG.*)*

*I had always envisioned his having the kerchief looped around head and jaw (as people with the mumps used to be pictured), but I am reliably informed that a Chinese folk remedy for indispositions of various sorts is to tie a kerchief tightly around the head, so that seeing a person with a headcloth tied that way would indicate illness of some sort.

Now how about the likes of you! Nobody asked you a thing and you begin babbling. If there'd been anyone in the place to hear you they could have robbed and killed you in a trice. Then where would your sales trip have got you? You don't even know what kind of man *I* am. You know what they say: "Drawing a tiger you draw the skin; to draw the bones is the hardest part. When you know a man you know the face, who has ever known a heart?"*

TE-CH'ANG:
How could there be any robbers here! But look, old one, I have caught this bad chill and when I go down I won't be able to get up again. My only hope was that you would take a message to my wife to tell her to come nurse me. If you won't deliver the message and I die, it will have been because you tampered with my destiny!

KAO:
You crafty beggar, you certainly can lay traps. All right, I'm breaking a lifelong vow, but I'll deliver your message. Where do you live, what does the store look like and who are your neighbors? Tell me, then go rest.

(Hou-t'ing Hua 555345..5.)

TE-CH'ANG:
(sings)

I live
In a two-room house with a roof of tile.
The door
Is newly made from top to sill.
Next door is a hot food shop
And across the road from that is the 'pothecary's store.
Old one, if by chance
You cannot find the place,
Ask someone:
"Where's the dry-goods shop of Li Te-ch'ang?"
And anyone along the street can point it out.

*Another cliché. Used in *Ku-chin Hsiao-shuo* as well. See Birch, *Stories From a Ming Collection*, Grove, 1953, p. 68.

KAO:
All right, I understand. Now rest.

TE-CH'ANG:
While it's still fresh in your mind, old one, hadn't you better go?

(Chuan-sha 55676347447)

(sings)
Keep the memory safely locked in your head—
Never hesitate, never wonder "Am I right?"
(I do not mean
To command you again to remember instructions just given,
But what can I do? I can now no longer raise myself or move!)
Tell her to borrow a horse or find a mule and hurry here—
(I have no paper, I have no pen,
I cannot write so much as "Safe journey, I wish you well.")
Old one, you must let nothing stop you.
Speak to the clumsy mistress of my house,
Tell her she must hasten here to help this sick man home.

KAO:
I've gone through the door and I see the rain has stopped. Since I am going to the city to sell my Mo-ho-los, I'll take Li Te-ch'ang's message. *(exit)*

ACT II

(Enter LI WEN-TAO.*)*

WEN-TAO:
I am Li Wen-tao and having nothing in particular to do I'll just go to the door of the shop to see who's passing by.

(Enter KAO SHAN.*)*

KAO:
I am old Kao Shan finally arrived in Honan city, but I wonder where Vinegar Alley is? Let me put down my hampers and enquire of someone. *(Sees* LI WEN-TAO.*)* Brother, could I trouble you to tell me where Vinegar Alley can be found?

WEN-TAO:
Why do you ask?

KAO:
Well, a certain Li Te-ch'ang lives there. He went to Nan-ch'ang to sell his wares, returned a hundred times richer, and is now in the Temple of the Guardian General south of the city quite ill. He asked me to carry a message for him.

WEN-TAO:
(aside)
Things *are* improving! *(turns)* Old one, where you are now is Little Vinegar Alley but there's another called Big Vinegar Alley and to get there you head east and then walk westward until you are facing south. Then go north. When you've gone around a corner you'll see a great sophora tree in front of a gate and a large house with a red-painted door and green-painted windows. Above the door you'll see a bamboo screen and under the screen will be a little tyke of a dog fast asleep—that will be Li Te-ch'ang's house.

KAO:
Thank you, brother. *(shoulders his burden and goes muttering)* All right, he said go east and walk west; face south and go north, turn corner, big Sophora tree, great house, red door, green windows, bamboo screen and underneath a little tyke sleeping—but suppose that dog should wake up and leave—? *(exit)*

WEN-TAO:

How true is the saying, "What man wants heaven grants." There he lies sick! I'll say nothing to his wife but mix a draught, go straight out of the city, and poison him with it. Then his wife and money will *both* be mine! It must be the goodness of my nature that has prompted heaven to give me this nice little kettle of rice!* *(exit)*

(Enter YU-NIANG *and child.)*

YU-NIANG:

I am Liu Yü-niang and since the day my husband Li Te-ch'ang left to sell his wares in Nan-ch'ang I've heard nothing. Well, I must open the shop again today and see who comes.

(Enter KAO.*)*

KAO:

I've walked myself to death! I could take that whoreson and—he said there was a Big Vinegar Alley but there is no such thing! *(puts down his hampers)* I could take that jackass-begotten, ugly whoreson—*This* is Vinegar Alley and he sent me right around the city! And all the time it was here!

*(*YU-NIANG *comes out the door and sees him.)*

YU-NIANG:

See here old man, don't you know any better than to stand in the doorway of a shop that's trying to do business? What are you doing there anyway?

KAO:

Now we know my entire fate! I am doomed to be walked to death by a whoreson or talked to death by a woman! Kao Shan, you've no one to blame but yourself for this! Had you refused to deliver Li Te-ch'ang's message it would never have happened!

---

*Same villainous gloating to be found verbatim on *YCH* 671.

YU-NIANG:
Old one! Where did you see Li Te-ch'ang? Please, come in and have a cup of tea!

KAO:
[*sarcastically*]
What? And interfere with business!

YU-NIANG:
Father, where did you see Li Te-ch'ang?

KAO:
Are you perhaps Liu Yu-niang, madame?

YU-NIANG:
Yes, I am.

KAO:
And this child is Fo-liu?

YU-NIANG:
He is, in truth! Father, how do you come to know these things?

KAO:
Sister, Li Te-ch'ang is back from Nan-ch'ang, a hundred times richer and at this moment lies ill in the temple of the Guardian General. You must find a beast and go fetch him immediately.

YU-NIANG:
Oh, many, many thanks, old one; when Li Te-ch'ang has got back home I will find time to thank you properly.

CHILD:
Mama, I want one of those Mo-ho-lo dolls.

YU-NIANG:
(slaps child)
You stupid child! We've hardly enough for food, where would we get the money for that?

KAO:
Don't scold the child. I'll *give* him a Mo-ho-lo. Take good care of it now, son, don't break it playing with it. Look, here on the bottom—my name. It says "made by Kao Shan." And when your father comes home and sees it he'll have proof that I delivered his message. *(exit)*

YU-NIANG:
Who could have imagined Li Te-ch'ang lying sick in the temple of the Guardian General? I'll leave the child next door, lock up, borrow a beast and go to him. *(exit)*

(Enter LI TE-CH'ANG, *ill.)*

LI:
I caught this bad chill on my way home from Nan-ch'ang and have lain here ever since. I asked Kao Shan to tell my wife to come and take care of me. Where is she? Li Te-ch'ang, your time has come and your fate and your destiny. What the soothsayer said has come true.

(Hang-chung, Tsui-hua Yin 76565 (53))

(sings)

In vain
I traveled far to Nan-ch'ang and sold my wares for a handsome profit.

Hurrying home
I am now laid low, trapped by the delirium of disease.
Looking homeward
Each foot of the journey seems further than the edge of heaven
Which so vexes my fearful heart
That I cannot quiet the caged fawn plunging inside my breast.
But,
Hardest of all to bear now
Is the bolt of
Blinding pain that splits my skull apart.

(Hsi Ch'ien ying (55) 46245344)

And who could I call upon to treat me?
No man would enter this lonely, abandoned shrine—
Think again!
The likeliest visitors are cutthroats and thieves.
Once more my mind and heart grow vexed and fearful.
Involuntary tears start.
Again and again
My will deserts me and my spirit sinks.
Wildly
My whole body trembles once more.

(Ch'u Tuei-tzu 43777)

This tottering, this staggering
Raises the darkest thoughts—
Now I sense
A dim, dark belly pain—an awl is slowly thrusting through,
And now
A searing wave of heat as though a fire burnt within,
And then
A marrow-chilling wave of cold, like an icy torrent flows.

(speaks)
Oh, wife, where are you?

(Kua Ti-feng 747444334334 (55))

(sings)
No matter how I yearn for my wife and child, there is only silence.
Impatience is an itch that can't be scratched.

(speaks)
I've got to go look out the temple door.

(sings)
Slowly I force myself to pass through the door of my empty temple
Raise my eyes and force a look—
I managed
The rough tread of the steps and now
Beneath the eaves I stand and watch.
Now faintness comes.
I reach behind me for the door
To rest and lean against its wood.
I thought it tightly shut;
But
The latch-bar was not caught
And when I leant upon it
It burst inward with my weight
And I have toppled backward and fallen in a heap.

(Ssu-men Tzu 55335334)

As ever,
"The hardest frost smites the weakest reed!"
Alas!
The fall has made my illness even worse.

How much it aches!
How deep it burns!
(Once more wealth has brought misfortune in its wake.)*
How much it aches!
How deep it burns!
I can do nothing now
But beseech the god of an abandoned shrine.

(Enter LI WEN-TAO *hastily.)*

WEN-TAO:
Well here I am at the temple. Brother! Where are you?

*(*TE-CH'ANG *sees him.)*

(Ku Shui-hsien-tzu 374456775)

TE-CH'ANG:
(sings)
Ya, ya, ya!
Someone bursts upon the scene.
Hai, hai, hai!
And my soul and all my spirits shrink in sudden fear.
I, I, I
Move behind the paper offerings,
I, I, I
Crouch behind the earthen image,
And, and, and
Quickly hide myself away from view.

---

*Or, "Alas for my wealth!
Bitter Misfortune's brought it all to nought."

WEN-TAO:
I've come only to help you. Come out and accept your brother's bows.

TE-CH'ANG:

(sings)

He, he, he
Walks in here displaying every sign of confidence.
I, I, I
Now I look with care and scrutinize his every feature,
It, it, it
Is the brother I left at home—he at least looks well.
Please, please, please
Li Wen-tao, dispense with formal bows!

(speaks)

Oh, brother, on my way back from Nan-ch'ang I caught a severe chill and could go no further—but where is my wife?

WEN-TAO:
She'll be here presently. Tell me, good brother, how long have you had this?

(Sai-erh Ling 337445)

TE-CH'ANG:

(sings)

If not last night
Then early this morning I think
I was touched by the chill of the wind or breathed in some summer miasma.

WEN-TAO:
Let me take your pulse. *(pantomimes taking pulse)* I know this disease well, brother, and I have brought just the potion for it. *(pantomimes mixing the draught and giving it to* TE-CH'ANG*)*

TE-CH'ANG:
One moment, brother, let us wait for my wife.

WEN-TAO:
You shouldn't wait—the sooner you drink it the sooner you'll feel better. (TE-CH'ANG *pantomimes drinking.*)

TE-CH'ANG:

(sings)

I have drunk the potion down
And now a hot and oily flood
Burns my viscera with a violent fire,
Searing the sphincters of the stomach.

(speaks)

Brother,

(sings)

Surely this drug was never meant for chills!

(Shen-chang'erh 444 444(4) 33?)

He prepared and mixed his fluids,
I took them up and gulped them down.
Suddenly I'm faint and fall—
Struck down by his drug.
Mists cloud all my senses
And an icy sweat bathes my limbs.
Who could have guessed
Behind that smile a dagger lay
Or that my eyes
Beheld my own lonely gravesite? *(He falls.)*

WEN-TAO:
He's down! I'll gather up all his things and get home fast! *(exit)*

(Chieh-chieh Kao 444 3336)

TE-CH'ANG:

(sings)

There goes one who
Destroys his fellow men that he may prosper,
Immune, it seems, from heaven's laws.
But that much money there never was;
Had he wanted it, he could have said so plainly.
Why must he take his brother's life?
Where lust for gold grows, pity dies.
What a shameful contrast to
Kuan-tzu sharing his gold with Pao Shu-ya!*

(Che-tz'u-ku 545454 445 (?))

Fever's fetters bind my legs
So I can neither move nor flee.
Claws of poison clutch and close my throat
So I can neither cry nor call.
I trust that Heaven in its secret ways
Will find some perceptive spirit to avenge me,
To show that good begets more good
And evil acts have evil ends.
Oh, heaven!
This *was* for me the year of baleful omination.

(Kua Chin-so 45454545)

I thought his draught would cure my fever
And never guessed what poison lay within it!

**The Book of Lieh-tzu* (Graham translation): "I used to trade in partnership with Pao Shu-ya. I took the larger share of the profits for myself but he did not think me greedy." But, see the *ju-hua* to story #7 of *Ku-chin Hsiao-shuo* where it is greatly elaborated. It is this story which becomes proverbial among the common folk as an allusion for close and unselfish ties between friends.

For wealth he'll even take a life!
We've raised a slave-whelp to bite its master's hand.
When suspicion first arose
I would not believe my own wife.
How generations hence will laugh
As scornfully as Kuan Yü or Chang Fei.*

(Wei 767)

Not a single bauble left of everything I owned!
No slightest trace of wealth remains here as I die—
He has managed to cram every last thing on his horse somehow!

(falls back under altar table)

(Enter LIU YU-NIANG.*)*

YU-NIANG:
Here at last! I must get down from my beast and go into the temple. But where is my husband? Oh!—he's lying under the altar table and he's terribly ill. *(pantomimes helping husband to rise and get to the animal)* Oh, Li Ta, you must get on the beast and I'll take you home! *(Exeunt and then* YU-NIANG *enters distracted.)*

YU-NIANG:
No sooner had we reached the door of home when blood gushed from all his portals and my husband died! I'm afraid I'll have to tell my brother-in-law so arrangements can be made. *(calls)* Brother!

(Enter LI WEN-TAO.*)*

WEN-TAO:
Now she's frightened and calling *me*! What is it, sister?

*I don't understand why the allusion was thought apposite, but the overall sense is clear.

YU-NIANG:
Your brother's returned and . . .

WEN-TAO:
Ask him to come out.

YU-NIANG:
But Li Ta had just reached home when blood suddenly gushed from him everywhere and he died!

WEN-TAO:
Dead!? My brother? Now everything is clear! He goes away on a business trip. You take a lover. And when the two of you heard he was coming back you conspired to poison him!

YU-NIANG:
We were betrothed as children; what could ever make me poison him?

WEN-TAO:
My brother is dead; now, we can settle the matter privately or publicly, as you like.

YU-NIANG:
What do you mean privately, publicly?

WEN-TAO:
Publicly, I will report to the *yamen* that you must pay with your life for my brother's. Privately, if you marry me we'll forget the whole thing.*

---

*Perng Ching-Hsi points out to me that this "which poison would you like" offer from the villain to the victim is characteristic of this kind of "overturned-judgement play." Note *YCH* 567, 1114, and 1507.

YU-NIANG:
What are you talking about! I'd rather die than marry you!

WEN-TAO:
Then we're off to the *yamen*.

YU-NIANG:
But I *want* to go to the *yamen*. Oh, Li Ta, I shall die of grief.

(Exeunt, WEN-TAO *dragging* YU-NIANG.*)*

(Enter comic-villain official [ku] *leading* CHANG CH'IEN.*)*

JUDGE:

(recites)

When I'm the judge I hear each plea
With fine impartiality.
I take my gold with an open mind
From defense and plaintiff equally.
The senior judge would (if he knew)
Flog me till the cocks all crew.*

(speaks)

I am the magistrate of Honan Fu and this is the day we hold early court. Chang Ch'ien, see if there are any litigants and if so, send one in.

CHANG:
Yes sir.

(Enter WEN-TAO *and* YU-NIANG, *talking.)*

---

*This comic entrance verse by the bad judge is also part of the stereotype. See the identical quatrain on *YCH* 767 where the text is mispunctuated.

WEN-TAO:
—think it over.

YU-NIANG:
I tell you I *want* to go to court.

WEN-TAO:
Very well, then court it is! Justice, justice!

JUDGE:
Bring them over.

CHANG:
Kneel! *(The judge kneels.)* No, no, your honor, the litigants kneel! Why are you kneeling to them?

JUDGE:
Ah, you don't understand at all! Litigants beget my daily bread—for which parentage I have great respect!

(CHANG *forces* YU-NIANG *to kneel.)*

JUDGE:
What complaint do you bring?

WEN-TAO:
We are residents of Honan Fu. There are five in my family. This is my sister-in-law, I am Li Wen-tao, and I had a brother, Li Te-ch'ang, who went to Nan-ch'ang to sell his wares and returned this day with a hundredfold profit. His wife had been keeping a lover in his absence, and the two of them poisoned her husband. Have pity, your honor, and give me justice.

JUDGE:
Let me ask you one question. Is this brother of yours dead?

WEN-TAO:
He's dead.

JUDGE:
He's dead, well that's an end to it, isn't it?

CHANG:
But you can make judgments and set reparations!

JUDGE:
Who, me? *(Turns to* CHANG.*)* Get me my clerk!

CHANG:
(calling)
Where is the clerk of the court?

(Enter CLERK *in clown* [ch'ou] *makeup.)*

CLERK:
(recites)
Hearts of judges? Pure as water!
Clerks? Clean flour from the mill!
You put these two together and the kind of mess they make
Will gum things up as bad as paste or sizing will.

(speaks)
I am Hsiao the bailiff and clerk. I was just putting papers in order in the offices when I heard a great hoo-haw. I suppose the judge is finding it impossible to judge again. *(sees the plaintiff)* Oho! Where have I seen that one before? I know, it's the "second physician of

Lu." I was there the other day to see what I could pick up and he wouldn't give me so much as a seat on his bench—but now *he's* in *my* place! Chang Ch'ien, bring him over and flog him!

*(*CHANG CH'IEN *pantomimes seizing* LI WEN-TAO *who holds up three fingers to the clerk.)*

WEN-TAO:
I'll give you this much silver!

CLERK:
What a pity! It seems two of your fingers have rotted off!

WEN-TAO:
All right, brother, but just take care of this for me—

CLERK:
I understand perfectly, say no more. Now then, what is the complaint and who is the plaintiff?

WEN-TAO:
I'm the plaintiff.

CLERK:
You are the plaintiff. State the circumstances of your complaint.

WEN-TAO:
I am a resident, Li Wen-tao by name, and my older brother Li Te-ch'ang went to sell his wares in Nan-ch'ang and on his return (he had made a hundredfold profit) my sister-in-law and her lover conspired to poison him. Please, good clerk, be my advocate!

CLERK:

[*shows him a sheet on which he has been writing*]*

These are the facts? Sign here. (WEN-TAO *signs.*) Chang Ch'ien, bring over the woman. Woman, why did you poison your husband? Confess!

YU-NIANG:

Have pity, your excellency, I am Liu Yü-niang and Te-ch'ang was my man. He returned from Nan-ch'ang and near the temple of the Guardian General of the Five Ways he took a chill and fell sick. I found a beast and went there, spoke to him—though he said nothing in reply—took him home where blood suddenly flowed from all his orifices and he perished in an instant. I called my cousin to ask him what must be done and he accused me of keeping a lover. But I was betrothed to Te-ch'ang as a child and could never have brought myself to harm him. Excellency, I have no lover!

CLERK:

No flogging, no confession. Chang Ch'ien, lay on!

(CHANG *pantomimes flogging.*)

Now will you confess.

YU-NIANG:

I have no lover!

CLERK:

Will not confess without flogging! Chang Ch'ien, flog her for me.

(CHANG *pantomimes flogging.*)

---

*These additions are needed here though no edition of *Mo-ho-lo* has them.

YU-NIANG:
Stop, stop, stop! I was never going to confess, but how can anyone stand such a beating! I might as well make one up—I, I poisoned my man.

JUDGE:
Don't confess, woman, you'll die if you do!

CLERK:
The confession is made! Bring a cangue and take her away to the cells for the condemned.

JUDGE:
Bring the cangue, Chang Ch'ien, and lock her into it.

CHANG:
It's done. Off to the dungeons.

YU-NIANG:
Oh, heaven, who will speak for me?

JUDGE:
Clerk, come here. I saw your client open up his hand. How many pieces of silver did you get?—and you'd better tell me the truth.

CLERK:
I wouldn't lie to you, your honor, it was five.

JUDGE:
That's two for me and three for you. [?] *(exeunt)*

ACT III

(Enter the PREFECT *in* wai *makeup leading* CHANG CH'IEN.*)**

PREFECT:

(reciting)

Fat-rumped mounts with silken reins
wastrel officials ride,
In billowing robes of gossamer their
artful henchmen stride.
The sowers and reapers never know why
they must keep less grain
For they are told that crops decreased
from blight and lack of rain.

(speaks)

I am a Wan-yen Jurched—the Wan-yen now call themselves Wang and the P'u-ch'a call themselves Li. While still young I learned to read and later became proficient in warfare. Because my ancestor gained great merit, his descendants have inherited his honor and for generations have been officials and generals.

Now this area of Honan Fu is suffering under corrupt officialdom which has been snaring and harming citizens in every fashion. His Sage Presence appointed me Special Prefect here. I am to root out evil and sustain justice; armed with the "sword of authority and the seal of power" I have permission to punish first, if need be, and notify the throne afterward. I have been installed for three days now and am holding early court this morning. But where is the clerk and bailiff?

CHANG:

Clerk! His honor is calling for you.

---

*Only in the fourth act does it become clear that nearly a year has passed between the second and third acts during which time Yü-niang has been languishing in jail.

CLERK:
Coming, coming! *(pantomimes seeing the* PREFECT*)*

PREFECT:
Are you the court clerk?

CLERK:
I am, your honor.

PREFECT:
Then hear me, knave, I've been sent here by the Sage Presence to root out the corrupt officials of Honan Fu and I am empowered to order summary execution. Believe me, if so much as half a dot is out of place in your records the first thing I shall do with my "sword of power" is to separate you from your asinine head. Now, if there are any cases which should be examined, bring them to me immediately.

CLERK:
There are, there are, and I have brought one with me for your honor to read.

PREFECT:
(looking at the papers)
What is this all about?

CLERK:
A certain Liu Yü-niang, adultress, poisoned her husband. She has confessed to it and it needs only your honor's signature.

PREFECT:
But killing one's husband is one of the Ten Unpardonable Crimes—why didn't the former judge pass sentence?

CLERK:
He was awaiting your honor's arrival.

PREFECT:
Where is the prisoner?

CLERK:
In the cell for the condemned.

PREFECT:
Bring her here and I will reexamine her.

CLERK:
Chang Ch'ien, fetch the prisoner.

CHANG:
Yes sir.

(Enter YU-NIANG *and speaks to* CHANG CH'IEN.*)*

YU-NIANG:
What do you want me for, good brother?

CHANG:
You're supposed to see his honor.

CLERK:
Listen woman, there's a new judge here now, and if you so much as open your mouth and say one foolish word I'll have you beaten to death. All right, take her in.

CHANG:
Kneel, woman! *(*YÜ-NIANG *kneels.)*

PREFECT:
Is this the accused?

CLERK:
It is.

PREFECT:
Prisoner, you are called Liu Yü-niang, is that right? Now then, why did you poison your husband? It may be that the judge before me judged ill and there may be things you were not able to speak of. If you tell the truth now, you may be sure I will act in your behalf.

YU-NIANG:
I have no statement to make.

PREFECT:
Since the prisoner will add nothing to her statement, there is no profit in questioning her. Bring me the brush and I shall note that she is to be executed. Take her to the square and put her to death.

(CHANG *leads her out of the chamber.)*

YU-NIANG:
Oh, heaven, is there no one to speak for me?

(Enter chief bailiff CHANG TING *in the singing role,* cheng mo.*)**

CHANG TING:
I am Chang Ting, my courtesy name is P'ing-shu, and I now serve as chief clerk and bailiff of Honan Fu in charge of all records. I have

*The *ya-men* underling who solves cases of violent crimes seems to have been a well liked theme within the general class of *kung-an* (crime case) stories. Chang Ting appears in another play in this role—*YCH*#39; see p. 674 for his entrance. Story #15 in the collection *Hsing-shih Heng-yen,* and #36 in the collection *Ku-chin Hsiao-shuo* both have similar situations; however, the agent is not the same in either.

just returned from inspecting the area and encouraging its agriculture as I was bidden by his honor. Today I must go to court for there are a number of cases awaiting his honor's decision. Oh, when I think of how the petty official can twist the crooked till it seems straight, or call the tune that words must dance, or fiddle the law! How many men have been stabbed to death by the point of a pen!

(Shang tiao, Chi Hsien-pin 7566 667655)

(sings)
Recently, despite the press of daily matters within our courts,
I had to leave my post to settle other things.
But now I'm back, responsible again for public weal and private woe.
And from my pen must flow decisions on life and death.
("Examine this guilty woman, whose act was evil and wrong,*
Who with this stubborn man destroyed the public peace.")
He who acts as keeper of the judge's rolls, bailiff of the judge's court
Cannot allow disorder or be himself in disarray.
But now I hear the "doong-doong" of the drum for morning court
The solemn answers and the call to order.

(Hsiao-yao Lo 4444676444)

I raise my head and look;
The officers ascend the dais
Silently, respectfully,
As if they heard their teacher speak.
I carefully adjust my robes while
Decorously I raise my eyes attending each detail.

**Yüan-k'an* has: "Now examine this guilty woman fallen into thievery,
Now this impudent youth who destroys the public peace."

Martial and fierce as tigers the lictors push and shove a guilty woman.
See her furrowed brow, her tears,
The manacles, the cangue she wears:
I suppose it must concern
Some rustic discord, some country quarrel.

(speaks)

Over against the "petition wall" I see a woman awaiting justice. I don't understand why, but her distress goes straight to my heart.

(Chin-chü hsiang 77745)

(sings)

I can see the
Wet, sticky stain of blood across her ruined robes—
Mute, cruel witnesses to cudgel wounds that lie beneath.
Worse yet,
The heavy cangue twists her back into the mockery of a camel's hump
And her white neck stretches forth;
As heart-break tears flood her eyes.

(speaks)

Look at her, I'll swear she's innocent—wearing that cangue, crying her eyes out. The ancients said: "Nothing will tell you the nature of a man so well as the eye—eyes can never conceal what evil lies within."* And also, "Observe his acts, listen to his words, then judge his crimes and fix his punishment."†

(Ts'u Hu-lu 337747)

(sings)

Let me carefully
Watch her closely a while,

**Mencius*, "Li Lou," 15.

†Probably also a garbled paraphrase of *Mencius loc. cit.*

With clear sight
Examine her face a moment.
I see there
Unfair accusation hidden unspoken deep in an innocent heart.
Ah, poor woman,
How did you fall so far into the net of injustice
That now you stoop under cudgel and cangue?
Enough! I busy myself, no doubt, with concerns that concern me not.

(Yao p'ien)

And so I slowly walk here
Through the two porticoes
And slowly, abstractedly
Reach the Hall of Justice.
She remains there
Sobbing, weeping as though her mouth could release the pain within.
Thrice I've kept myself from questioning her case!

CHANG:
Liu Yü-niang, why don't you talk to good brother clerk and he will be your advocate.

YU-NIANG:
(clutching CHANG TING'S *garments)*
Brother, save me!

CHANG TING:
(sings)
But see, she catches my robe and holds me fast
And whether I will it or not I find myself giving my promise now.

(speaks)
Chang Ch'ien, bring the woman before me. I will question her.

CHANG:
Come forward, Liu Yü-niang. *(She kneels.)*

CHANG TING:
Woman, state your complaint and I will hear you.

YU-NIANG:
(recites)
I pray, good clerk, indulge me for a time
While I set forth the sequence of the crime:
Te-ch'ang, who left to flee malignant fate,
Brought back a purse ten times its former weight.
But in a temple sheltering the day
A morbid illness seized him where he lay.
He hemorrhaged then, and all his portals bled.
We'd barely reached our gate when he was dead.
He died from poison, so much I knew.
I called his brother, asking what to do,
But he straightway accused *me* of the crime
And claimed I kept a lover all the time
Te-ch'ang was south. Before I could protest
He hailed me into court. You know the rest.
They flogged me till I made a false confession. (I'm only a woman!)
I could not stand their cruel inquisition.
But sir, from childhood I was always Te-ch'ang's wife.
How could I bring myself to take his life?
His brother acts from some malign intent—
Please help, good clerk, for I am innocent!

CHANG TING:
Woman, I will speak to the judge for you, but you must be neither overjoyed if he grants me time to investigate nor importunate if he does not. Chang Ch'ien, take charge of the prisoner.

CHANG:
Yes sir.

CHANG TING:
(pantomimes seeing the judge)
Your honor, Chang Ting, whom you sent to investigate farming conditions locally, has returned and having heard that your honor has begun holding court wishes to present a number of cases which need your review.

PREFECT:
(aside)
Ah, my chief clerk and bailiff, Chang Ting, a very able man. *(turns)* All right, tell me what cases need my attention. *(*CHANG TING *hands the* PREFECT *a sheaf of papers.)* What are these?

(Chin-chü hsiang 77745)

CHANG TING:
(sings)
This one a case of booty stolen by one convicted of assault and robbery.
And these
Details on untaxed salt and tea transported here.
And here are two which most pertain to us and our district:
A newly arrived talley-half
And a
List of official tax-grains stored and sent.

PREFECT:
And what is this batch?

(T'su Hu-lu 337747)

CHANG TING:

(sings)

This concerns
A new-made bridge for Yen-ho circuit,*
And this
The new-built storehouse for Sui-chou town.
This concerns
Wang Shou and Ch'en Li who laid false claim to another's farm.†
And this
Chang Ch'ien's assault and the injury of his neighbor Li Wan.

(speaks)

They feared you might not believe them so

(sings)

I brought them here
To face one another and lodge their complaints.
And here is A-chang, wife of Wang,
Who repeatedly used abusive words on a public thoroughfare.

PREFECT:
Then is there anything else?

CHANG TING:
Nothing else, your honor.

PREFECT:
All of these will be sent to various officials for proper disposition. But Chang Ting, I'm going to give you a ten-day leave and I want you to rest. Afterwards you can come back and take up your duties.

---

*Or, "a new-made bridge for River Road."? Perng Ching-Hsi suggests (and there is much to be said for the interpretation) "Where bridges were needed for crossing they were built; where granaries were lacking in towns we had them constructed."

†*Yuan-k'an* has: "The sale of a farm between Wang Shou and Ch'en Li."

CHANG TING:
Thank you, your honor. *(pantomimes going out door)*

CHANG:
Brother clerk, did you speak to his honor about the other matter?

CHANG TING:
I forgot all about it!

(Yao-p'ien 337747)

(sings)

I wasn't
Overburdened with my duties,
It worries me
That I was so distracted.
What if I'd
Neglected some great affair and called down heaven's wrath?
Chang Ting could not call to mind this minor matter—
Is it not said in truth:
"The greater the position the shorter the memory"?
Chang Ch'ien,
Tell her to wait a moment longer and not surrender to despair.

(speaks)

I was so intent on other work I forgot. I'll go back and speak to his honor.

CHANG:
Speak to him now for her, brother, in the name of mercy.

*(*CHANG TING *pantomimes coming before* PREFECT *again.)*

PREFECT:
What brings you back, Chang Ting?

CHANG TING:
Your honor, when I left the *yamen* I saw a woman under sentence at the "petition wall" crying for justice. Those who know about these things realize that she simply fears for her life. But the ignorant might believe that our *yamen* has caused some miscarriage of justice. Will your honor think about this matter?

PREFECT:
That was a case decided by my predecessor. Clerk Hsiao should have managed that one.

CHANG TING:
Clerk Hsiao, *I* am chief clerk now and this was a capital offense. I should have been informed.

CLERK:
You were off looking after the farming and you could have been gone a year. Was I supposed to do nothing but wait for you?

CHANG TING:
Well, bring me the record now.

CLERK:
Here it is, read it.

CHANG TING:
(reading)
"The accused, Liu Yü-niang, 35, under the jurisdiction of the Honan Fu Bureau of Records. Her husband, Te-ch'ang, with a capital of ten pieces of silver went to Nan-ch'ang to sell his wares and was gone nearly a year without word. In the seventh month an

unidentified man brought word that Li Te-ch'ang lay ill in the temple of the Lord Commander of the Five Ways unable to travel. The accused, upon hearing this, secured a mount and went quickly to the temple which lies south of the city. She brought him home but he expired as he entered his own gate when he hemorrhaged through all orifices. Accused notified her brother-in-law, Li Wen-tao, who states that accused planned, together with her lover, to mix a potion and poison her husband. This he deposes and states to be the truth." Your honor, this deposition is useless—

CLERK:

(aside)

He can't buy anything with it so of course it's useless!

CHANG TING:

. . . . We lack support in any form—

CLERK:

His honor, I suppose, is sitting in the air?

CHANG TING:

. . . . and the deposition is full of holes—

CLERK:

That's where mice got at it.

CHANG TING:

. . . . and if your honor doubts this for a moment, let me point them out one at a time.

PREFECT:

Go ahead, I'm listening.

CHANG TING:
Here, "A certain Li Te-ch'ang with a capital of ten pieces of silver. . . ." Now, this silver, was it confiscated by the court? Did the bereaved get it?

CLERK:
It was never found.

CHANG TING:
So much for that, then. Now here, ". . . unidentified man brought word. . . ." Your honor, how old was this man, and was he brought in by the court?

CLERK:
We didn't bring him in.

CHANG TING:
How could he be questioned if he was not brought in? Also, ". . . . Her brother-in-law deposes that the accused planned this with her lover." Who is this lover, your honor, Mr. Li? Mr. Chao? Mr. Wang? And has the court ever brought him in?

CLERK:
Well, if we're missing a lover, will I do?

CHANG TING:
And then, ". . . mixed a potion and poisoned her husband." Where was this poison mixed, your honor, there had to be a source for the poison. . . .!

CLERK:
If we can't find a potion-preparer then I did it!

CHANG TING:
. . . . So, your honor, consider everything; the silver was not found, the messenger is missing, no lover has been discovered, the co-poisoner and co-conspirator are lacking—if we lack such a host of witnesses what grounds have we for executing the woman?

PREFECT:
Mr. Clerk, Chang Ting says the deposition is useless.

CLERK:
You know, brother bailiff, you're an awful busybody. What concern of yours is it anyway?

CHANG TING:
Let me tell you, clerk Hsiao, a human life concerns all of heaven and earth. This is not a small matter:

(recites)

One day in jail is like autumn's entire length.
Outside his body suffers blows; hope inside fights with waning strength.
If you would beat or flog a man, give banishment or transportation,
First see you've granted him the fairest examination.

Rewards and punishment are the tools of power; affection and anger are constants in man. Reward not those whom you love nor punish those who vex you. To reward out of affection is to invite remorse and if punishment were given all who anger others, who would not be judged guilty?*

---

*A series of aphorisms in fours and sixes with occasional rhyme.

"When frost fell, men knew how a virtuous woman suffered,
Falling snow finally proved that Tou Ngo was wronged."*

(Yao 337747)

(sings)
Because the former
Judge's heart was stony
And his
Bailiff's vision short
The entire deposition is reduced to nought; a worthless shambles!
No investigation made for the bearer of the news; unheard-of neglect!
(I'll not even mention the missing lover's deposition.)

(speaks)
Your honor, think of it,
(sings)
In the midst of idiocy like this, they blithely sent a woman to her death!

CLERK:
Ho! Your honor! He accused you of idiocy!

PREFECT:
See here, Chang Ting, whose idiocy—

CLERK:
He said it was your honor's.

---

*These sound exactly like *cheng-ming* and *t'i-mu* for the play "Snow in Midsummer" but they are not the ones we have today. They are *tui-lien,* however, having no connection with the preceding verse and apposite only because Tou Ngo was also a helpless woman, falsely accused, who aroused the concern of "all of heaven and earth."

PREFECT:
Chang Ting, who is idiotic?

CHANG TING:
Your honor! I would not dare—

PREFECT:
See here, Chang Ting, the case of Liu Yü-niang and her lover poisoning her husband was judged by my predecessor and clerk Hsiao was responsible for any imperfect deposition. You have no call to speak of my idiocy! I've been on duty only three days, and yet you have me playing the idiot. When the case was heard I wasn't even here! Now, attend me, you knave! I am ordering you to investigate the whole matter and *you* clear up *your* case in three days! If you've not succeeded by then, I'll deal with you myself! Ai!

(recites in tz'u*)*

Now then, you glib, insubordinate clerk,
You've led me a chase and impugned my work!
The lover, the spouse, the woman transgressor
All had been judged by my predecessor.
But you've discovered untruth and omission
In every line of the deposition:
"Who mixed the poison, Li Ssu or Chang San?
Who was the lover, Chao Erh or Liu An?
Who was the messenger, who brought the news?
How many did the conspiracy use?"
Since none of that's the concern of this court
I designate *you* to prepare a report.
In your search for the facts you have nothing to fear
To judge by the way you have badgered us here!
But let me warn you once again:
Investigate three days, but then
Your search must stop and the depositions
Must all fulfill the law's conditions!

(speaks)

If you succeed, I shall compose a dispatch and send it by fast courier through the bureau at the capital to the Sage Presence, after which you may expect great reward. If, however, you should fail—you latter-day Sui Ho, you argumentative Lu Chia—having gone stiff-necked against the rulings of this court, I will test my "sword of authority" on that very gallows-neck which fastens on your foxy head! *(exit)*

CLERK:
Be of good cheer, Chang Ting. Your stiff neck may be so hard that it'll turn the edge of the sword!

(recites)
Who does not stop when stop he should
Will find himself in jail for good!
An open mouth is calamity's gate
If you stick out your neck they will amputate! *(exit)*

CHANG TING:
Alas, Chang Ting, you've brought all this on yourself!

(Hou-t'ing Hua 5555345--5--)*

(sings)
I've set my hand to
An obscure, uncertain, sordid matter.
Today
I spoke to keep the guiltless free from harm—
You have been lucky so far, Clerk Hsiao,
And you may yet condemn another man, Liu Yü-niang.†
But let me
Deliberate and weigh my task:
His honor wants
Judgments free of ambiguity;
To prove murder the witness must see the wound.
By law the thief and his booty must both be found.

*This and the following aria do not appear in *Yuan-k'an*.

†*I.e.*, Chang Ting may lose his head because of her.

The adulterous couple must once have been seen together.
How much questioning is needed to discover such a crew!

(Shuang Yen-erh 73733)

So much was baseless in the report—the result of lack-brained inquiry—
I all but rejected the task.
But now I've accepted the case,
Three days' limit to find the truth seems but a moment's grace.
I fight back panic
But I'm panicked still.
I choke down fear
But am still afraid.

(speaks)
Chang Ch'ien, take the woman back to her cell.

CHANG CH'IEN:
Yes sir.

(Lang-li-lai sha 337747)

CHANG TING:
(sings)
Liu Yü-niang's an innocent;
Hsiao the clerk's a sophister.
I will hear
All cries for justice (and right all things that now seem wrongs)
For Li Te-ch'ang, who, foully murdered, perished far from home,
And discover
Why he died and in what way,
Then save the lives of the blameless ones and make the guilty pay!

ACT IV

(Enter CHANG TING.*)*

CHANG TING:
I am Chang Ting and I have been given three days by his honor to complete this inquiry; if I succeed I shall be rewarded, if I fail I'll die in Liu Yü-niang's stead. Oh, Chang Ting, you've only yourself to blame for that!

(Chung-lü, Fen-tierh 46633446)

(sings)
Until the time
I've solved this violent crime, so long
Will deep and anguished concern rend my very bowels,
Depression steal my sleep, distraction rob my meals.
How am I to
Examine every fact?
How difficult to judge,
Not knowing each detail.
I must use every mechanism of the mind,
Ransack my brain to search out every strategem!

(Tsui Ch'un-geng 55711444)

Charity bade me urge this action on others,
But urging brought a charge upon myself!
(The open mouth—calamity's gate, Chang Ting)
Regret!
Regret!
To you
The purport of every law must be clear,

But never a
Guiltless person will be free
Unless your mind is clearer still!

(speaks)
Chang Ch'ien, bring the woman Liu Yü-niang here.

CHANG CH'IEN:
Yes sir. Kneel, woman! *(She kneels.)*

(Chiao-sheng 52237)

CHANG TING:
(sings)
"How fiercer than the ravening beast is an evil magistrate."
Scurry, scuttle
To push and hustle,
Hustle and push her
To kneel below the dais
So I may behold
The hidden hostility, the unuttered mutterings, the hangdog head.

(speaks)
Chang Ch'ien, undo her fetters.

CHANG CH'IEN:
Yes sir. *(Pantomimes unfastening her cangue.)*

YU-NIANG:
(rising and bowing)
Thank you, brother clerk, I'll remember to send you a basket of fried cakes one day. *(She starts to leave.)*

CHANG TING:
Where are *you* going? If you disappeared I'd forfeit my head!

YU-NIANG:
Oh, I thought you'd freed me.*

CHANG TING:
Woman, let me hear your deposition. Remember, now, if you speak the truth all is well; if you say one untrue thing—Chang Ch'ien, fetch the heavy rod.

(Hsi Ch'un-lai 77735)

(sings)
You say you are
Wronged and have been made to suffer all that can be borne,
But then who did do both murder and robbery?
When you've been beaten till
Your skin parts, your flesh puckers, it's far too late for regrets.
I would not try to
Force you to implicate yourself
But, the sooner you tell the truth the better.

YU-NIANG:
Your honor, you could flog me to death but all you would get is a false confession.

(Hung Hsiu-hsieh 667335)

CHANG TING:
(sings)
I am strictly limited by the judge: two days and a night.
You steadfastly resisted confession—ten times and more—
And disrupted the court with six examinations and three denials.

*Here again, the stage horseplay is preferred over sustained illusion—no matter how serious the plot.

I have heard your plea
But if it contains
No bit of substance,
Can you hope it will get past me?

(Ying Hsien-k'o 3373345)

Before
The thumbscrew-cord is tightened
It is
Thoroughly steeped in brine,
The wrist that wields the flogging rod is capable of violent strength;
You'll be
Beaten till you're black and blue
And red welts
Show between the bruises,
Then if you've needlessly
Brought the staff on yourself again
You may regret it but you'll repent in vain.

YU-NIANG:
You can beat me to death but it will still be a false confession.

(Po Ho tzu 5555)

CHANG TING:
(sings)
You tell me if you die you die wronged,
You insist again the confession you gave was false.

(speaks)
I'll ask you only this, then.

(sings)
What was in your heart as you left the city wall
And why did he die as he reached the door of his home?

(speaks)
And tell me this, woman,

(Yao)

(sings)
Was the messenger a new acquaintance in the same trade?

YU-NIANG:
I don't know!

CHANG TING:

(sings)
Could it have been an old drinking companion?
And tell me again why would he carry this news?

[*(speaks)*
Woman, do you remember the messenger?]*

YU-NIANG:
Good brother clerk, I've even forgot what the man looks like.

CHANG TING:

[*exasperated*]†
Come over here and I'll knock a likeness of him into your head!

YU-NIANG:
The time's too long past. I've simply forgotten.

(Yao)

---

*Added from the *Yuan-k'an* ed.

†My addition.

CHANG TING:

(sings)

But think again; was the fellow tall or short?
Was his frame well-fleshed or thin?
His complexion, was it dark or was it sallow?
Had he whiskers, had he a beard?

YU-NIANG:
Something is coming to me!

CHANG TING:
Wonderful! As the sage said, "Examine a man's acts, mark his motives; know what makes a man uneasy, then can he hide his character from you?"*

(Yao)

(sings)

By the time I discover where the criminal went to earth,
Searching and seeking to conclude this case,
I will be harrowed till my hair is turned gray.
It troubles my mind and viscera so they threaten to crack.

(speaks)

Woman,

(Yao)

(sings)

Perhaps he lives east of some small lane,
Perhaps his home is west of the high road?
What village is his, what town is he from,
What is his surname and how is he called?

---

*This rather inapposite quote is from the *Analects of Confucius,* II, 10, and is introduced simply to confirm the fact that the clerk is really a learned man.

(pantomimes thoughtfulness)

(speaks)
Well, what was the date he brought you the message?*

[YU-NIANG:
On the seventh of the seventh month.]†

CHANG TING:
On the Seventh of the Seventh?

(Yao)

(sings)
Perhaps he bought oil and noodles for the festival meal,
Or a length of cloth to make himself clothes for fall?
But I ask you why he would leave his home that day
And come inside the city walls—

(speaks)
But, Chang Ch'ien, isn't tomorrow the Seventh of the Seventh?

YU-NIANG:
Good brother clerk, I've remembered! It was the Seventh of the Seventh last year and he had come to sell Mo-ho-lo figures for the festival and brought me the news on his way—he even gave me one of his Mo-ho-lo dolls.

CHANG TING:
Woman! Do you still have it? If so, where is it?

YU-NIANG:
It's still on the little altar in my house.

**Yuan-k'an* has these lines and *Ku Ming-chia* ed. has them copied in by hand, but in the wrong place, I believe. See Yang 1-4573.

†I reconstruct this line.

CHANG TING:
Chang Ch'ien, get it for me.

CHANG CH'IEN:
Yes sir. *(pantomimes making trip)* I'm out the door and, having got to Vinegar Alley, I've asked which house is hers. I open the door, and there on the altar piece is the Mo-ho-lo. I take it, leave, and here I am at the *yamen* again. Brother clerk, here is the Mo-ho-lo.

CHANG TING:
And a handsome one it is! Chang Ch'ien, light incense. Oh, Mo-ho-lo, what man took a life for the sake of wealth? Why did Li Te-ch'ang die the moment he entered his gate? Tell me—

(Chiao-sheng 52237)*

(sings)
You have taken a stupid, foolish child
And
Taught him,
Taught him
Till his mind grew clear.
If you explained this base, this cruel injustice to our judge—

(Tsui Ch'un-feng 55711444)

How much better, Mo-ho-lo,
Than having maidens ply for you the needles you inspire,
Or
Encouraging beauties at their fine embroidery!

---

*Note the two 2-character lines, like cries, and the brevity of this aria. (See also the earlier use of Chiao-sheng in this act above.) There must be a connection between this and its title, "The Cry." Further, Chiao-sheng and Tsui Ch'un-feng go well together because of the likeness in meters—repeat 2's in the first and repeat 1's in the second.

How much better, Mo-ho-lo,
To clarify this dark and mortal crime!
Mo-ho-lo, it rests with
You,
You!
Rescue this woman from false witness
And I will make *men* worship you.
How much more worthy this, Mo-ho-lo,
Than being simple inspiration for children's games!

(speaks)

Speak, Mo-ho-lo. Indeed, why should you not? Don't people still talk of the dog, Black Dragon, who wet his body and threw himself down on the burning reeds where his master slept?* And the horse which knelt on the river bank to trail its reins so its master could save himself from drowning? If dumb beasts can so express themselves, why not you? Men burn money and incense to you; surely then, you should manifest your godhood to them. Have pity on that poor spirit which must be grieving over wrongful death and point out to us the one who did the murder.

(Kun Hsiu ch'iu 33663366774)

(sings)

They can paint your image
With curving blue brows,
Dress your statue in
Flowing red robes
And set
Upon your head a glittering crown and sunset cloth,
But
What purpose would it serve lavishly to clothe you thus!?
When comes again
The Seventh of the Seventh Month
With its
Contests of skill and cleverness

---

*The story is told of Li Hsin-ch'un's dog and also that of a certain Mr. Yang of Kuang-ling. See *Man Who Sold a Ghost*, p. 86, where the *Sou-shen Hou-chi* is the source.

Then
Everyone takes you home—a mere bauble for his wife and child.
There you become god for a day
And all their wishes come true.
But if before you
Opened your jade-fingered hand to thread others' needles,
You
Parted your carmined lips to say what is true here and what is not,
Then men would
Remember your act for *all* time to come!

(speaks)

Mo-ho-lo, who murdered Li Te-ch'ang? Tell me.

(T'ang Hsiu-ts'ai 667334)

(sings)

Deceitful clay! You so resemble Kuan-yin in form
I wonder you lack her finest virtue, compassion.
You let me invoke you, yet vouchsafe us no word.
But I must once again
Look you up and down with care
To satisfy myself you give no sign.

(He sees the characters.)

(speaks)

I have it!

(Man ku erh 22 334)

(sings)

I pondered
Where a sign would appear
And all the time
The words were graven here!

Who could have guessed that
Hid in the carved base of the doll lay the murderer's name?
Here! To the dais!
Summon everyone!
Who among you knows Kao Shan?

(speaks)
Chang Ch'ien, do you know a Kao Shan?

CHANG CH'IEN:
Yes, I do.

CHANG TING:
Then flog him all the way here to the *yamen*.

CHANG CH'IEN:
Yes sir! Now I am going out of the *yamen;* let me see what I can see.

(KAO SHAN *enters.)*

KAO:
I come to the city to make me a little money from my Mo-ho-los again.

CHANG CH'IEN:
(pantomimes seizing KAO*)*
Off we go! The *yamen*'s waiting for you!

KAO:
Aiyo!
You're killing me! *(pantomimes seeing* CHANG TING *and kneeling)*

CHANG TING:
Are you Kao Shan?

KAO:
I am, yes, but I've done nothing to make this clown beat me here like he was paddling a boat upstream!

CHANG TING:
Old one, did you ever deliver a message for anyone?

KAO:
Three things I steer clear of, sir: acting as go-between, going bond, and delivering anyone's messages! I've never delivered any message.

CHANG TING:
(*to* CHANG CH'IEN)
Have him sign this statement.

KAO:
Why? I told you I delivered no messages!

CHANG TING:
Old one, who carved this Mo-ho-lo?

KAO:
I did.

CHANG TING:
Bring in the woman.

YU-NIANG:
(*Looking at* KAO)
Do you recognize me, old one?

KAO:
Why, aren't you Liu Yü-niang? Is Li Te-ch'ang well now?

YU-NIANG:
He's dead!

KAO:
Oh, no! He was a good man!

CHANG TING:
You told us you delivered no messages.

KAO:
Just that *one*—

CHANG TING:
All right, old one, tell us the truth. How did you rob and murder Li Te-ch'ang?

KAO:

(recites)
Good brother clerk please listen to me
While I describe things carefully.
The Seventh of the Seventh was when I made
My trip to the city to ply my trade;
At the Five Ways Shrine to the south of here
I said my prayers and dried my gear.
There Li Te-ch'ang, who was very ill,
Wept and explained he'd caught a chill.
He sounded so sick I feared for his life,
So I promised him I'd tell his wife.
(For him I broke my lifetime vow,
For all the good it does him now!)

My hampers of images don't conceal
A pinch of arsenic or an inch of steel.
Now why would a rustic peddler plan
The robbery and murder of another man?*

CHANG TING:
Old one, you had better tell me just how you worked it.

KAO:
Oh, well, front face the head should have a winged helmet, the body is clad in chain mail and there's a sword in the right hand. Left hand view shows a "black pagoda" hat, body draped in a green robe and left hand holding a brush-pen and a tablet is under his arm: right hand view, blue face, long teeth, red hair, and holding a club of "wolf's tooth"—†

CHANG TING:
That's not clay, is it? Look, I'm talking about murdering men, not molding clay!

KAO:
But you said worked it—‡

CHANG TING:
Chang Ch'ien, flog him till he confesses.

(pantomimes beating)

---

*Ku Ming-chia ed. (*Yang* 1-4578) has very different wording for this *tz'u*.

†This is mostly nonsense, of course; all that matters is that the audience understand that Kao Shan and Chang Ting are talking at cross purposes. It is hard to determine, however, whether Kao Shan is describing three views of one image or three separate images.

‡The Chinese double entendre which brings on this byplay is untranslatable. *Shih-su*, "make an honest confession," is taken by Kao Shan to mean *shih-su*, "mold a likeness."

(K'uai-huo san 5575)

(sings)
The Mo-ho-lo was shaped by you
And Kao Shan is your name.
If we "use the booty to catch the thief" who else could it be?
Try your stubborn best to answer that!

(Pao Lao-erh 7575444 (444))

I'm certain you poisoned the husband to implicate the wife.
Ya!
How cleverly you managed to lay the blame on others.
But when you toss a tile in the air, where and when will it come to rest?
It must always land in *someone's* field.*
Let us have no
  Wild speech or slanderous talk
  No glib lips or nimble tongue,
  Nor hasty-mouth excuses.
I want only
  A settled story begun at the start,
  A precise weight for every word,
  Responsible charges, a careful picture—

KAO:
Oh, I can do better than that! I'll make you a "living portrait." *(Begins to paint.)*

CHANG TING:
Come over here, old one, and listen to me carefully.

*Following *Yüan-k'an*. This proverbial wisdom also appears on *YCH* 947. It is also used in *Chin P'ing Mei*. (see *P'ing wai Chih-yen*.)

(Kuei San-t'ai)*

(sings)

From the
Time you left
To deliver the news
Did you meet a soul along the way?

KAO:
No, I didn't see anyone.†

CHANG TING:
But, before you saw Liu Yü-niang did you do anything else?

KAO:
Oh, now I remember! When I reached the city wall I took a good leak.

CHANG TING:
Nobody asked you about that!

KAO:
Well, when I got *into* the city I asked directions of a shopkeeper and in front of his place was a torture shell.

CHANG TING:
You mean a tortoise-shell.

KAO:
I guess I know when something was a torture. And beside the door stood this mortal pester—

*The scansion of this aria precludes its being Kuei San-t'ai. It in all probability is San-t'ai, the base form of which is 334333 33335.

†Note replies to questions that have only been sung, not asked in plain speech.

CHANG TING:
You mean mortar and pestle.

KAO:
Maybe I do, but what he did was pester me to death. Anyway, inside the place there sat this veterinarian—

CHANG TING:
You mean physician.

KAO:
No, horse doctor!

CHANG TING:
How could you tell that?

KAO:
He could never have played such jackass tricks if he hadn't been. Anyway, he called himself "Second Physician of Lu."

CHANG TING:
Liu Yü-niang, do you know any "Second Physician of Lu?"

YU-NIANG:
Oh yes! He's my brother-in-law.

CHANG TING:
Did you get along well together?

YU-NIANG:
We did not!

(Kuei San-t'ai, continued)

CHANG TING:

(sings)

Now
I've heard him through,
The gloom I felt
Gives way to joy.
This honorable court
Has finally heard the truth.
Come, each and all,
I must find out,
Is this physician known to one of you?

(speaks) [*exasperated*]:
Chang Ch'ien, give Kao Shan eighty strokes because he shouldn't have made the Mo-ho-lo.*

CHANG CH'IEN:

(pantomimes flogging)
Sixty, seventy, eighty—out you go!

KAO:
What was that for?

CHANG CH'IEN:
For making a Mo-ho-lo.

KAO:
Eighty strokes for a Mo-ho-lo—I bet I'd have lost my head if I'd made an Indra! *(exit)*

---

*I have not the remotest idea what reasoning lies behind this line. In terms of this drama it is an opening for the gag line about the Indra statue. The violent pantomime of flogging seems to have been well liked by Yuan audiences and is often introduced seemingly for its own sake.

CHANG TING:
Chang Ch'ien, take Liu Yü-niang elsewhere and then summon the Second Physician for me.

CHANG CH'IEN:
I've left the *yamen*. Here's the right gate. Is the Physician of Lu at home?

WEN-TAO:
Who is it? I'll open the door and see. What do you want, brother?

CHANG CH'IEN:
I am Chang Ch'ien from the *yamen* and the bailiff wants to see you.

WEN-TAO:
I'll go with you right now.

CHANG CH'IEN:
Here we are at the *yamen* gate. I'll go in first. *(reports)* The Second Physician is here.

CHANG TING:
Bring him in.

WEN-TAO:
(pantomimes seeing CHANG TING*)*
Good clerk, why do you want me?

CHANG TING:
His honor's wife is ill; take these five pieces of silver which should certainly pay for any drugs you need. I hope you'll take it.

WEN-TAO:
But what medicine do you wish?

(T'i Yin-teng 6676334)

CHANG TING:
(sings)

Hers is
No stubborn ailment of long standing—
A touch of something chill she ate that harmed her appetite.
Your sanatory broth, I think, will surely do her good;
Go,
Get your monkshood and your mountain fennel.

WEN-TAO:
I carry all those drugs on my person. [*mixes drugs*] Here, it can be taken to madame right now.

CHANG CH'IEN:
Give it to me. I'll take it in to her.
(pantomimes carrying it off and returning)

CHANG TING:
(pantomimes whispering in CHANG CH'IEN's *ear)*
(aloud) Chang Ch'ien, see if mistress has taken her medicine and how she is.

CHANG CH'IEN:
Yes sir. *(exits and reenters hastily.)* Brother bailiff, mistress took the potion and suddenly blood gushed from everywhere and she died!

CHANG TING:
Aha! Did you hear that, Mr. Apothecary!? The Mistress took your drugs and blood flowed from all her portals and she died!

WEN-TAO:

(terrified)

Good clerk, save me!

CHANG TING:
In case I should save you, tell me how many there are in your family?

WEN-TAO:
Only my aged father.

CHANG TING:
How old is he?

WEN-TAO:
He's eighty.

CHANG TING:
Ah, "the aged must not be harmed" so I would only fine him. All right, if you'll denounce your father I'll save you; if you refuse, I'll do nothing for you.

WEN-TAO:
Oh, thank you brother, thank you!

CHANG TING:
So when I say to you, "Physician," you will answer, "Here, sir." I will say "Who mixed that poison?" "My father did, sir," you will say. "Who thought up the idea?" "My father did, sir." "Who took the silver?" "My father did, sir." "You did none of this?" "Oh, it had nothing to do with me, sir." If you answer me in exactly this fashion, I will save you.

WEN-TAO:
Oh, thank you, brother!

CHANG TING:
Chang Ch'ien, take him into the courtroom and fetch the old man here on the end of your stick!

(T'i Yin-teng, concluded)

(sings)
In person I shall hear
The truth from him.

(speaks)
Chang Ch'ien,

(sings)
Say to him only,
"Someone has accused you here at court."

(Man Ching-ts'ai 5527)

(sings)
Say only:
"Bailiff Chang, a new broom sweeping clean,
Demands your speedy arrest and presence at the court.
He told me to
Arrest you at once,"
And if he does not
Comply in every particular
Clap him straightway into jail!

CHANG CH'IEN:
I'm leaving the *yamen*. Is Li the Elder here?

YEN-SHIH:
Who is calling?

CHANG CH'IEN:
You're wanted in the *yamen*.

YEN-SHIH:
All right, I'll go with you. *(pantomimes seeing* CHANG TING*)* Why did you call me?

CHANG TING:
Old one, someone has made a complaint against you.

YEN-SHIH:
Who? What have *I* done?

CHANG TING:
Your own son, Li Wen-tao, has denounced you and if you doubt me you will hear it coming from his own lips.

(Ch'iung Ho-hsi 5752?)

(sings)
Who came to court
To point the finger of accusation?
None other than that filial Tseng Shen,* "Second Physician" himself.
No new-got ingrate foundling was here,
But the flesh of your flesh.
Ai, old clown,
Your guilt could hardly be more clear!

YEN-SHIH:
I don't even believe Wen-tao is here.

CHANG TING:
You've only to listen. Second Physician!

*The paragon of all filial sons.

WEN-TAO:
Here, sir.

CHANG TING:
Who mixed the poison?

WEN-TAO:
My father did.

CHANG TING:
Who thought up the plot?

WEN-TAO:
My father did.

CHANG TING:
Who took the silver?

WEN-TAO:
My father.

CHANG TING:
Who did everything?

WEN-TAO:
My father; I had nothing to do with it.

CHANG TING:
Now then, old one, hadn't you better give me a true confession?

YEN-SHIH:
Brother bailiff, he did the whole thing himself and now he is trying to put the blame on me!

CHANG TING:
Will you sign a statement saying he did it? *(*YEN-SHIH *signs.)*

CHANG CH'IEN:
Now that he's signed, I'll open this door.

YEN-SHIH:

(beats WEN-TAO*)*

You! You poisoned your cousin, you took his property, and you lusted after his wife. All of it was your doing, yours!

WEN-TAO:
No, no! I only admitted poisoning his honor's wife.

YEN-SHIH:
Aiya! But I've admitted that you killed your cousin and everything else!

WEN-TAO:
Confessed?! I'm dead! You stupid old fool!

(Liu Ch'ing niang 447---333)

CHANG TING:

(sings)

I've used this trick
To gull our poor old innocent.
He may spend his life-substance regretting,

But spilled water remains forever on the ground.
He is so frightened his face has turned cracked and yellow like earth.
But as the ancients* said,
"A team of four cannot drag back one spoken word."
A confession once made
Cannot be struck out;
Innocence lost once is gone forever. *

(Tao-ho 33----?)

The truth is known,
Truth is known!
Falsehood can't parade as fact.
Surpassing strange, this case;
It challenged me, and challenged me
To find the roots of truth.
It challenged me, challenged me
To risk my neck and use my wits.
To lay my traps and snare both right and wrong.
None could resist
Nor answer me
Nor deny each fact
With certainty.
How deep, how deep the pleasure went
To wield my nimble wit
Till each confessed his crime.
Had not, had not heaven's will and mine concurred
This worthy court in three days time
Would set the execution blade
First against my neck!

---

*From *Yüan-k'an*.

(speaks)
All of you come with me and we will go before his honor.

(PREFECT *enters.*)

PREFECT:
How have you made out with the case, Chang Ting?

CHANG TING:
It is solved and ready for your honor's judgment.

PREFECT:
I am aware of all the circumstances.* All of you, attend me while I pronounce judgment. The former magistrate and his henchmen were corrupt. They are to be given one hundred blows and never again summoned to official duty. Li Yen-shih, you failed to control your family for which the punishment is eighty blows, but because of your age you will be fined instead. Your crime will be redeemed by the payment thereof. Liu Yü-niang who underwent unjust beating and interrogation will be presented an Imperial Testimony to Merit for mounting on her gateway. Li Wen-tao, the murderer of his elder cousin, will be carried forthwith to the marketplace and there beheaded. I shall personally see that Chang Ting gets three months' extra salary as a reward.

(recites)

I was promoted here by Imperial Decree,
Chang Ting was assigned to investigate for me.
Liu Yu-niang is innocent; she'll retain the estate.
Imperial Commendation will be mounted on her gate.
Offenders of propriety and public sentiment
Are driven to the marketplace and condign punishment.

YU-NIANG:
Thank you, your honor.

*Note how swiftly the Yuan playwright *can* pass over the story and *not* recapitulate when he wants to.

(Sha-wei 3377)

CHANG TING:

(sings)

Kinsmen should be close as hand and foot,
How dared you take his life?
When we have beheaded his murderer
Let it satisfy his much-wronged ghost!

T'I-MU. Li Wen-tao poisons his brother, Hsiao the clerk extorts much wealth.

CHENG-MING. Kao the Elder is wrongly brought to Honan-fu. Chang P'ing-shu solves the case of the Mo-ho-lo.

PART III

Program Notes

Finding List

(from *YCH* and *WP* page numbers to play numbers and romanized titles)

page	play	
1130	# 65	Yüan-chia chai-chu
1146	66	Tsou Mei-hsiang
1172	67	Tan pien to shuo
1187	68	Ch'eng nan liu
1200	69	Sui Fan Shu
1221	70	Wu-t'ung yeh
1234	71	Tung-p'o meng
1251	72	Chin hsien ch'ih
1265	73	Liu hsieh chi
1280	74	Ch'i Ying Pu
1299	75	Ko chiang tou chih
1321	76	Liu hang-shou
1335	77	Tu Liu Ts'ui
1353	78	Wu ju t'ao yüan
1368	79	Mo-ho-lo
1389	80	P'en-erh kuei
1410	81	Yü shu chi
1425	82	Pai hua t'ing
1442	83	Chu wu t'ing ch'in
1456	84	Pao chuang ho
1476	85	Chao-shih ku-erh
1499	86	Tou Ngo yüan
1513	87	Li K'uei fu ching
1532	88	Hsiao Shu-lan
1543	89	Lien-huan chi
1567	90	Lo li-lang
1584	91	K'an ch'ien nu
1608	92	Huan lao mo
1625	93	Liu I ch'uan shu
1639	94	Huo lang tan
1656	95	Wang-chiang t'ing
1670	96	Jen feng-tzu
1684	97	Pi t'ao-hua
1703	98	Chang-sheng chu hai
1716	99	Sheng chin ko
1737	100	Feng Yü-lan
WP 1	101	Hsi-shu meng
WP 7	102	Pai-yüeh t'ing
WP 18	103	P'ei Tu huan tai
WP 42	104	K'u Ts'un-hsiao
WP 58	105	Tan tao hui

page	play	
WP 71	#106	Fei yi meng
WP 81	107	T'iao feng yüeh
WP 91	108	Ch'en mu chiao tzu
WP 108	109	Wu-hou yen
WP 129	110	Yü shang huang
WP 144	111	Hsiang-yang hui
WP 162	112	Mien-ch'ih hui
WP 184	113	Chin feng ch'ai
WP 202	114	Tung ch'iang chi
WP 219	115	Yi ch'iao chin lü
WP 243	116	Chiang shen ling-ying
WP 259	117	Hsi hsiang chi
WP 324	118	P'o-yao chi
WP 337	119	San to shuo
WP 345	120	Tzu-yün t'ing
WP 355	121	Pien Huang-chou
WP 368	122	Pien Yeh-lang
WP 379	123	Chuang Chou meng
WP 394	124	Chieh Tzu-t'ui
WP 405	125	Tung ch'uang shih fan
WP 416	126	Chiang sang-shen
WP 448	127	Ch'i-li-t'an
WP 456	128	Chou-kung she cheng
WP 467	129	San chan Lü Pu
WP 497	130	Chih yung ting Ch'i
WP 515	131	Yi Yin keng hsin
WP 530	132	Lao chün t'ang
WP 545	133	Chui Han Hsin
WP 554	134	Ts'un-hsiao ta hu
WP 568	135	Chien fa tai pin
WP 581	136	Huo Kuang kuei chien
WP 590	137	Yü Jang t'un t'an
WP 604	138	Ching-te pu fu lao
WP 617	139	Feng yün hui
WP 633	140	Hsi yu chi
WP 695	141	Sheng hsien meng
WP 707	142	T'i sha ch'i
WP 716	143	Hsiao Chang t'u
WP 725	144	Po-wang shao t'un
WP 748	145	Ch'ien li tu hsing
WP 767	146	Tsui hsieh *ch'ih-pi-fu*

page	play	
WP 782	#147	Yün ch'uang meng
WP 795	148	Tu chiao niu
WP 808	149	Liu Hung chia pei
WP 834	150	Huang-ho lou
WP 854	151	Yi ao ch'e
WP 867	152	Fei tao tui chien
WP 883	153	Wang-chiang t'ing
WP 899	154	Ts'un lo t'ang
WP 914	155	Yen-an fu
WP 934	156	Huang-hua yü
WP 949	157	Yüan t'ing ching
WP 961	158	So-mo ching
WP 971	159	Lan Ts'ai-ho
WP 981	160	Fu Chin-ting
WP 1000	161	Chiu shih t'ung chü
WP 1012	162	She liu ch'ui wan

Glossary

an-shang
暗上

ch'a-tan
搽旦

Ch'a-t'u-pen Chung-kuo Wen-hsüeh-shih
插圖本中國文學史

ch'ang
唱

Chang Chi
張繼

Chang Chu
張翥

Ch'ang-lun
唱論

chang-man
帳幔

chang-ngo
帳額

ch'ang tao-ch'ing ch'ü-erh
唱道情曲兒

Chang Te-hao
張德好

Chao-shih Ku-erh
趙氏孤兒

ch'ao-ko
嘲歌

Ch'en Chen-ai
陳真愛

Ch'en-chou T'iao-mi
陳州糶米

Chen-ting
真定

ch'en-tzu
襯字

ch'en-yin
沉吟

ch'eng-an
承安

Cheng Ch'ien
鄭騫

ch'eng-ch'in
成親

cheng-ke
正格

cheng-kung
正宮

cheng-ming
正名

cheng-mo
正末

ch'eng-ta
呈答

cheng-tzu
正字

chi
疾

ch'i
騎

ch'i chu-ma
騎竹馬

ch'i ho shang sheng
騎鶴上升

ch'i-ma
騎馬

ch'i-p'ai
旗牌

Chi-wang
稷王

chia-yi tai-fu
嘉議大夫

Chiang Juei-tsao
蔣瑞藻

ch'iao
喬

Chien-fu Pei
薦福碑

chien kuai
見怪

chien-pan
簡板

chien-tzu
簡子

chih-chih wei chih-chih; pu chih wei pu chih
知之為知之，不知為不知

ch'in
琴

Chin An-shou
金安壽

Chin Hsiang Shuo
巾箱說

Chin-hui Shih-liao (See *Yuan, Ming, Ch'ing San-tai Chin-hui Hsiao-shuo Hsi-ch'ü Shih-liao*.)

chin-jih chi-jih liang-ch'en
今日吉良辰

Chin P'ing Mei
金瓶梅

Chin P'ing Mei Chih-yen
金瓶梅巵言

(Tsang) Chin-shu
(臧)晋叔

chin-tou
觔斗

ching
淨

Ch'ing-lou Chi
青樓集

ch'ing-ming
清明

Ch'ing-ming Shang-ho T'u
清明上河圖

Ch'ing-p'ing Shan-t'ang Hua-pen
清平山堂話本

Ch'ing-shih
情史

chiu-lung k'ou
九龍口

ch'ou
丑

Chou Te-ch'ing
周德清

Chou Yi-pai
周貽白

ch'ü
曲

chu-kung-tiao
諸宮調

chu-ma
竹馬

chu-ma teng
竹馬燈

Ch'u-tz'u
楚辭

chuan-kuo yü-t'ou, mo-kuo wu-chiao
轉過隅頭，抹過屋角

ch'uan tso ti men
椽做的門

chuan wan mo chiao
轉弯抹角

Chuang-chia Pu-shih Kou-lan
莊家不識勾闌

chüeh-chü
絕句

Chung-kuo Hsi-ch'ü Shih Chiang-tso
中國戲曲史講座

ch'ung-mo
冲末

Chung Ssu-ch'eng
鍾嗣成

Chung-tu
中都

Chung-tu Hsiu
中都秀

Chung-yuan Yin-yün
中原音韵

ding dong
玎璫

erh-mei
二妹

erh-pen
二本

Erh-shih-ssu Ch'iao Ming-yüeh Yeh
二十四橋明月夜

fen-fen yang-yang hsia-che hsüeh
紛紛揚揚下著雪

Feng-ch'iao Yeh-po
楓橋夜泊

Feng-liu T'i
風溜體

Feng Yuan-chün
馮沅君

fu
賦

fu-ch'in
父親

Fu Hsi-hua
傅惜華

Gen Zatsugeki Kenkyū
元雜劇研究

ha-ma yang-te
蛤蟆養的

Hao Shu-hou
郝樹侯

Hei Hsüan-feng
黑旋風

hei-niu
黑牛

Hei Tieh-tieh
黑爹爹

heng
哼

heng-hsing
橫行

Hou-t'ing Hua
後庭花

Hou-t'u Miao
后土廟

hsi
兮

Hsi-ch'ang hsiao t'ien-ti; T'ien-ti ta hsi-ch'ang
戲場小天地，天地大戲場

Hsi-chi-tzu
息機子

Hsi-chü Yen-chiu
戲曲研究

Hsi-hsiang Chi
西廂記

hsi-ma
躧馬

Hsi-yu Chi
西遊記

Hsia T'ing-chih
夏庭芝

Hsiao-heng Chi
小亨集

hsiao-mo tso pai k'o
小末做拜科

Hsiao-shuo Chih-t'an
小說枝譚

hsieh-hou yü
歇後語

hsin-su
心疎

Hsin Yuan
辛愿

hsing
醒

Hsing-shih Heng-yen
醒世恒言

hsiu
修

-hsiu
秀

hsü-hsia
虛下

Hsü Wei
徐渭

Hsüan-ho Yi-shih
宣和遺事

Hu Chi
胡忌

Hu Ch'i-yü
胡祇遹

hu-shao
胡哨

hu-yi
虎衣

hua chao-erh
花招兒

Hua Li-lang
花李郎

huan-hui
歡會

Huan-men Tzu-ti Ts'o Li-shen
宦門子弟錯立身

huan ni pu wei pieh shih
喚你不為別事

Huang-liang Meng
黃粱夢

Hung-tzu Li Erh
紅字李二

Huo-lang Tan
貨郎旦

"Huo Wu-ch'ang"
活無常

Jen-min Wen-hsüeh
人民文學

ju-hua
入話

kai-pan
改扮

k'ao-pei
靠背

Kao Wen-hsiu
高文秀

keh-poo
可撲

ko
歌

k'o
科

kou-lan
勾闌

Ku-chin Hsiao-shuo
古今小說

Ku-ch'ü
(See Ku-ch'ü Chai.)

Ku-ch'ü Chai
顧曲齋

Ku-chü Shuo-hui
古劇說彙

Ku-ch'ü Tsa-yen
顧曲雜言

ku-men tao
古門道

ku-shih
古詩

Ku-tai Hsi-ch'ü Hsüan-chu
古代戲曲選註

Kuan Han-ch'ing
關漢卿

Kuei Ch'ien Chih
歸潛志

kuei-men tao
鬼門道

kung-an
公案

k'ung-mu
孔目

kuo
裹

kuo-chiao
裹角

Lai-chiang Chi
酹江集

Lan-ku
蘭谷

"Lan-lu Hu"
攔路虎

Lan Ts'ai-ho
藍采和

Li Hsin
黎新

Li K'uei
李逵

Li Lou
離婁

Li Shih-chung
李時中

Li T'ing-hsün
李廷訓

li-wa
裏瓦

Liang-yuan
梁園

Liu-chih Chi
柳枝集

Liu Nien-tzu
劉念茲

Lo Li-lang
羅李郎

lou
樓

Lu Hsün
魯迅

Lu-kuei Pu
錄鬼簿

lu-t'ai
露台

Lun-chu
論著

Ma Chih-yuan
馬致遠

ma-pien
馬鞭

Ma-shang Jih-chi
馬上日記

Mai-wang Kuan
脈望館

Man-chiang Hung
滿江紅

Mang
蟒

Meng-hua Lu
(See *Tung-ching Meng-hua Lu Wai Ssu-chung*.)

Ming-jen Tsa-chü Hsüan
明人雜劇選

Ming-ying Wang Tien
明應王殿

mo
末

Mo-ho-lo
魔合羅

mo-hsieh
摹寫

mo-hui
摹繪

mo-ni
末泥

Mo-nien Chin-chung
抹撚盡忠

mo-pen
末本

Nan-tz'u Hsü-lu
南詞敘錄

nei
内

nien
念

Nü-chen
女真

pai
白

p'ai-ch'ang
排場

Pai-yüeh T'ing
拜月亭

pan
搬

pan (?)
[illegible]

pan t'iao
搬調

pao, chien k'o
報見科

p'ei
呸

p'eng
棚

Ping-wai Chih-yen
瓶外巵言

P'ing-yang
平陽

P'ing-yang Nu
平陽奴

P'ing-yao Chuan
平妖傳

Po Hua
白華

Po Jen-fu
白仁甫

Po P'u
白樸

Po Wen-chü
白文舉

pu-hsien hsing-chen
步線行針

san-ch'ang
散場

san-ch'ü
散曲

san-t'ao
散套

sang-luan
喪亂

Shan-erh
山兒

shan-hsia
閃下

shan-ma
跚馬

Shansi Chung-nan-pu ti Sung, Yuan Wu-t'ai
山西中南部的宋元舞台

Shao Tseng-ch'i
邰曾祺

"She Hsi"
社戲

shen-cheng
神幀

shen-lou
神樓

shih
詩

shih
士

Shih T'ien-ni
史天倪

Shih T'ien-tse
史天澤

shih ts'ai tsa
試猜咱

shih-tzu
獅子

shih-yün
詩云

shou chiu
守舊

shu-hui
書會

shuo
說

Sou-shen Hou-chi
搜神後記

Sui Hsüan-ming
睢玄明

Sun K'ai-ti
孫楷第

sung
誦

Sung Yuan Ming Chiang Ch'ang Wen hsüeh Shih
宋元明講唱文學史

Sung-Yuan P'ing-hua Pa-chung
宋元平話八種

ta-chan
打戰

ta-hang
大行

ta-hang-shou
大行首

ta-hang-yuan
大行院

Ta Hsi-chü-chia Kuan Han-ch'ing Chieh-tso chi
大戲劇家關漢卿傑作集

ta hua-lien
大花臉

ta pei k'o
打悲科

Ta-tu
大都

Ta-tu Hsiu
大都秀

t'ai
擡

t'ai-chi ch'üan
太極拳

T'ai-ho Cheng-yin P'u
太和正音譜

T'ai-ting yuan-nien
泰定元年

tai-yün
帶云

tan
旦

?-tan hang-yuan
回淡行院

tan-pen
旦本

Tanaka Kenji
田中謙二

T'ang Chieh
唐介

tao-ch'ing
道情

tao-ch'ing ch'ü
道情曲

tao-hua-ch'ien
倒花錢

t'ao-shu
套數

te-yeh-ma
得也麼

teng-yün
等韻

ti
弟

ti
第

t'i-mu
題目

tiao
吊

t'ieh-niu
鐵牛

tieh-tieh
爹爹

T'ien-jan Hsiu
天然秀

t'ien-na
天阿

t'ing
聽

t'ing-ch'a
聽差

Ting Ming-yi
丁明夷

t'ing-tso
聽左

Tōhō Gakuhō
東方學報

tou-tzu
斗子

tsa-chü
雜劇

ts'ai-tsa
猜咱

tsai tz'u tso-ch'ang
在此作場

Ts'ang-chou Chi
滄州集

Tsang Mou-hsün
臧懋循

tso
坐

tso-ch'ang
作場

tso nu k'o
做怒科

tso p'ai-ch'ang
做排場

tso pei k'o
做悲科

tso shou-chih k'o
做手指科

tso tso-yung k'o
做作用科

tso-yi (erh)
做意(兒)

Ts'ung Shih Tao Ch'ü
從詩到曲

Tu-ch'eng Chi-sheng
都城紀勝

Tu Mu
杜牧

Tu Shan-fu
杜善夫

tu-wei na-t'ou
都維那頭

t'uei
㖠

tui-lien
對聯

Tung Chieh-yuan
董解元

Tung-ching Meng-hua Lu Wai-ssu-chung
東京夢華錄外四種

Tung-p'ing-fu
東平府

Tung-t'ang Lao
東堂老

tz'u
詞

Tzu-chih T'ung-chien
資治通鑑

tz'u-hua
詞話

tz'u-pen
次本

Tzu-shan
紫山

Tzu-shan Ta-ch'üan-chi
紫山大全集

wai
外

wai-ch'eng k'o
外呈科

wai ch'eng-ta
外呈答

Wai-pien
外編

Wang Chin-pang
王金榜

Wen-wu
文物

WP
(See *Wai-pien*.)

wu-chiao
屋角

Wu Hsiao-ling
吳曉鈴

wu-t'ai
舞台

wu-t'ing
舞厅

wu-t'ying
舞停

ya-nei
衙内

Yang Hung-tao
楊弘道

Yang Wei-chen
楊維楨

yao-mo
幺末

yao-p'eng
腰棚

yao-p'ien
幺篇

Yao-tu
堯都

YCH
(See *Yuan-ch'ü Hsüan*.)

YCHS
元曲選釋

yeh-p'o
也波

Yeh Te-chün
葉德鈞

Yen Shih
嚴史

Yen Tun-yi
嚴敦易

Yi-chai
已齋

Yi-shih Hsiu
一時秀

yin
吟

yin-lü
音律

Yoshikawa Kojirō
吉川幸次郎

yu
又

Yü Ch'iao Chi
漁樵記

yü-ku
愚鼓

yü t'ou
愚頭

yü t'ou
隅頭

Yuan-chü Chen-yi
元劇斟疑

Yuan-ch'ü Hsüan
元曲選

Yuan-ch'ü Hsüan Wai-pien
元曲選外編

Yuan Hao-wen
元好問

Yuan Hao-wen Shih Hsüan
元好問詩選

Yuan, Ming, Ch'ing San-tai Chin-hui Hsiao-shuo Hsi-ch'ü Shih-liao
元明清三代禁毀小說戲曲史料

Yuan-jen Tsa-chü
元人雜劇

Yuan-k'an
元刊

Yuan-k'an pen
元刊本

yuan-kung
院公

yuan-pen
院本

yüeh-chang
樂章

yüeh-ch'uang
樂牀

yüeh-fu
樂府

yün
云

yung
咏

Yung-lo Ta-tien Hsi-wen San-chung
永樂大典戲文三種

Notes

1. The Society: The Barbarians and Chinese Drama

1. Marco Polo. *The Travels of Marco Polo* (The Marsden Translation Revised and Edited). Rochester, N.Y.: Leo Hart, 1933, pp. 190–91.
2. Most recently Cavanaugh gives a good biography and bibliography of Po P'u studies.
3. Igor De Rachewiltz. "Personnel and Personalities in North China in the Early Mongol Period." *Journal of Economic and Social History of the Orient* IX/1-2 (1966).
4. H. D. Martin. *The Rise of Chingis Khan and His Conquest of North China.* New York: Octagon, 1970.
5. *Yuan Hao-wen Shih-hsüan,* edited by Hao Shu-hou (Peking, 1959). Pien-liang was the southern capital to which the Chin rulers had retreated. Pien-liang soon fell.
6. See *Chin-hui Shih-liao,* p. 3.
7. See Chambers, vol. 1, pp. 36–41, especially p. 38: "It may be fairly said that the history of minstrelsy is written in the attacks of ecclesiastical legislators, and in the exultant notices of monkish chroniclers when this or that monarch was austere enough to follow the example of Louis the Pious and let the men of sin (minstrels) go empty away."

8. West, p. 171.
9. *Lun-chu*, p. 241.
10. *Lun-chu*, p. 159.
11. *Lun-chu*, p. 13.
12. Yoshikawa, p. 148.
13. Preface dated 1324; *Lun-chu*, p. 231. See also West, p. 188.

2. Stages and Theaters

1. The date should be 1324, *i.e.* the first year of the *T'ai-ting* reign period.
2. Lawrence Sickman. "Wall Paintings of the Yuan Period in Kuang-sheng ssu Shansi." *Revue des Arts Asiatiques* (Musée Guimet) 1937:53–67.
3. For the whole history of the *Orphan* in Europe, see Liu Wu-chi, "The Original Orphan of China," in *Comparative Literature*, vol. 3, 1953, pp. 193–212, and for the vagaries attendant upon the era of chinoiserie, see Appleton's work, especially chapters 5 and 6.
4. *Hsi-ch'ü Yen-chiu*, p. 75.
5. It should be noted that Feng Yuan-chün (p. 74) at one time thought this was the troupe's advertising, but she herself "had never seen the wall painting."
6. For a translation of Act I, see the section on "Theaters," this chapter.
7. Ting Ming-yi, p. 50.
8. Ting Ming-yi, pp. 47–50. The term *wu-t'ing* is probably most accurately translated "performance hall."
9. Ting Ming-yi, p. 49.
10. *Meng-hua Lu*, p. 35. See Gernet, pp. 189–90, for a full description of these high jinks.
11. See Feng Yuan-chün, p. 32, n. 1.
12. *CYSC*, p. 1109.

13. *CYSC*, p. 547. The most helpful edition of Kao An-tao's composition is certainly Hu Chi's (pp. 312–25), since he not only has descriptive notes but hazards guesses and speculations on the parts that are least intelligible. Other *san-ch'ü* which deal tangentially with the theater are "The Drum" by Ch'ü Hsuan-ming (*CYSC*, pp. 547–48) and "Visit to the Players," an anonymous piece (*CYSC*, p. 1821). These last have been translated and annotated by Tanaka in Japanese and in Dutch by Wilt Idema (*Forum der Letteren*, Leiden, December 1972).
14. Translator's addition.
15. See Hu Chi, p. 314.
16. Also translated by Tanaka Kenji (1969).
17. For a full translation of this scene, see chapter 3 below under "Horses and Other Critters."
18. See 21, 49, 492, 1580, *WP* 127, and *WP* 852.
19. Hawkes, p. 70.

3. The Actor's Art

1. In *WP* 43 after Ts'un Hsin *tso pei k'o,* his father asks him why he is crying, and in *Li K'uei Carries Thorns* (translated in part II of this volume), Wang Liu's daughter is described as "shaking," *ta chan.*
2. From Kalvodová (1972), p. 40. For even more Gothic examples, see Kalvodová (1970, pp. 511–15) and Scott, vol. 1, pp. 140–44.
3. The occasion for Chou Yi-pai's note on the empty exit above.
4. See also *WP* 942, where exactly the same thing is done.
5. See Crump (1971), pp. 22–23, for a translation of this scene.
6. *YCH* 264, 411, 585, 695, 777, 951, 962–63; *WP* 259, 277, 772, 583, and 1026.
7. As usual with these lectures, Chou Yi-pai gives no authority for his *chu-ma teng*.
8. See West (pp. 177 *ff.*) for an interesting examination of the possible origins and uses of the "Jurched suite."

9. I have pursued the matter (Crump, 1973), *q.v.* if you're "into" (as we say) that sort of thing.
10. Yeh Te-chün (pp. 43–49) claims that the verse form was used by performers of an entertainment form he postulates and calls "Yuan dynasty *tz'u hua*" and was later adopted into Yuan drama by the playwrights. *Tz'u-hua* by Yuan times was just a general term for entertainment involving verse and prose, I fear, and the lack of even a single example of a Yuan dynasty *tz'u-hua* in the form he proposes badly weakens the argument for the existence of such a genre.
11. Under the title "Lyricism in Yuan Drama," Helmut Martin has some interesting things to say about the function of *shih-* and *tz'u-yun* in Yuan drama. See *Prušek Festschrift,* pp. 248–58.
12. See p. 481 (e.g. line 11) of the Jen-min Wen-hsüeh edition of *San-kuo Chih Yen-yi* (available in English as *Romance of the Three Kingdoms,* translated by C. H. Brewitt-Taylor, 2 vols., Rutland, Vt.: C. E. Tuttle, 1959). This is also its modern meaning in spoken language.
13. Crump (1958), p. 430.
14. See *Journal of Chinese Society of the University of Singapore* X (1969), 85–116, where Ch'en Ch'en-ai expands on Feng's work.
15. See Kalvodová (1970), p. 515.
16. For examples, see 283, 521, 736, 738, 752, 941, 981, and *WP* 182.
17. See 142, 528, 1203, and *WP* 769.

4. Background of the Plays

1. Shih, chapter IV, does a good job of laying out what we know in an orderly fashion.
2. E. Bruce Brooks, "Chinese Aria Studies," Ph.D. dissertation, University of Washington, Seattle.
3. T. Tzu-shan. See *Tzu-shan Ta-ch'üan Chi* (Complete Works of Tzu-shan), p. 43b, but more accessible in Yoshikawa, p. 65.
4. Quoted in Chiang Juei-tsao's *Hsiao-shuo Chih-t'an,* vol. 2, p. 150.
5. The *Register* says Kao-Wen-hsiu alone wrote seven plays featuring him.

Bibliography

All Men Are Brothers
Pearl S. Buck, tr. *All Men Are Brothers,* 2 vols. (by Shui Huchuan). New York: John Day, 1933.

Appleton
William W. Appleton. *A Cycle of Cathay: The Chinese Vogue in England During the Seventeenth and Eighteenth Centuries.* New York: Columbia University Press, 1951.

Birch
Cyril Birch. *Studies in Chinese Literary Genres.* Berkeley: University of California Press, 1975.

Book of Odes
Shih ching. The Book of Odes. Chinese text, transcription, and translation by Bernhard Karlgren. Stockholm: Museum of Far Eastern Antiquities, 1950.

Cavanaugh
J. T. Cavanaugh. *Dramatic Work of the Yuan Dynasty Playwright Pai P'u.* Ann Arbor: University Microfilms, 1975.

Chambers
E. K. Chambers. *The Mediaeval Stage,* 2 vols. London: Oxford University Press, 1963.

Chao
Chao Ching-shen. *Tu Ch'ü Hsiao-chi.* Peking, 1959.

Cheng Ch'ien
Cheng Ch'ien. *Ts'ung Shih Tao Ch'ü.* Taipei, 1961.

Chiang Juei-ts'ao, *Hsiao Shuo Chih-t'an* Shanghai, 1936.

Chou Yi-pai
Chou Yi-pai. *Chung-kuo Hsi-ch'ü Shih Chiang-tso.* Kowloon, n.d.

Crump (1958)
J. I. Crump. "The Elements of Yuan Opera." *Journal of Asian Studies* 17/3 (1958): 417–33.

Crump (1970)
J. I. Crump. "Yuan-pen, Yuan Drama's Rowdy Ancestor." *Literature East & West* 14/4 (1970).

Crump (1971)
J. I. Crump. "The Conventions and Craft of Yuan Drama." *Journal of American Oriental Society* 91/1 (1971): 14–29.

Crump (1973)
J. I. Crump. "Spoken Verse in Yuan Drama." *Tamkang Review* 4/1 (1973): 41–52.

Crump and Malm
J. I. Crump and William P. Malm. *Chinese and Japanese Music Dramas* (Michigan Papers in Chinese Studies No. 19). Ann Arbor: University of Michigan Center for Chinese Studies, 1975.

CYSC
Ch'üan Yuan San-ch'ü. 2 vols. Taipei: Chung-hua, 1969.

Dudbridge
Glen Dudbridge. *The Hsi-yu Chi.* England: Cambridge University Press, 1970.

Feng Yuan-chün
Feng Yuan-chün. *Ku-chü Shuo-hui.* Peking: 1956.

Gernet
Jacques Gernet. *Daily Life in China on the Eve of the Mongol Invasion: 1250–1276.* California: Stanford University Press, 1962.

Hawkes
David Hawkes. "Reflections on Some Yuan *Tsa-chü.*" *Asia Major* 16 (1971): 69–81.

Hsi-ch'ü Yen-chiu
Liu Nien-tzu. *Hsi-ch'ü Yen-chiu* (Drama Research). No. 2, 1957.

Hu Chi
Ku-tai Hsi-ch'ü Hsüan-chu. 3 vols. Shanghai: 1964.

Johnson (1968)
Dale R. Johnson. *The Prosody of Yuan Ch'ü.* Ann Arbor: University Microfilms, 1968.

Johnson (1970)
Dale R. Johnson. "The Prosody of Yuan Drama." *T'oung Pao* LVI/1–3 (1970): 96–146.

Kalvodová (1970)
Dana Kalvodová. "The Baroque Spirit of the Traditional Chinese Stage." *Literature East & West* 14 (1970): 511–15.

Kalvodová (1972)
Dana Kalvodová. "Theater in Szechuan." *Interscaena '72* (Acta Scaenographica, Prague) 3 (1972): 40.

Kalvodová (1976)
Dana Kalvodová. "Village Theater of Shao-hsing in Lu Hsun's Work." *Acta Universitatis Carolinae, Series Philosophica et Historica* 3 (1976): 132 *ff.*

K.M.
The *K'ai-ming Shu-tien Erh-shih-wu Shih* (9 vols.), Shanghai, 1935. Serially paginated from the *Shih-Chi* through the *Ming-shih.*

Li Tche-houa
Li Tche-houa (editor and translator). *Le Signe de Patience et Autres Pièces du Théâtre des Yuan.* Paris: Gallimard, 1963.

Lun-chu
Chung-kuo Ku-tien Hsi-ch'ü Lun-chu Chi-ch'eng. 10 vols. Peking: 1959.

Ming-jen
Chou Yi-pai. *Ming-jen Tsa-chü Hsuan.* Peking: 1962.

Prušek Festschrift
Études d'Histoire et de Littérature Chinoises: offertes au Professeur Jaroslav Prušek. Bibliothèque de l'Institut des Hautes Études Chinoises, vol. xxlv. Paris: 1976.

Register
Chung Ssu-ch'eng. *Lu-kuei Pu* (*Lun-chu* ed.).

Rosten
Leo Rosten. *Joys of Yiddish.* New York: McGraw-Hill, 1968.

Scott
A. C. Scott. *Traditional Chinese Plays.* 2 vols. Madison: University of Wisconsin Press, 1967 and 1969.

Shao Tseng-ch'i
Shao Tseng-ch'i (Ed.). *Yuan-jen Tsa-chü.* Shanghai: 1955.

Shih
Shih Chung-wen. *The Golden Age of Chinese Drama: Yuan tsa-chü.* New Jersey: Princeton University Press, 1976.

Tanaka
Tanaka Kenji. *Tōhō Gakuho.* 40 (1969).

Ting Ming-yi
Ting Ming-yi. "Shan-hsi Chung-nan-pu ti Sung Yuan Wu-t'ai" (Sung and Yuan Stages in S. Central Shansi). *Wen-wu* (Cultural Artifacts) No. 4 (1974): 47–56.

Ts'ang-chou Chi
Sun K'ai-ti. *Ts'ang-chou Chi.* Peking: 1965.

Tzu-shan
Tzu-shan Ta-chüan Chi. Ssu-pu Ts'ung-k'an edition. Shanghai: 1936.

Waley (1931)
Arthur Waley. *Travels of An Alchemist.* London: 1931.

Waley (1964)
Arthur Waley. *The Secret History of the Mongols, and Other Pieces.* New York: Barnes & Noble, 1964.

Wells
Henry W. Wells. *The Classical Drama of the Orient.* New York: Asia Publishing House, 1965.

West
S. H. West. *Studies in Chin Dynasty (1115–1234) Literature.* Ann Arbor: University Microfilms, 1972.

Wittfogel and Feng
K. A. Wittfogel and Feng Chia-Sheng. *History of Chinese Society: Liao 907–1125* (vol. 36 of Transactions Series). Philadelphia: American Philosophical Society, 1946.

WP
Yuan-ch'ü Hsüan Wai-pien. Taipei: Chung-hua.

Wu Hsiao-ling *et al.*
Wu Hsiao-ling *et al. Ta Hsi-chü-chia Kuan Han-ch'ing Chieh-tso Chi.* Peking: 1958.

Yang Chia-lo
Yang Chia-lo. *Ch'üan Yuan Tsa-chü (ch'u, erh, san,* and *sai-pien).* Taipei, n.d.

YCH
Yuan-ch'ü Hsuan. Taipei: Ch'eng-wen, 1970.

YCHS
(Yuan-ch'ü Hsuan Shih), i.e. Genkyokusen Shaku. In 3 collections, 1951–76. Kyoto (Jimbunkagaku Kenkyūjo).

Yeh-shih Yuan
Sun K'ai-ti. *Yeh-shih Yuan Ku-chin Tsa-chü K'ao.* Shanghai, 1953.

Yeh Te-chün
Yeh Te-chün. *Sung, Yuan, Ming Chiang-ch'ang Wen-hsüeh Shih.* Peking, 1962.

Yoshikawa
Yoshikawa Kojirō. *Gen Zatsugeki Kenkyū.* Translated by Cheng Ch'ing-mao. Taipei, 1962.

Yuan chü Chen-yi
Yen Tun-yi. *Yuan chü Chen-yi.* 2 vols. Peking, 1960.

Yuan-k'an pen
Chiao-ting Yuan-k'an Tsa-chü San-shih Chung. Cheng Ch'ien (Ed.). Taipei, 1962.

Acknowledgments

I wish to express my gratitude to the Center for Chinese Studies, University of Michigan, for their help and particularly for making possible the excellent set of line drawings of stage types. My thanks to Dana Kalvodová for her stimulating work and photos and in particular for permission to use the painting of the village theater in Shao-hsing (Fig. 5). My thanks to Lawrence Sickman for permission to quote extensively from his 1937 article and from his letter to me of March 9, 1973—beyond those two items, however, I wish to thank him for expressing his obvious pleasure with my book. My thanks to the University of Virginia Libraries, especially to Joyce Kroll, for letting me use their copy of *YCH* to provide a sharp reproduction of the stringing up of Judge Pao (Fig. 6). My thanks to Professor John C. Wang who arranged for the handsome *k'ai-shu* calligraphy of the Teatrum Mundi lines. The original hangs in my office and is one of my proudest possessions. I also want to thank the University of Arizona Press for effecting publication of this work.

Finally, I am beholden to Professor William Schultz—he not only spoke kind words about the book into the ears of those who could help it, but in the fair name of friendship took a burden of minutiae off my back when that particular piece of anatomy was badly in need of a rest.

J. I. Crump

Index